PASSION BEYOND THE STARS

Aidan let his fingertips float lightly across the portion of the exotic line that encircled her waist like a narrow belt. "What do you call this form of decoration? Is it no more than another tattoo?"

"No, it is a Love Vine," Kara revealed, pronouncing each of her words with exaggerated care.

"That is precisely the name it should have." He moved down to the foot of the bed and began at her ankle to trace the vine's delectable path with teasing kisses.

Suddenly Kara realized she was no longer wrapped in her towel and made a grab for it. Aidan simply ripped the towel from her grasp and tossed it aside.

"It's far too late for modesty now," he teased. "The fun has already begun."

◆

Beyond the Stars

Phoebe Conn

Beyond the Stars

POPULAR LIBRARY

An Imprint of Warner Books, Inc.

A Warner Communications Company

POPULAR LIBRARY EDITION

Popular Library® and the fanciful P design are registered
trademarks of Warner Books, Inc.

Cover design by Dave Gatti
Cover illustration by Pino Daeni

Popular Library books are published by
Warner Books, Inc.
666 Fifth Avenue
New York, N.Y. 10103

 A Warner Communications Company

Printed in the United States of America

First Printing: February, 1988

10 9 8 7 6 5 4 3 2 1

Beyond the Stars is for you, Bill. Thank you for giving so generously of your invaluable expertise, your marvelous enthusiasm and, best of all, your unwavering love.

Beyond the Stars

When I gazed beyond the stars,
Doomed to view distant worlds from afar,
I never dreamed their radiant beauty
Would come to me, Kara.
From worlds apart we've become one,
The passion of our love hotter than the sun.
I am the dragon, you are my wings.
Together we'll ride the stars' blinding light
Until the whole universe sings . . .
Our love song.

Together

Come share my days,
From the first bright ray of dawn
Until the sunset's last rosy glow.
Each hour will be ours to savor, together.

Come share my nights,
So the magic of the darkness
Flavors your kisses and makes your touch divine.
I want to see the sparkle of the stars
Reflected in the blue of your eyes
While we stroll moonlit gardens, together.

Come share my life,
So I may learn your secrets
Better than I know my own.
Let's fill the heavens with our love
And build an empire from our dreams, together.

CHAPTER
◊ **I** ◊

Aidan had just posted the last shift of guards along the city wall when a shooting star sent a shimmering trail of light across the eastern sky. The powerfully built warrior leaned against the heavily fortified wall, his gaze intent upon the heavens until the last spark of the dying star had dissolved in the mist. It was not an unfamiliar sight, and yet tonight Aidan found it strangely compelling, as though that splendid shower of beauty had been meant for him alone. He wondered if falling stars ever reached the ground. Would the same fiery brilliance that shone in the cool night air glitter as brightly on land? This one had been so close. Surely if he went out now he could find some small part of it still glowing. What a treasure that would be. An impulsive young man despite his heavy load of responsibility to oversee the city's defenses, he called to the guard at his side. "I am going out, Juno, open the gate."

The soldier did not question the wisdom of his commander's order aloud, but moved to obey it immediately. He struggled to lift the heavy steel beam that barred the single entrance to the city, then opened the gate only far enough to allow the tall warrior to slip through. It was not until after he lowered the beam into place to restore the tightly guarded city's security that he dared take a deep breath and wonder if Aidan were exceedingly brave or merely a star-crazed fool.

The warrior was so familiar with the rugged mountain terrain that the darkness did not impede his long fluid stride and he traveled swiftly down the narrow trail that led to the eastern desert. If there were some small fragment of the star left to find, then he would carry it back up to the city for all to see. He wanted to share whatever he found, for he knew his companions' lives were as devoid of beauty as his own and they would love it as dearly as he.

The path to the desert was seldom used, for none wished to retrace the steps condemned men had once taken before being left alone to die upon the blistering white sand in what surely had to have been the cruelest of all executions. He shuddered at the dark memory of his grandfather's tales. Aidan believed, as all did, that ghosts still walked the desert screaming in an agony of thirst and pain, but he was too excited to let fear of those tormented souls influence him now. As the rising sun broke over the horizon he was rewarded for his courage. He caught sight of a flash of light just ahead and, certain it was a tiny bit of the falling star, he ran toward it.

While the mystery of the starlit sky filled Aidan with wonder, a most unwilling visitor was beginning a desperate approach to his planet. Fighting valiantly against the suffocating stranglehold of stark terror, a scout with the Fifth Squadron of Alado's Expeditionary Force punched the coordinates of Mother, her base ship, into her spaceship's onboard computer.

"Come on, Sonia, come on!" Kara urged in a frantic whisper, thumping the instrument panel with the heel of her hand. The blinking green lights of the sweeping search beacon completed their sequence and turned not a comforting bright blue but a blood-chilling red. When channeling every gram of the ship's rapidly dwindling power to broaden the sensors' range still failed to yield any trace of Mother's presence, the distraught pilot had no choice but to begin the series of commands which had been the first lesson she had been taught but the last she had ever thought she would have to use. Knowing the required procedure for a scout unable to contact Mother brought her scant consolation, however. Fear continued to rise in her throat until its sharp metallic sting choked her, and she had to swallow hard to force it away. "Where are you, Mother, where?" she cried aloud although she was the sleek ship's sole crew member.

She had been on a routine flight, updating the geographical surveys of a remote planet in the Altair System whose only known inhabitants were thought to be the ragtag descendants of a penal colony abandoned in 2186, at the dawn of intergalactic travel some sixty years earlier. Alado Mining Colony 329 had been an ambitious disaster almost from its inception as far as Kara could tell from its brief entry in Mother's vast history files. Chosen as the site of a maximum security prison because of its remote location, the colony had soon proven to be far too costly to maintain when all efforts to make it self-supporting ended in failure. Chronically short of provisions and dangerously understaffed when the facility had been partially destroyed by an earthquake, it had been taken over by the inmates during a brief but murderous revolt. The few guards who had survived the bloody massacre had fled in the lone operative shuttle. Since the convicts lacked any means of transport to enable them to once again prey upon civilized worlds, the board of directors of the Alado Corporation had simply left the planet in their control and declared it closed. Since it had become both a political and social embarrassment, any interest in Mining Colony 329 was effectively suppressed and its existence all but forgotten.

However, the recently intensified competition among the six corporations engaged in space exploration had forced action by the directors of Alado. While searching for a way to solidify the corporation's influence in that sector of the galaxy, the planet still noted on their navigational charts simply as 329 had come up for review. Sent on a survey mission, Kara's initial metallurgical observations gave no indication that a return to mining precious metals would be profitable for Alado, but the small planet's parched and barren landscape meant it would require little in the way of surface preparation in order to become an immense launching station for the powerful corporation's spacecraft. There were no tropical regions with dense jungles to tame and the one mountain range, which was clearly volcanic in origin, could be swiftly reduced to rubble so the entire planet would share the same featureless terrain. That a mission yielding nothing more than the promise of a likely base to support Alado's quest for expansion could have brought her to the brink of disaster galled Kara.

Her ship's impressive array of ultrasensitive scanners continued to confirm what the highly skilled pilot already knew: there was no sign of the immense base ship where her calculations repeatedly indicated Mother should be. Kara's abilities, both as a navigator and pilot, were unquestionably superb. She had graduated at the top of her class after three years of intensive training. Her experience as a scout confirmed her belief that she could not possibly be lost. Mother had to be the ship that had strayed off course.

The small but aerodynamically perfect Banshees piloted by scouts were medium-range reconnaissance vessels. Their life support systems and fuel supply were designed for exploratory flights, not great distances. Kara had been reprimanded more than once for stretching her ship's capacity to the limit before returning to Mother, but the accuracy of her observations had justified the risks she'd taken time and again.

"Every time until now!" Kara moaned in despair. Mother was gone. There was no other explanation for the absence of the base ship which had been her only home since birth. Mother never changed course with scouts in flight. Never! It was unthinkable . . . yet Mother wasn't where Kara knew she had to be.

"You must regain your composure, Kara. Breathe deeply, loosen the knots of tension and your inner peace will be restored." Sensing the pilot's distress, the sweet feminine voice of Sonia, the on-board computer, offered her distraught companion advice in a soothing tone and adjusted the flow of oxygen accordingly.

Grateful for even that small amount of comfort, Kara began to inhale and exhale with a practiced rhythm which if continued would lead her into deep meditation.

"Panic is the enemy of reason," she reminded herself. She closed her golden eyes to shut out the gleaming red lights on the control panel as well as the darkness of the universe which stretched endlessly before her.

Her orders couldn't be more specific. A scout unable to return to Mother was to land wherever possible, activate the ship's distress beacon and await the arrival of a rescue sled. As usual, she had made an extra sweep of the planet she'd been assigned to insure the robot scanners caught every detail of its surface. That meant she had burned all but her small reserve tank of fuel. In an effort to conserve what little remained for the reentry into 329's atmosphere, she fed the computer the planet's coordinates, flipped all three switches to shut down the engines that powered the superbly engineered craft and prepared simply to coast in on the planet's gravitational pull the same way glider pilots in ancient times had sailed their craft through the sky borne solely by wind currents. With luck she still had enough fuel to reach the surface without disintegrating, but as she again leaned forward to search the heavens for Mother, she had the sinking feeling her usually extraordinary luck had finally run out and knew that in all the universe it could not have happened in a more forbidding place.

Despite her justified fears, 329's thick blanket of white sand cushioned the Banshee's crash landing, enabling Kara to emerge safely from her craft. While the landing had been by no means smooth, she was too grateful she'd survived it to complain.

Kara had known the planet's atmosphere, while thin, would sustain life, but she had no desire to meet whatever creatures the inmates of the long forgotten penal colony might have spawned.

"Undoubtedly lumbering jackals with less intelligence than Martian lizards," she muttered under her breath.

Lowering the visor on her helmet to protect her eyes from the painful glare of dawn, she surveyed the vast panorama of sparkling white sand. Far in the distance the gentle curve of the horizon was broken by the rugged peaks of the planets' single mountain range, but the Banshee's sensors had detected no sign of civilization to cause alarm. The robot scanners were far more accurate in space than on land, however, so Kara preferred to stay on guard and rely upon her own vision rather than their optic panels.

After the incessant whirring hum of her ship's many instruments, the still desert air was nearly deafening, but she hoped she would not be marooned on 329 long enough to grow accustomed to the pervasive silence. As she was obviously alone, she removed her helmet and ran her fingers through her closely cropped curls. She felt secure enough to remain outside her half-buried craft and set up the heat-reflecting awning contained in her survival gear. Certain the worst was now over, she sat down in the wide patch of shade it cast and calmly awaited rescue. The morning was very warm, the distractions nonexistent, and Kara soon grew drowsy and dozed off.

When the wedge-shaped ship's sensors sounded a piercing alarm she was wide awake and on her feet instantly, calling upon years of training and poised to repel what she was certain would be a vicious attack by a band of renegades with an insatiable lust for blood.

To her exquisite delight, what she saw instead was a single man who appeared to be more astonished than dangerous. He was a ruggedly handsome brute, deeply tanned with a flowing mane of thick blond hair which had been bleached by the blazing light of Altair until it was nearly as white as the sand upon which he stood. He was wearing no more than a pair of tan shorts which were suspended precariously low on his narrow hips and crudely fashioned leather boots. What appeared to be a battered canteen dangled from a knotted strap slung across his shoulder. Although he carried a long spear with a wickedly sharp steel tip, Kara hoped he would not prove violent since she wished him no harm.

Aidan had spent his entire life training to repel an invasion, so he knew spaceships existed even though he'd never seen one. Now that he was so close, however, he realized the glimmering object he had mistaken at dawn for a fragment of a star had been Altair's reflection on the metal craft. There were no tracks in the sand to show from whence it had come, so the only direction possible was the sky.

His attention was quickly diverted from the wonder of the

spacecraft by the iridescent fabric of the owner's suit. Nearly transparent, the soft swells it so enticingly revealed proclaimed the pilot loudly as a female despite the short cut of her astonishingly bright red hair. To go searching for a star and find a woman from the sky instead was a difficult happenstance to grasp, but since women were highly prized in his city, Aidan simply ignored the standing order to kill all invaders on sight and stepped forward. He smiled broadly so she would not be afraid.

Kara reached into the cockpit to silence the alarm, but remained close enough to the Banshee to leap inside if the man's actions proved threatening. While they undoubtedly shared nothing in common but the human form, she knew she would have to explain her presence in a manner he could readily understand, and without further delay. She had received only the minimal amount of diplomatic training that all scouts received. Straightening up proudly, she sent the scantily clad man the Alado Corporation's message of greeting.

A tidal wave of intense pleasure dazzled his senses and weakened his knees as it swept clear through Aidan's well-muscled body. The most beautiful voice he had ever heard flooded his mind with celestial song. The words were incredibly sweet, and the tenderness of their meaning brought tears to his eyes. It was an overwhelming message of profound love, and he felt his highly prized spear slip from his grasp but knew he had no reason to bend down and retrieve it. He had lain with a woman, and the warmth that now filled his heart was the very same sensation of perfect peace the aftermath of that union brought. He could do no more than stare wide-eyed at the red-haired female, fascinated not only by her remarkable powers but also by her extraordinary appearance. She was the first woman he had met who was his equal in height, but she was very slender, her features of such delicate perfection he thought she must surely be a princess in her own world. Her eyelashes were so long and thick they cast shadows upon her cheeks, and the color of her eyes was a startling amber hue. She was incredibly lovely, and it was not until his eyes had swept over her several times that he realized while he heard her voice clearly, her lips had not moved.

"How can you talk without speaking?" he asked in dismay.

"I am projecting my thoughts directly to your mind; no words are required," Kara explained, sending out the thought with another mental wave of incredible beauty. It was a skill all Alado scouts possessed, an invaluable self-defense tool developed to shield them from harm whether the threat came from hostile personnel of a rival corporation or an as-yet-undiscovered enemy from space. This planet was so remote she knew this man would know nothing of modern techniques of mental manipulation. She was surprised, however, that they had understood each other without difficulty. His language was her own, only in a slightly archaic form, and she had not expected that kinship. "If you would like me to respond with words, I will."

Aidan was no fool. This woman was the most remarkable being he had ever encountered, and any way she wished to communicate with him would please him. Though it would make her seem more like himself if she used words. "Please speak as I do," he asked politely.

He was such a pleasant person that Kara saw no reason not to move closer to make their conversation more friendly. She was well aware the young man's glance was focused solely upon her figure, but she could not imagine why. When she stood directly in front of him, she formed her words slowly so he would be sure to understand. "I have missed the rendezvous with my mother ship. I should be rescued shortly. My orders prohibit me from contacting your people. I know you will want to tell them we have met, but I must ask that you wait until I am gone."

"Why must you leave?" Aidan asked sharply, having no intention of losing such a delightful female without a fight to the death.

Kara felt his hostility but could not discern its cause, for while she was adept at projecting her own thoughts, he was protecting, not projecting, his. It was extremely difficult to analyze accurately the thoughts of others, especially when they did not want their thoughts read as this young man clearly did not. She tried once again to reassure him that she posed no threat to his survival. "You have nothing to fear. I've come here as a friend. I've made new maps of your planet and now that task is complete I must return to my base ship for another assignment."

"I am a warrior. I am never afraid," Aidan boasted proudly, but as he leaned down to pick up his spear, the woman's elegantly fashioned silver boot drove it deep into the sand.

"You'll not need your weapon," Kara commanded firmly. "I am a friend."

Aidan straightened up slowly, his expression fierce now. "I do not take orders from women," he vowed through clenched teeth. "Do not make me harm you."

Kara did no more than smile sweetly as she stepped back, but she repeated Alado's message of greeting in her thoughts and was pleased when she saw the defiance which had filled the man's gaze dissolve into wonder. "I am your friend," she again repeated aloud.

Aidan tried to take a deep breath, but his lungs were slow to expand. He knew how to fight other men, how to keep on fighting when the pain of his wounds would have been unbearable to others, but he had no idea how to fight the heady waves of pleasure this slender woman in a shimmering suit of constantly changing colors could send jolting through him with no more than a seductive glance. "How do you do that?" he asked in an anguished gasp, thinking her a priceless treasure, worth far more than any fragment of a star.

"It is one of the most difficult skills to acquire, but eventually it can be mastered. It just takes practice, like learning how to read or—"

"What is that?" Aidan asked quickly, not recognizing the word and not wanting her to think him stupid if he gave a wrong reply.

Kara frowned slightly, for she could not even imagine how he could have grown to manhood without learning to read. His scant apparel and crude weapon clearly declared his life-style as primitive, but surely he could read. "The words we speak can be written down. Do you do that here? Do you leave messages for your friends?" The young man appeared confused by that explanation, so Kara bent down and wrote her name in the sand. "This is my name, Kara. What is your name?"

"Aidan," the young man answered as he bent down by her side. He watched as she printed the word in capital letters. Then he traced the letters with his fingertips. "I have seen marks like these, but no one knows what they are. You say they are words?"

His eyes were a bright blue, nearly the color of the lights on her navigational console when the homing beacon locked in on Mother. Physically, he appeared to be a perfect specimen. Intellectually, his curiosity showed him to have the capacity to learn, but why hadn't he been taught? That was a question for the diplomats, Kara reminded herself. Her job was to make maps, not to befriend the inhabitants of the planets she surveyed.

Still, she had to do something to pass the time. She rose slowly so as not to startle him, then returned to her ship to check the reading on the communication panel, but there was still no signal coming in from Mother. While she had a small store of provisions for just such highly unlikely emergencies, she was forbidden to share them.

"I'm sorry, I can't offer you anything to eat or drink," she explained as she rejoined Aidan outside. "I would like to talk with you for a while longer, though. Someone should come for me soon, but if you will answer my questions, I will try to answer yours."

"How many will come?" Aidan asked suspiciously, wanting some idea of how many men he would have to kill to keep her for himself.

Since Kara knew he could have no possible use for such information, she merely shrugged. "If you are still here, I will introduce you to my friends. Would you like that?"

"Can they all work your magic?"

"What magic?" Kara asked with a lilting laugh. "I don't know any magic."

"You can speak with thoughts," he reminded her, hoping

she might do it again while they were alone since it was so very pleasant.

Rescue sled mechanics didn't receive the same training as scouts, so Kara shook her head. "Probably not. They seldom have need for that skill, so few do the work to acquire it."

Aidan nodded thoughtfully, enormously pleased his adversaries would have no such powers. "I have many questions. May I look at your ship?" Even knowing nothing about such things, he assumed the gleaming triangular craft must fly superbly and he longed to know how.

"Yes, but you may not touch it because the instruments concealed in the shell are extremely sensitive. The ship itself is indestructible, built of an alloy a thousand times stronger than steel but so lightweight you and I could carry the vessel easily."

Aidan found that impossible to believe, but since she would not allow him to touch the craft he did not think he should try to lift it. Squatting by the open hatch, he peered inside and was immediately fascinated by the bank of instruments illuminated by hundreds of tiny lights, all glowing brightly with more colors than he could name. "What makes this fly?"

As her body was still adjusting to the thinness of 329's atmosphere, Kara needed to take a deep breath before she could reply. "It is powered by a synthetic fuel," she stated simply. The truth was that space exploration was a viciously competitive field. No one knew the formula for the Banshee's fuel but the chemists who made it. Its composition was a highly guarded secret, and she knew that should the few drops remaining in her ship's tanks fall into the wrong hands the delicate balance that now existed between the half dozen corporations which sought to colonize space would be upset for generations. None of those fears showed in either her expression or tone, however, for she did not want to relay them to him.

While he readily accepted the ship as being powered by some type of fuel, Aidan's curiosity was far from satisfied. "May I please go inside?"

While he appeared to be several years older than her

twenty-six years, he behaved like a good-natured child. Her orders expressly forbade such a thing, but Kara decided there would be no harm in giving him a brief tour. "All right, but let me go first, and watch your head."

She took the three steps with agile hops, bent down to enter the cockpit and waited for Aidan to follow her inside. Since he had obviously never seen a spacecraft before, she let him look around a bit before she spoke.

"This ship is called a Banshee. It's designed for exploration and geographical surveys, so instead of weapons it carries the equipment to make accurate records of terrain. In an emergency it can be armed and pressed into service as a fighter."

"You've fought in wars?" Aidan asked incredulously.

"No, there's been no need," Kara explained matter-of-factly. "Disagreements between corporations over territory have become more frequent of late, but we've been able to avoid combat so fierce that Banshees are involved."

Aidan nodded, but he was still completely unable to believe women might be required to fly combat missions under any circumstances. He walked toward the rear of the ship marveling that it held such a wealth of technology. That he could comprehend none of its functions pained him greatly. Grasping for something about the elegant ship he could understand, he asked, "Where do you sleep, or cook your food?"

"I do neither," Kara explained with a smile. "My flights aren't long enough to require me to eat or sleep on board."

While Aidan didn't understand how that could be possible, he didn't want to sound ignorant, so he again kept his thoughts to himself. "This is a very pretty ship," he finally said. The compliment was sincere, even if it was motivated by frustration.

"Pretty?" Kara asked skeptically, clearly amused by the word. "It is a masterpiece of form and function, but pretty? Well, I suppose it truly is." She was used to being all alone in it, however, and while she knew Aidan couldn't possibly harm her, the Banshee's equipment was both delicate and expensive and she didn't want to risk having any of it damaged. He was a remarkably handsome man, and while his actions were not in the least bit threatening, she felt a growing sense of unease and moved toward the open hatch. "I'd like to go back outside now if you don't mind."

Aidan gave the control panel one last lingering glance, hoping to memorize all he'd seen before following Kara down the steps. Gesturing toward the awning where he'd found her, he smiled invitingly. "I'd like to stay awhile longer. May we sit down please?"

Since it would be very rude to ask such a polite person to leave, Kara had no choice but to agree. "Why yes, of course." She made herself comfortable in the shade and waited for Aidan to take his place at her side. "Tell me something about your people," she said, encouraging him with a charming smile. "It's been a long while since the colony established here had visitors."

Aidan knew his family's history well, but had no desire to reveal it. "No, now that you've shown me your ship, I'd like to know about your world. From where have you come?"

Kara had received no training in how to manage such a conversation since she was not expected to land and converse with the inhabitants of the planets she surveyed. Everything about her present situation was extraordinary, and since she had no precise orders in how to handle it, she saw no reason not to tell the curious young man the truth. Then she suddenly realized he had to be descended from escaped prisoners, prisoners who had been given life sentences of hard labor in Alado's mines. If she did not choose her words carefully, he would surely regard her as an enemy. She could protect herself from physical attack, but not without harming him which she was extremely reluctant to do. After all, violence would only confirm his mistaken belief that she was his foe.

"Well you must have something to tell!" Aidan prompted impatiently. "Do you have a mate? Children?"

That he would ask such personal questions made Kara laugh, and her momentary tension vanished. She had a very pleasant laugh, as light and sweet as the voice Aidan had heard inside his head. "No, of course not. I am a scout. I live on a base ship with other scouts. We are mapping the universe." *For the Alado Corporation, which imprisoned your people's forefathers,* she was far too cautious to add.

"The entire universe?" Aidan whispered incredulously, for he had spent many a lonely night gazing up into the heavens wondering if somewhere there were others like him as the old tales said there were.

"Yes, that's our mission."

"How long will that take?"

"Forever," Kara replied with a careless shrug. "Our task will not be completed in a thousand lifetimes."

"You make maps and then move on? You never stay in one place?"

"No, Mother—that is my base ship—is my only home. I was born and raised on board and have never lived elsewhere."

Aidan picked up a handful of sparkling white sand and let it sift slowly through his fingers. "I do not think I would like your life."

Insulted by an opinion she considered insufferably ignorant, Kara swiftly defended her choice. "Being a scout is a great honor. It's the only life I've ever wanted to live. Now tell me something about yourself. You said you are a warrior. Tell me what it is you do."

Aidan looked out over the barren landscape as he attempted to channel the riotous confusion of emotions swirling within him into a coherent stream of thought. "I do not even know where to begin," he admitted shyly. "There are no strangers here, no one who does not know our history as well as I do."

They were already in trouble, Kara realized instantly, for it was highly possible she knew far more than he did about his past. Trying to be as tactful as possible, she offered some help. "Let me tell you what I know. My charts show Mining Colony 329 was established here in 2184 but was abandoned two years later as economically inefficient to maintain."

"What does that mean?" the young man asked with a sullen frown, certain it had to be insulting.

"The mines did not produce sufficient quantities of precious metals to make them worth operating in such a remote location."

Aidan stared at the flame-haired woman, astonished she knew so little about his home. "Mining Colony 329 was the most barbaric prison ever built. Don't your charts tell you that as well?"

Afraid no matter what she said would insult him, Kara simply nodded slightly while she silently cursed the fact that she had mastered so few diplomatic skills.

Aidan flashed a predatory grin, revealing sparkling white teeth which provided a sharp contrast to the warm bronze of his skin. "Oh, so you did know that. Did you also know that being sent here was considered far worse punishment than being condemned to death? That the men and women confined here suffered far worse torments than they would have had to endure in hell?"

The man by her side was becoming far too agitated, and Kara had been taught that such a show of uncontrolled emotion often led to violence. To avoid such an unfortunate consequence, she extended her hand. "Will you allow me to touch you? Will you permit that?"

Confused by her irrelevant question, Aidan took a moment to reply, but he knew if this beauty's touch was anything like her thoughts he certainly wanted to feel it. He raised his hand slowly to take hers, not knowing what to expect but hoping it would be pleasant. Her skin was soft, her grasp warm, and in no more than an instant he had shed the anger of his memories as easily as raindrops slipped off leaves. He closed his eyes and leaned back against the side of her ship to savor the splendid sense of calm her presence brought and silently vowed he would die before he gave her up.

Kara's golden gaze swept over the muscular warrior, noting he bore the evidence of his profession in numerous jagged scars. She reached out to trace one that crossed his forearm as she encouraged him to continue. "Tell me what else you know, Aidan, please." She remembered to add the word please, even though that old-fashioned courtesy had long been absent from her vocabulary. She had been taught

that anyone sent to a mining colony deserved no better than
a life sentence of hard labor and death if they refused to
work, but she dared not voice that opinion since he would
violently disagree. Besides, sixty years had passed since inmates had been sent there, so this man was no criminal, or at
least as far as she knew he wasn't. "I know there was an
earthquake followed by a riot," she mentioned casually, sub-
tly encouraging him to confide in her.

Aidan nodded. "Yes, when the quake sent everything into
confusion, my great-grandfather and his friends knew they'd
never have a better opportunity to break free and swiftly
made the most of it."

"What was his crime?" Kara asked curiously, for surely
the man had to have done something hideously evil to be
sent there.

Aidan's reply was preceded by a patronizing chuckle. "It
doesn't matter. Good men sometimes do bad things, but he
was good all the same." Noting that she seemed skeptical,
he continued. "There were all kinds of men sent here, Kara,
from evil to courageous. Their only bond was a conviction
which carried exile to a mining colony. The women were no
different. Many killed themselves rather than become the
guards' whores."

"What? But that is forbidden! No woman may be taken
against her will, not even in prison!" Kara insisted emphatically. Seeing the clear light of rage again darken the blue of
his eyes, she qualified her statement. "I'm certain that must
have been the law even then, wasn't it?"

"Of course, but like all laws it was ignored here." He
shook his head sadly. "Prisoners were made to work such
long shifts in the mines that they never saw the light of day.
They were housed in cramped cages, fed garbage and
clothed in rags. Those who fell ill were given no care. Any
man or woman who objected to such harsh treatment was
left out here in the desert to die. Did you not see their ghosts
last night?"

Amazed to realize he considered that a serious question,
Kara did not scoff as she replied, "No, I did not. Have you
seen them?"

"No," Aidan admitted reluctantly, "but there are many who have." He tried to smile then, but failed. "Convicts were sent here so they would no longer prey upon society, but here they became the guards' prey. No one cared how cruelly they suffered or how many died of starvation or worse."

While Kara dared not drink his water for fear of falling ill, he took frequent sips from his canteen as he continued to calmly recount the shocking events of his great-grandfather's time. She sat spellbound as he recited the lives of the inmates in minute detail. He knew each one by name, what they had looked like and how some had fought simply to endure lives of unspeakable misery without any hope they would ever be set free. Others had no such strength of character and, their spirits broken, their bodies weakened by overwork and neglect, they had simply died of despair. Kara had never heard such a moving account of personal courage in the face of impossible odds. She was so totally absorbed in Aidan's tragic tale she did not realize how much time had gone by until the last rays of the setting sun began to cast long shadows around them. He had not only succeeded in relating his ancestors' anguish in a compelling fashion, he had also convinced her his view of history was a far more accurate one than the one she had read. She had not expected to be stranded there so long, but now she knew she wanted to hear all of what this young man had to say and she was certain he'd barely begun. As the darkness deepened around them, she remembered to excuse herself before again checking the instrument readings in the cockpit, but there was still no signal from Mother that a rescue sled was on the way.

Aidan was as startled as Kara that their conversation had run so long, for he was known by all as a quiet man who kept his thoughts to himself. "I must go home now. I am responsible for the city's guards at night." Rising to his feet, he offered his hand. "Please come with me," he invited graciously, knowing that with his protection she would be safe.

Kara wasn't surprised to find that she truly wished to join him, but such a choice was impossible. "No, I am not allowed to leave my ship. I must wait here for my friends to come," she explained nervously, confounded by the absence of any logical explanation for Mother's disappearance. Still, she was certain a rescue sled, although long overdue, would soon appear.

Aidan slung the strap of his empty canteen over his shoulder, then walked out to pick up his spear before returning to face her. "Are they late?" he asked sympathetically.

"Very late," Kara admitted, but she forced herself to smile. "They should come soon."

"Now that you have made your maps, will others finally come here to live?"

Since she was not positive 329 would soon become a supply base, she kept that possibility to herself. "I'm not sure. Perhaps. Would you like that?"

"Only if they are like you," the warrior confessed with a charming grin. He would never reveal how quickly the men would be slaughtered, but the women would all be most welcome.

Kara could not recall ever having spent an entire day talking with anyone; in fact, she had never met anyone who could hold her interest even half that long. She had not been bored for an instant and she still had so many questions to ask that she hated to see him go. "You must not tell anyone I am here," she reminded him. "But if I am still here tomorrow, will you come to see me again? I would like you to tell me more about your people."

"And I still know far too little of yours," Aidan pointed out with a slow smile. He had a difficult choice, he realized. He could walk away and pray she would be there when he returned, or he could try and force her to come with him now. How he would do that when she used pleasure so effectively as a weapon he didn't know, but if there was a way to keep her he vowed he would find it. "If your friends come, will you please ask them to wait so you can tell me good-bye?"

While she could not honor that request, Kara knew she was long overdue for a furlough. None of Alado's resorts appealed to her as much as flying, so she seldom used her allotted time for recreation; but perhaps she could get permission to come back here. Such an idea would be considered ridiculous, she knew, but still, she would like to learn more about how the few inmates who had survived the bloody battle to seize control of the prison had fared. Yet to make Aidan such a promise would be cruel when she was so uncertain she could keep it. It would be better to say goodbye now than to leave him with hopes she couldn't fulfill, but she found the words impossible to say. She could now appreciate the wisdom of her orders not to contact the inhabitants of any planet not under Alado's control. If she had obeyed that directive she would have been spared the painfully conflicting emotions that bothered her so greatly now. She had not gone looking for Aidan, however, he had come to find her. "I will promise only that if it is possible for me to see you again, I will."

Discouraged that he had found such a bright and beautiful female only to lose her all in the same day, Aidan wished there were some way he could stay with her. "If I do not return to the city before nightfall I will be considered a deserter," he explained regretfully.

"Then go, hurry!" Kara knew it must be some distance since she could see no sign of a settlement. "I don't want you to be punished for talking with me."

"I would not merely be punished," Aidan informed her calmly. "I would be executed."

"Then you must not risk being late!" Kara put her hands on his broad chest to give him an encouraging shove. "Please go!"

The magical sweetness of her touch only made that action all the more difficult, but knowing he had little choice, Aidan made one last plea for her to remain. "Please wait for me to come back tomorrow. I will be here with the dawn."

Kara nodded. "I will try. I really will," she promised sincerely. As he turned away he broke into an easy run which swiftly carried him out of view, leaving her alone in a vast desert believed to be haunted by the tortured souls of prisoners of long ago. That was not a pleasant thought, but it remained with her as she ate a small portion of her food and

sipped the mineral-rich beverage that would keep her from
becoming dehydrated. After again setting the ship's sensors
to warn her of approaching danger, Kara lay down beside it.
Soothed by the warmth retained in the sand, she fell asleep
before she realized she had not asked the ruggedly handsome
warrior with whom he had been fighting to get such brutal
scars.

CHAPTER
◊ II ◊

Aidan dashed through the gate with only seconds to spare
before the city was secured for the night. The first shift of
guards was already in place, and he walked down their line
with a word of encouragement for each of his friends, hoping none had noted the tardiness of his arrival. No man enjoyed this tiresome duty but all shared it without complaint.
He was far too excited to feel tired, but Aidan knew if he
again stayed awake all night he would fall asleep when he
went to see Kara, if by some miracle the lovely space traveler was still there when he reached the desert in the morning. The likely probability she would be gone was so
frightening that he doubted he could get any rest no matter
how diligently he tried.

He paced restlessly up and down the walkway behind the
high wall that protected the mountain fortress from assault.
He had lost count of how many times he had had to defend
his home, but prayed he would not be called upon to do so in
the next few hours. When he was finally satisfied the night
would be a calm one, he walked the short distance to his
quarters, the only ones permanently occupied in the guards'

barracks. The other men came and went as they took their turns in an endless rotation, but since Aidan was responsible for their performance, he had never seen any point in maintaining a home elsewhere.

As he entered his apartment, he wondered what the elegant creature he had met in the desert would think of his home. The main room was open to the sky so that Altair's light could nourish the garden which grew in the center and provided the major portion of his diet. A smaller room opened onto that spacious courtyard. It contained his bed and the carved chests that held his belongings. Opening off it was an elaborate bath where the bubbling hot springs which flowed from deep within the mountain provided an endless supply of hot water. He had never thought until that very moment that a warrior's home was not the best of all possible places to live. He had to admit now it was stark, devoid of the soft decorative touches a feminine hand would provide. Forcing himself to rest, he stretched out on his bed to pass the time before the guard would change and he would again have to make certain all the posts were manned.

Propping his head on his hands, he closed his eyes and lazily recalled each exquisite detail of Kara's delicate features. There were a few redheads in his city, but none with hair of such a bright hue. Nor had he ever met anyone with eyes of such an incredible golden shade. While she was undeniably a natural beauty, she wore more makeup than the women he knew. Her eyelids were frosted with a pale lavender, her cheeks kissed with a sweet pink blush and her lips brushed with the most tantalizing shade of rose. He and Kara had talked the whole day away and her appearance had been as fresh when he left her as when he had first arrived. Rubbing his hand over the stubble on his chin, he wondered how she had managed to look so cool and fresh in such blazing heat. Was her appearance always perfect, no matter how high the temperature or trying the occasion?

"Oh my God!" he shrieked with a sudden terrible realization. Despite the fact that they had no written materials on 329, he had spent his youth listening to his elders reminisce and knew the universe was filled with many marvelous things which, even though he had never seen them, existed not merely in people's minds but in reality. The inhabitants of 329 considered memories of other worlds a precious treasure to be passed from one generation to the next until the descendants of those exiled resumed their rightful place in the Confederation. From his grandfather's tales he knew there had once been androids on the prison staff, robots with an amazingly human form. They had been communication specialists and office workers, but they had not functioned well in 329's hot, dusty climate and had soon been replaced by self-contained computers with the usual machinelike form.

Badly shaken by these thoughts, he sat up straight and swung his legs over the side of his bed. He was horribly ashamed by how easily he had been duped. Kara was perfection all right, but he should have realized her extraordinary appearance was too perfect. She had communication skills far beyond the human level, too.

"How could I have been such a colossal fool?" he berated himself sternly. He had spent the whole day conversing with a machine with an attractive façade, for surely that's all Kara was, a lovely computer with long, thick eyelashes. His friends would never cease laughing at him if they ever learned of it! She had undoubtedly recorded every word he had said so it could be analyzed by experts when she returned to her base ship. Humiliated to have been taken advantage of by a robot disguised in a seductive feminine body, he cursed the loneliness his choice of occupation required. What he needed was a woman, a real flesh-and-blood creature, not just some complex machine programmed to elicit information from talkative strangers.

Furious with himself for being so gullible, Aidan stormed into the bath, peeled off what little he wore and descended the half dozen steps into the bubbling pool. The warm water swirled around his hips with a sensuous grace which made his longing for feminine companionship all the more intense. The churning water caressed the powerful muscles of his thighs and back like teasing fingertips until he could stand no more. What fiend had designed such an enticing creature and set her loose on mankind? He wanted to meet that inventor and tell him exactly what he thought of the perverse little joke before he methodically broke every bone in his miserable body.

Since the heat of the pool was only fueling his anger, he climbed out, grabbed a towel and dried himself off with a vigorous circular motion. Standing nude before his mirror, he shaved quickly, then went to the chest which held his clothes and pulled out a pair of the soft, woven shorts he preferred to wear at night. He knew which of the men standing guard had obliging wives who would be home alone and eager to welcome him, but as he reached his door a truly evil thought struck him. An android of such incredible beauty would undoubtedly be programmed to make love. He burst out laughing then, a hearty laugh that rumbled from deep within his broad chest and graced his lips with a beguiling grin. If Kara was still there in the morning he would find out the extent of her programs and then make certain he took advantage of every one.

As the warm evening breeze caressed his bare chest, he left his quarters, realizing only then that there were many who would accuse him of treason for not reporting what he had seen that day. Invaders were to be promptly slain, not entertained with the romantic tales of 329's history! Were Kara human, such a charge would be justified, but surely she was no more alive than her marvelous ship. She had used him that day, but it would be his turn to use her the next.

Kara slept poorly, for throughout the night she kept expecting Mother to begin broadcasting the signal of the rescue sled. Anxious to be ready for it, she dared not nap too long. Each time she got up to check Sonia's screen it was blank, however, and she grew increasingly depressed. Something had to be wrong, dreadfully wrong, but what it was she could not even imagine. They all knew the procedures and followed the same set of rules. When Mother set her course she kept it. Always. Or at least she always had until yesterday.

Long before dawn Kara was up and rapidly working a
detailed series of computations. Mother had certain speed
limitations which she used to calculate the base ship's location in every possible direction. Time and again the answer
was the same. Mother could not possibly have escaped
Kara's scanners' range in the time she had been mapping
329. It simply wasn't possible. Even if Mother had completely reversed her course she would still have been within
range.

When the sensors shrieked a warning, Kara knew before
she shut them off that Aidan was back; but she was positive
she would never be able to concentrate on questioning him
now that she was faced with such distressing facts.

Just as Aidan had expected, Kara was as impeccably
groomed as she had been the previous day. Her sheer suit
was unwrinkled and her features as beautifully touched with
color. Her creator was undisputably a genius, but Aidan still
wanted to tear him limb from limb since that bastard's skill
had resulted in his suffering the most humiliating of practical
jokes. He knew the symptoms well even if he had never
before experienced them, and to have caught himself on the
brink of falling in love with a pretty creature who was a
masterpiece of technology rather than a lovely example of
femininity was more than he could bear.

"We have few machines here," he said, greeting her
warmly. "The air is too frequently filled with sand for them
to function properly. If you remain out here in the desert,
you'll not be in good working order yourself much longer."

"I beg your pardon?" Kara thought the man's comment
strange. She looked out over the barren terrain but saw no
sign of a dust storm. "Are high winds predicted for today?"

"It is a rare day that we are without them. Yesterday was
unusual in many respects," Aidan revealed with a rakish
grin. Despite his intention of spending the evening in the
arms of another man's wife, he had been so fascinated by the
challenge of capturing Kara that he had spent his time saun-
tering about the city rather than making love. Since he preferred not to share his women with others, he had decided
the lovely android would make him the perfect companion.

Her owners might come for her ship, but they would be unlikely to waste their time searching for her since they would undoubtedly have dozens of similar models. Such a high level of technology was impossible in his world, but obviously it wasn't in hers.

Kara frowned anxiously, worried a sandstorm might harm the Banshee's wide array of delicate instruments. "That's all I need," she moaned softly. While Aidan seemed in a playful mood, she most certainly was not. "Perhaps I should tell you good-bye right now. I've made an effort to determine where Mother might be, and since I've come up with nothing conclusive I'll have to try again. There must be something I'm overlooking, or I'm constantly making the same careless error; but until I find out what's wrong, I'm afraid I'll be very poor company for you."

"I'd like to watch," Aidan offered graciously. "I won't disturb you, I promise."

Kara licked her lips thoughtfully, the action making their lush rose tint shine. She knew she should simply send him on his way. "That's very kind of you, but I know you must have more important things to do."

"Not today," Aidan assured her. His eyes swept her slender figure with a calculating glance. How he could not have realized no living woman could have such splendid proportions he didn't know. He wondered how long she was scheduled to stay on his planet. Since a mechanism as intricate as she was undeniably delicate, and 329's conditions extremely harsh, he feared she was at risk already. She was a lovely toy, and one he intended to prize highly rather than abuse. Since he thought it unlikely she would have been programmed to lie, he asked a straightforward question. "Where are your recorders hidden?"

Hoping that if she satisfied his curiosity he would leave her in peace, Kara gestured toward the cockpit. "Sonia, my computer, contains a recorder to monitor significant details of my flights. The Banshee carries no others."

Aidan frowned slightly, for while that answer was logical, he had been certain every word he spoke to her was being

saved for others to hear. "Can what you and I say be overheard?"

"No," Kara admitted distractedly. She chewed her lower
lip nervously, preoccupied with locating what she hoped was
merely an error in her calculations. The Banshee's solar
panels provided the power for its instruments, and if there
truly were a danger of high winds, they might be severely
damaged. She had no time to lose. If she asked for his help,
they could bury the lightweight ship so it would not be
tossed about, but such a precaution would also shut down
her source of power, and she wasn't ready to sacrifice that
when her whole future still lay in doubt. "You needn't worry
about being overheard," she assured him. "I've really no
time to talk with you today."

As the distracted redhead quickly reentered her ship, a
startled Aidan took a moment to follow. He leaned nonchal-
antly against the open hatch and wondered if Kara had already started to malfunction. If she had been sent there to
determine the extent of their defenses she had failed in her
mission, for that was information he had not supplied. She
had not asked how many lived in his city, nor many other
details a military leader plotting strategy would want to
know. Perhaps her inventor had not been nearly so clever
after all if she could do no more than chat like a pretty
teenager rather than perform with the cleverness of a human
spy.

Confident his discovery of what she was had given him
the upper hand, Aidan studied her expression as she typed a
long series of commands for Sonia to process. He had to
admit she had remarkably expressive features. In fact, all of
her actions were so close to human, he rationalized, it was
no wonder she had fooled him so easily the day before. As
he continued to watch her closely, Kara sat back and her
sensuously feminine form adjusted itself perfectly to the
contours of her thickly padded seat. She then raised her hand
to shade her eyes until Sonia provided a one-line response.
While he could not make any sense of the figures on the
screen, Aidan could readily see from the sudden stiffening
of Kara's posture that she had not received the answer for

which she had been hoping. Even as he cursed his own stupidity for actually caring about her, he found himself too caught up in her struggle to remain coolly detached. Far too curious to remain silent, he leaned forward and asked in a sympathetic tone, "What's wrong?"

Huge tears welled in Kara's golden eyes but she was too embarrassed to let the handsome man see her distress and turned to avoid his glance as she brushed them away. "There's no way to explain what's happened, no way at all," she confessed unhappily. She sat back in the comfortable pilot's seat, her long oval nails digging into the fabric of the softly cushioned arms, her terror every bit as great as it had been when Mother's comforting image had first failed to appear on her navigational screen.

Aidan was perplexed by the savagely conflicting emotions Kara created within his breast, but he found his pretty companion's downcast mood deeply disturbing. She was nothing but a damned machine, he kept reminding himself silently, but surprisingly that made no difference in the empathy he felt for her plight. "There's still no signal from your friends?" he prompted helpfully.

Kara turned slightly to regard her visitor with a weary glance. While he carried no spear that day, Aidan was again clad in a worn pair of shorts and old boots. The frayed strap of his canteen was carelessly slung over his right shoulder, and what appeared to be a net of some sort was fastened to his belt. "What do you plan to do with that net?" she asked with casual interest, seeking only to distract herself from the horror of her predicament by focusing her attention on him.

Forgetting for the moment that he had brought it, Aidan looked down to see what she meant. "Oh this?" he lied with a cunning smile. "Sheep sometimes stray out into the desert, and I use this to catch them. I don't want anyone becoming curious about why I'm spending so much time out here, so I'll use a search for lost sheep as an excuse should anyone ask."

"Sheep?" Kara asked incredulously. "Do you actually raise sheep here?"

Insulted by her tone, Aidan straightened to his full height.

More than six feet tall, he attempted to use his size to his advantage as though they were having a physical rather than a verbal confrontation. "No, I do not waste my time raising sheep," he responded sarcastically, "but sometimes I'm hired to recover strays."

Kara leaned forward, her tone conciliatory. "Forgive me, I did not mean to offend you. I was merely surprised to hear you have livestock of any type here. It was my understanding that all efforts to raise animals and crops met with such dismal failure they were abandoned."

Before he had time to recall he was speaking to an attractive robot on a mission to gather information, Aidan replied, "You'd be surprised how much more successful free men are than prisoners in any endeavor, especially when their very lives depend on them being able to produce enough food to survive."

Intrigued, Kara swiveled her seat around so she might face him. "Then there was some livestock still here at the time of the revolt?"

Aidan caught himself suddenly, angry he had not done so sooner. "I'll answer no more of your questions until you answer some of mine." Turning his back on her, he sat down on the steps, his mind clearly made up on that point.

Kara rested her palms on her knees as she tried to think of a reason why she shouldn't humor the young man. She was getting nowhere with her intensive search for Mother and she knew from experience she might as well rest until some other direction of inquiry occurred to her. "What is it you wish to know?" she asked sweetly.

Aidan shot her a dark glance, knowing he would have to lure her outside to use the net effectively. Should anything go wrong in his attempt to capture her, he would have no other chance to ask questions. He wasted no time now, praying that despite her attractive form she did not have the skill to lie. "From where does Mother come? How many like you are on board? What's the real reason you were sent to 329?"

His expression was so hostile that Kara was instantly reminded of what she knew of his heritage. In spite of the kind words he had had for his great-grandfather, she doubted the man could possibly have been considered good in any respect. Mining Colony 329 had housed the most despicable sort of criminal, from the celebrated Cameron Burke, an assassin who sold his considerable talents to the highest bidder, to Joaquin Zacatón, a terrorist whose zeal for his cause had resulted in the slaughter of hundreds of innocent people. The death penalty was a thing of the past except for crimes committed in prison, but surely no men had ever deserved such a fate more, and they were only two of the many prisoners she recalled. The crimes of the women, while generally not nearly as violent, were no less damaging to society. As she had read the list of prisoners in a cozy cubicle in Mother's spacious library, she had shivered with dread, for the names of the more fiendish of the villains were still remembered. It had been lunacy to gather them all together no matter how remote the location, and as she gazed through the Banshee's open hatch toward the stark mountain range in the distance she could not help wondering which ones had survived the atrocities Aidan had described. Surely their already perverse spirits had been twisted beyond redemption by then.

Her dark musings too disconcerting to continue, Kara glanced over at Aidan and she thought again how remarkably handsome he was. His features were well defined, so attractive they were almost classical, while the fair curls which brushed his shoulders lent his appearance an innocence she doubted he deserved. His obvious strength was comforting rather than threatening, though, and since he had done nothing to cause her alarm she again refused to give in to prejudice and dislike him simply for his lineage. She rose gracefully to her feet and slowly descended the three steps to the sand. "Since the wind isn't blowing yet, I'd rather talk out here again if you don't mind."

Fingering the net suspended from his belt, Aidan got to his feet and waited for her to precede him. The time was not yet right, but she had walked right into his trap and he couldn't have been more pleased. Recalling she had not accepted anything to drink, he was certain she would refuse again. He unscrewed the cap of his canteen and offered her a sip of water, but she replied with another polite, "No, thank you" and sat down, confirming his suspicions that she had no use for the liquids without which humans could not survive.

Once she had gotten comfortable in the shade provided by her awning, Kara waited for Aidan to take his place by her side and tried to recall his questions. She then decided to give her replies what she considered a necessary preface: "It would be just as ludicrous for you to hate me because of my background as it would for me to hate you for yours. If I tell you something about my people, will you try to remember that?"

Puzzled by her request, Aidan swiftly asked for clarification. "Since we are responsible for the future, not the past, why do you think I'd be so unfair?"

"I'm hoping you won't be," Kara assured him with a bewitching smile, "but perhaps after you've heard a bit of my story you'll understand my concern."

Impatient for her to begin, Aidan gestured with a gracious sweep of his right hand. "Say whatever you will, I'll not take offense."

While she had seen no evidence he had such control, Kara decided to give the man the benefit of the doubt, but she took care to phrase her remarks in the most neutral manner possible. "Mother is part of a corporate expeditionary force. As I told you, our mission is to map the universe while others are responsible for colonization. Despite the high hopes of the explorers of the twenty-first century, we've yet to make contact with creatures having intelligence equal to ours, let alone superior. Since we are thus far alone, there is quite naturally a heated rivalry between the six corporations which make up the Confederation of Populated Worlds. Natural resources are always at a premium, as well as desirable lands for colonization."

Before she could continue, Aidan interrupted excitedly. "Wait a minute, just which corporation do you represent?"

Stalling for time, Kara instead asked him a question. "Do you know how the corporations were formed?"

"Yes, of course." Aidan replied impatiently, frustrated because she seemed to think him stupid. Even if she were no more than a hypnotically attractive robot, he was insulted for he'd been tutored in history with great care. "The quest for domination of Earth created six great alliances which superseded all former national boundaries. All-out nuclear war was still a constant threat, however, and was undoubtedly averted only by the common discovery of the means to conquer space. Rather than continue to prey upon one another, the people of Earth agreed to form six corporations and charged them with the responsibility of exploring and colonizing space. Each was to be independent and was to be free of any interference from the others for all time." He would have continued, but he was shocked to find Kara staring at him, mouth agape, displaying the most perfect teeth he'd ever seen. Of course, he scolded himself, why would anyone create an android with less than perfect teeth? "What's the matter?" he asked sullenly. "Is that story so different from the one you were taught?"

Kara shook her head. "Why no, but since you can not read, how did you learn so much?"

Aidan looked away, disgusted with himself for caring what an android thought of him in the first place. "A man who fails to learn the lessons of the past will never control his future," he snarled angrily.

"Yes, that is certainly true," Kara agreed in the most soothing tone she could manage. Without asking for his permission this time, she slipped her hand in his and was pleased to see the tension leave his deeply tanned features almost immediately. Knowing she could no longer hide the truth, she spoke it proudly. "As you must know, what became the most successful of the corporations was the one sponsored by the alliance created by the countries of North and South America. It is called Alado, and Mother belongs to them."

Aidan's first impulse was to yank his hand from hers, but to his dismay he found he could not move. Thoroughly disgusted to learn what he was doing was indeed treason, he felt sick to his stomach as a wave of revulsion left him too stunned to speak.

On 329 nothing was more despised than the memory of Alado's insufferable domination. There was not a single person who did not live in eager anticipation of the day they would hear the news the Alado Corporation and everyone ever associated with it had been consumed by the fires of hell. Once their desert world had been abandoned by Alado, the newly freed prisoners had prepared to fight off invasions by the other corporations whom they had expected to stake their claims to 329, but the blessed isolation that had extended for three generations had been complete, until now. Why had he had the misfortune to meet their first visitor? the young warrior asked himself through a deep haze of pain. Dear God, why did Kara have to be from Alado? Would those fiends come again to enslave his people? The horror of that prospect paralyzed his senses, plunging him into a sea of darkness despite the brightness of Altair's light.

Aidan was never frightened, never, but his hatred for Alado was so intense it simply closed his throat and threatened to suffocate him. As if she sensed the depth of his distress, he felt Kara increase the pressure of her fingertips on his hand, and although he tensed to shut it out the intense pleasure that shuddered through his body only deepened his shame. He had disgraced not only himself, but also his entire city. He had betrayed every principle he had ever been taught and, dear God, he could never even lift his hand to rip Kara's gorgeous head from her lovely mechanical body.

"Aidan! Aidan!" Fearing he had been overcome by some unseen peril to which she was immune, Kara ripped the canteen from his shoulder and tore off the cap. She poured the cool water into her hand and then splashed it on his face. "Aidan, can you hear me?" When that tactic brought no response, she tossed the canteen aside, placed her hands on his shoulders and shook him soundly. "Breathe, damn it! Breathe!" She had no idea what had caused the man to enter what appeared to be a deep trance, but she wanted him out of it immediately! She doubted he could have choked on anything since they had not been eating, but just to be certain she moved behind him to try the series of maneuvers guaranteed to dislodge a blockage from a person's throat. Aidan made no response at all to that effort, so she lay him down in what she hoped was a comfortable position and prayed that he would not die in the few seconds it took her to leap inside the Banshee, yank the small emergency tank of oxygen from the first-aid kit and return to his side. She placed the mask over his nose and mouth, then turned on the valve full blast. After what seemed to be an eternity, his eyes fluttered open and, relieved to find the handsome man had not died in her arms, Kara laid the nearly empty oxygen canister aside and burst into tears.

Uncertain just what had caused him to black out, Aidan raised up on one elbow and watched the lovely young woman weep for several minutes before he realized that, no matter how cleverly it was programmed, an android would not have the emotions Kara was displaying with such spectacular profusion. She was crying real tears, her distress obviously genuine, and he sat up and drew her into a warm embrace. He was still so confused he could not think of a single comforting word to repeat, but he did know enough to cradle her protectively in his arms until she at last regained her composure and looked up at him with a shy smile.

"I'm so sorry, but you gave me an awful fright. Do you pass out like that often?" Kara whispered hoarsely, wiping away the last of her tears. "The atmosphere here seems very thin to me, but I thought you'd be used to it."

Aidan shook his head. "No, I never pass out, or at least I never have before today." He tried to think of some way to describe adequately how she had made him feel, but he was so fascinated by her sparkling golden eyes that he was easily distracted. The soft violet shadow which graced her eyelids was still lovely. Her torrent of tears had not dimmed the delightful blush in her cheeks, nor had the fact she was chewing nervously upon her lower lip smeared their inviting rosy hue. He had never seen any woman cry as hard as she had, and yet it had left her spectacular beauty untouched. He reached out to caress her cheek lightly. "You are human,

aren't you? Not some marvelous invention sent here solely
to torment me with desire?"

Taken aback by so forward a remark, Kara tensed slightly
in his arms, but she was still trembling with fright and did
not move away. "Of course I am human. What did you
think?"

Knowing such a conversation was surely ridiculous in the
extreme, Aidan told her the truth. "I thought you were an
android."

"You didn't!" Kara gasped in dismay.

Knowing he had evidence aplenty, the young man quickly
shared it. "Why wouldn't you drink my water?"

"I'm sure it's very good, but while it might not upset your
system, there is a great risk that it would upset mine. I told
you I have my own rations. Didn't you believe me?"

Aidan shook his head slowly. "No, but listen, there's
more. Your face and figure are perfect. You can even cry
and it does not dim your beauty. How long do your cos-
metics last?"

Self-conscious now, Kara tried to put more distance between them, but he refused to release her and she had no
choice but to relax in his arms. "Do you know what a tattoo
is?" she asked breathlessly, all too aware of his warm bronze
chest.

Aidan frowned slightly. The word was familiar, but not its
meaning. "No, what is it?"

"Tattooing is a method for putting color on the body so it
will be permanent. It can be designs, patterns, or simply a
subtle hint of color. It's an ancient art. You don't do it
here?"

"No," the handsome warrior admitted reluctantly. He
lifted his hand to allow his fingers to comb through her
crimson curls, curious about their color. "Is nothing about
you real? Do you dye your hair this shocking color?"

Offended, Kara said firmly, "All of me is real. My hair
truly is this red." She looked down at the fullness of her
breasts which were pressed against his arm and was about to
remark that the contours of her figure were clearly her own,

too, when she thought better of it and swiftly changed the subject. "I'm glad you're not ill. Your people have been isolated for so long it's possible contact with me might cause you problems. I hope it doesn't."

"Oh, you've caused me problems all right," Aidan whispered as he leaned down to brush her lips with his. She tried to draw away, but he wound his fingers in her soft tangle of curls so she would not escape him until he was ready to set her free. For an instant he thought she might bite him, or foolishly flood his body with the indescribable pleasure which would inspire him to never let her go, but then she relaxed and opened her mouth sightly to return his kiss. As her tongue curled seductively around his own, he was the one to draw away, startled she would be so bold.

"What's the matter?" Kara asked curiously. "Don't people enjoy kissing here?"

The blond warrior provided a compelling answer, crushing her in his arms as his mouth again met hers for a slow, sensuous kiss which she returned so joyously it ended in a low moan of surrender when he drew away. For the first time in his life Aidan found himself with an irresistibly attractive female whom he dared not lead any further. For a few moments he had forced the thought of who she was to the back of his mind, but lovely though she was, she was his sworn enemy. He could no longer hide from that fact. Regretfully he released her and rose to his feet. He bent down to pick up his canteen and replaced the cap while he tried to think of some way to tell her good-bye. Even knowing what he did about her, the realization that he would never see her again was unbearably painful. "I hope your friends arrive for you today. If they don't, stay right here until they do. If you go any closer to the mountains you might be seen. The word Alado would be your death warrant. Don't even whisper it to the wind." With that sorry bit of advice he turned away and, breaking into a brisk run, soon disappeared into the shimmering waves of heat dancing above the sparkling white sand.

CHAPTER
◇ **III** ◇

Stunned by the ominous ring of Aidan's farewell, Kara sat for a long while fighting back the compelling urge to break the desert's oppressive silence with a loudly shrieked curse. He hadn't told her a damn thing she didn't already know. She had crash-landed on a planet whose environment and inhabitants could not have been more hostile. For some ridiculous reason she had expected better of him, though. She had made a point of requesting his assurance he would not react badly to her disclosures, but she had not expected him to lose consciousness over them! Perhaps she had overreacted, she admitted grudgingly. He would probably have revived on his own if she had just allowed him to rest quietly. She was positive she had handled their entire encounter very badly, but he had done far worse and she was sorry now she had not said so to his face.

Kara knew that, had she become so upset in the cockpit of her Banshee, Sonia would now be offering tender words of sympathetic advice to restore her calm. Determined to take care of herself, she took several deep breaths in hopes of improving her mood before she reentered her ship. As if to mock her efforts, she felt the first warm rush of heat which heralded the arrival of a blistering westerly wind. Disgusted by the fact that even the elements refused to cooperate, Kara rose, dismantled the awning which had provided much needed shade and stored it away with her survival gear. "I should have asked for that blasted net!" she swore regretfully, knowing she could have used it to secure the Banshee in place so it would not be buffeted about should the winds grow stronger. Lacking that, she assembled a small shovel and scooped up enough sand to cover the remainder of the fuselage which had not been buried when she had made her landing. Knowing it could easily be refilled, she replaced the oxygen canister in the first aid kit before walking around the Banshee one last time to be certain there was nothing more she could do to protect it. Without a backward glance at the bleak desert landscape she mounted the steps, pulled them inside and secured the hatch. The damn wind could blow until the rescue sled arrived for all she cared; she would not venture outside again when 329 offered so little in the way of hospitality. She had emergency provisions for a week, and since she had little appetite, she knew she could make them last far longer. Since Aidan had been so blunt, she was surprised he had not asked if the ship had a toilet, but there was a lavatory concealed behind the widest panel in the aft. If the wind did not clog them with sand, the vents would provide her with a steady stream of air. Resigned to the wait, she swore she did not need Aidan or any of his despicable kind to survive.

Kara collapsed into the pilot's seat, leaned down to pull off her soft silver boots, then slung one long shapely leg over the armrest to get comfortable and lazily wiggled her toes. The sorry outcome of her meeting with Aidan reminded her of one of her instructor's favorite sayings: The problem with people from the provinces is that their attitudes are always provincial. That oft-quoted line had made no sense to her at the time since she had had so little contact with people outside Mother's crew, but she understood it completely now and savored its truth. Aidan might know what had happened in his great-grandfather's time, but he was dreadfully ignorant about his own. She had been right about him from the beginning; he had proven most emphatically that they did not share anything but the human form. She was a child of the stars, her attitudes generations ahead of his. Aidan was a captive of the past, as much a prisoner of 329 as his great-grandfather had been. Straightening her posture proudly, she forced his handsome image from her mind and turned her attentions to the problem at hand: finding Mother and going home.

As he posted the first shift of guards that night, Aidan wore a long woolen cloak with the hood pulled forward to protect his eyes and face from the needlelike particles of sand which filled the air to a near suffocating density. The close weave of the dark brown garment made it uncomfortably warm, but he was not so foolish as to risk going without it in such a fierce wind. The hem whipped about his ankles as he walked along the wall with a carefully measured stride. He needed all his considerable strength to combat the fiery gale's efforts to send him into hiding. The guards were huddled down behind the wall, as miserable as he, yet none would desert his post that night, and he would not leave them alone to suffer the hot wind's wrath. In truth, he was so depressed that the nastiness of the weather did not faze him.

The dawn brought no respite from the storm, but Aidan's tour of duty was over and he made his way through the golden haze of sand-filled air to his quarters. He had securely covered the opening in his roof, but sand driven by the relentless wind had still found its way into his rooms. Knowing it was pointless to begin cleaning until the weather returned to a more placid state, he shook the sand off his blankets, tossed his dark cloak aside and stretched out on his bed.

Succumbing to the dreariness of his routine was something against which he constantly fought, but to discover that Alado still had the same power to torture him as relentlessly as it had his ancestors was a bitter realization indeed. Even after so many years of freedom, he felt the anguish of his great-grandfather's pain. He had never questioned what he had been taught about Alado's many evils. He had always considered everything about the hateful corporation cursed, right down to the most insignificant scout, so why couldn't he despise Kara as he knew he should? The elegant redhead had burst into his carefully constructed world with the searing heat of a shooting star, and in two brief days had reduced his superbly structured life to a mangled heap of impossible dreams. She had brought a vibrant streak of color to his bleak days, but the joy of her company was something he was forbidden to share. Horribly depressed, he let the bitter tears he could no longer contain roll down his cheeks unchecked. The thought that Kara would soon be gone was the only comfort he had, but he doubted Alado would have sent her to make maps had they not intended to use them. While disastrous for his emotions, her visit had provided him with the means to warn his people that an invasion was imminent. How he would go about that task without revealing the details of her visit he did not know, but he was confident a plausible explanation would occur to him soon. He would wait a few days to be certain she was gone before he'd make a report of their meeting. He would make it sound as though he had been the clever one and had feigned friendship only to gain knowledge of Alado's plans. If someone wanted to accuse him of treason, he was positive he could defend himself well enough to prove that charge a lie. Satisfied he could still fulfill his primary duty to safeguard his city, he closed his eyes and sighed softly as the face of the most beautiful woman he had ever seen teased his imagination with an impossibly lovely and totally unforgettable smile.

When Aidan awoke in the early afternoon, his head ached painfully from the oppressive heat while his stomach noisily protested its long deprivation. He simply ignored the throbbing pain in his temples while he steamed half a dozen succulent squash and ate them with a mound of brown rice. As he finished the last of his meal, he could not help but wonder at Kara's comments. Did Alado truly think the prisoners of 329 had starved to death after their cowardly guards had run away? That thought made him laugh, for he considered his diet more than adequate regardless of what the imbeciles of Alado imagined to be true.

The wind's high-pitched whine had not lessened, and as he bathed to remove the fine layer of silt from his skin he did not look forward to spending another night outside in what would surely be more sweltering discomfort. As his fingertips moved slowly across his chest, the memory of the cool sweetness of Kara's tears as they had splashed onto his bare skin was too compelling to ignore. His breath caught in his throat then as he suddenly realized that the force of the restless wind would shift the sparkling dunes, constantly rearrange the drifts, and change the face of the desert until the entire landscape would be unrecognizable by the time the storm had passed. What if Kara had not been rescued before the full fury of the winds had struck? What if she were still exactly where he had left her, all alone, huddled inside her ship while the sands swirled ever deeper around it? He shut his eyes in a futile attempt to combat that horrible image, but the possibility that she had been buried alive and at that very minute was struggling to draw her last breath was one he found impossible to force away.

Leaping out of the bath, he did not bother to dry off but simply yanked on a pair of shorts and his boots. Grabbing his cloak and the shovel he feared he would need, he ran to his door, but it took all his strength just to pry it open wide enough to permit him to slip through. The wind's fearsome howl was as piercing as the Banshee's sensors, and while several excellent reasons not to go to Kara's aid presented themselves, he knew he could not live with himself if he failed to do so. Haunted by the memory of her tears, he dared not risk allowing her to die all alone, lost and afraid in a world where she had heard no words of welcome. The streets were deserted. The astonished sentry did not question his order, but had he been unable to open the door in the massive gate, Aidan would have vaulted the wall rather than abandon Kara. Fighting the force of the stiff wind, he wrapped his cloak more tightly around himself as he made his way slowly down the steep mountain trail and out onto the vast desert. Having relied all his life on the jagged mountain peaks as a reference point, he had never used a compass. He had always considered it impossible to become lost, but he knew it was a real danger in such a fierce wind. The horizon was obscured by swirling sand, but he pushed on, praying he could find the exact spot where the Banshee had lain half-buried. It took him more than an hour to cover the same ground he would have traversed in a quarter of that time on a calm day, but the terrain was constantly shifting beneath his feet and each step was torturous. He turned often to be certain his direction was still correct, but the tall mountain range that protected his home was no more than a faint shadow in the distance. Fearing he had gone too far, he turned back and began to walk in an ever-widening circle, but there was no sign of the Banshee. Whether Kara and her gleaming craft had taken flight or been buried beneath the drifts he didn't know, and the agony of that uncertainty brought him to his knees.

"Kara!" he screamed. The wind instantly swallowed the sound of his deep voice, then spit it back in his face as a terrified shriek.

Feeling utterly defeated for the first time in his life, Aidan struggled to his feet and began to trudge slowly back toward his home. The constantly shifting sands tugged at his boots like malevolent fingers and he tripped and fell forward, bruising his shoulder on the handle of his shovel. He cursed loudly until he looked down and saw a piece of metal and realized he had stumbled over the edge of one of the Banshee's backswept wings. With energy born of desperation he began to dig with a frantic rhythm, but for each shovelful of the flowing white sand he scooped away, three seemed to replace it. He refused to give up, however, and through sheer perseverance he finally succeeded in uncovering the hatch. The ship's sensors were muffled by the weight of the sand, but he did not rely on them to alert Kara to his presence and pounded his fists on the oval doorway with savage blows.

Kara yawned widely, so dazed from lack of oxygen she had little interest in entertaining callers. Finally the beating on the hatch became so deafening she struggled to her feet and switched on the viewer to see who the ill-mannered guest might be. The Banshee's power reserves were so low that she could make out only a shadowy profile on the screen, but certain it was Aidan who was making all the racket, she released the hatch. The sand instantly poured in around the bottom and made it impossible to lower the steps, but he scrambled over that barrier and, after brushing back his hood, pulled her into an enthusiastic embrace.

Aidan covered Kara's sweet features with light kisses as he exclaimed in delighted surprise, "Thank God you're alive! I was terrified I'd find you dead."

The open hatch permitted a much needed influx of oxygen which quickly cleared Kara's befuddled mind, but the slender beauty failed to realize Aidan had arrived just in time. While she found his enthusiastic affection quite enjoyable, she had no desire for a repeat of his bitter farewell. As gracefully as she could, she withdrew from his embrace. "For some reason I can not imagine why you would even care if I did meet with an untimely end. What brought you back, unbearable guilt?" she inquired sarcastically.

"Guilt?" Aidan gasped incredulously. Of all the emotions the striking beauty created within his heart, guilt was most definitely not one of them. "Don't be ridiculous!" he responded harshly. "It simply became obvious to me that if your friends hadn't come to get you before the storm struck, you'd not survive it. I couldn't let your ship become your tomb!"

Kara looked away, certain he was overdramatizing her situation, but the lights that usually lit the Banshee's cockpit were very dim, so she knew the ship's power was shockingly low. She had come no closer to discovering the secret of Mother's disappearance, and worn out by the effort she had dozed off, but surely the Banshee would not have been her tomb. "Well, now that you've satisfied your curiosity about me, I'll thank you to leave."

Aidan was ready to wring the lovely space traveler's slender neck. "The sand has the Banshee completely buried. Had I not tripped over one of the wings I never would have found you. You won't be able to dig yourself out if I leave you here. You've got to come with me."

"No thank you," Kara replied coolly, although his description of her ship's plight had shaken her. "Scouts are not permitted to leave their ships, and from what you've said I know I wouldn't be welcome in your home. I'll not go willingly when it's likely there is a bounty on my head."

Cursing her stubbornness, Aidan still knew she had every reason to expect the worst after what he had told her. "I am a warrior and I'll give you my protection. You'll not be harmed. No one will forcefully drag you from my home."

Apparently he had forgotten just how easily she could turn anger aside, but there was a limit to the number of people she could influence at one time, and Kara feared she would be helpless in the face of a hostile crowd. That was something she would never admit, however. "No one is going to forcefully drag me from here, either. Now I'll thank you to get out and leave me alone," she demanded with a smoldering glance which clearly illustrated her hostile mood.

Aidan shook his head. "If I leave you here the risk is too great that you'll die."

"And if I go with you the risk is even greater that I will!" the hot-tempered scout replied. "Since the outcome will be the same no matter what I do, I prefer to remain here where my friends can find me." As if to emphasize her point she sank down into the pilot's seat and gripped the armrests firmly. "Good-bye."

"How many days had you been here before I found you?" Aidan asked with a renewed burst of determination, nowhere near ready to give up on his cause.

Kara shrugged. "I'd landed early that same morning. Why?"

"Then you've been here for three days and still have had no contact with Mother?"

The redhead hated to admit that was true, but since she was certain he already knew it, she didn't argue with him. "No, but I'm sure I soon will," she insisted defiantly.

Aidan knelt by her side, seizing the only alternative he thought she would accept. "Come home with me now. In this storm no one will see you enter my house, and I'll keep you hidden there until it's safe for you to return to your ship. Your friends can't find you if the Banshee's buried, can they? Even if they could, would they risk their own lives to land in this storm?"

The wind that howled steadily through the half-open hatch added credence to his words, but Kara needed a long moment even to begin to consider his invitation seriously. If the ship were buried it would be difficult, but not impossible, to find. She needn't tell him that, however, as it would only encourage him to bury the Banshee deeper. He was right, though; the question was whether or not rescue sled mechanics would brave the wind to save her. She knew there were a few who would, but the vast majority most definitely would not. Her greatest fear was that her calculations had been correct and that for some inexplicable reason Mother had simply ceased to exist. That was the only plausible theory for the base ship's sudden disappearance, and no matter how reluctant Kara was to accept it, if it were true then no one was likely to come for her—ever. That possibility unbearably dismal, she turned her piercing golden gaze upon her visitor. If she was forced to remain on 329, then it was definitely going to be on her own terms and she wanted him to understand that. "If this is some sort of an elaborate trap, Aidan, Alado will make every last person on this misrable planet extremely sorry. Do you understand what I mean?"

That the stranded scout would threaten him was somehow wildly amusing, and Aidan did no more than scoff at her challenge. "It is no trap. You will be safe in my home, and I'll bring you back here as soon as the weather clears."

He had always seemed to be a sincere man, but Kara hoped the consequences of trusting him would not prove fatal. She leaned forward and typed a brief entry for Sonia: I AM WITH AIDAN. IF I FAIL TO RETURN I HAVE BEEN SLAIN. RETALIATE. The computer had barely enough power to record the message, but when she was positive her fate would be communicated to Mother or another base ship, Kara reluctantly agreed to accompany Aidan, although she doubted his home could possibly be any place in which she would enjoy staying. She reached out to touch his long cloak. "I have no coat and I dare not let anyone see me wearing my helmet."

Relieved that she had finally realized his offer was her only logical choice, Aidan graciously offered to share the long garment. "This is large enough for both of us. Now let us hurry. There's no time to lose as we dare not be late."

"Why does your city have such strict security? Of whom are you afraid?" Kara struggled to pull on her boots, then stood to face him.

"I'm not afraid of anyone," Aidan boasted with a rakish grin, "but I will have to describe our enemies another time. Now let's go. When we get outside, I'll wrap my cloak around you."

Her decision made, Kara preceded him, but even with his warning she had not expected the force of the wind to be strong enough to slam her back into the side of her ship. It was impossible to be heard, but she grabbed his arm and gestured toward the partially open hatch. She dared not leave it ajar for fear the Banshee would fill with sand while she was gone. Despite both of them pushing with all their might, they had great difficulty sealing the hatch and had to rest a moment before turning in the direction Aidan was certain the mountains lay.

Kara slipped her arm around the handsome young man's waist, snuggling close as she matched her stride to the length of his. She would have to report that the climate of 329 was far worse than what she had expected. It would make an extremely poor base for spacecraft if the wind was frequently so violent. She tripped more than once, but Aidan caught her each time and kept her upright. Their journey seemed interminable, but when at last they reached the gate, Aidan kept Kara hidden in the folds of his cloak as they hurried inside. While the stone walkways were heaped with sand, the footing was at least secure there and he rushed her the short distance to his home. Opening his door, he shoved her inside, but did not venture in himself.

"Do whatever you like. Have a bath and something to eat or take a nap. I'll be back as soon as I can."

Before Kara had a chance to reply, the door swung shut and she was left alone in the spacious apartment. It took a moment for her to wipe the flecks of sand from her thick lashes and dump out her boots, but then she walked slowly through her host's home, amazed to find there was no sign of the squalor she had imagined. While a thin coating of sand covered everything in sight, the furnishings were remarkably handsome. She knelt down to brush off the mosaic tile at her feet, fascinated by the intricate abstract design. "Of course," she mused thoughtfully, "with so much sand they'd be bound to make glass." The half-inch mosaic tiles were predominantly gold, adding a richness to the geometric pattern that decorated the floor far more attractively than woven carpets ever would.

Pleased with that unexpected display of artistry, she rose and walked around the garden, but hesitated to sample some of the many vegetables she found or the large red strawberries. Thinking herself very foolish to have forgotten to bring along her own rations, Kara moved swiftly into the bath where the warmth of the bubbling water was so wonderfully inviting she quickly peeled off her sparkling rainbow-hued suit and the delicate lavender lingerie she wore beneath. She used a curious lump of transparent soap to rinse out her garments in the sink. Then she draped them over a towel rack to dry before turning her attention to herself. The floor of this room was also decorated in gleaming mosaic tile in shades of gold, but here the pattern was accented with silver. The sunken tub was nearly large enough for swimming and Kara stretched out in it, letting the water's swirling warmth caress her bare skin until she was again yawning widely and feared she would fall asleep in the water. There were large white towels stacked upon a shelf within easy reach, and as she stepped from the luxurious tub she wrapped the top one around herself before continuing her exploration of Aidan's home.

The walls were all a soft white, allowing the colorful tile floor to dominate each room, but by the time Kara realized there was but a single bed, she was too tired to wait up for her host to tell him she had no intention of sharing it. While she wasn't hungry, she was quite thirsty and realized she now had no choice about drinking Aidan's water. Noticing a carafe beside the bed, she filled one of the small glasses with the clear liquid which she mistook for harmless spring water. She was astonished by the fiery sensation that greeted her first long swallow. *I should have known*, she thought lazily with a sigh. She had tasted spirits on occasion, but had never enjoyed them. This drink left a deliciously sweet taste in her mouth, however, and since its initial searing heat had dissolved into a comforting warmth, she poured herself another glass and sipped it more slowly. After the troubles she had faced in the last three days, she thought she deserved a drink or two since they would undoubtedly prove relaxing. When she bent down to replace the glass on the tray, it slipped clumsily from her fingers and rolled across the beautiful tile floor, but retrieving it seemed totally unimportant when the large bed looked so inviting. Built for Aidan's impressive height, it was also perfect for her. It was too warm to slip beneath the covers, so Kara did no more than sweep off the sand which seemed to be everywhere and lay down on the bed still wrapped in the towel. She was in a dreadful mess, she remembered sleepily, but until she could return to Mother, she prayed that Aidan's promise that she would be safe in his home would prove to be true.

Despite his hopes for a swift return home, several hours passed before Aidan was able to leave the guards to tend the walls without him. He entered his apartment quietly, thinking Kara might be resting, and when he glanced in his bedroom and found her stretched languidly across his bed, he was pleased to see she had made herself so at home. He went to bathe before joining her, but as he approached his bed he found he could do no more than stare in astonishment. That tattoos were responsible for the soft touches of color that highlighted her features so attractively had been shocking news, but he had never dreamed she would have others. Fascinated, he bent down to study the sensuously coiled vine which began at her right instep. The pale green tendrils of the elegantly tattooed plant caressed her ankle, encircled her shapely calf with its narrow dancing line, then wound around her slender thigh and disappeared beneath the towel veiling the rest of her splendid figure from his view. Aidan was so intrigued by the lifelike quality of the vine and its few tender leaves that he knew he had to see it all. As he stepped forward his toe brushed against the overturned glass, and bending down to return it to the tray he realized with a devilish delight that she must have sampled the potent liqueur known on 329 as the Nectar of Oblivion. He had no idea how much she had consumed, but since she was unlikely to recall anything that transpired between then and dawn, he leaned down to draw away the towel.

Kara lay on her stomach, her right knee drawn up slightly, and Aidan reached down to trace the path of the delicate vine as it wound its way over the smooth flesh of her hip. It encircled her tiny waist, crossed her back with a graceful diagonal swirl, then disappeared over her left shoulder. The redhead's skin felt delightfully warm to his touch; a pale golden shade, it was the smoothest he had ever felt. While her exotic tattoo struck him as being unbelievably strange, he thought it the perfect decoration for a young woman as uniquely beautiful as she.

Placing his hand gently on her right shoulder, he applied light pressure to encourage her to roll over on her back, and when he called her name softly, she did. "Oh my God," Aidan whispered hoarsely, for when the pale green vine reached the fullness of Kara's breasts it burst into a wild profusion of lavender and pink blossoms. The details of the tattoo were so intricate he knew he would have been able to name the spectacularly beautiful flowers had he ever been privileged to see them growing wild. Overwhelmed with desire, he let his own towel slip to the floor and sat down by her side.

"Kara," he encouraged persuasively, "wake up."

Her dreams were so sweet that Kara was reluctant to respond to Aidan's call until it grew quite insistent. Her golden eyes opened slowly then, and her lashes seemed so heavy she wondered how she usually managed to bear their enormous weight. "Hello, Aidan," she whispered seductively. She lay her hand on the taut muscles of his thigh, not yet realizing he was also nude.

Aidan let his fingertips float lightly across the portion of the vine that encircled her waist like a narrow belt. "What do you call this form of decoration? Is it no more than another tattoo?"

"No, it is a Love Vine," Kara revealed, pronouncing each of her words with exaggerated care.

"That is precisely the name it should have," Aidan hastened to agree. Inspired by that title, he moved down to the foot of the bed and began at her ankle to trace the vine's delectably appealing path with teasing kisses.

After exerting considerable effort, Kara raised up on her elbows so she could watch him. "Whatever are you doing?" she asked with a charmingly innocent giggle.

Aidan paused only a moment, leaned down to pick up the carafe containing the hypnotically affecting liqueur and poured a tiny amount on her dimpled knee. He spread the fiery liquid up her thigh with his thumb, then continued his pursuit of the delicious vine's ravishing owner, this time using the tip of his tongue.

The young warrior's rakish grin and tender touch had lulled Kara into a warm sense of complacency, but when she suddenly realized she was no longer wrapped in a towel, she made a grab for it in a futile attempt to cover herself.

Aidan simply ripped the towel from her grasp and tossed it aside. "It's far too late for modesty now," he teased. Moving closer, he put his hands on her waist to turn her toward her left side. "The fun has already begun."

Kara knew she should argue, but she couldn't seem to form the words. Lying in Aidan's fond embrace, her usually agile mind stubbornly refused to function logically, while perplexingly her senses had never seemed more acute. As Aidan bent down to nibble playfully the fullness of her hip, the sensation of his lips on her fair skin was simply exquisite, light and yet unbearably tantalizing. "When do I get to kiss you?" she asked in an enticing whisper.

Aidan was enjoying himself so thoroughly he hated to stop to reply. Despite a far higher tolerance for the liqueur he was massaging into her creamy soft skin, he was beginning to feel its mind-numbing warmth. "Do you enjoy taking turns?" he finally asked with a quizzical glance.

Kara found the startling blue of his eyes greatly enflamed

the already dangerous level of her desire, but she could not honestly recall what her preferences were. "I don't know what I like, but I know I'd like to kiss you."

Even in his euphoric mood, her indecision sounded a tiny signal of alarm in his brain and Aidan sat up slowly. "What do you mean you don't know? Surely I am not your first lover."

"Lover?" Kara purred softly. The word rolled off her tongue, but it brought no image of another man to her mind. She frowned slightly, attempting to concentrate more fully on his question, but she continued to draw a complete blank. It was like looking for Mother, she thought with a flicker of her usual intelligence, and knowing how hopeless that had proven to be she gave up the quest. "I'm sorry, I just don't know."

Aidan found her confusion enchanting. "I have never made love to a woman who could not recall whether or not she was a virgin." He was inspired then to press his advantage and discover what else she might have forgotten. "Can you say something to me with your mind?" Splashing more of the delicious Nectar of Oblivion on his thumb, he began to tease the flushed tip of her right breast, then leaned down to savor the taste of her fragrant flesh with his tongue.

Kara wound her fingers in his flowing blond hair to press his face closer to her heart as she tried to comply with his request, but her thoughts, while loving, reached him as no more than a teasing flutter of desire.

Aidan's grin widened as he straightened up. While he knew he could not keep this delightfully loving creature drunk all the time, the fact that her remarkable powers were significantly diminished by strong spirits pleased him greatly. It made her seem far more human, more like himself somehow. He raised his hand to encircle her throat and drew her rosy lips to his. Her mouth opened easily, and this time he was not at all shocked by the eagerness with which she returned his deep kiss. Enjoying her flavorful affection too greatly to draw away, he clasped her gently in his arms as he stretched out beside her. He had never made love to a woman with her height, and it was a very pleasant sensation indeed, for she immediately entwined her long legs with his as her arms wrapped around him in a loving embrace. She was no virgin—he was certain of it—for no woman possessed such remarkable grace without considerable knowledge of passion's finest art. That she had forgotten all her previous lovers suited him just fine, but he wanted to make certain she never forgot him.

Alado's men wore their hair as short as hers, but Kara liked everything about Aidan, including his thick mane of damp curls whose tips reached clear to his shoulder blades. She combed the silken strands away from his face as she kissed his temple sweetly. She nibbled his earlobe, then used the tip of her tongue to catch a drop of water trickling down his neck. Freshly shaven, his face was very smooth and, like a cat rubbing against his owner, she caressed his cheek with her own. She then lowered her lips to his throat, tempted to leave clear evidence of her possession with playful love bites, but recalling dimly that he went without a shirt and might be embarrassed by the telltale bruises which would linger for days, she did no more than kiss him lightly. Her fingertips slid tenderly over the firm flesh of his bare chest before she traced their path using her nails with such gentle pressure his deeply tanned skin remained unmarred. His scent was fresh and clean yet distinctively male, and as she continued her tantalizing exploration of his well-developed body, she was certain there could be no more superb example of his kind on 329 or anywhere else in the universe.

Aidan prided himself on many things, and his prowess as a lover was most definitely one of them; but he soon began to suspect Kara possessed knowledge far superior to his own, and with a cocky grin he lay back to enjoy her attentions. She was not merely a passive partner despite her clouded mind, but a woman so loving he felt as though he were floating on a bed of pleasure as her kisses trailed their unique fire down his throat and across his broad chest. Her lips tarried at his nipples, her tongue taunting the sensitive nubs as she silently promised still more affection of the most lavish kind. Moving lower, she caressed the flat planes of his stomach with teasing nibbles as her nails began to slowly stroke his inner thighs.

The handsome warrior had never met a woman who was so obviously at home in a man's bed. She had aroused him with a remarkable talent for seduction. There was no trace of shyness in her touch, no hint of doubt in her kiss. When at last she drew the velvety smooth tip of his manhood into the warm, moist sweetness of her mouth, he knew in another moment his very soul would be lost, and he pulled her back into his arms before he lost the last bit of self-control he possessed.

Her slender body was so warm and soft, still flavored with the Oblivion's irresistible taste. He traced each of her luscious curves with his fingertips and tongue until he could no longer hold back his need to possess her. The boldness of her gestures had removed all doubt about the state of her virtue, but his touch was still tender, his impressive strength channeled into a superb masculine grace. His motions were slow and sure as he let the heat of their mutual desire build to a molten fury which fused their bodies into one. His conscious mind gave way to pure instinct then, and encouraged by Kara's soft moans of surrender and fevered embrace, he brought her swiftly to the brink of rapture, then abandoned himself to his own. She clung to him, taking all he could give, and then gently lured him again to passion's peak. She knew many uniquely beautiful ways to make love, and shared them all with him so willingly that his heart was filled to overflowing. Too content to ask more of the graceful beauty in his arms, Aidan lay adrift in their shared pleasure. When at last sleep overtook him, he knew he would never spend a more exquisitely erotic night nor find a more deeply satisfying mate. But even as the memory of her lavish affection filled his dreams with splendor, he knew the greatest challenge of his life would be to keep Kara for his own.

CHAPTER
◇ IV ◇

Kara awakened gradually with a languid sigh and a graceful feline stretch before she cautiously opened one eye. Pale rays of golden light bathed the bedroom in a sumptuous glow, but her surroundings were completely unfamiliar to her. What she did recognize immediately, however, was that her left cheek was resting comfortably on a distinctively masculine shoulder. The man was deeply tanned and the muscular arm that lay carelessly draped over her waist was covered with a thick growth of blond hair. She combed those fine strands lazily with her fingertips as she tried to recall what curious set of circumstances had brought her to this man's bed. When not a single thought filled the perplexing void where her memories should have been, she raised up slightly on her left elbow to look at her companion's face in hopes she would know him.

"Aidan?" she whispered softly, pleased to find she at least remembered his name if not how she had come to be lying nude in his arms. She knew there had been a sandstorm and he had come to help her, but she had no recollection of what had happened after that. Dismayed, she lay back down and closed her eyes, certain if she just gave herself a bit more time she would remember everything she had forgotten. Her mind rebelled against such strenuous labor at such an early hour, though, and refusing to concentrate on the elusive past, her mind filled again with the comforting warmth of dreams.

More than two hours passed before Kara awakened once

more. Aidan was reclining on his right side with her head cradled on his outstretched arm. His blue eyes were alight with mischief and his grin one of such unabashed glee that the mere sight of it infuriated her completely. He was also nude, and they were lying atop his bed in such casual poses it was painfully obvious they had been intimate; but an even greater shock was that Kara still couldn't remember any of it. That appalling fact infuriated her all the more.

"In addition to pleasure, it is possible to send mental waves of unspeakable agony. Unless you have a logical explanation for what happened between us last night, you are soon going to feel as though that magnificent body of yours is being ripped to shreds by a million birds with razor-sharp beaks!"

Aidan's satisfied smirk vanished instantly with that gruesome threat, for he had no doubt the feisty scout not only could, but would carry it out. "You've no reason to be angry with me," he insisted in his own defense, but as he recounted their romantic interlude, he stretched the truth to the absolute limit. "When I came home after posting the last shift of guards, I found you in a playful mood. You'd been sampling a liqueur known as the Nectar of Oblivion which accounts for your lapse of memory—but believe me, my memories are extremely pleasant and yours, if you had them, would be very nice, too."

Kara stared coldly at the handsome man, certain that tale was a flat-out lie. "There is no way I would sleep with you willingly. Had I thought there was even a remote possibility you'd try and take advantage of me I would never have come here!" she snarled angrily.

Insulted that she obviously considered herself too good for him, Aidan's savage frown mirrored Kara's rage. "I brought you here because you would have died had I left you in your ship!" he reminded her in a harsh whisper. "No matter what you might try and make yourself believe this morning, last night you wanted me every bit as much as I wanted you!"

"Don't be absurd!" Kara denied hotly. "You offered me a place to wait out the storm. That's all I wanted from you." She sat up then, meaning to scramble off the end of Aidan's bed, but a blinding wave of pain sliced through her head and then shot down her spine with a crippling effect which left her quivering in a limp heap by his side. Hot tears of frustration rolled down her cheeks, but she felt far too wretched to expend the energy necessary to wipe them away.

That she was plainly hurting, and badly, caused Aidan real pain too, since he feared her suffering was all his fault. He reached out to smooth her bright red curls away from her forehead with a gentle, sympathetic touch. "Oblivion tastes delicious but it gives some people a vicious hangover. I should have warned you not to sit up so quickly."

Kara's eyes filled with loathing as she looked up at him. "What you should have done is warn me I'd be far safer remaining in my ship than coming here with you. Just as soon as I can catch my breath, I'm going back there, since it's plain you aren't to be trusted!" How she could have been so stupid as to have trusted him in the first place she didn't know. Female scouts were always at a greater risk because of their sex, but their training provided them with more than a dozen ways to immobilize an attacker whether his intentions were amorous or otherwise. She had the skills to avoid compromising situations such as this one, so why hadn't she used them? That she'd been drugged was obvious, but she refused to believe she'd done it to herself.

Despite the ferocity of her mood, Kara was still so incredibly beautiful it took all of Aidan's concentration to focus on defending himself against her accusations. The enticing swell of her breasts was terribly distracting; the delicate lavender and pink blossoms adorning their lush fullness seemed to come alive each time she took a deep breath. He longed to lean down and again caress her sweet flesh with the tip of his tongue. Instead, he dared do no more than feast upon her with his eyes, and his glance was full of desire. "You told me that pretty tattoo is called a Love Vine, and it was clear to me that you're no stranger to the art of making love," he complimented her softly.

Thinking his assumption accurate, if totally beside the point, Kara nevertheless responded emphatically. "I'll not deny that, but I do not make love to strangers!"

Aidan gasped sharply, reacting as though she'd struck him. "I risked my life to save yours and you dare to call me a stranger?" That was one insult too many as far as Aidan was concerned. He rolled from his oversized bed, grabbed his towel from the floor and wrapped it snugly around his hips. "Get out of my bed. I didn't save your life so you could insult me. I don't want you here anymore than you want to be here!" He strode out of the bedroom and went to the front door to yank it open, but the howl of the wind was still so loud he knew he would only be filling his home with sand rather than effectively emphasizing his demand that she leave. Rather than appear a fool by making such a ridiculous gesture, he leaned back against the still-bolted door and tried to think of an alternate plan.

It was difficult to know how to act since he had never met another woman like Kara. There simply wasn't a female even remotely like her on 329. She was totally unique, for she had a man's fiery spirit and courage plus the beauty and grace of the most exquisitely feminine woman. That was an appealing combination to a warrior, but one which continually caused him pain. Women always liked him, so he had quite naturally assumed she would, too.

"Damn it! She did like me last night!" he swore under his breath. He had known she was drunk, though. He had known that and used it to his own advantage, he realized with a sudden twinge of guilt, but he had not once considered what her mood would be like that morning when he had awakened in such high spirits. He was so thoroughly depressed by their argument that it took him a long while to recall she had referred to his body as magnificent. The warmth of that no doubt unconscious compliment brought a smile to his lips, for it made it plain she was no more immune to the strength of his physical appeal than he was to hers. His spirits soaring with that new burst of insight, he realized he could do little to ease the strain between them until she regained her health. With just such a plan in mind he went into the corner of the main room that served as his kitchen. He reached into the large bowl containing freshly picked strawberries and other produce from his garden and extracted a knobby purple fruit. After peeling it, he sliced it into quarters and carried it into his bedroom on one of the delicate circles of glass which served as his best dishes.

Despite his hostile demand that she leave his bed, Kara had not moved. She had not even struck a more modest pose, and the elegant lines of her long-legged figure were so incredibly alluring that Aidan was afraid the fact that the mere sight of her filled him with desire would be all too obvious. He would not have won his first fight, let alone all the rest, had he let his emotions overrule his reason, however, and attempting to think only of her distress rather than the charm of her beauty, he sat down by her side.

Since it was all he could do to stifle the impulse to reach out and trace the exotic swirl of the Love Vine where it encircled her slender thigh, he gripped the plate so tightly his fingers soon began to ache, but he considered that pain a welcome distraction. Yet when he spoke, his voice betrayed his true mood, sounding far too deep even in his own ears. "Oblivion is made by distilling the juice of these pears. The fresh fruit will stop your headache, but I'm afraid there's no antidote that will restore your memory."

Kara knew better than to sit up this time, but she still didn't trust him. "I've never seen a lavender pear," she remarked skeptically. "How does it taste?"

Aidan was tempted to dump the slippery fruit into the delectable hollow of her bare stomach, but restrained himself at the last second. "This fruit is produced by one of our hybrid succulents so it might look a bit strange to you, but it tastes very good. I'm not trying to poison you. Is that what you're thinking?" He picked up one of the juicy lavender wedges, popped it into his mouth, then hastily wiped the juice from his chin. "See? I'm not afraid to eat it myself, so you've nothing to fear."

Kara felt too ill to argue and reached out to pick up a slice for herself. Guardedly she took a tiny bite, but when she found the pear tasted very good despite its peculiar color, she finished that piece and took another, thinking surely it could make her feel no worse. Much to her delighted surprise, by the time she had finished the third wedge her pain-

ful headache had faded somewhat, so that it was no longer
blindingly painful.

"Thank you," she offered gratefully, somewhat surprised
that he had been so kind after the terrible trick she was certain he had played on her during the night. "If you'll just
give me another few minutes to rest, I'll be strong enough to
leave."

Aidan set the empty plate at his feet as he explained why
that was impossible. "The wind is still blowing much too
hard for us to venture out, so we might as well talk awhile.
The only birds we have here on 329 are chickens, and I
don't think they would attack anyone even if they did have
razor-sharp beaks. What sort of birds can you conjure up
with your mind?"

Still a bit shaky, it took considerable effort for Kara to
focus her eyes on Aidan's face so his expression became
clear enough to analyze and judge sincere. Perhaps it was
the clear sapphire blue of his eyes that was so reassuring, but
despite his height and muscular build he did not appear in
the least bit threatening. He had the exuberant charm of an
inquisitive child, and she couldn't fault him for that when
she was just as curious about his life as he was about hers.
She would not be so foolish as to remain on his bed while
they talked, though, and used the first excuse that came to
her mind to put more distance between them. "I'd like to
bathe first please. I seem to be all sticky. I didn't realize I'd
made such a mess of myself with that pear."

Aidan chuckled slyly. "There's nothing wrong with your
manners. I rubbed some Oblivion on your skin last night and
I guess I didn't quite lick it all off."

That admission was scarcely what Kara wished to hear,
and she felt her cheeks flood with a blush far brighter than
the subtle shade that usually graced her cheeks. She slipped
by him hurriedly without comment and went straight into the
bath. The sheer curtain that covered the doorway provided
little in the way of privacy, but she didn't glance back over
her shoulder to see if Aidan was watching her. She stepped
into the bubbling tub and, finding another transparent sphere
of soap handy, first washed her hair before scrubbing herself

clean with long deliberate strokes. Since she had no bruises she knew Aidan had not taken her by force, but she was chagrined she had believed herself to be safe in his home. A scout always had to be on her guard, but somehow she had been tricked into lowering hers. She was not only embarrassed by that failing, but she was also disappointed in herself as her behavior showed a shocking lack of discipline. Aidan might have gotten the upper hand once, but she would see that it never happened again.

When she heard him call her name she wheeled around, ready to defend herself vigorously, but he had not entered the room. "Yes, what is it?" she called out nervously.

Aidan tossed a light woolen robe through the curtain. "You can wear this. We can't risk having you seen in your suit, but I've no women's clothes to offer you."

"Since I've no intention of being seen by anyone, I'll wear my own clothes, thank you." Kara watched in dismay as Aidan swept back the curtain and stepped into the beautifully tiled room. He grabbed her multicolored suit from the rack and left as quickly as he had entered, leaving her no choice but to obey his command.

"Damn you!" she called out in protest, but a wicked laugh was his only reply.

Kara sat down on the steps until the soothing warmth of the constantly churning water restored her calm. A quick review of her options brought the uncomfortable realization that if Aidan did not swiftly become more cooperative, she would have no choice but to force him to do so with pain. She had found it a simple matter to manipulate his behavior through the use of pleasure, so she knew pain would be equally effective, but she hated to unleash that cruelty upon him. That she had been stranded on the desert planet certainly wasn't his fault any more than it was hers. Each was an unfortunate victim of circumstance and, since she would prefer to have him help her willingly rather than because he was terrified not to, she decided to try using logic with him first. That question settled for the moment, she slipped back into the water to soak a few minutes more before getting dressed. After donning her own whisper-light lingerie she pulled the delightfully soft white robe over her head.

Returning to his bedroom, Kara did her best to give Aidan a disarming smile. "I'll answer your questions now, but you must again agree to answer mine."

Aidan replied curtly as he moved past her, "It will have to wait until I've bathed. Sweep up the place if you get bored."

Kara stared wide-eyed at the muscular planes of the young man's back. She had no intention of playing the role of housekeeper no matter how bored she got. Deciding she could justify searching the apartment since he had had no right to take her suit, she looked through the room's two carved chests hoping he had hidden it there. The first contained clothing, but it was all his, while the second held only linens. The tray with a bottle of clear liquid and several small glasses by the head of the bed caught her eye, but fearing that might be the cursed Oblivion, she did not touch it.

Frustrated by her lack of success, she left the bedroom and entered the cooking alcove. He had had plenty of time to use the cupboards as a hiding place, and she began with the cabinet beneath the counter on the left side of the sink hoping she would find the garment. The bottom shelf held two neat stacks of dishes, one made of ceramic and the other hand-blown glass. Heavy glass tumblers along with delicate crystal goblets filled the top shelf, but there was no cloth of any kind. The center cabinet beneath the sink held an assortment of scrub brushes and soap while the cabinet on the right contained several copper pans along with sacks of flour, bottles of beans, rice and other grains she didn't recognize and didn't care to examine. She quickly slammed the doors shut.

There was a stove with an oven below it built into the end of the long tile counter and when she flipped the switches, the burners came on with the bright blue glow of natural gas. A wide door at the opposite end of the alcove opened to reveal a refrigerator which contained only half a bottle of milk, a bowl of eggs and a plate with several wedges of dark orange cheese.

There were no drawers in the cooking area, but a small chest placed beside the stove held a wide array of utensils and cutlery. Picking up an elegant gold serving spoon, Kara wondered if the residents of the long-forgotten colony still worked the mines. They had every right to the precious metals, but it surprised her they would want them after Aidan's tales of the prisoners' suffering. Thinking the gold implements might be old and treasured heirlooms, she carefully replaced the spoon and closed the chest so Aidan would not suspect she had been rummaging through his belongings.

Leaning back against the counter, Kara could not help but marvel at the tiny kitchen. It was functional, but so primitive it made her feel as though she were touring one of Earth's folk museums. Alado's policy had always been to build colonies which would exist in harmony with a given planet's natural environment. Each planet was different, and so had different facilities. As 329 had an abundance of natural gas, that had been the obvious choice for cooking and refrigeration. Apparently, the inhabitants of 329 had managed to preserve the technology that provided these conveniences, even if so much else about their life was so primitive.

Indeed, Kara was impressed that Aidan's people had successfully maintained even the simple technology represented in the small kitchen. After all, the inmates had been sent to the exile facility because of their crimes, not because they possessed the necessary skills to create an advanced society. From what she could recall, only a few professions had been represented by the prisoners. There were perhaps three physicians, a couple of attorneys (who had amassed huge fortunes operating on the wrong side of the law) and a wide assortment of entrepreneurs who had possessed more in the way of diabolical cunning than fine education. The rest had had such violently antisocial natures that she couldn't imagine them contributing anything constructive to 329's society.

Kara couldn't recall a single mention of an engineer, scientist or inventor who would have had the expertise to refine and advance the spartan living conditions of the original

prison once it fell into the inmates' hands. No, clearly the
survivors of the revolt had had to make do with the minimal
technology Alado had provided for the penal colony and had
taken great care to preserve it. That Aidan's home was in
such excellent condition was undoubtedly a tribute to how
highly that technology was regarded.

Aidan's home was remarkable in all respects. The proportions of the stark apartment were classical in design, evoking
a mood of times long past. But rather than being soothed by
the simple elegance that surrounded her, Kara felt dreadfully
out of place. She longed to return to Mother, where every
inch of space was put to excellent use. Her cozy quarters
there provided maximum comfort in a minimum amount of
square footage, unlike Aidan's spacious home where the living room was so large that voices echoed with a hollow ring
against the bare white walls.

Had it not been for the thriving garden in the center, the
long rectangular room would have had all the charm of one
of Mother's docking bays, for other than the covered opening in the ceiling, the apartment had no windows. It was
well illuminated, however, by recessed light panels near the
ceiling. Solar energy was remarkably easy to harness, and
clearly Alado had shown the inhabitants of 329 how to do
so, at least for the purposes of providing lighting, before the
revolt. Given the strength of Altair's rays and the planet's
dry, desert climate, Kara was certain the residents of 329 had
an unlimited supply of power to provide light for their
homes. She hoped they enjoyed happy lives, but she simply
felt homesick and, now that her headache was gone, extremely hungry too.

Since she had suffered no ill effects from eating the
strange-looking pear, Kara decided to try a few of the luscious, ripe strawberries in the bowl on the counter. She carefully rinsed a handful and removed the stems but rather than
simply pop them into her mouth, she again opened the cabinet on the left and took out a small glass bowl. Not wishing
to be an inconsiderate guest, she then filled another bowl for
Aidan and carried them both over to the low table sur-

rounded by large cushions where she assumed he took his meals.

Making herself comfortable on one of the amply sized pillows, she began to eat the juicy strawberries with her fingers. When Aidan walked into the room, she was on her third bowl and looked up with an embarrassed smile. "These are delicious. I hope you don't mind that I've taken a few."

"Of course not," Aidan scoffed as he stretched out on the cushion opposite hers. "I might ravage all my female guests, but I always give them a nice breakfast before I send them on their way."

That he would tease her about the night they had spent together shocked Kara so badly she nearly hurled the glass bowl at him before she recalled her plan to win his help precluded such an impulsive act of violence. "I think the less said about last night the better. It shouldn't have happened because it complicates things unnecessarily, and I certainly don't think it's a fit subject for jokes."

Instantly defensive, Aidan's expression grew stern. "Why not? You're laughing at me, aren't you?"

"Of course not!" Kara insisted, but his question was strangely disconcerting and she felt compelled to give him a more detailed reply. "A scout is required to follow a strict set of procedures. I should not have spoken with you in the first place let alone come to your home. Once here, I meant to make my stay brief and, well, no more than a friendly one."

"The women here do not consider me ugly. Why do you find what happened between us so revolting?" Aidan asked accusingly, hoping to again force her into paying him compliments since he enjoyed the way she phrased them.

Kara's golden glance swept over the powerfully built warrior while she frantically searched her mind for a suitably tactful response. Aidan was clad as usual in no more than a pair of badly scuffed boots and worn shorts, but despite his numerous scars, he was as handsome a man as she had ever seen. His remarkably attractive appearance had nothing to do with her problems, however, and she said so. "I have no idea what actually happened between us, Aidan; all I can do is guess. What I do know is that a scout is forbidden to contact the residents of a planet not under Alado's control. I would not even be on 329 had it not been for Mother's disappearance. The fact that I am here is difficult enough for me, and I would never have involved you in my problems had I had any choice. I think you're extremely handsome and you've been so kind to try and help me, but since I'll be leaving soon, it would be cruel of me to begin a physical relationship with you when I have no intention of continuing it."

Aidan regarded the vibrant redhead with a perplexed stare for a long moment before he was finally satisfied he had grasped her point. "Wait a minute. Do you mean just because you don't know how long you'll be here, we can't enjoy the time we do have together?"

Seeing that he still didn't understand, Kara rose with tantalizing grace and, after licking the last drops of strawberry juice from her fingertips, began to pace in front of the low table. She gestured dramatically as she asked several questions of her own. "What are the customs here, Aidan? Do men and women engage in casual affairs? Is anyone married?"

"I asked if you had a mate!" Aidan replied crossly.

Kara stopped pacing and turned slowly to face him. "Had I told you I had a husband, would it have made any difference to you last night?"

Embarrassed that his thoughts were so transparent, Aidan looked down as he shook his head. "No."

She'd hurt his feelings again, Kara realized sadly. For some inexplicable reason, she was tempted to kneel at his side, to run her fingertips through his soft blond curls and offer what comfort she could. But knowing that would only compound their difficulties, she resisted that sympathetic impulse and kept her distance. "It's very flattering that you like me, Aidan. I can't help but like you, too, but that doesn't mean I'll begin an affair since there's no way it could possibly end happily. I'd never wish to hurt you, nor myself, either."

When Aidan looked up he was surprised to find her lovely features marred by the shadow of a troubled frown. "Why do you think we'd cause each other nothing but pain?" he asked thoughtfully. He could not recall ever having had such a frank discussion with a woman, but he much preferred encouraging Kara to talk with him in a reasonable tone than listening to her scream hysterically about betraying her trust as she had earlier that morning.

The wind had such an eerie howl that Kara shivered slightly despite the warmth of Aidan's flowing robe. She rubbed her hands quickly up and down her arms to dispel that sudden chill before she turned away and resumed her restless pacing. The fine grains of sand that had seeped into the apartment during the storm covered the bright mosaic tile floor with a thin layer of grit. Barefoot, each of her footsteps made a soft shuffling sound which accented the easy rhythm of her speech as she moved slowly back and forth. "I told you I love being a scout, but it's a life that demands total freedom. Opportunities for exploration do not present themselves on a regular basis, and yet I must always be ready to take advantage of them. I have never met a man who did not eventually demand that I choose to stay with him when I wished to go on a flight."

"And what do you do in that case?" Aidan asked curiously.

Kara halted in mid-stride but did not flinch as she looked him directly in the eye. "I've always said good-bye," she stated bluntly.

Aidan thought again how unlike the women of 329 this lovely creature was. She was tall, but so slender he had mistakenly considered her delicate. All her gestures were feminine, inviting his caress if not much more, but her appearance was maddeningly deceptive, for she had an inner strength that continually amazed him. He knew many men with the total commitment to duty she had described, but never a woman with such singleminded devotion, and he simply could not bring himself to believe there would not be a point at which she would make the other choice. The charming vixen who had shared his bed the previous night would most surely have chosen love. "What if you loved the man? Would your answer be the same then?" he asked with a knowing smile.

Kara's softly painted lips were graced with a sad, sweet smile as she replied, "You don't understand, Aidan. I have always loved them, but I've always said good-bye."

"I can't believe that, not when you make love so beautifully." The memory of her generous affection made him long to recapture the thrilling hours they had shared, and he was determined to make her want that, too.

Rather than respond as he had hoped, Kara laughed at his compliment but did not really sound amused. "Making love is a skill like any other, Aidan. I've been taught to do many things well—making love is merely one of them. It's not the least bit remarkable that you enjoyed being with me, but it won't happen again."

The defiant tilt of her chin finally convinced him she meant exactly what she said, but he couldn't accept her rejection gracefully. "Oh, now I see." Aidan rose to his feet, ready to bring their discussion to a close since it had taken such a disagreeable turn. "First you accused me of betraying your trust by making love to you when you'd had so much Oblivion it didn't occur to you to say no. Then you tell me you'll not be here long enough to make an affair worthwhile. Now you say you regard flying more highly than love anyway, so even if by some miracle you did learn to care for me it would not make the slightest bit of difference! You seem to have plenty of skills, Kara, but no emotions." Disgusted with her endless string of excuses, Aidan grabbed his long brown cloak from the peg beside the door and went out into the storm.

The tall warrior was gone before Kara could open her mouth to argue that she was not as despicably self-centered as he had made her sound. Despite his insult, there was no place for emotions in her decision. The audacity of the man was appalling, but she would not allow him to make her feel guilty for standing by her principles, the only ones a scout could possibly have. Clenching her fists tightly at her sides, she simply refused to allow him to do that.

Noticing he had not touched his strawberries, the distraught scout sat down and devoured them herself with a savage abandon. She had certainly learned one thing from her stay on 329: If she ever had the misfortune to crash-land on another planet she vowed never to speak to a single soul. Meeting Aidan had only deepened her predicament, not eased it. When the storm cleared and he took her back to her ship she would be ecstatic when she told him good-bye. The sand was undoubtedly ruining her instruments, to say nothing of what it was doing to the engines. When a rescue sled arrived, she feared her Banshee would have to be towed to Mother. That was the worst of embarrassments for a scout, but she would be so grateful to get home she would not object to the teasing she would surely receive.

Far too restless merely to recline on the comfortable cushions until the storm began to subside, Kara carried the two empty bowls to the sink, rinsed them out and put them away. Once that chore was complete she had nothing to do but stroll about aimlessly. The golden mosaic tile floor continually attracted her eye, for it was an artistic masterpiece, but other than the table where they'd talked and the surrounding cushions, Aidan seemed to have little need for furnishings.

Finally recalling she had yet to find her flight suit, she entered the bathroom. There were shelves for towels and she unfolded each of them thinking Aidan might have hidden it between them, but he hadn't. Glass shelves beside the mirror above the sink held his shaving equipment and a surprising variety of colognes contained in hand-blown glass bottles, but nothing of hers. She left the room disgusted that her search had been so unsuccessful, but the fabric of her missing suit was so fine he might simply have folded it up and carried it away in his pocket rather than leaving it behind for her to find. Tired of searching for it, she began to wonder how Aidan spent his spare time since his home was so devoid of amusements.

She knew he couldn't read, but she was surprised she had come across no sound system to provide soothing music, no screens upon which films could be viewed. There was so little in the apartment other than Aidan's clothes and a few personal items that she would have sworn it was vacant. She was accustomed to spending a great deal of time on her own, but there were plenty of tasks to keep her occupied in her Banshee and numerous entertainments on board Mother. Here there was nothing to catch her interest and she swiftly grew bored and then sleepy. Determined not to repeat the mistake of using his bed, she stretched out upon the cushions beside the low table and closed her eyes. With no distractions, she soon found herself reviewing their last conversation. She had not meant to insult Aidan by refusing his affection, but she didn't want him to misunderstand her views, either. That he had had such a hostile reaction was but another reminder of how deficient her skills were in diplomacy. She had obviously been too blunt in explaining her reasons for remaining aloof, but still, the truth remained the truth no matter how poorly she had stated it. She just hoped the storm would soon be over so she could leave his home before the vast differences between them grew even more painfully acute.

Bracing himself against the driving force of the wind, Aidan took a firm hold of his cloak and made his way through the narrow streets to his favorite tavern. Like all public houses in the city the tavern had a double entrance so the full force of the wind which frequently plagued 329 did not intrude upon the lively atmosphere of the establishment. Sighting his best friend leaning against the bar, Aidan tossed his cloak upon the heap near the door and started across the crowded room to join him. He had to stop often to reply to loudly called greetings, but he had a ready supply of teasing jests with which to respond. When finally he reached the bar, a dark-eyed young man with thick black curls reached out to slap him soundly on the back.

"Where have you been keeping yourself? For the last three days Tory has asked every man who came through the door if he had seen you. It isn't like you to neglect a pretty woman like that," he teased with an engaging grin.

Cringing visibly at the mention of the inquisitive barmaid's name, Aidan turned to glance briefly over his shoulder and was relieved to find her occupied on the far side of the room with a large table of boisterous customers. He had to admit he had found her passably amusing upon occasion, but this was most definitely not one of them since he was in no mood for her silly giggles. "The nights have been far too rugged to leave me with enough energy for Tory, Zac. Why don't you look after her for me?"

Zac shook his head emphatically. "Sorry, but she's definitely not my type. Duke's been looking for you, too. How many times does he have to tell you to stay away from his wife?"

Aidan brushed that question aside as unworthy of response. He had not seen the woman in more than a month anyway so he knew the man had no legitimate complaints. "I don't have long before my shift begins. Have you no more important news than that to share?"

Eric, the sandy-haired man on Zac's left, leaned forward to tell a joke which at another time would have struck Aidan as being hilarious, as it did all those standing nearby. Now he reacted with only a slight smile. A sense of humor was essential to survival on 329, but he was far too tense to appreciate the complicated tale which had made the others laugh. He turned slightly, hoping Tory would be too busy to get over his way before he left, but she was walking straight toward him with such an enthusiastic smile that he did his best to look pleased to see her. He reached out to give her a warm hug when she reached him but then quickly released her.

"What can I get for you?" the petite barmaid asked sweetly, hiding her disappointment that he had not noticed her new gown. A clinging sheath of pale blue knit, it was slit up the side from ankle to thigh as all her gowns were. The top of her head was even with his shoulder, and as she turned to stand next to him her long blond curls brushed against his bare chest. It was a gesture she repeated often for she had found that most men loved the silken feel of her flowing hair, so she allowed it to fall unbound in loose waves which reached her tiny waist.

"You know I never drink in the afternoon," Aidan reminded her with what he hoped would pass for his usual good-natured chuckle.

Clasping her tray tightly against her side, Tory leaned close to ask, "You'll be back later, won't you?"

Aidan shrugged. "Can't say."

"Well then, who can?" the pretty woman demanded in a childish whine, her annoyance with Aidan now too great to hide.

Overhearing that complaint, Eric turned around to join in. "I'll be here all night, sweetheart. I'll see you don't get lonely."

Since Eric was very nice looking if not rakishly handsome like Aidan, Tory warmed instantly to his offer. She planted a light kiss on his cheek as she went to answer another patron's call, hoping that gesture would not only encourage his attention, but also serve to make Aidan jealous.

Aidan winked at Eric. "Thanks. She's very cute, I know you'll enjoy yourself."

"You didn't look too interested so I figured you wouldn't mind."

"You're right, I don't." In fact, Aidan was delighted Eric had shown some interest in the overly possessive barmaid since he no longer had any. Turning back to Zac, he asked again, "Nothing happening on the day watch?"

His friend started to comb his dark curls back from his forehead, but finding them so tangled that that careless gesture caused real pain, he dropped his hand to his side. "No, but this storm has everyone on edge. Watch your back."

"I always have," Aidan assured him with a friendly wink. He had an unusual schedule which allowed him to come and go at odd hours, but that also provided jealous husbands and others who had grudges against him with more than the usual number of opportunities to find him alone. The few men who had been so stupid as to jump him had instantly regretted it, however. Still, Zac was right; a storm never improved anyone's mood. "It doesn't sound like I've missed much."

Not wanting his tavern's reputation to suffer, the owner, a burly red-haired man named Dodge, leaned across the bar to argue. "There was a fight in here last night I'll not soon forget. Stefan and Blair set it off, but I had to finish it myself."

Aidan's glance filled with casual disgust as he surveyed the scarred tables and scattered benches that furnished the room. "Can't have been much of a fight. Doesn't look like there was any damage."

"Oh, well, no," Dodge admitted with a hearty laugh. "It was nothing like the time you and Zac tore up the place. That was the worst brawl we've ever had in here."

As Aidan caught his best friend's eye, he realized while he could recall the spectacular fight down to the last bone-bruising punch, he couldn't remember the reason why they had come to blows. It had to have been a woman, but he would be damned if he could recall which one. Rather than ask, he just shook his head as he agreed with the barkeep. "Yeah, that was some fight." At the moment, the only woman he regarded worth paying such a painful price for was Kara, but he knew she would not be impressed with a mere physical display when she could do such incredible things with her mind. Fascinated by his thoughts of her, he didn't respond until Zac had called his name for the third time. "Hmm?"

Zac threw a teasing punch to his buddy's midsection. "They catch you daydreaming like that tonight and you'll be out of a job."

"I'm the captain, remember? There's no one to catch me," Aidan replied with a broad grin. "But you're right, I better get going."

"See you later?" Zac asked.

"Now you're beginning to sound like Tory!" the tall warrior grumbled as he turned away, ready to leave his friends to continue their revels without him.

"Hey, what's gotten into you?" Eric called out.

Aidan turned back to wave and reply, "Not a thing. It's the storm that's making everyone's temper short." Yet as long as the wind blew, he knew Kara wouldn't be able to leave his home and, despite the bitterness of their last argument, that thought brought a wide grin to his lips which he made no effort to repress.

CHAPTER
◇ **V** ◇

By the time Aidan returned home he had had a long and exceedingly torturous night during which to reflect on Kara's coolly detached explanation of how she chose to live her life. He was chagrined to realize what had angered him most was how close she had come to describing his own philosophy. He had never promised any woman more than the pleasures of the moment. He had not allowed even one to imagine he might take her for his wife. No indeed, he had always ended an affair the instant a woman had begun to presume upon his time or affection. He had never deliberately refused to fall in love; he had just not found any woman's charms so tempting that he wanted to claim them permanently for his own. That was the major difference between Kara and himself, he decided. She refused to begin affairs when she knew the anguish the inevitable end would cause, while he had always wrung every last ounce of pleasure from life without a thought of the price he or his lady of the moment might eventually have to pay. Her approach to love was painfully honest, and while his had never been so devastatingly direct, the resulting heartbreak each wrought was exactly the same. They were an amazing pair, he mused with a touch of pride. Now if only he could convince Kara they were more alike than different so she would accept his way of life as the far better one for them to share.

The weary warrior opened his front door just wide enough

to slide through, then stood perfectly still for a moment to allow his wind-numbed senses to adjust to the blissful calm that welcomed him home. Breathing a deep sigh of relief, he turned to hang up his cloak. Desperately hungry, he started toward the kitchen at the opposite end of the long room. It was not until he had passed the garden that he spotted Kara curled up on the floor cushions. She was hugging one tightly, but he dared not hope that he might be the lover who filled her dreams and graced her expression with a wistful smile.

As he stood watching, she turned in an attempt to find a more comfortable position but succeeded only in rolling off the overstuffed pillows. The hard sandy surface of the mosaic tile floor awakened her with a bone-jarring jolt, and as she sat up she swore with an oath he had never known a woman to use.

Laughing at her bawdy outburst, no trace of his parting anger remained. "You're always welcome to my bed," he offered graciously.

"No thank you." Kara replied much too quickly, afraid their argument would now continue as though it hadn't been interrupted. She knew it would take her body several days to adjust to 329's thin atmosphere, which made her so sleepy all the time, but she was still annoyed to have been caught sleeping. She fluffed out her curls with her fingertips then rose shakily to her feet. She wondered how long Aidan had been watching her before she awakened and hoped it had not been more than a few seconds. She was surprised she had not heard him come in since she was usually a very light sleeper. Feeling far from refreshed, she knew she was at a disadvantage for she would need all her wits about her if she were to avoid another nasty confrontation with her handsome host. She was horribly uncomfortable in his home but could tell by the seemingly perpetual whine of the wind that the storm had yet to abate and she would be forced to remain there longer.

That his lovely guest would now be so ill-at-ease around him saddened Aidan terribly, and he flashed his most charming grin to reassure her he meant her no harm. "The storm has not let up any. It could last for days, but I'll do my best to make the rest of your stay far more enjoyable." He took the long way around the low table and cushions to avoid alarming her as he entered his kitchen. "Let me cook you some breakfast. Do you like omelets?"

Kara covered a wide yawn as she nodded. "Yes, very much, but I don't want to be any trouble."

Aidan put a copper teakettle on the stove, then removed the milk, eggs and cheese from his refrigerator. "You're no trouble at all to me, Kara. I'm sorry I got so angry with you yesterday afternoon. You're absolutely right. You'll be here only briefly and the less impact we have on each other's lives, the less painful our good-byes will be. I'm just not used to a woman caring so much about my feelings. You took me by surprise."

"You're not still angry with me then?" Kara asked apprehensively. She couldn't believe his reaction to her comments could possibly have changed from the wild anger with which they had parted to this calmly displayed acceptance. Although she scarcely knew the man, he had not struck her as the type to change his opinions capriciously, if at all. If he were merely acting, he was doing a superb job of it, for both his expression and voice were sympathetic and conciliatory.

"No, not at all," Aidan insisted. "Like I said, you're right. We should simply stick to conversation. You answer my questions, and I'll try and answer yours. That should keep us busy." While conversation was most certainly not all he hoped they would share, Aidan knew better than to press his luck and for the moment was attempting simply to regain her trust.

"I'd like my suit, please," Kara announced calmly, recklessly testing the sincerity of his friendly mood.

Surprised by this unexpected request, Aidan turned around and leaned back against the counter. He folded his arms across his chest and shook his head with obvious regret. "You look very comfortable in my robe. Are you certain you'd rather wear that tight suit?"

"It's not in the least bit tight!" Kara responded crossly. "But even if it were, I am supposed to be dressed in my uniform when I'm on a mission, not in some—" she looked down at the robe which flowed with a graceful fullness from her shoulders to her toes. "In some helpful man's clothes," she finished tactfully.

Aidan reached into his hip pocket and with a gentle tug slowly withdrew her shimmering suit. He held it out and waited for her to come close enough to take it from his hand. The impulse to catch her in a fierce embrace from which she would never escape was nearly overwhelming, but he relaxed against the counter and smiled invitingly. "Well, here it is."

Exasperated that her suspicion he had taken her suit with him had been confirmed, Kara took two long strides and snatched the silken garment from his outstretched hand. "I'd like to bathe before breakfast. Is there enough time?"

"Take all the time you need. I won't cook the eggs until you're ready to eat," Aidan replied agreeably, as though her question had been politely worded rather than a hostile inquiry.

Kara still thought his smile far too wide but prayed his more reasonable attitude was not a ruse of some sort. Her smile was faint as she left him. She had meant to bathe hurriedly, but as soon as she entered the bubbling water what little energy had not been sapped by the almost constant ordeal of the last few days began to seep away, and she was content to float in the bath's enveloping warmth until Aidan finally drew the curtain aside and asked if she'd fallen asleep.

"No, I'll be right there," she apologized, but still she made no great haste. It took such effort merely to rub soapy lather up and down her arms that Aidan had had time to bake bran muffins before she rejoined him. When he offered her a cup of freshly brewed herb tea, she took it eagerly and went to sit down at the table while she sipped it. Just being able to wear her uniform again lifted her spirits immensely, and she tried to be coolly professional once more. "I didn't mean to take so long," she offered sincerely. "I'm not usually as tired as I am today."

"That's not surprising. You've been through a lot in the

last couple of days. What did you fix yourself for supper?" Aidan asked casually as he began to crack half a dozen eggs into a mixing bowl.

"Nothing," Kara admitted with a shrug. "It was stupid of me to forget to bring my own rations with me."

"Well, it's far more stupid not to eat mine," he scolded without losing his smile. When she didn't respond, he grew curious. "You do know how to cook, don't you?"

Kara licked her lips thoughtfully. The tea had the sharp tang of mint combined with an enticing sweetness, but she hoped it had no unusual powers like the Oblivion did. "Cook?" she asked absently. "Well, actually, I've no need for that particular skill. Scouts all take their meals together in one of Mother's dining rooms. I have no facilities for cooking in my quarters."

"So what are you supposed to do if you find yourself stranded as you are now if you're forbidden to rely upon, how did you put it, 'helpful strangers'?"

He was plainly teasing her, but Kara answered seriously, "There's a generous supply of rations stored on board each Banshee. Scouts never starve to death before they're rescued."

"You mean one hasn't yet," Aidan replied with a playful wink.

Kara didn't bother to argue as she watched him prepare their morning meal. He moved with an admirable economy of motion, as though he often cooked for himself. She knew nothing of his life and, since he was in a talkative mood, she encouraged him to answer her questions while he worked. "Why is your city so heavily guarded, Aidan? I didn't see any other settlements when I was making my maps."

Aidan raised a brow quizzically as he glanced toward her. "Just exactly what did you see?"

Kara took another comforting sip of the soothing herb beverage before she replied, "There's very little to see. Except for this one range of mountains, the desert landscape is unbroken. But you're simply evading my question. If you're a warrior, then whom do you fight?"

Aidan sighed as though the answer was too obvious to

merit an explanation, but then he realized 329's customs would undoubtedly sound strange to her and she would never understand them unless he finished the tale he had begun the one full day they had spent together in the desert. "As you might expect, when the prisoners broke free the last thing they wanted to see established here was any sort of authority. Each man wished to live out his life totally independent of the others. That worked just fine until the first time two men wanted the same woman for a wife. Since men outnumbered women by about five to one then, it was a problem the survivors knew they would face often. It was decided the only way to settle such a dispute was with hand-to-hand combat."

"Wait a minute," Kara interrupted anxiously, already caught up in the continuing drama of his ancestors' lives. "Why didn't the woman just say which man she wanted? Wasn't she given any choice in the matter?"

Aidan poured the lightly beaten eggs into the pan he had heated and answered her question as best he could. "Well, even if she had had the sense to choose one, I doubt the other man would have backed down, but apparently it made no difference to her."

"But it must have!" Kara exclaimed in disbelief, her bright golden eyes mirroring her dismay.

"Just believe me, it didn't." Aidan placed several thin slices of cheese on top of the bubbling mixture and when he was satisfied the eggs were fully cooked, he carefully folded one half neatly over the other. He divided the omelet into two equal portions, placed them on glass plates and carried them over to the table. "Try and remember what hell this place was, Kara. Everyone had been so badly abused they were numb. For that matter, they didn't know but whether Alado's forces would retaliate at any minute for what they had done." He went back to the counter and returned with two golden forks, napkins and the plate of muffins. It took another trip to get his cup and the teapot. Finally ready to enjoy his breakfast, he made himself comfortable on the cushion opposite hers and continued. "Do you know what a zombie is?"

Kara was so hungry she took a large bite of her omelet before she even considered giving Aidan a reply. The eggs were flavored with a sharp tang of cheese and the result was utterly delicious. "Zombies are walking corpses, aren't they? I don't know much about those ancient voodoo cults. I thought they had all disappeared long before 329 came into existence. Do they practice that sort of thing here?" Nothing would surprise her, but she certainly had more than enough problems trying to handle Aidan without the threat of zombies to worry about, too.

"No, of course not!" Aidan denied with an exasperated sigh. He had not expected her to have taken his remark so literally. He remembered the first time they had talked and he had been so nervous he had not known where to begin. Now everything had changed between them. They were in his home which naturally gave him confidence. She had shared his bed, so he felt no more reluctance to share his life; but he wanted her to understand how difficult survival on 329 had been. "You've got to remember that most of the prisoners were only one step away from the grave. That's what I meant about zombies. It was obvious that not everyone would survive the hardships they still had to face, so it was decided a man who wasn't strong enough to win a woman in a fistfight had no right to have one."

"You don't mean it!" Astonished, Kara's fork slipped from her fingers and clattered noisily on her plate. Aidan looked so shocked by her question that she hurriedly promised to be still. "I'm sorry, go ahead. I won't say another word. Just tell me what happened." She found his story fascinating and, while she couldn't help but have questions, she vowed to keep them to herself until he finished.

Aidan was certain Kara was pushing his explanation in entirely the wrong direction and paused to eat a muffin in an attempt to regain control of their discussion before he dared continue. He considered the history he was attempting to relate a simple, straightforward tale, but clearly she didn't. Now he tried to slant his comments to win her sympathy. "Women were quite naturally in short supply since there hadn't been that many of them here to begin with. None could be wasted on a man who might be too weak to father a healthy child. You see, the more children the women were able to produce, the better everyone's chances for survival would be."

"Oh, of course," Kara replied sarcastically, the fury of her anger barely disguised. "Why is it so many men refuse to believe women are good for anything but breeding?"

"You just promised not to ask me any more questions," Aidan reminded her crossly. Recalling her technique, he extended his hand. "Will you permit me to touch you?" he asked with an enticing grin.

"Oh, Aidan, I'm so sorry." Kara reached out to take his hand, but gave his fingers no more than a quick squeeze before releasing them. "If I were a diplomat I'd be so well trained I'd be able to sit here for days listening to you without ever making a single judgmental remark. Forgive me. There's no reason for me to be angry with you just because someone thought having lots of children was a good idea three generations ago."

Aidan's grin took on a decidedly sheepish slant as he admitted the truth. "It was my great-grandfather's idea, actually. He wanted to show Alado that given their freedom, even the most despicable criminals could build a harmonious society and raise peace-loving children." As he watched Kara's beautifully expressive features, he knew she would never be able to accept that statement without comment. "Go ahead and say it. It must be obvious that if I am a warrior, he failed."

Kara shook her head. "No, those are marvelous goals for any society. Just because they have yet to be achieved does not mean his ideas were a failure."

"That's an unusual way to look at it, but yes, I suppose you could say that." Aidan refilled their cups with tea, then returned the pot to the stove to heat more water. When he came back to the table he tried to complete his explanation as briefly as possible.

"The challenges began with the question of wives, but it became the standard way to settle any argument. There's still an aversion to authority here. As Captain of the Guard, I have only the authority needed to see the walls are manned and the responsibility to command should we be attacked. I'm not expected, nor allowed, to do anything more. We all take care of ourselves. We have no police force, no judges, most certainly no jails."

"No one ever does anything wrong?" Kara asked skeptically.

"Of course they do, all the time. But it is up to the wronged party to handle it. Let's say there's a riot in a tavern, then the owner handles it himself. It's a very efficient system," Aidan insisted proudly.

Kara found that difficult, if not impossible, to believe. "It might be for you. You're young and strong and can obviously take care of yourself. Is that true for everyone? Are there no elderly people here, or others who might be easy prey for bullies?"

"I told you I was a warrior. Should anyone need help in resolving a dispute, then I handle the challenge."

"You're paid?" Kara inquired between bites of the savory omelet.

Aidan gave her a critical glance, then decided she was just curious, not deliberately trying to insult him. "Why else would I risk my life?"

Kara nodded thoughtfully. "You're a mercenary then. A soldier who offers his talents to the highest bidder?"

"I prefer the word warrior to mercenary, but yes, that's exactly what I am."

Intrigued by the implications of his vocation, Kara phrased her next question as tactfully as possible. "So what happens if two people wish to hire you to settle the same dispute? What do you consider most important, the size of your fee or seeing that justice is done?"

With that question she had backed him into a very tight and uncomfortable corner, and Aidan quickly excused himself to check on the teakettle to give himself a moment to think. He knew her well enough to know what she would prefer to hear, but that wouldn't be the truth. He added the herbs to the hot water so they would begin to steep, then turned around to face her. "Look, it was decided a long time ago that whoever wins is right. We don't debate issues end-lessly here, we settle them quickly and forget them."

Kara could scarcely believe what he was saying was true and persisted in her questioning. "So if I had a disagreement with someone, but he could pay you more to take his side than I could pay you to take mine, the fact that I was right wouldn't influence you? You'd simply take the other man's side if he could pay you more?"

Kara was as usual maddeningly direct, but Aidan saw a way out and took it. "I'd take your side for free, Kara," he offered with a teasing wink as he returned to the table.

The redhead thought the gleam that brightened the blue of his eyes to a dazzling azure was far too predatory for such a show of sentimentality. "Oh, no you wouldn't. You'd expect to be paid all right, only not with money," she challenged with a defiantly tilted chin.

He had learned her mannerisms quickly, and while he found them charming, he had no desire to spend the entire morning in a bitter debate with such a determined opponent. "Our system of justice works here because we all agree upon it. It's as simple as that. There's no point in arguing about what is right when the question can be settled to everyone's satisfaction in a few minutes."

"Can it?" Kara asked with a knowing smile. "You already know you can not fight me and win. Does it frustrate you to know your physical prowess isn't enough where I'm con-cerned?"

Aidan stared at the lovely scout for a long minute, his mind awhirl with the utter insanity her presence in his home represented. With her mind alone she could twist every rule on 329 until it suited her sense of order rather than theirs. Such awesome power was terrifying, and he rebelled in-stantly. "You told me you were forbidden to interfere in our lives," he threatened coldly.

"I have absolutely no intention of meddling in your life or anyone else's, Aidan," Kara responded flippantly, waving his concern aside. "I am a scout and I came here to make maps, not laws to govern your society. Now please tell me what happened to the men who weren't able to win wives. Were they doomed to a life of loneliness?"

Aidan frowned in annoyance, for she had made him confront the issue of her remarkable gifts and then just as swiftly had lost interest in the very real threat she presented to the status he had fought long and hard to win. "What I'm doing is treason, Kara. Sitting here, entertaining you at breakfast, would be considered treason by everyone. Don't make the mistake of thinking I'm doing it lightly," he cautioned sternly.

"You insisted I come to your home, remember? I didn't beg you to bring me here," Kara reminded him with an equal edge of disdain in her voice.

Aidan rested his elbows on the table for a moment and cradled his head in his hands. Only by shutting out her captivating image could he gain control of his thoughts. He had given away no secrets worth having. He had told her nothing that could be used against them by Alado, nothing at all. Satisfied in his own mind that he had done nothing wrong, he looked up and smiled. "I'm sorry, I didn't answer your question. Things weren't as difficult for the bachelors as you might imagine. Some did keep to themselves and lived quietly. Some proved to be so tough once they had regained their health that they were alive to marry some of the first girls born." He paused then, sensing what her next question would be. "No, the girls weren't forced to marry anyone. When they turned sixteen they were permitted to decide whether or not they would accept the winner of a challenge as their husband."

"Could they do no more than pray that the man they loved would win?" Kara asked softly, that imagined heartbreak plain in her golden glance.

Aidan shook his head. "No, it works the other way. They fell in love with whoever won."

Kara found that impossible to believe, for she knew the girls must have had some feelings for the men before the fight began. Afraid he would never understand her confusion, she decided to keep silent for the moment. Doing a few fast calculations in her head, she swiftly discovered the original imbalance between males and females had had sufficient time to correct itself. Children would have been born in approximately equal ratios of male to female and surely all but the youngest of the original inmates were dead. "This is 2246, Aidan. There's been enough time for the population to even out so there should be a sufficient number of women for the men now."

"Yes, that's true, but it's only been in recent years. For a long while it wasn't unusual for men to share their wives with their friends. It's a practice that's still not uncommon." He recalled Zac's warning about Duke, but knew better than to discuss his own affairs with her.

With the addition of that bit of information the inquisitive redhead was certain she would never understand the finer points of his perplexing culture. "Women married men who won them in fistfights, but the women sometimes took the losers as lovers? Is that it?"

"Well, not exactly. A man didn't have to have lost a challenge to become a woman's lover. He might never have fought for a woman of his own."

"He'd just be content to share one with another man?" Kara asked incredulously.

"Yes. It might sound peculiar to you, but it works well for us here. Really it does," Aidan insisted.

Kara frowned as she pursued their discussion more aggressively. "If the purpose of the challenges was to insure that the stronger men fathered the children, then to allow women to have lovers who hadn't passed that test put the whole community at risk. It makes no sense at all. How could any woman be certain who had fathered her child?"

"It really didn't matter, Kara. Children were considered vital to survival, I told you that. Besides, most women didn't take lovers until they had already had several children by their husband."

That fact made Kara curious about a point she thought he had overlooked. "How could these men who married the first generation of daughters be certain they were only husband to the girls and not father as well?"

That Aidan had not once considered such an obvious

question shocked him quite badly. He had never thought of himself as stupid until he had met this infuriating beauty who asked such difficult questions and gave such astonishing answers. "I don't know," he admitted reluctantly. "I just don't know."

Since she had not meant to upset him, Kara reached out to caress the long scar that crossed his left forearm. "Is the city fortified merely as a defense against Alado's return?" she asked softly.

Aidan covered her hand with his to enjoy the magical spell of her touch more fully. "The city's defenses are something I'll not discuss," he replied firmly.

"The residents of 329 are in no danger from Alado, Aidan. Were the corporation to contact you, it would be through diplomats who are trained in establishing dialogue without generating hostilities. You needn't spend another night guarding your city from Alado. There is no threat other than that in your imagination."

Aidan gripped her hand more tightly as he explained the threat was very real indeed. "You don't understand. I told you my great-grandfather wished to establish a harmonious society. Not everyone agreed with him. In fact, the majority didn't. After years of bitter conflict the survivors of the revolt split into two factions. Our city is built upon the ruins of the prison. The others occupy the caverns of the abandoned mines. They are a far greater threat to our survival than Alado has ever been because without fail every few months they attack us."

Astonished by that news, Kara leaned forward slightly as she spoke. "Does your side never attack theirs?"

"Never!" Aidan scoffed emphatically. "They have nothing we want, and there is no value in killing the miserable creatures merely for sport."

Since that was the first custom she had found admirable, Kara finally gave her handsome companion a warm smile. "Alado does not kill for sport, either. At least on that major point we agree."

"Is that a comfort to you when our views differ so widely

on the question of justice and adultery?" Aidan inquired with a cocky grin.

"I told you I was sorry for asking so many questions," Kara reminded him with an embarrassed blush. "I never even considered becoming a diplomat because I lack the ability to observe a culture without comparing it with my own."

"Isn't that merely a skill to be learned like all your others?" Aidan asked pointedly. He still regarded her as a very puzzling creature, not simply as a collection of useful skills in a lovely form.

"No, not really," Kara admitted readily. "The talent must be there initially or it can not be developed no matter how excellent the teacher."

"That at least makes sense."

"And nothing else I say does?" Kara tried to pull her hand from his grasp, but he refused to let her go. Since his mood was so playful, she relaxed and did not fight his affectionate display.

"Look how much I've told you, and you've told me nothing."

"What is it you wish to know? You've seen my ship, and I have explained that I spend my time flying it and making maps. There's little more to tell."

"But that's just your occupation. I still know very little about you. Tell me about your parents, about your childhood, things like that," Aidan encouraged with a warm smile. When Kara's expression filled with such deep anguish he felt her tears flood his heart before they had begun to fill her lovely golden eyes. "Kara, what's wrong?"

The usually graceful young woman yanked her hand from his as she leapt to her feet. She gathered up the dishes and rushed toward the sink as if clearing his table were the most important task she would ever have to perform. In her haste, the glass plates slipped from her arms and shattered as they struck the tile floor. She bent down and grabbed for the jagged pieces so quickly that she slashed her right index finger badly and cried out in pain. This was apparently one disaster too many, and she could no longer hold back her tears.

Aidan had no idea what ghastly thing he'd said or done to upset his beautiful visitor so suddenly, but he pulled her to her feet and led her over to the sink to inspect her wound. "I know somehow I caused this, and you must believe I'd never knowingly hurt you." He used his napkin to bandage the profusely bleeding cut, then gripped it tightly. "I've never tried putting stitches in a wound myself, but if we can't make this stop bleeding, it looks like I'll have no choice but to try that."

Even more sickened by that suggestion than by the cut itself, Kara began to argue immediately. "No, you needn't do that. I have medicines on board the Banshee which will help it heal." His expression was so tender as he lifted the edge of the cloth to check the bleeding that she could not allow him to take the blame for a stupid accident she had caused herself. "This was all my fault, not yours."

Aidan disagreed. "No, it was something I said. You were smiling and talking with me so pleasantly until I asked you to tell me something about your life. Then you went to pieces faster than the plates when they hit the floor."

"I'm so sorry about the dishes, too. Can they be replaced? If they're very expensive, I'll—"

"Kara!" Aidan was tempted to shake the vibrant young woman, but when the tears continued to stream down her cheeks he did no more than pull her into his arms and hold her tightly. The curves and hollows of her lithe body fit so perfectly against his own he felt as though he had made love to her on a thousand nights, rather than only one. He closed his eyes to savor the stirring warmth of that memory.

She was trembling all over, clinging to him helplessly, and he still had no idea what was causing her emotional pain. When next he checked the cut, the bleeding had slowed considerably.

"Come on," he said softly. "I have some fabric I can use as a bandage in my bedroom." He slipped his arm around her waist and guided her into his room and saw that she was seated comfortably on his bed. He opened the chest containing linens and rummaged around for a long scrap of white cotton which he tore into two-inch strips. "I am pretty good at wrapping up cuts. I've had plenty of practice at that."

"Aidan?" Kara whispered anxiously. She raised her left hand to cover her mouth. "I'm afraid I'm going to be sick."

The agile warrior dropped the bandages, grabbed Kara around the waist and half-carried, half-dragged the limp young woman into his bathroom. That he had prepared such a splendid breakfast and she had not been able to keep it down did not upset him nearly so much as her ghostly pallor.

Lifting her into his arms, he carried her back to his bed and laid her down. "Now don't think I'm going to attack you. I don't plan on doing more than bandaging your hand and letting you sleep." He could recall none of the compelling arguments he had thought of while on duty the previous night to entice her back into his bed. His only thought now was that somehow he had upset her so badly she had not only been injured, but had also become physically ill. "Was your childhood so gruesome you can not bear to think of it? Please forgive me for asking if it was. I thought it was a very innocent question, but clearly it was not."

His touch as he bound the cut was surprisingly gentle for such a strong man. Kara did not want him to feel responsible for her injury or illness and so told a soothing lie. "It was nothing you said. I am used to eating my own specially prepared rations rather than the fresh food you served. You see, Alado's rules are wise ones, but I've broken them all and have no one but myself to blame that I'm suffering now."

"Did the pear and strawberries make you ill, too?" Aidan asked anxiously as he wrapped the ends of the bandage around her wrist and secured them in a square knot.

Kara closed her eyes to shut out his troubled frown. He was being so wonderfully warm and sympathetic, but she was not even remotely tempted to share the secrets of her past, so she embellished the lie she'd begun. "No they didn't, but I'm very tired. I tried to sleep while you were gone, but—"

"I know," Aidan whispered. "I shouldn't have walked out

on you like that. That was no way to treat a guest, especially such a lovely one from so far away." He brought her bandaged hand to his lips and kissed it lightly. "Let's try and get some sleep now."

Kara's lashes swept her delicately painted brows as she looked up at him. "What do you mean by 'let's'?"

The blond warrior gave her a playful nudge. "Just move over, the bed is plenty big enough for us both. I won't take advantage of you."

Kara studied his expression through a tear-filled gaze. "Androids don't bleed, Aidan, and they don't get sick, either. It would have been better for you if I'd actually been one."

"Nonsense." After taking off his boots and then hers, Aidan stretched out beside his reluctant guest and slipped his arm beneath her head so she would have to rest her cheek on his shoulder again. "I like you just the way you are." He held her in a light embrace, and while her tears continued to splash on his chest and roll down his side to dampen the bed, he did not ask her again to tell him what was wrong. She was lost in a world where clearly nothing made sense to her, and he gave her a loving squeeze so she would know she wasn't truly alone.

CHAPTER
◇ **VI** ◇

When Kara awakened she opened her eyes cautiously, praying the room would not take a sudden painful lurch. Finding herself alone in Aidan's comfortable bed was reassuring in itself, and she needed no more than a moment's reflection to realize she not only felt wonderfully rested but completely well. A delectable aroma filled the air, giving clear evidence of Aidan's whereabouts. The thought of him busily preparing another meal for them to share brought a sweet smile to her lips. In every way he was a remarkable man, and she knew despite the brevity of their friendship that she would miss him. She lay languidly, enjoying the pleasant warmth of his bed and trying to decide whether or not it would be worth expending the energy to investigate the source of the enticing scent when she realized the only sound she heard was the soft bubbling of the bath water in the adjacent room.

"The wind, Aidan. The wind's stopped blowing!" the lithe beauty shouted with glee as she leapt from his bed. She dashed for the doorway, and they nearly collided when he came running to meet her. While she was surprised to find him clad in no more than a low-slung towel, she ignored his maddeningly distracting physique and forced herself to concentrate on the blue of his eyes. "Listen," she urged with unabashed delight, her expression aglow with an instantly rekindled hope of a swift return to Mother. "The wind's finally died down and I can go back to my ship!"

That she would be so overjoyed to leave him ripped

Aidan's already ragged emotions to agonizing shreds. He knew he would soon lose her, but in his mind he screamed, *not yet, not yet!* Soup ladle in hand, he used it to gesture dramatically. "You get right back into that bed, Kara. You're far too ill to make that long trek through the desert. Even if you were well, we'd still have to dig your Banshee out of the drifts, and that will take more time than we have left today. Just get back in bed and I'll bring you some soup when it's ready."

The fierce expression on the muscular warrior's finely chiseled features served to emphasize his sharp command. He was serious in his demand, but Kara knew it wasn't a reaction to his food that had caused her to be sick, it was an aversion to the memories she would not willingly relive. She couldn't bring herself to admit she had lied to him, however, but now changed her story slightly to bring it closer to the truth. "I was just overtired, Aidan, but I feel ever so much better now. I'm not ill, really I'm not. It is so nice of you to be concerned, but I can handle the walk to the ship and even if I have to wait until tomorrow to dig it out, I'd at least be there when the rescue sled arrives."

The prospect of the imminent loss of his fascinating and impossibly elusive companion was more than Aidan could bear to face calmly and he emphatically refused to grant her request. "I won't take you today and that's final! There's not enough daylight left for me to get back safely even if we have no great difficulty finding your Banshee. It's as simple as that. There's too great a risk to make going now worth my while."

Shocked that Aidan was furious with her when he had absolutely no reason for such anger, Kara took a step backward to put more distance between them. "If there is not enough daylight, all you need do is say so and I'll understand. I'll not put your life at risk. Even if that's how you usually earn your living, I'd never ask that of you."

Aidan looked away, ashamed he had sounded like he placed a higher value on his own life than hers, but he would use any excuse to keep her with him no matter how ridiculous it made him look. "I promised to take you back out to the desert after the storm and I will. There just isn't enough time to do it right now," he apologized curtly.

Certain he wasn't revealing the true cause of his anger, Kara placed her palm just above his heart. The deeply bronzed skin of his broad chest felt smooth to her touch, but the tension that had tied fierce knots in the underlying muscles took several seconds to dissipate. As her silent gift of tranquility flooded through him, his expression filled with awe and he leaned back against the doorway to retain his balance. He covered her bandaged hand with his, then raised it to his lips and gave her wrist a brief kiss before breaking into a wistful smile.

"I was worried about you," he admitted readily, but that was the only part of his anguish he would reveal.

The impulse to step into his arms and give him a reassuring hug was surprisingly strong, but rather than give in to it Kara pulled her hand from his grasp and slid past him to enter the cooking alcove. "I'm sorry you were so worried, but really I'm fine again. Your soup smells absolutely delicious. What's in it?" She leaned over the simmering pot to savor the aroma more fully. "Vegetables, spices, anything else?"

"It's my secret recipe, and you'll never guess all the ingredients," Aidan boasted proudly, but truly he had no idea exactly what he had tossed into the pot—his mind had been so filled with thoughts of her. As she moved around his kitchen, the rainbow hues of her iridescent suit danced invitingly under the soft lights. From every angle Kara was an incredibly attractive female. "Now that I see you in that suit again, I do think it's more flattering than my robe. What do your men wear?"

Kara gave her uniform a cursory glance. She had worn it for years. It was as comfortable as her own skin, and she gave it as little thought. "The men wear exactly the same thing. Would you like to try this on?" she asked with a teasing grin.

"We're not anywhere near the same size," Aidan pointed out quickly, but he had no wish to don such a revealing garment. It was difficult enough hiding how easily she aroused him; in that flimsy suit it would be impossible.

"Our uniforms come in only one size and the fabric is so fluid it conforms to the contours of the wearer. This suit would fit you very nicely, really it would. Since you have such a splendid body, it would be very handsome on you."

That she had complimented his build again made Aidan chuckle self-consciously. "Well, at least you like the way I look, if nothing else."

Kara frowned, sorry he would have such a mistaken notion. "I like you very much, Aidan. I hope I haven't insulted you in any way, or made you feel that I don't enjoy your company, because I do."

Not impressed, since her words bore no relationship to her actions, Aidan straightened up, walked over to the stove and gave the pot of bubbling soup an attentive stir. They had only a few more hours to share, and he knew exactly how he wanted to spend them. "I'm a grown man, Kara, and if you'd insulted me I'd have said so. Since you give me no choice about telling you good-bye, I should at least be allowed to do it in my own way."

That remark confused the young woman so completely that she stepped around to his left so she could study his expression as they spoke. "Do you have some sort of a farewell ceremony? Do you exchange gifts or do something like that? Is that what you mean?"

Kara was the brightest woman he had ever known, but her question was so damn stupid Aidan didn't believe she had asked it, and he snarled his reply. "Of course we don't have any elaborate farewell ceremony. No one has ever gone anywhere from here!" He saw her begin to reach out to him again and swiftly blocked that move. "Stop it! That's not how I want you to touch me, can't you understand that?"

The flame-haired scout was stunned by his outburst, but since it was simply impossible to turn her back on the man and walk away, she stood her ground. "Even an innocent friendship between us is forbidden, Aidan. What you ask of me is impossible. I want to leave immediately, but you say it's too dangerous. Well, now it appears it's too dangerous for me to stay here as well."

"You are in absolutely no danger here!" Aidan denied sharply. He threw the ladle on the counter and started for his room. "I'm going out. Have all the soup you want. I'll take you back to your Banshee at dawn. Be ready to leave when I return."

In a matter of minutes he had dressed in what few clothes he usually wore, stormed past her and slammed the door soundly on his way out. Kara had made no effort to stop him since she considered their conflict completely beyond her ability to resolve peacefully. She turned the fire off under the soup, then walked over to the garden and sat down on the low wall surrounding it.

How would a diplomat have handled the meeting with Aidan? What would a person trained in avoiding conflict have done that she hadn't? There had to be an answer, but she was afraid she already knew it: Avoid all contact. It was as simple as that. Once she'd broken the first of Alado's rules, the rest of her problems had been inevitable. "I despise rules!" she growled to the empty room. Suddenly an almost fiendishly clever idea occurred to her. There was a way to please Aidan without complicating things between them, and she didn't understand why she had not thought of it sooner. Well, at least it wasn't too late, for she was certain he would listen to her idea when he came home, and she couldn't imagine any reason why he would not agree to it.

Aidan went not only to Dodge's Tavern, but also to three others to make certain he was seen by anyone who might wonder where he had been. He told hilarious jokes, soundly kissed thirteen different women and started two fights which swiftly turned into savage brawls before he slipped away to begin the night shift as Captain of the Guard. If he failed to return from the desert in time to visit his usual haunts the next afternoon, then it would just be assumed he had gone to one of the others or could be found at home nursing his wounds. He had been forced to accept the sorry conclusion that there was no way to avoid taking Kara back to her Banshee at dawn. He would not simply abandon her, though. He would return every day until she was rescued, and if there were any way he could wring a promise to return to 329 from her, he vowed he would do it.

To spare himself additional anguish, Aidan did not return to his apartment until the first rays of dawn had already lit the sky with a pale orange glow. He knew Kara had nothing to pack and he had expected her to meet him at his door ready to go; but to his surprise, she was nowhere in sight.

"Kara?" he called softly. When there was no response, his first thought was that she had gone without him. He ran to his room fearing he would confirm that suspicion. He didn't expect to find her sound asleep in his bed, but that was exactly what he found.

Thoroughly confused, Aidan sat down beside his perplexing guest and ran his fingers through her short curls with a loving caress. "Kara, wake up. Why aren't you ready to go?" The sheet had been pulled up to her chin, but as she raised her hand to cover a yawn it fell away to reveal a shapely, blossom-covered breast—he was shocked to see that she was nude. "Kara—" Aidan whispered hoarsely, unable to think of anything other than how much he wanted to gaze on her spectacular figure one last time, to begin at her instep and trace her exotic tattoo with his adoring lips again. He reached for the sheet to pull it away, but she placed her hand over his to stop him.

"I was hoping you would come home before this," Kara purred sweetly. "I had an idea I think you'll like."

While he doubted that, Aidan was eager to hear it. "What sort of idea?" he asked breathlessly.

"I know what Oblivion does to me. Does it have the same effect on you?"

Aidan was disappointed in that question since he didn't see its purpose. "It doesn't give me headaches, if that's what you mean," he replied with an impatient frown.

"No," Kara assured him with an enticing smile. "I want to know if it wipes away your memory as cleanly as it did mine."

Aidan gave her a rueful grin. "Oh yes, it does that quite

well. I don't dare drink it anywhere but right here in my own home."

Kara curled up into a seductive pose and rested her arm across his bare thigh. "If we were to drink it and then make love, we'd not be complicating our relationship any because we'd not remember it, would we?"

Aidan's first reaction was astonishment, but that was swiftly followed by the most furious anger he had ever felt. He grabbed Kara by the wrists and yanked her into a sitting position. He pulled her so close their noses were touching as he snarled, "You bitch! How can you even imagine I'd want to forget you!" When she did no more than stare at him in wide-eyed wonder, he shook her. "Well come on, try and hurt me! Where are your damn flesh-ripping birds?"

Kara knew she had made several serious mistakes with Aidan, but she would not compound them with an even more senseless show of violence. Instead, she focused her thoughts solely on the pleasures she had meant them to share, if not remember. He shut his eyes tightly as though he could block out the tendrils of rapture she sent curling around his bare chest, but they slid over the flat planes of his stomach, then tugged at his loins with an irresistible allure.

"Dear God," Aidan whispered hoarsely. If this was her idea of excruciating pain, he wanted even more.

Kara felt him begin to relax and leaned forward to kiss his eyelids sweetly. She let the erotic images that filled her mind flood his senses with sensations too delicious to ignore. When he released her wrists, she placed her hands on his chest and rubbed tiny circles around his nipples with her thumbs. At the same time her teasing kisses moved down his temple until she slid her tightly curled tongue into his ear. He tried to grab her then, to toss her down and pin her beneath him, but she was too agile to be caught so easily and eluded him with a charming giggle. "You've been up all night, so let's bathe first," she invited considerately. Taking his hand, she led the way into the adjoining room and then knelt at his feet to remove his boots.

Aidan wound his fingers in her fiery curls to force her to look up him. "Are you trying to drown me?" His question was no jest, for he feared entering the water would be a grave risk with such an enchanting creature at his side.

Kara stood up to help him remove the rest of his scant apparel. "I want only to drown you in pleasure, Aidan. Is that a crime here?"

She asked the question with such casual aplomb that he wondered if she seduced men with such astonishing ease every day. He quickly forced that thought aside, for he didn't want to think of her as having been with others or how swiftly she would return to them. He slipped his arms around her waist and pulled her close. "No more of your tricks, please. Just make love to me."

Kara lifted her arms to encircle his neck and slipped her fingers through his blond curls as she had so often longed to do. "That is what I am doing, Aidan." She gave his lower lip a playful nibble followed by a long, slow kiss which sent his already smoldering passions bursting into a riotous brilliance of flames. She did not draw away as she felt him grow hard, but moved her hips against his in a slow circular invitation whose purpose he could not possibly mistake.

Unable to stand such blatant teasing, Aidan gathered the long-legged beauty into his arms and carried her down the steps into the tub. The warm water in itself was relaxing, but his mood most assuredly was not. He again pulled Kara close, crushing the lush fullness of her breasts against his hard muscular chest as his kisses turned from tender to bruising. He held her captive in his arms, unwilling to release her until he had savored not only her delectable taste but her very soul as well.

While Kara made no effort to break free, her mind was full of playful affection in the luxurious setting of his invitingly bubbling tub, not the desperate desire that filled Aidan's embrace. She wasn't frightened, for while she hoped he had merely been teasing, she knew she could drown him quite easily despite his ardor. Much preferring the gentleness she knew he possessed to fierce passion, her fingertips traveled down the muscular planes of his broad back with a light, soothing rhythm which she hoped would inspire the tenderness she longed to share.

Although his mouth covered hers, Aidan clearly heard the sweet sound of Kara's enticing whisper. She was paying him a series of successively more lavish compliments until he was so embarrassed he could no longer keep silent. He leaned back for a moment, then fixed her with a teasing gaze. "What are you trying to do, make me so conceited no other woman will have me?"

Kara reached up to nibble his right earlobe. "What do you mean?" If anything, she thought the man had an exceedingly casual regard for his extraordinarily handsome appearance. "I don't think you're the least bit conceited."

Aidan couldn't contain his laughter. "No, I'm not conceited, but I have an 'extraordinarily handsome appearance'? Isn't that what you're thinking?"

A sudden mist of confusion filled Kara's golden eyes, then she began to blush brightly. "Oh no, you weren't supposed to hear that!" she confessed in a mortified squeal.

"Well I did," Aidan revealed with a rakish grin, enormously pleased to think he had at last gotten the upper hand. "I love it when you say nice things to me, but if you can only think them in your mind, then I'll enjoy that, too."

They were standing chest-deep in rapidly churning water with Kara's arms encircling Aidan's neck protectively as she tried frantically to find some way to avoid appearing like a silly, love-struck fool. "There's one technique for projecting thoughts and another for keeping them private. Your affection is so delightful, it's obvious I'm unable to make that distinction right now. I hope I didn't shock you."

"Shock me?" Aidan was so amused he couldn't stop laughing. "Sapphires must be gems of remarkable beauty if they match the blue of my eyes. That the warmth of my skin is like liquid amber, or—"

Appalled to find him so amused by her thoughts, Kara made no effort to escape him, but she did silence his teasing with a hasty kiss which she then deepened until he was left gasping for breath. With a gentle nudge she guided him into the nearest corner where he would be sure not to lose his footing; then she wrapped herself around him with serpent-like grace. He was fully aroused, and she brought their sleek bodies together with such ease he had time to do no more than shudder before he found himself compelled to thrust deep within her. He had never encountered such an aggressive female, but he scarcely considered that a flaw when she gave him such immense pleasure. He did not fight her possession, but instead surrendered completely to the tide of emotion that crested within his heart. Since the first moment he had seen her he had longed to make her his own. That she had so easily made him hers mattered not at all since the resulting rapture was exactly the same. As he stood drowning in the flood of pleasure she had promised to provide, he could not imagine a more glorious death.

Kara felt each wave of ecstasy that rippled through Aidan's powerful body, for it echoed in the very depths of her own. The splendid joy throbbed within her with a heat so intense she knew not even the water in which they stood would quench its flames. The protective veneer of a well-trained scout slipped away as she exalted solely in the joy of being a woman. For a few thrilling moments there were no differences between them, simply the intensely satisfying bond created by mutual pleasure. She knew how to give peace with her mind, but he had brought a magnificent calm to her soul with the strength of his body alone, and she wanted to savor that gift for as long as the last tingle of bliss remained in her heart. With her mind still filled with thoughts of him, she was content to rest quietly in his arms until he spoke.

"I know you'll feel it your duty to reveal all that you've learned of 329 when you return to Mother, but what can you possibly tell them about this?"

Much to her dismay, his question cut through her with the pain of a well-sharpened blade. Since the first moment she had thought of a way to make love to him, Mother had ceased to exist. But he had just brought reality crashing down upon her with stunning force. She placed her palms on his chest, meaning to push free of his confining embrace, but he refused to release her. "I will tell them nothing, Aidan, nothing!"

He knew she had enjoyed their erotic escapade as greatly

as he, and he was thoroughly confused by her sudden show of anger. Rather than argue, Aidan slid his fingers through her damp curls and pressed her cheek to his shoulder. For a woman with such a magnificent store of skills, she had a surprisingly volatile nature, he thought, and he was sorry he had again upset her. He did not want to let her go, but since he knew he must, he had not thought his question improper. "We should get out of the water so I can rebandage your cut," he suggested in a soothing whisper. "Then we can decide what else we'd like to do."

Kara clung to him, not trusting herself to speak. She had done exactly what she swore she would not do. She had come to care for him, and the prospect of telling him good-bye overwhelmed her with sorrow. "In a minute," she replied softly.

She was so light that holding her took no effort, and Aidan decided he would just continue to lean against the side of the tub until she asked to get out. If he were lucky, they would spend a very long time making love and there would be no time left to take her out to the desert. His thoughts as romantic as hers, he nearly screamed in alarm when someone began to pound frantically on his door. He placed his hands around Kara's narrow waist to help her to stand. "Stay here if you like. I'll see what the trouble is and be right back."

"Could it be an attack?" she asked apprehensively, knowing his home lacked a good place to hide.

That he could not tell whether she was worried about him or more concerned about getting back to her ship pained Aidan greatly, but he didn't ask her to clarify her question. He grabbed a towel as soon as he stepped from the water and quickly knotted it around his waist. "No matter what it is, I'll come and tell you about it. I'll not risk facing any sort of danger clad in no more than a towel!"

His levity made Kara feel a little more at ease, and she stayed in the water to await his explanation. Picking up the soap, she found it impossible to touch herself without thinking of Aidan's caress. "Another rule broken," she whispered to herself, but he was very wrong if he thought she would ever confess the truth of their encounter to another living soul.

When Aidan pulled open his front door, Zac pushed his way inside without waiting for a formal word of welcome. "Hurry and get dressed. You've got to come with us!" he shouted excitedly. "Blair went out early this morning to search the desert for Duke's ram and found what he says is a spaceship! Well come on, let's go! Don't you want to see it?"

"A spaceship?" Aidan gasped hoarsely, for he was certain the only one Blair could possibly have found was Kara's. "Would Blair even recognize one if it landed on him?"

Disgusted by such an unenthusiastic response, Zac put his hands on his hips. His proportions were as sleek and handsome as Aidan's but he was not quite as tall. "Well, he swears he found some sort of fabulous machine and he wants us to go out and take a look at it. I thought you'd insist on going along, but if you've something you'd rather do, then go ahead and do it." He winked, then glanced toward the bedroom door as though he were certain Aidan weren't alone. "You are Captain of the Guard, and if there are any decisions to be made you'd naturally make them, but if you're too busy to investigate—"

Aidan yanked open his door and gave his best friend an encouraging shove. "I'll meet you at the gate as soon as I'm dressed. Don't let anyone leave until I get there. I don't want this 'fabulous machine' damaged before I can examine it."

Noting that his friend was now extremely serious, Zac wasted no more time with teasing innuendoes and stepped into the street. "Good. If there's a ship, then there's got to be a pilot, and I don't want to have to fight him without you."

"I'll be right there!" Aidan called after him. He slammed his door, then leaned back against it in hopes the frantic beating of his heart would subside to its normal rhythm. He had two choices: one, to tell Kara the truth; the other to lie. As he walked toward the bathroom, he made what he hoped was the wisest choice. He bent down by the tub and began to explain the sudden crisis in the most soothing manner he could. "Do you remember the net I had the second day I saw you?"

"The one you use to catch sheep?" Kara recalled aloud.

"Yes, that's it. Well this morning a young man named Blair went out to look for a ram that had wandered away. He found what he insists is a spaceship, but that doesn't mean that's what it really is, or that it's yours."

Kara wasted no time climbing out of the sunken tub. She reached for a towel and wrapped it around herself, but that modest action covered only the middle portion of her colorful tattoo, while the vine that swirled up her leg was a teasing reminder of the astonishing beauty she had just hidden from his view. "My first thought is that you must have told him exactly where to look. Did you?" she asked accusingly.

Appalled by her question, Aidan rose slowly. When he stretched to his full height he did have a slight advantage over her in stature. That she would imagine he would betray her infuriated him so completely he scarcely knew where to begin to deny it. "All I planned to do this morning was to take you back to your ship. That Blair had time to find it is your fault, not mine! You're the one who distracted me so thoroughly by suggesting we make love. It wasn't my idea!"

"It most certainly was your idea," Kara protested immediately, "but I will admit I'm responsible for the timing." She thought it strange indeed that each time she broke one of Alado's many rules she was instantly punished. Still, she did not feel the slightest bit of guilt for her actions despite the impossible mess in which she now found herself. "So what do you plan to do?"

Aidan turned away, entered his bedroom and began rummaging through his chest for a clean pair of shorts. "I am supposed to lead this farcical expedition. I have scant hope he hasn't found the Banshee, and if he has, I'll be damned if I know what to do about it."

Kara walked up behind him, slipped her arms around his waist, then lay her cheek on his shoulder. "You have done a great deal for me already, Aidan. If you can do no more I'll understand."

The confused warrior took her hands in his as he turned

around to face her. His clear blue eyes were shadowed by the troubled nature of his thoughts. "Do you honestly believe I'd turn you over to them?"

Kara took a deep breath and let it out slowly. The concern in his expression was so painfully sincere she knew he would not do it willingly. "You may have no other choice."

Aidan shook his head. "You're forgetting this is 329 where I can enforce whatever type of justice I choose. Even if I am accused of treason I'll have to fight only one man, and I've never met one who can beat me. Everyone knows that."

"Is that why you're Captain of the Guard? Because there's no one who can make you follow his orders?" Kara whispered in dismay.

"Of course. Did you think the post went to the best-looking man rather than the strongest?" Aidan teased with surprising good humor considering the dire nature of their plight. He was dressed in an instant, then had to step back into the bathroom to fetch his boots.

Kara sat down on the edge of his bed and forced herself to consider his options thoughtfully. "Your friends will quite naturally be curious, but if you can keep them from damaging the ship, then I'll still be able to transmit a signal to Mother and be picked up."

Aidan nodded. "Right. I'll not let it be destroyed."

Kara licked her lips thoughtfully, certain he would not harm her, but not nearly so certain he wouldn't dismantle the Banshee himself to keep her from leaving. "Aidan, no matter what happens to my ship, Mother will still come for me. I told you Alado does not kill for sport, but it will with provocation. Don't give them any."

"Do you honestly think I would?" Insulted when she did not reply, Aidan strode out without saying good-bye.

He found a group of twelve anxious men waiting by the gate. Much to his credit, Blair had not run through the streets yelling the news of his astonishing discovery, but had gone straight to Zac, who commanded the watch during daylight hours. Zac had, of course, reported to Aidan, who was, as Captain of the Guard, his superior. While Aidan knew he could handle his friend and Blair easily enough, several of the older men who had gathered would be extremely difficult to fool if he weren't careful. Knowing he would have to play his part well, Aidan drew Blair aside, praying what he had found was some battered relic of the revolt rather than Kara's Banshee. "Tell me exactly what you found, Blair. We should be fully prepared to defend ourselves if need be."

Blair was a young man barely out of his teens. Of medium height and build with shaggy brown hair and brown eyes, there was nothing in the least bit remarkable about his appearance, but he was constantly in trouble of one sort or another. Looking up at Aidan's serious frown, he immediately complied with his request. "Duke offered me a nice reward if I could find that big ram of his, but I had no luck spotting him. I just kept walking, not paying much attention to where I was going until I saw something shiny where I knew nothing should be."

"And what was it?" Aidan encouraged helpfully as his heart again began to pound fiercely with dread.

Blair swung his arms wide as he explained, "It's a spaceship! It looks like a triangle. Part of it was covered with sand, but I brushed it off to get a good look at it. You'll have to see it yourself—there's no way I can describe it any better than that."

Aidan knew without any doubt that it had to be the Banshee. "Yes, I do want to see it very much. It was clever of you to come back and get help rather than alarm the whole city. Let's go." He grabbed his spear from the guard hut and pretended to let Blair lead the way as they started off down the mountain trail. The wind must have changed directions more than a dozen times, blowing the drifts this way and that, constantly covering and uncovering it, but he was furious the blasted ship hadn't stayed buried where it belonged! It was going to be difficult, but he decided the best approach would be an extremely cautious one, as though he knew no more about the Banshee than the others. When it came into view, he stopped the group and whispered a warning. "The ship has to be occupied, and we don't want to frighten the pilot and get ourselves killed. Let's all stay together and let me do the talking."

"Just what are we going to do with the pilot, Aidan?" Zac pushed by Blair to step to his friend's side. "You want to stake him out right here and let the heat dry his brains to dust? That's what Alado used to do here, so he deserves no better."

While that suggestion was met with a hearty cheer by several of the others, Aidan shook his head emphatically. "We don't even know if that's Alado's ship. Even if it is, it would be stupid to kill the pilot before we learn all he has to tell."

Disgusted with his own impatience, Zac agreed. "You're right, of course. He might not be alone. Hundreds of those things might have come in during the storm."

"An invasion?" Blair asked in a terrified gasp. His words prompted most of the group to scan the horizon hurriedly for signs of other craft, but they saw nothing other than the usual bleak landscape.

"Let's just walk up and see what we can find out from this ship before we start worrying about any others." Aidan moved closer, but kept a respectful distance. If the Banshee had suffered any damage in the storm, it wasn't apparent to his eye. The sleek craft still looked brand new. There were no lights on the exterior to give a clue of the dazzling array of instruments inside and, as he walked around it, he thought the ship looked every bit as forlorn as its beautiful pilot had when he had left her. Even to a casual observer the neglected craft was obviously abandoned, and when the others came up to join him, Aidan made a suggestion he hoped they would accept.

"Not all ships need pilots, do they? Doesn't that look too small to have a human crew?"

Zac moved closer still, his curiosity not nearly satisfied. "It has what looks like windows. Why would it have windows if there's no one inside?"

Since that was an extremely good question, Aidan shrugged as he replied, "Maybe they're for cameras."

"Yeah, could be." Zac agreed. He reached out to touch the hull, then brought his hand back quickly.

"What's the matter?" Blair asked anxiously, looking ready to run all the way back to the mountains at the slightest provocation.

Zac reached out again and this time left his hand on the hull. "Nothing. It just doesn't feel like anything we have, that's all. It looks soft, but it isn't." When he pressed on it more forcefully, the ship rocked slightly and he jumped back. "Did you see that? It moved!"

"It didn't move," Aidan assured him. "You pushed it."

Zac used both hands this time and found he could rock the ship back and forth easily. He shouted for Blair and the ×‰å – ™Bothers to come help him. "Well come on, Aidan, give us a hand here."

Aidan lay his spear aside and took a place beside his friend. "Just what is it you're planning to do?"

"Let's see if we can lift this thing." Zac was so excited he didn't wait to get everyone ready but just took hold and yanked the Banshee right off the ground himself.

Aidan remembered that Kara had said two people could carry her ship, but he had not believed her then. Now he did, for Zac had raised the craft off the sand with astonishing ease. "Wait a minute. Put it down, we've yet to decide just where we're going with this thing." Now that he and Zac had touched the ship without suffering any harm, the others were running their hands over it, examining it with the same care he had shown. Since the large oval hatch was obviously the door, Aidan walked over to it and, after some pretended difficulty, pulled it open. As the solar panels became fully exposed to the light, the ship's instruments were at full power, their lights blinking brightly. Aidan feigned the same fascination as the others as they took turns standing at the open hatch to peer inside.

Standing back to give his friends a better view, Aidan's mind was filled with images of Kara. She would undoubtedly be pacing his home with that restless stride of hers which he enjoyed watching as much as a wonderfully erotic dance. He could not think of her without smiling, but surrounded by men he had known all his life, the warrior wondered if he was being a stupid fool as well as a traitor not to consider her presence a threat to his world. He had chosen from the very beginning to shield her from harm, and he knew now it was far too late to question the wisdom of his actions. Although his conscience nagged him painfully, he knew it was far more than mere desire that had shaped his decision. Kara was not only a beautiful woman; she knew more than all the rest of them combined. Cut adrift from the Confederation, 329's technology had fallen further and further behind. The knowledge she possessed was therefore far too precious to those on 329 to risk losing. She was so unique it was imperative they be friends, and Aidan could not bear to think how swiftly many of the others would have put her to death. When everyone had had the opportunity to look inside the Banshee, he reached in and picked up the helmet she had left beside the seat. "It looks like there was a pilot all right. Did you see his tracks, Blair?"

The youth shook his head nervously. "No, not a one. The ship must have landed before the end of the storm."

"It might have landed several years ago for all we know. Look around." Aidan gestured broadly. "The drifts shift constantly. This strange craft might have been buried here for decades and only been swept free of the sand yesterday."

"That's possible but unlikely," a gray-haired man named Fermin suggested thoughtfully. "I think the ship landed during the last storm, but the real question is: what's happened to the pilot? He couldn't have just vanished, so where is he?"

Fermin was acknowledged by everyone as possessing considerable wisdom, and Aidan did not regard his comment lightly, but he tried to slant the man's thinking in the direction of his own. "I'll wager all we ever find is his body since he couldn't have survived out here in the desert for long. He might have started toward the mountains, but if he had reached them we would certainly know it."

Since they all knew how treacherous the arid terrain was —and how alert their guards—there was no argument to that until Zac suddenly spoke up. "Not if the moles got him!

They could have him down in their caves and we'd never know about it!"

"Not unless the bastard began to lead their attacks," Fermin suggested with a shudder.

Blaming the pilot's disappearance on the moles was so brilliant that Aidan was furious with himself for not thinking of it first. "Yes, of course," he agreed enthusiastically. He turned to look back at the stark mountain range which concealed their fortified city from view. "He must have expected a hostile welcome and, staying well away from our trails, stumbled right into one of the mines. If the moles didn't slit his throat instantly, then they might well be planning to use him against us."

"Well, no matter where he is, he'll not go anywhere else if we have his ship," Zac insisted firmly, ready to carry it back to the city himself if the others wouldn't agree.

Aidan knew if they left the Banshee where it was everyone would soon hear about it and trek out there to see it. If they took it into the city, however, it would be studied rather than vandalized, so he didn't object to Zac's suggestion. He tossed the helmet back inside, slammed the hatch shut and secured the latch. When Zac regarded the ease of his actions with an incredulous glance, Aidan spoke to distract him before he could ask how he had managed to do that so rapidly. "Take the tail section, Zac, but first make certain the edges aren't sharp. I don't want anyone to get hurt lugging this blasted thing home."

"Do you think we can make it fly?" Blair asked excitedly as he took up a position at Aidan's side. "I'd give anything to be able to fly."

Aidan grinned at the young man as he agreed. "I'd like a closer look at the stars, too." He remembered then that Kara preferred flying to making love. "It must be wonderful to fly," he remarked wistfully, but he didn't understand how anything could possibly be better than making love to Kara, no matter where or how she chose to do it.

CHAPTER
◇ **VII** ◇

Aidan sprinted through his front door and, as he had hoped, found Kara standing near the garden. "I've no time to answer any questions now," he greeted her breathlessly. "We've brought your Banshee into the city but it will be far safer here than out in the desert now that others know about it. I'm supposed to be conducting a house-to-house search for the pilot, but it's already assumed he's been captured by the moles."

"My God," Kara gasped in dismay, "who are the moles?"

Surprised she didn't understand the derogatory term, Aidan explained it as he rushed back out the door. "Moles are little creatures who live below ground. That's what we call the people who live in the abandoned mines."

He was gone as quickly as he had come. Kara went over his brief but horribly disturbing news time and again, but was unable to decide what to do about this sudden worsening of their situation. It was precarious at best and dire at worst, but she needed far more information than he had had time to impart. She had hoped to be rescued without the residents of 329 ever suspecting she had visited their planet. Now she would be unable to leave without attracting a great deal of notice, all of it hostile. If Aidan was expected to canvass the entire city, then he would have no time to return before dawn, which meant she might have a thousand questions to ask by then and he would not be there to answer them. She had already swept up all the sand and watered the garden and had no idea how she would occupy herself until his return. She clenched her fists at her sides and swallowed the furious scream that threatened to explode from deep within her chest. Even if none of Aidan's people had ever left 329, she was determined she was going to go—and soon!

Aidan hurriedly covered the sector of the city he had assigned himself, made certain the first shift of guards was posted, then returned to his home. He wanted to offer Kara what reassurance he could that she would come to no harm under his protection, but he needed only one look at her distraught expression to realize that might be a nearly impossible task.

The lovely scout was again dressed in his robe. Her red curls were a mass of damp ringlets, but he knew if she had bathed in an effort to relax, the soothing waters had had no noticeable effect, for the strain she was under was plain in her troubled gaze and tightly clasped hands. Before she could bombard him with questions, he led her over to the cushions, saw that she was comfortably seated and then knelt behind her and began to rub her back. The tension in her slender body made his fingers tingle with desire. He wanted to crush her in his arms and smother her with kisses, but knew better than to abandon himself in that forceful affection when her emotions were in such turmoil.

His voice was soft and low as he tried his best to ease her mind. "The search of the city turned up no trace of the pilot, which I am sure is no surprise to you. My friend, Zac, he's the one who came to get me, suggested the moles must have taken the man prisoner, and I did my best to see the others believed that was true. When it was suggested we search the city to be certain the pilot wasn't hiding anywhere, I went along with that plan, but since I gave out the assignments, I took my own home myself."

Kara's posture was not merely proud, but also painfully stiff. Aidan's hands were warm and the motions of his fingertips gentle, but she resisted his efforts to soothe her troubled spirit. "Everyone just assumed the pilot was male?" she asked incredulously.

Aidan was taken aback by that question since it struck him

as being irrelevant. "What difference does it make? Everyone believes the pilot is with the moles, so you'll be safe here. That's all that's important."

"I can understand how your people could make such a mistake since you were forced to build a society from a group that was predominantly male." That was an error which could be used against them, Kara reasoned wisely. If Mother were to send females to rescue her, and preferably pretty petite ones, their reception clearly would not be nearly as hostile as the one brawny males would undoubtedly receive. "How many survived the revolt, Aidan? How many were in the initial group and how many people live here now?"

While the subject of her questions astonished him, Aidan kept up his slow, tender message, but his thoughts strayed to how easily he could snap her slender neck as he replied, "I won't help you gather intelligence to use against us, Kara. I refuse to do that."

When Kara tried to turn around to look at him, Aidan placed his hand on her shoulder to force her to look straight ahead. Rebelling at his show of brute strength, the redhead began to argue. "I am not trying to gather intelligence. I am merely trying to figure out some way to return to Mother without getting us both killed. Now where is my Banshee? Can you help me get to it without being seen?"

Aidan ran his fingertips slowly down her spine, then rested his hands on his thighs as he sighed wearily and said, "The ship is in an open square right in the center of town. It's under heavy guard. There's no way you can get to it." He could not help but marvel at the irony of his situation, for she obviously expected him to help her arrange an escape from 329 while he desperately wanted her to stay with him forever. Since only one wish could come true, he was determined it would be his. "Aren't you forgetting something? You're not the only one who's lost. Mother's gone, too."

"She was for a time, that's true," Kara admitted reluctantly, "but she might be trying to signal me at this very minute. If she is, then I must answer."

"What will happen if you don't?" Aidan was glad she

couldn't see his face, for he knew the hope in his expression would swiftly betray his true feelings.

"A scout is not presumed lost until an extremely thorough search is made. The Banshee is sending out a distress signal so they'll know where to find me. They'll come for me. It's only a matter of time," she assured him confidently. When he did not speak, she turned slowly to glance at him over her right shoulder. That gesture would have been seductively teasing at any other time, but now was merely curious. "I'm not only worried about my safety, but yours as well. If you are certain you could win a fight against anyone who accused you of treason, why did you tell me you'd be executed if you did not return to the city before dark?"

Aidan gave a careless shrug as he replied, "You have touched on two entirely different issues, Kara. Those of us who live within the city don't stray outside the walls unless there is some compelling reason to do so."

"Searching for lost sheep is considered compelling?" Kara asked skeptically.

"Yes, it is," the determined warrior replied. "We take very good care of everything we have here—our women, our children and also our animals."

Kara couldn't allow that remark to go unchallenged. She made an attempt to keep the anger out of her voice, but failed. "Do you honestly believe women and children belong in the same category with animals?"

"No, of course not," Aidan insisted impatiently, but he realized too late that was exactly how he had made it sound. "Look, you were right when you said our society began with mostly males. Had there been no women here, then the pitifully few men who survived not only the horrors of the prison, but also the violence of the revolt would have died with no heirs. Quite naturally then, women and children are precious to us. Sheep are merely necessary for food and clothing, so it's important to keep track of them, but we certainly don't love them."

Since it was difficult to carry on their conversation with her back toward him, Kara turned to face him before he continued. "I am merely trying to understand your customs,

Aidan, so I will not unwittingly cause you problems, or at least more problems than I already have," she added with an apologetic smile. "Isn't it possible that someone might go out after sheep and not return before dark? Execution seems far too stiff a penalty for such a minor offense."

"It is not considered minor here, Kara, because anyone who ventures out in the desert runs the risk of being captured by the moles. He could then be held for ransom, or used to gain other concessions from us, and we want to avoid such an unfortunate situation at all costs."

Kara still considered such reasoning flawed. "Just how many people have been executed for violating the curfew?"

"None that I know of," Aidan admitted after a moment's hesitation. "It is a very good law in that everyone obeys it so there is no need to enforce it."

"Thank God. I am almost afraid to ask who the executioner might be should your people need one. Is it you?"

Aidan was surprised to see she was serious and that his answer would obviously matter a great deal to her. "I've tried to explain that we have as few laws as possible here. No one has ever been executed for anything as far as I know, so who the executioner would be makes no difference."

"It *is* you, isn't it?" He had admitted as much by refusing to give her a straight answer. "Well, isn't it?" she repeated persistently.

"It is one of the duties of Captain of the Guard, but you needn't fear I'd ever harm you, or allow anyone else to, either." He slipped his hand around her throat to incline her lips to his for a light kiss. "You are as safe here with me as you were on board Mother."

While she knew that could not possibly be the truth, Kara did not argue. She took his hand from her throat and laced his fingers in hers. "If I can get to my ship, I can check to see if Mother's received my signal. If she has, I can arrange to be picked up far enough away from the city that my rescue will cause no notice, but it would have to be done at night. I've seen nothing of your city but the inside of your home. I know we're close to the gate, and since you were able to sneak me inside the walls, can you get me out just as easily?"

"I promised to take you back to the desert, didn't I?" Aidan reminded her through clenched teeth, disgusted that her only thought had been escape even as he kissed her.

Startled by his sudden hostile mood, Kara began to chew her lower lip thoughtfully as she nodded. Not only did she have to see if Mother was sending a signal to her, she also had to modify the one she had left for the base ship requesting retaliation against Aidan. "Yes, and I know you'll keep that promise, but I'll have to get to my Banshee first. That's imperative. Can you send the guards away? Even if you could only take them aside or distract them for just a few minutes, it would give me all the time I need to receive a message and transmit a reply."

Without answering her question, Aidan rose to his feet. "I must remove the tarp I placed over the opening in the roof. The garden needs the light. I really should have done it right after the wind died down," he explained as he hurried toward the door. "It will take me only a minute."

Kara was so amazed by Aidan's sudden concern for his garden that she didn't argue. The plants looked vibrantly healthy to her, and as robust as those raised for food on board Mother, but she had never before tended a garden until she had begun to water his. It was plain what the man needed was time alone to think about her request and he had used the first excuse that occurred to him to dash outside. Her presence in his home placed him in an extremely awkward position, but she had thought she had made her concern for him clear. Obviously she hadn't.

When finally he returned, she walked forward to meet him. "I've broken all of Alado's rules and I'm certainly paying for it now. I don't want to cause you the same misery. If you can not grant any of my requests because to do so violates your city's laws or your own sense of honor, then just tell me and I will understand." She was far too clever to reveal that with or without his help she intended to visit her Banshee.

The very fact that she was so wonderfully sympathetic to

his plight made Aidan's decision all the more difficult. Venturing outdoors had been a stupid mistake since it had only given him the chance to catch a glimpse of the stars to which she longed to return. For some ridiculous reason he felt ashamed for not immediately offering the help he truly did not want her to have. He scarcely recognized the sound of his own voice as he heard himself volunteer it. "I could relieve the last group of guards just before dawn. That would give you a few minutes to try and send a signal before the next shift reports for duty. I can't do more than that, Kara, but I can provide those few minutes. If you wear my cloak and stay in the shadows, you shouldn't be seen."

While her delight at his offer was immense, Kara was still worried about him. "I think it's too dangerous for me to wear your cloak. What if I were caught? I don't want anything to tie my presence in the city to you."

"My cloak is no different from anyone else's, but if there's any trouble I'll see that you get away. Now, do you want to do this or not? If you do, then we'll have to make our plans quickly. I don't usually check the guards more than once, but on a night like this when everyone will be thinking about the discovery of your ship, it might seem strange if I don't appear more often."

"Yes, of course. You don't want to make anyone suspicious by deviating from your usual routine," Kara agreed. "I wish you had a map to show me. Is the town square difficult to find? If you're going to take the risk of sending away the guards, I don't want to get lost on my way there."

"You won't need a map," Aidan confessed with a sly grin. Bending down, he traced a semicircle on the tile floor. Realizing it was no longer covered with a fine layer of sand, he looked up and smiled more broadly. "Thanks for cleaning up. I'm sorry I didn't notice when I first came in."

"I like to keep busy." Kara brushed his apology aside as easily as she had the sand and bent down next to him. "Go on. What were you about to show me?"

She had moved so close their knees were touching, and Aidan could think of only one thing he wanted to show her: how much he enjoyed her affection. Since he knew her thoughts were focused solely on escape, however, he forced himself to adopt a strictly professional manner. "You know the city is perched on the mountainside. It's shaped like half a wheel with six main streets forming the spokes. They all meet in the center. That's where the Banshee was put on display. All you need do is walk out my door, turn to your right and just follow the street. It ends at the square so you can't possibly get lost."

Kara nodded thoughtfully. "How is the city arranged, with homes closest to the wall and businesses near the hub?"

Aidan stared at her a long minute, wondering what had prompted that sudden bit of curiosity. "Isn't that how most cities are planned?" he asked sarcastically. "It would make no sense to have the commercial interests spread around the edge and the houses at the center."

Kara rose to her feet with her usual willowy grace. "My only interest is in knowing where your people will be concentrated during the night. If the central portion of the city will be relatively deserted, my task will be much easier than if I have to worry someone suffering from insomnia might glance out his window and see me entering the Banshee. Are you going to regard all my questions as clumsy attempts to gain intelligence I'll use against you later?"

Aidan straightened up so he could look her directly in the eye. "You were going to answer my questions and I'd answer yours. That was our agreement, but I'll give you no answers that will give Alado an advantage over us they don't already have."

Exasperated that he would be so stubbornly shortsighted, Kara turned away and took several paces in an attempt to walk off her anger. Then she replied, "Your society would be totally helpless against Alado's forces, Aidan. Whether you tell me every last secret you possess or nothing at all won't change that. You will simply have to trust me when I tell you your people are in no danger from me or Alado. The threat is entirely in your imagination, while apparently the danger I'm in is very real. Just exactly what would have happened if my whereabouts had been discovered today? Since you warned me the word Alado would be my death warrant, I'm sure my reception would have been anything but cordial."

"No, it most certainly wouldn't have been pleasant," Aidan assured her. "We never expected you to be stranded here for so long when we talked about it, though. Now I'm fairly confident I can keep you hidden here until, well, until you're able to return to Mother; but if your presence should be discovered, then you'll have to say you're from Europa's forces. That will at least be believable and no one here has any reason to despise them."

"The Europa Corporation?" Kara scoffed in disgust. "I'd sooner fly for the devil himself than that avaricious crowd!"

"What does avaricious mean?" Aidan asked with a puzzled frown.

"Greedy, miserly. They have no interest in establishing colonies. Their sole quest is to make enormous profits by plundering natural resources regardless of the cost in human lives. I would choke trying to say I represented them."

"This is a ridiculous argument. You realize that, don't you?" Aidan pointed out sharply. "It makes absolutely no difference which corporation you mention as long as it isn't Alado! Tell them you're with the Asian Alliance, or the Lenin League, any damn thing you want—just don't mention Alado!"

Reacting instantly to that unwanted advice, Kara's golden eyes blazed with a molten fury. "All I need is a few minutes to signal Mother and set up a location for a rescue. Since you have generously arranged to give me those minutes, I would prefer to rest quietly until it's time to leave."

"Fine!" the handsome warrior responded in a hoarse shout. "I will come back to awaken you before I relieve the guards. I can risk doing this only once, Kara, and if it doesn't work tonight—"

"It has to!" Kara insisted with equal fervor. She turned away and went into his bedroom and stretched out on his bed. She had no choice but to trust Aidan, and yet it was obvious he didn't trust her. It was a hopeless situation, one from which she hoped to remove herself with all possible haste.

Aidan didn't understand what he'd done wrong. He had agreed to help Kara contact Mother in spite of the danger involved, and still she was angry with him. "Women!" he snarled savagely under his breath.

He didn't waste another minute attempting to make peace with the impossible redhead before he left, but he chose the longest route possible back to the wall so that by the time he returned to speak with the guards he had had ample opportunity to burn away the fury of the temper she so continually aroused.

Wrapped in the dark folds of Aidan's long woolen cloak, Kara crept silently down the street toward the town square. Hugging the rough sides of the stone buildings, she remained in the shadows, the pounding of her heart echoing wildly in her ears. Aidan's home was at the far end of the city's easternmost street, but she knew she dared not return there should someone see her and give chase. She would seek refuge in some dark crevice like a homeless spider rather than endanger Aidan's life in any way. She frowned in concentration, trying to recall the details of the lessons in espionage she had completed as part of her training as a scout. She had always been given maps to memorize before entering a city for the test missions she had regarded as silly games. Since childhood her only interest had been in flight, and she was chagrined to think that now not only her own life but Aidan's as well might depend upon how well she had learned those lessons she had taken so lightly and never expected to have such a desperate need to use.

Knowing this was no test that, if failed, could be repeated, Kara discarded her former excuse of lack of interest and forced herself to breathe deeply and think calmly. As in any covert mission, timing was the critical element. Aidan would relieve the three men guarding the Banshee a few minutes before their replacements arrived. The danger lay not only in the imminent arrival of the new shift of guards, but also in the coming dawn which even now threatened to fill the square swiftly with brilliant light that would render her vital errand impossible to complete. Aidan believed he could give her five minutes, but she vowed to take no more than one. Either Sonia would have Mother's message or she wouldn't. That much Kara could determine in seconds. She would then make her reply to the base ship extremely brief. She went over their plans again and again as she darted from one shadow to the next. If all went according to plan, she would enter the Banshee, request messages from Sonia, cancel her order for retaliation and give coordinates for her rescue. *If all went according to plan,* she thought, but she couldn't bear to think what would happen if it didn't.

When she reached the edge of the square, Kara found Aidan talking with three men beside the open hatch of her Banshee. They were laughing together, their spirits high. When he dismissed them, one of the guards remained behind and continued to chat. Kara licked her lips anxiously, knowing the minutes she would have with Sonia were precious few, and now some fool who wouldn't go home seemed determined to totally eradicate her chance to contact Mother. What could he possibly have to discuss with Aidan that was so damn urgent?

With each passing second the approaching dawn raised the veil of darkness that much more, and soon she would have no hope of success. Aidan had said he could give her only one chance, but it was rapidly slipping away as the shadows began to fade. Kara was infuriated to be standing within sight of her Banshee and not be able to reach it.

Perhaps it had been only a ruse on Aidan's part, her troubled conscience whispered. Perhaps he had never had any intention of helping her. He might have started this ridiculous conversation himself just to thwart her attempt to send a signal to Mother! Fighting against accepting what she feared might be the truth, Kara's spirits soared as Aidan put his arm around his friend's shoulders and walked with him toward the front of the ship. They were both facing away from her now, leaving the hatch clear, and Kara knew he had given her what could well be the only chance she would have to reach her ship. Not caring if it was a trap, she quickly sped across the smooth cobblestones of the square and leapt aboard. She had typed the command to Sonia clumsily with her injured hand before she slid into her seat, but to her dismay the computer responded with the heartbreaking reply that no messages had been received. She quickly checked out the system, fearing it might have been damaged by the storm, but Sonia was functioning with her usual perfection. Once again it was Mother who had failed to respond.

While stunned by this devastating realization, Kara had no time to waste in tears. She quickly erased her request for retaliation and sent instead the standard plea for assistance any downed scout would transmit. Then, since she did not know when she would be able to return, she slipped the small box containing medicines from the Banshee's first-aid kit under her left arm before opening the compartment containing rations and grabbing a handful of the small packages. She turned back to the hatch and, after checking to make certain Aidan and his friend were still facing the opposite direction, jumped down and dashed away just as Altair's first blinding rays burst over the horizon.

She had not bothered to take a firm grip on the cloak and it fluttered behind her with a majestic flourish; but once she entered Aidan's street, she slowed her frantic pace to a sedate walk to avoid attracting attention from any early risers who might chance to see her passing by. With the hood pulled down low to hide her flame-red hair and striking features, she again stayed to the inside edge of the walk. Although an occasional voice broke the silence, the bits of conversation she overheard were the usual morning talk of household members and did not cause her any undue alarm. At the end of the long street she stepped through Aidan's door and tossed his dark cloak on its peg. Then, with a deep sigh of disappointment, Kara went to light the fire under the teakettle. When Aidan arrived she had little to offer other than the warmth of the spicy herb brew.

The tall warrior was frowning deeply when he came through his door, but he relaxed immediately and gave Kara an easy grin when he saw her seated at his table. "Why Eric chose this morning to praise Tory in such lavish detail I will never know. What happened? Were you able to send your message while I was talking with him?"

"Yes," Kara replied, uncertain how much to reveal about its contents. "Who is Tory?" she asked after taking a sip of soothing tea.

"She's a barmaid at Dodge's Tavern, a tiny blond Eric suddenly decided he loves."

"What makes you think he doesn't love her?" Kara inquired, eager to discuss any topic other than the desperate state of her own situation.

"Kara, I don't care about Eric and Tory!" Aidan knelt beside her and leaned forward to brush a stray curl from her cheek with his lips. "I want to know what happened when you tried to signal Mother. Did she finally answer?" He held his breath, terrified he would have no more than this one last day with his maddening guest.

The expression etched on Aidan's handsome features matched the fear in her heart so closely that Kara felt no further need to hold back the torrent of emotion churning within her breast. Tears spiked her long lashes as she replied truthfully, "No, there's been no signal from Mother in all the days I've been with you. She's simply disappeared, vanished. It's as if she's ceased to exist, but I know that can't possibly be true!" she insisted in an anguished sob.

Aidan reached out to pull the tearful scout into his arms and cuddled her sweetly. He stroked her soft curls and kissed her cheeks as he tried to imagine what Mother must be like. "Mother is a large ship, isn't she?" he finally asked softly.

"Immense," Kara replied. "There is nothing in space that even compares with Alado's base ships in either size or function range."

After a long thoughtful silence, Aidan asked quietly, "Could a base ship like Mother explode?"

Kara sat back to look up at him, her gaze as troubled as his. "Were Mother to explode, Aidan, the entire universe would not only hear it, but feel it, too. Yet there was not even a ripple, not one whisper of trouble on the day she disappeared."

"But still, she's gone," Aidan pointed out matter-of-factly, confused and yet elated that Kara would have to remain with him indefinitely. It took considerable effort on his part not to let the joy flooding his soul show in his expression. "Are you certain the trouble isn't with your Banshee? Maybe it's not sending the messages it should."

"Sonia has never malfunctioned, and she doesn't appear to be doing so now. My signals are being transmitted, they just aren't being received." Frustrated by the failure of her mission and annoyed by the throbbing ache in her index finger, Kara began to pull at the bandage secured around her wrist. Aidan quickly untied it for her.

"How is your cut doing?" he asked solicitously before bringing it to his lips. Her skin felt too warm, and he knew the deep gash wasn't healing properly. "We've got to do something about this today, Kara. Bandaging it obviously wasn't enough. I should have stitched it up first."

"No!" Kara replied adamantly. "I brought some medicines back with me. They're in the box over on the counter. I'll get it!"

"No, you sit still." Aidan eased her from his lap and went for the flat metal box himself. It was filled not only with rolls of sterile cloth he recognized as bandages, but also with numerous small vials and tubes of ointment. "Do you know what to put on the cut?"

First aid was another subject to which she had paid scant attention, but Kara sorted through the tubes for an antibiotic she had used once before. "This one will be fine." At Aidan's insistence, she soaked her hand in warm water for a few minutes before he applied the salve and again bandaged the cut. "You'd make a very fine physician," she complimented him sincerely.

"No I wouldn't," Aidan argued. "My talents definitely do not lie in the art of healing."

He had been so kind, yet Kara knew it was only a matter of time before their friendship cost him his position as Captain of the Guard, if not his life, despite his constant protestations that he was in no danger. If the citizens of 329 despised Alado, it was only logical they would despise not only her, but him as well for helping her. She would not ignore that threat even if he did. "No, I understand. You're a warrior and I'm certain a very fine one. Since it's your responsibility to protect your city from invasion, you must know it well. Is there a place near my Banshee where I could hide? A store or warehouse that isn't in use? I doubt the ship will be heavily guarded very long and I'll need to check it frequently. There's got to be an explanation for what's happened to Mother, and I want to find it."

"You want to leave me, leave here?" Aidan asked, knowing he had revealed far too much with that unintentional slip.

They were still seated on the cushions, an arrangement Kara found much too intimate for the type of discussion she hoped to have. "Aidan, I've relied upon your help far too long already. I had hoped to reestablish contact with Mother as soon as the storm passed. Now that I have no idea when I'll be able to do that, I can't stay here. It presents far too great a risk to you."

"That's nonsense," Aidan insisted. "I'm in no danger at all, but you soon will be if you think you can hide in some dank hole and sneak out each night to try and contact Mother. If you left here, I'd have to bring you food, and that would call attention to your hiding place. No, it wouldn't work. You're far safer staying here with me."

"I brought some of my rations back with me so food will be no problem. Besides, you told me you couldn't give me any more help reaching the Banshee after last night, and I can accept that. The problem is, I still have to try and contact Mother. I have to! I have no choice in the matter; it's something I must do to reach home."

Aidan searched his mind frantically for an argument that would convince her to stay in his home and finally found one. "If it's only messages you want to send, then I could do it for you, couldn't I? You could teach me how to transmit them. No one would think it odd if I entered the ship occasionally, or even every day if I chose different times. Wouldn't that be a better plan? You can stay here where you'll be safe, and I'll send your signals until there's a reply."

There were several excellent reasons why Kara couldn't accept such an offer, but she chose to explain the most obvious one. "You'd have to know how to read to be able to type in the commands and then understand the responses."

Exasperated, Aidan was tempted to wring her pretty neck, but he flashed a charming smile instead and used her own terms in his reply. "Reading can't be such a difficult skill to master. Why don't you teach me how to read, if that's all I'll need to know to send messages?"

"Teach you to read?" Kara mumbled numbly. "That's not something I can do in one day, Aidan."

The young man shrugged his broad shoulders. "What other choice do you have? You can't wander the city alone while you pray for opportunities to enter your ship. I can go in and out of the Banshee at will without causing comment. All you have to do is show me how to send your messages. Look, if I'm willing to try and learn how to read just to help you, can't you make the effort to teach me? Regardless of what you think, I'm not stupid. I can master any skill you have the patience to teach me," he declared proudly.

When he put his offer in those terms, Kara dared not risk insulting him by refusing. "I've never thought you lacked intelligence, Aidan," she assured him immediately. "It's only that when I was forced to land here I expected to be rescued in a matter of hours, not days or weeks. I really don't know what to expect since nothing has gone right for me lately."

"Nothing?" Aidan asked in a challenging snarl. "Am I part of that nothing?"

Kara shook her head. "No, of course not. I didn't mean that at all." She knew she wasn't making a bit of sense, but the last thing she would ever want to do would be to hurt him after the kindness he had shown her. She rested the fingertips of her left hand lightly on his shoulder as her voice took on a seductive warmth. "I don't know what I'd have done had I not met you. Perhaps I wouldn't have survived the storm or an encounter with that group you took out to the desert yesterday. I feel as though I'm cheating fate with every step I take and I don't want you to come to any harm because you gave me assistance. I knew the life of a scout was a perilous one when I began my career, but I can't bear to involve you in that danger, too."

Aidan knew the only danger that faced him was an emotional one. He raised his hand to cover hers as he asked a teasing question. "A warrior's life is filled with danger, too, and that doesn't scare me. Now, are you going to teach me to read or not?"

Kara thought the twinkle in his bright blue eyes was impossibly appealing and began to smile as she nodded. "Yes, I'll teach you everything you'll need to know." She leaned forward then, sealing their bargain with a kiss. Now that they had become lovers, she knew there was no way to return to mere friendship. He would be deeply insulted if she asked that of him, so she kept still. But Kara knew in her heart that the risk involved in loving him was every bit as great as any of the others she faced on the cursed planet known as 329.

CHAPTER
◇ VIII ◇

Aidan placed his hands on Kara's shoulders to force her an arm's length away. "You needn't pay for my help with affection you don't feel," he warned her sternly.

Shocked by his flare of temper since it was completely unwarranted, Kara nevertheless refused to respond in kind. Her golden gaze wandered over his remarkably attractive features, then strayed to his bare chest and muscular arms before returning to his face. "I think you are easily the handsomest man I have ever met. You are bright and charming, and you have willingly offered the help I doubt many others in your city would be inspired to give. You couldn't be more mistaken if you think I would seek to repay that kindness with sexual favors. I think far too much of myself, as well as you, to stoop to that."

Aidan watched in rapt silence as in one fluid motion Kara brushed his hands aside and rose to her feet. What he had been trying to achieve he wasn't quite certain, but he had clearly failed to evoke any sort of declaration of feeling for him from her lips. He had to admit he was spoiled where women were concerned since they had always come to him so willingly and spoken of love so readily. They were no challenge at all, or at least none had been until he had met Kara. She had been so reluctant to sleep with him that he had not expected the unmistakable invitation in her kiss. None of her actions were predictable. That was the problem, he told himself. She continually surprised him, and as usual he had reacted like a witless fool.

He rose and followed her to his bedroom, but called to her from the door, "What I should have said is that I want you to be comfortable here. For as long as you can stay, I want us to be together in every way possible, but it would kill me to think you didn't want me as much as I want you. I'm paid for fighting other people's battles, but I would never demand or accept any kind of payment from you."

If her present pattern continued, Kara knew her predicament would worsen regardless of the decision she made. It would be impossible to pretend they hadn't been intimate, so if she chose to return to being an aloof stranger, the tension she would create between them would be unbearable. If she continued to welcome Aidan's affection, then the heartbreak when they parted would be equally unendurable. The choice was either to suffer now or merely postpone the pain until later—and that was no choice at all.

Since her life was clearly in danger, Kara knew she would be a great fool not to savor each precious moment to the fullest. With that tempting thought in mind, she removed her boots, then reached for the closure strip concealed in the left shoulder seam of her suit and unfastened it with a gentle tug.

"Not only do these suits fit whoever tries them on, they

are wonderfully easy to put on and remove." To demonstrate, she pulled her left arm from the sleeve, then her right. She rolled the rest of the slinky garment down the elegant contours of her spectacular figure and stepped out of it with her usual graceful ease. Now clad only in shimmering lavender silk and lace, she dangled the rainbow-colored suit from her fingertips. "Are you certain you would not like to try it on?"

That she had peeled away the stunning garment as easily as he peeled a banana was something of a shock, but Aidan was positive he was far better off wearing his own tattered shorts than the revealing suit. "No, thank you," he again declined politely.

Kara walked over to the bathroom door to toss the suit into the tub. "The fabric provides warmth in cold weather and a delightful coolness in desert climates. It's not only worn by Alado's forces, but also by civilians since it's so practical."

Aidan was simply amazed that his lovely guest would extol the merits of some wonderfully versatile synthetic fiber while she did the most erotic striptease he had ever witnessed. When she came forward as she reached for the straps on her teddy, he didn't trust himself to speak. His adoring gaze traced the undulating curves of the Love Vine from her ankle to the spot where it disappeared beneath her sheer undergarment. Kara was undoubtedly the most magnificent female ever born. Elusive one moment, brazen the next, she kept him constantly off guard; but this time when her lips met his, he did not stop to analyze her motives.

Whatever her reason for wanting him, he abandoned himself in the pleasure of their contact. His lips never left hers as he helped her step free of her flattering lingerie. Without bothering to check his aim, he tossed it in the direction of the tub, then swept her up into his arms and carried her the short distance to his bed.

He pulled off his boots and stripped away his shorts with such careless haste that Kara began to laugh. "Take your time, Aidan, you know I'm not going anywhere," she teased playfully.

"Oh yes you are," Aidan insisted as he stretched out beside her and drew her into his arms. "You're coming with me to paradise." He nuzzled the smooth curve of her throat, then let his lips slide over the fair skin of her shoulder before seeking the flushed tip of her right breast. "You taste delicious," he murmured hungrily as his lips traced the outline of the exotic pink and lavender blossoms which adorned her creamy smooth skin. Hugging her even more tightly, he spread tender kisses around her pale pink nipples before pausing to draw first one and then the other into his mouth.

Far from being passive under his tender assault upon her senses, Kara's hands moved through Aidan's blond curls and over the powerful muscles of his shoulders, silently encouraging him to sample still more of her slender body's ample gifts.

Certain he was pleasing her as well as himself, Aidan shifted his position slightly so his tongue could tease her charmingly dimpled navel. Her stomach was flat, the muscles taut. Her pale golden flesh was drawn tightly over her hip bones and he strayed lower to rest his cheek in their warm hollow as he paused to drink in her body's marvelously fragrant perfume. His hand slowly caressed the path of the Love Vine where it encircled her tiny waist before his fingertips invaded the soft triangle of bright red curls nestled between her thighs.

He made his touch superb: light, yet knowing, drawing forth the first ripples of ecstasy before he positioned himself between her long, shapely legs. She made not the slightest protest as he pressed on toward total intimacy, but lay completely relaxed in his arms. Her thick lashes fluttered slightly as she closed her eyes and her breathing deepened while her fingers combed lazily through his hair. It was not the peace of contentment he had meant to bestow, however, and he longed to again ignite the fires of her passions since he could barely contain his own. Slipping his hands beneath her hips to tilt her toward him, he used the tip of his tongue to caress her exquisitely sensitive flesh lightly before plunging into the velvety soft center of her being. When she began to push against him, the motion of her hips drawing him ever deeper

into her warm, moist sweetness, he drew back for a moment
to allow the rapture swelling within her loins to be overtaken
by the fiery throb of increasingly intense desire.

Again and again he brought her to the glorious brink of
fulfillment only to draw away for a few agonizing seconds
which seemed to Kara to stretch into eternity. When she
could stand no more of his erotic teasing, she spoke his
name in an anguished plea, and his fevered kisses descended
upon her in a final flurry that sent her soul soaring on the
broadest wings of pleasure she had ever known.

Eager to share the passionate splendor of her joy, Aidan
moved over her, caressing the whole length of her trembling
body with the unrestrained heat of his own until at last their
lips met. Kara's welcoming kiss was filled with an abandon
so wild he came dangerously close to surrendering his sanity
as well as he again made her his. He took her with a savage
grace that bordered so closely on violence that it left him
shaken by its power when at last a shattering climax brought
his own long-delayed release.

None of the women he had known had even come close to
making him feel so completely loved as this mysterious
stranger from the stars, and while he felt drained by the fury
of their joining, he was blissfully happy as well. Too content
to move away, he held her locked in his embrace as he
kissed her earlobes sweetly and tried to think of some way to
explain how much she meant to him without sounding like a
fool.

Kara held Aidan in a light embrace, her fingers slipping
slowly through his flowing curls as her spirit floated languidly upon a billowy cloud of contentment. He made love
beautifully, she reflected with a satisfied smile. He had an
imaginative artistry she was certain was not due merely to
practice but to the depth of his emotions. There was something so totally unique about the man. She was enormously
intrigued by him and wondered about the other women in his
life. When his lips began to tickle her throat, she bit his
earlobe playfully. "How many women have you been ne-
glecting since my arrival?" she whispered seductively. "Half
the female population of 329, or even more?"

When Aidan braced himself on his elbows to look down at her, his gaze held a taunting fire that reflected the stunning shift in his mood. "If that was another of your endless attempts to get information from me, it was a very clumsy one."

His misinterpretation of her teasing question astonished Kara, but she wasted no time in showing her displeasure at his insult. With a strength and agility born of years of intensive physical training she placed her palms on his chest and catapulted him right off the side of the bed. Before he could rise from a stunned heap on the floor she stepped over him and strode into the tub where she first gave her garments a furious scrubbing and then bathed hurriedly to remove all traces of his possession. When he followed her into the bubbling water, she scrambled out.

"I obviously made a disastrous mistake sleeping with a man who twists even my humorous compliments into clumsy attempts at spying. How can you possibly expect me to teach you how to read when you obviously already know everything!"

Rather than engage in a shouting match, Aidan washed with the same frantic haste Kara had shown. Then he left the tub and wrapped a towel around his hips. She had donned his robe and was pacing restlessly at the far end of the garden when he entered the main room of his dwelling. Aidan was appalled that he had again made a mess of things and made the only suggestion he could. "We've both been up all night," he called invitingly. "Let's go back to bed, get some sleep and talk about this later."

"I'm not tired," Kara insisted coldly.

Resting his hands on his narrow hips, Aidan gave an exasperated sigh before he made another attempt to reason with her. "Look, Kara, how many women I see is my own business and no one else's, but I certainly hadn't planned to be with any of them while you're here. You needn't be jealous."

Kara folded her arms across her chest as she turned to face him. "It is not a question of jealousy. I meant only that you are an attractive man. Whether you have dozens of girlfriends or only one doesn't matter in the slightest to me, but if you've changed your usual pattern of behavior, it will soon cause suspicion. What do you do with all your time? Surely you don't stay here and stare at the walls day after day."

Aidan frowned slightly, uncertain where their conversation was leading now but fearing he would again get the worst of it unless he could understand her point. "I usually sleep until mid-afternoon, then I either work out or visit a tavern or two to talk with my friends. At dusk I make certain the guards are posted and then I'm free to do as I please until the new shift comes on duty at midnight when I check them again." That he usually spent his nights with a wide assortment of both single and married women was something he thought he would be wise to keep to himself since her mood was obviously hostile. "I'm only here for an occasional meal and to sleep. I never sit around staring at the walls."

Sensing he was holding back something important, Kara paid scant attention to Aidan's words as she returned his accusing stare, certain his hatred for Alado was so elemental he would never trust her completely. Perhaps she had been a fool to expect that he could.

Horribly discouraged, she sat down on the garden wall and focused her troubled gaze on a meandering squash vine as she spoke. "We're attempting the impossible here, Aidan. You can't regard me as a woman one minute and an enemy the next. Perhaps you can separate me into two parts in your mind, but I can't live dual roles. I'll not say this again, but neither Alado nor I pose any threat to you; I will not allow you to treat me as though I am some devious spy sent here to learn all I can about 329 in order to help Alado destroy it." She held her breath as she awaited his reply, knowing he was a proud man. She needed his help desperately, but not at the cost of putting up with his unfounded suspicions. She would rather try to make it on her own than stay with him when he made only halfhearted attempts to understand her motives.

Aidan stood watching Kara's pensive expression for a long while, trying to decide what it was he truly wished to do. If she was a spy she was a damn clever one, for she had never shown much interest in anything other than returning to Mother. Nearly every question she asked related to that goal. Finally he walked over to her side and sat down on the low wall. When she looked up at him, the loneliness reflected in her golden eyes held a beauty so haunting it made his heart lurch.

"Don't ask me to visit other women because I simply couldn't do it. You're all I've thought of since the morning I found you out in the desert, but you've got to remember you're the first visitor our planet has had in three generations." When there was not the slightest softening of her expression, Aidan tried again to make her see his side of the situation. "I think my distrust of Alado is only natural after the brutal way our ancestors were treated. You can't fault me for having such a low opinion of Alado considering what we know of your corporation."

"I am not Alado, Aidan," Kara pointed out softly, "I only work for them. And as far as I know, no scout has ever abused anyone, let alone your great-grandparents."

Aidan was about to argue that they couldn't divorce themselves from their backgrounds when he recalled she had once asked him to do just that. When they had talked out in the desert, she had asked him to see only her rather than the corporation she represented. He had failed to do it then and he was failing miserably in that effort now. "I didn't mean to hurt you," he apologized sincerely. "You're the first woman I've ever wanted to impress, and I guess I don't even know how to begin to do it. That you're from Alado only makes everything more difficult for me, but I truly am sorry I hurt your feelings. Now please come back to bed with me, and when we wake up you can give me my first lesson in reading."

Although she had denied it, the night's excitement had left Kara exhausted, and there was no place she would rather be than in Aidan's bed, but she made one stipulation as she rose to her feet. "I don't mind sharing your bed, Aidan, but I don't want to make love again."

"Never?" the handsome warrior gasped in horror. "It was so special! Have I ruined everything for you?"

The depth of the man's sorrow was so easy to read in his

pained expression that Kara leaned down to give his cheek a
reassuring kiss. "I didn't say I would never make love to you
again, Aidan, just that I'd rather not do it now. There's a
great deal of difference between the two."

Aidan watched her walk slowly toward his room and
cursed his own stupidity which had ruined the loving mood
of the most beautiful morning of his entire life. Kara might
not want him now, but he still wanted her with an aching
need he knew it would take a thousand years to satisfy. To
distract himself from his impossible desires, he watered the
garden thoroughly. When he went into his bedroom to join
Kara she was already fast asleep.

He was disappointed to find she had just stretched out on
top of the bed still wearing his robe. Chiding himself to be
grateful she had not chosen to sleep elsewhere, he lay down
beside her and drew her into his arms so they could snuggle
together while they slept. Her short curls were still damp,
and he kissed her forehead tenderly before closing his eyes
and praying in his dreams that her mood would again be as
passionate as his own.

Kara found Aidan such an eager pupil that in a couple of
days he had mastered the sounds of the alphabet and begun
to read simple words. They had practiced by fashioning a
pen from a sharpened stick and writing the letters with a
vegetable dye he had made from the produce of his garden.
Since Aidan had no paper, they had written on cloth, then
washed it out each night so they could use it again the next
day. It was a tedious process compared with the animated
computer programs she had used as a child, but he was determined to learn despite the primitive methods she was
forced to use. She had taught him the command to bring up
messages on Sonia's screen, but each time he had tried it
there had been no response. Her resulting depression had not
lessened his enthusiasm to learn, however, and inspired by
his example she had kept up the tutoring.

To ease the uncomfortable strain which had existed between them since the morning he had stupidly accused her of
spying instead of answering her question about other women

with reassuring kisses, Aidan had begun staying out all night; but he had made a point of telling Kara the truth: he was patrolling the walls rather than enjoying the merriment in the city's many taverns or the charms of his usual feminine companions. Such a schedule allowed her to sleep alone in his bed at night while he found it unoccupied during the day. It was a far from satisfactory arrangement in his view, but Kara had become distant, her manner always preoccupied, and he had decided his best defense was patience. Regardless of what she believed, he thought it likely some terrible accident had destroyed her base ship and she would be stranded on 329 forever. With that constant hope in mind, he planned to wait for her desire to match his again. It was the incredible excitement of her affection he craved, and until her spirits improved he knew that magic would elude them. Having tested it fully, he would now settle for nothing less.

"I don't care what you say about nutrition, those rations of yours taste like sawdust," Aidan teased as he handed Kara a plate heaped with steaming noodles smothered in a rich tomato sauce. "Just enjoy my cooking while you can and be happy I'm so willing to share my secrets."

"You've given me too much," Kara protested as she did with each meal he served. "My appetite doesn't come close to matching yours, and I hate to see such good food go to waste."

"Nothing goes to waste," Aidan insisted as he took her elbow to guide her toward the table. "I usually finish up whatever is left when I come home in the morning; besides, this dish gets better each time it's reheated."

"That's impossible," Kara argued. "It's already delicious." Cooking was only one of his many talents, and she complimented him frequently even though she never finished half of what he gave her.

Since he knew from bitter experience that Kara would be unlikely to make any other attempt at dinner conversation, Aidan took on that task himself. "Tomorrow is market day," he remarked casually. "That's the only time moles are welcome in the city. Since they need the goods we exchange far more than we need theirs, there's no danger they'll attack us tonight." He looked up then, hoping she would suggest he stay home with her, but as usual her interest proved to lie in an altogether different direction.

"You mean your people and the moles have some sort of truce that allows you to carry on a trade?" Kara asked incredulously. She had been careful to ask no questions he could possibly construe as prying, but she was so surprised to hear about market day she had forgotten to be cautious.

"Sure. It's not a custom that's peculiar to us. Throughout history trade has gone on between tribes or nations that were enemies. The moles produce little in the way of raw materials. They manufacture glass and make jewelry from gold they take from the mines. They make boots from our hides and weave garments from our wool. They buy almost all their food from us although they do raise rice and fish in subterranean pools. The fish is rather good. I'll try to get some tomorrow."

Kara knew fish could be raised in rice paddies, but she was surprised to learn it could be done underground. "That would be nice. I haven't eaten fish in a long while."

"How do you spell fish?" Aidan asked with a sudden burst of curiosity. "You did not teach me that word."

Kara laughed since the reason was so plain. "I can't recall ever sending a message to Mother about fish," she explained before spelling the word for him. He nodded thoughtfully, and she knew he would remember it. He had an excellent memory, but she wished they had something to read so that he could practice all the words he learned. She made a mental note to see that he received some books once she was in a position to send them. "I'm really proud of you, Aidan. I never dreamed you would put so much effort into learning to read. You've really done well."

Her expression of pride pleased him and he flashed her a charming grin, but she seemed not to notice as she took another bite of the tasty dinner he had prepared. Inspired by her compliment, he paid one in return. "With you as my teacher, I'm sure I could learn anything. Want to teach me how to fly the Banshee next?" The enchanting light which filled her gaze at that suggestion made him long to reach out and hug her, but he forced himself to sit still.

"Why not? Without fuel you won't be able to take it aloft, but you could still learn the basics of piloting the craft without taking it off the ground."

Her smile was the first genuine one he had seen all week, and Aidan was sorry it was only the memory of her travels in space that had brought it to her face rather than her delight in being with him. "I'll look forward to it," he assured her before turning his full concentration to his dinner rather than making any further attempts to charm his distractingly beautiful companion.

He wanted her so badly, but he wanted to see the same enticing desire she had shown him before. Her manner so lacked passion now that he was at his wit's end about how to revive it. Sadly, he had come to realize his stunning success with the women of 329 had been due to their interest in him, not to whatever charm he might possess. Perhaps they had only admired his strength, or the power and influence he had as Captain of the Guard. It was obvious those assets meant nothing to Kara. She had expected something far different from him, namely trust, and he had been unable to give it. While he knew that might be wise for his people's sake, it had certainly proven disastrous for him. When they had finished their evening meal, he helped her clear the table and wash the dishes before he again set out to pass the night as best he could without her.

Since the town square where the Banshee was still on display was the site of the open market held each month, Aidan went there at dawn to make certain the guards understood that none of the moles was to be allowed inside the ship. When he saw the startled curiosity those arriving early from the underground city displayed, he knew he had made a grave error in not hiding the Banshee and decided to stay with the spacecraft himself. Already half a dozen moles who had come to barter were crowded around the sleek vessel hoping for a look at the interior, and Aidan realized with a sudden chill that it would be a miracle if the day passed without someone asking about the pilot. It was horrifying to realize that he had not foreseen such a serious complication.

The moles were an obnoxious and surly lot, but he knew their dismay if asked about the missing man would be too genuine to be mistaken for treachery. He wished now he had spoken with Kara about this new threat to her security, but it was too late for that now. He would simply have to station himself near her ship and hope he would be able to overhear all the conversations taking place around it.

Zac never missed attending a market day although he had never admitted the reason why to anyone. There was one mole who made exquisite gold jewelry, and he had bought several trinkets from him to use as gifts for his girlfriends before the elderly man had begun to appear with his granddaughter at his side. She had been little more than a pretty child then, possibly twelve but surely no older. All the moles had pale complexions since they so seldom came out into the light, but in spite of that fact this girl's creamy cheeks held a charming rosy glow. She had bright blue eyes fringed with dark lashes and wore her honey-blond hair in one long braid.

The first time she had come to market day Zac had been astonished, for he had never seen a more delightfully feminine little girl. That she lived among moles had become increasingly disconcerting with each passing year, for as she matured she grew ever more lovely, and he knew when she reached the age of sixteen some brutish mole would take her as his wife. There was nothing he could do about that sorry situation since no city dweller ever took a molewoman as a bride. Still, he looked forward to the brief glimpses he would have of her each month and wished with all his heart she had not been born a mole.

"Good morning, Domingo, Serafina." Zac nodded toward her, trying as always to include her in the conversation with her grandfather. "What have you to show me this month, anything special?"

The old man chuckled slyly, knowing full well the dark-eyed young man must have drawers full of his necklaces and bracelets at the rate he bought them. "Is there something in particular you'd like, Zac? I will be happy to make it up for you if there is."

As she listened to the two men talk, Serafina tried not to let her feelings for Zac show in the width of her smile. He was by far the nicest of the city dwellers, for he knew her grandfather was the best goldsmith on the planet and he never failed to compliment him on the high quality of his work and usually bought something pretty. Apparently he had many women friends; he was one of their best customers. He was tall and well built, quite handsome, she supposed, although the dark bronze of his skin had shocked her the first time she had seen him. Although her grandfather frequently teased her about being a flirt, she could never think of anything intelligent to say, let alone any flattering compliments to pay Zac. So she stood silently, waiting to wrap up his purchase.

When Zac glanced up, he saw Aidan standing by the spacecraft. Since he had known Domingo many years and considered him a reasonable man, he decided to ask him a few leading questions in hopes he might reveal the whereabouts of the pilot. "What do you think of that strange ship?" he asked lightly.

Domingo turned to get another look at it before he shook his head in wonder. "I do not know what to think, but until I see it fly with my own eyes, I don't believe it really can."

Zac gave Serafina an encouraging smile. "And what about you, little lady, does it look like a spaceship to you?"

In the three years she had known him, Serafina doubted they had exchanged more than a few polite sentences, but she was so fascinated by the triangular craft that she swiftly forgot the awkward shyness that usually overtook her when she was with him. "I think it's wonderful!" she responded enthusiastically. "I would love to meet the pilot, for he must have many exciting adventures to tell."

Her innocent delight was so convincing that Zac knew immediately the moles couldn't possibly have captured the ship's pilot as he had imagined. He had not expected such a lucky break in getting the information he wanted, but not wanting to alert the two pleasant moles to the motivation behind his questions, he merely smiled. "Yes, I'd like to meet the pilot, too, but apparently he was lost in the desert."

Serafina's gaze filled with deep disappointment at that news. "Oh, damn that abominable desert! I hate it!"

Zac could not help but laugh at this show of temper. He had not once considered that Serafina's sweet features might conceal the temperament of a spitfire, and he loved her all the more for that show of spirit. "None of us is fond of it, angel." While he longed to remain and talk with her until dusk, he considered the knowledge she had disclosed far too important to keep to himself. He picked out a narrow bangle bracelet and, when they had completed the transaction, slipped it into his pocket with absolutely no idea to whom he would give it.

"Until next month then," he offered by way of farewell. Seeing that Aidan was occupied, he gathered together several of their good friends and began to plot how best to use the startling discovery that the moles hadn't captured the missing pilot. Surely those who finally did find the man would be greatly admired, and Zac was eager to earn that prestige.

Kara was seated on the garden wall peeling one of Aidan's strange lavender pears when the front door flew open. As he stepped over the threshold, Zac stopped to call over his shoulder to a companion waiting in the street. He turned then, meaning to give the interior of Aidan's apartment a cursory search, but when his eyes locked with hers he gave a hoarse cry of alarm which swiftly became a strangled shriek.

Tossing the pear aside, Kara rose and walked toward him. The young man was hysterical, making the task of contacting him difficult, but she raised her hand in a gesture of friendship and sent him wave after wave of comforting, pleasurable thoughts. In such an agitated state he was not nearly so easy to influence as Aidan had been at their first meeting, but she resisted the urge to bombard him with pain and continued to send Alado's standard greeting of peace and love.

His mouth agape, Zac didn't cease his incoherent cries

until the two men who had been waiting outside lurched past him. Confronted by three powerfully built young men, the beleaguered scout began to back away slowly. She had no idea why Aidan had not returned home, but she knew instinctively he had not betrayed her. She regarded the two newcomers with a radiant smile, her silent message still wonderfully sweet. While her friendly expression slowed their progress toward her, she knew she lacked the mental power to stop three grown men as easily as she could have stopped one. She continued to back away until she had put the garden between them, cleverly drawing them a sufficient distance from the open doorway to make good her escape. She leapt over the wide planter then and rushed out the door with no more than a second's head start on the three men.

Knowing the center of the city held nothing but danger, she turned left and sprinted toward the wall. There were steps leading up to the walkway the guards strolled, and she mounted them two at a time. When she reached the walk she ran to the right, heading toward the mountain. Thinking they had her trapped, Zac and his friends remained at the top of the steps to block the way.

Kara had had no time to plan a sensible escape route, but she knew the mountains would offer many places to hide while the desert offered none. When she came to the end of the walk at the rocky face of the mountainside she did not turn back as the men had expected, but vaulted the high stone wall. She scrambled down the steep hillside, leaping boulders and sending loose gravel sliding in her path as she blazed her own trail. When she reached the base of the mountain, she again ran to the right, away from the city, hoping to get far enough ahead of her pursuers to find a good place to hide.

Gasping for breath in 329's thin atmosphere, she heard the men's frantic calls but they weren't able to close the distance between them; encouraged by that bit of luck, she skirted the opening of a small canyon and sped on. The rocky terrain made the going torturous, but fed by the fear of capture she drove herself past the limit of her considerable endurance and then some before pausing to rest. She had heard no shouting for several minutes, but since the men could have gone back to bring others she dared not tarry long. Knowing the city dwellers seldom strayed outside the walls, she hoped the mountains would be as unfamiliar to those giving chase as they were to her. That was scant consolation, but she now took great care to hide her trail by stepping wherever she could on outcroppings of rock rather than on the bone-dry soil.

Intent on making her way up to the crest of the mountain, she did not hear the large man who had fallen in step behind her until he groaned as he swung his heavy wooden club at her head. Tragically, it was far too late for her to avoid being struck by his vicious blow.

CHAPTER
◊ **IX** ◊

Aidan knew there was trouble the minute he saw Fermin working his way toward him through the crowd. When the man informed him tersely that his presence was needed in the guard hut at the gate, he paused only long enough to remind the men guarding the Banshee to make certain the hatch remained closed all day.

"What's wrong?" he asked when they had left the square and entered the wide street which led directly to the mountain fortress's single gate. He tried to sound only moderately concerned, but he had a sick feeling that something dreadful had happened.

Fermin cast a disgusted glance in Aidan's direction as he replied, "Your presence is needed. I can't tell you more than that."

While Aidan and the gray-haired man were not close friends, they had always had a mutual respect for each other. Now the coldness of the older man's manner made him wonder if that were still the case. The fact that Fermin had come to fetch him himself told him a great deal, but Aidan asked no more questions as they strode rapidly toward the gate.

The guard hut was not simply a small shelter for a single man but a spacious room where warriors stored their weapons and meetings were held to plot strategy for the city's defense. Aidan was astonished to find the room so crowded that he and Fermin could barely slip through the door; but as they entered a hushed silence fell over the all-male group and it parted to create a small clearing for them in the center.

Seizing the initiative, Aidan asked aggressively, "Well, what is the meaning of this hasty summons? If the city's under attack, the moles are being damn quiet about it."

Still shaken from that morning's shocking encounter, Zac pushed his way to the front of the crowd and addressed his best friend in an accusing tone. "I discovered the moles knew nothing of the spaceship's pilot and decided to search the town again. We found a strange woman in your house. She was easily seven feet tall, slender as a reed with bloodred hair. She was dressed in a shiny silver suit and cast some sort of spell on us to get away. She leapt over the wall and disappeared into the mountains. She seemed quite at home in your house, Aidan. Do not bother to deny you knew of this woman since none of us will believe it!"

Harsh rumblings spread through the room as the assembled group seemed automatically convinced of his guilt. Aidan, however, did not feel the least bit guilty. "You stupid fool, of course I knew she was there! I tricked her into believing I was her friend, and she has taught me all sorts of marvelous things. There's no limit to the information I could have gotten from her with my pretended friendship, and now you've ruined everything." He turned then, meaning to go after her, but this time the crowd surrounding him did not part.

"Get out of my way!" he shouted impatiently. "I've got to find her before she becomes hurt or lost."

"We have every intention of searching for her, Aidan," Fermin explained coldly, "but you'll remain in this room until we find her. I for one find your story impossible to believe. Even if you had sought only to trick the woman into confiding in you, you would have had no valid reason to keep her presence in the city a secret from us. Your silence alone proves you are a traitor."

Aidan straightened his shoulders proudly as he swiftly denied that accusation. "I am no traitor and I'll fight to the death any man who dares to call me one."

That challenge increased the tension in the crowded room tenfold, but rather than accept it Fermin continued with his explanation of what was to be done. "She's from Alado, isn't she? That makes her our sworn enemy regardless of what she knows. She's the one who will be put to death when we find her. When that chore is completed, we'll turn our attention to your punishment."

Aidan admitted nothing and refused to back down. "To despise a corporation that has left us in peace for sixty years is lunacy! You may consider me her champion. No one will touch that woman while I am alive to defend her. Is that understood?"

Confused by the ferocity of his friend's stand, Zac softened his accusing tone considerably. "Has she bewitched you, Aidan? Is that what's happened to you?"

While he knew Kara had indeed bewitched him it was most certainly not in the way Zac thought, and Aidan refused to admit it. "Don't be absurd. She is no witch, merely an unfortunate pilot who's been stranded here. She'll harm no one, and to threaten the life of such a gentle creature is obscene. I'll simply not allow it!"

Fermin scanned the puzzled expressions of the men gathered around him. There obviously was not a man present who would be eager to take up Aidan's challenge, but the defiant warrior could not go up against them all and survive. "Our contempt for Alado has never been questioned, Aidan, since it is so richly deserved. In choosing to take this woman's side against us, you have betrayed us all. When we find her, we'll bring her here. I think then you'll realize that giving your own life to save hers would be a pointless and stupid gesture. You'll not serve as her champion, but as her executioner." He called out the names of those who had volunteered to remain behind to guard him, then led the rest of the bloodthirsty men out the gate to begin a thorough search of the mountainside.

There wasn't a man on 329 who had ever gotten the better of Aidan one-on-one, and it was a testament to his skill as a warrior that he had been left so heavily guarded. He could readily discern from the hate-filled expressions of the six men who stood between him and the door that if he were so foolish as to take them all on, he would not leave the room alive.

They were men he had known all his life. Men who, if not as accomplished as he in combat, were nevertheless formidable adversaries, and he would not sneer at the threat they presented as a group. Since he would be of no use to Kara dead, he strode over to the bench that ran the length of the northern wall, sat down and made himself comfortable. Since Fermin had taken charge of the search party, he knew Kara would at least be brought back into the city alive, but that was scant consolation.

He couldn't believe Zac had shown such an uncharacteristic burst of ambition and had gone off on his own to search the entire city for the missing pilot. The source of his friend's inspiration mattered little now that Kara had been forced to flee for her life. He was certain he had given her ample warnings about his people's hatred for Alado that she would not be sweet-talked into surrendering. No, she was clever enough to find a place to hide and never come out willingly.

He prayed she didn't think he had had anything to do with Zac's search. God, if she thought he had betrayed her, he didn't know what he would do. He closed his eyes and rested his head against the hard stone wall. Fermin and the others were the ones who had made the stupid mistake, he told himself over and over, for he would gladly risk his life for Kara as many times as it took to set her free.

When dusk forced the search party to return to the city, Fermin dismissed the half dozen men he had left with Aidan and gave him the results of their search in private. "The only trace we found of the woman was blood spattered on the rocks near the entrance to one of the moles' many caves. I can not say for certain that the blood was hers since the moles are no strangers to violence, but I think it is likely they killed her and hid her body elsewhere."

Aidan stared at the man in stunned silence. Regardless of what Fermin believed had happened to Kara, Aidan knew she couldn't possibly have met with such a gruesome fate. Rather than argue, however, he realized if she were presumed dead there would be no further search, and since that would work to their advantage he kept still. He had risen to his feet when Fermin had entered the room, but Aidan now returned to the bench and held his head in his hands, hoping to appear stricken with grief while he tried to think how best to proceed.

Tired and dirty, Fermin was in no mood to deal with the disgrace Aidan had brought upon himself; but the men had readily agreed that their leader could not continue as Captain of the Guard, and he stated so abruptly. "You've been relieved of your right to command. Go to your home and stay there until it is decided what must be done with you."

Aidan responded with a savage frown as he looked up. "Nothing can be decided, as you put it, in such a manner. You know that as well as I do."

"Of course," Fermin agreed with a sneer of disdain, "if you've thought of some way to excuse the fact that you put the fate of one of Alado's women before that of the rest of us, we'll all be eager to hear it. Although she sounds like a peculiar-looking female, you obviously put your lust for her before your loyalty to us. You can not stand against us all, Aidan." Without waiting for a reply, the infuriated man stormed out of the room and slammed the heavy door behind him.

"Lust before loyalty?" Aidan murmured to himself as he

rose to his feet. Such an imaginative description of his situation was absurd, no matter how it looked to Fermin or any of the others. He cared little about his own reputation, however, when Kara would undoubtedly spend a wretched night huddled alone on the mountainside. Fermin had admitted they had no proof the blood they had seen was hers, but since she might easily stray into the moles' territory, he gathered up his weapons and carried them home.

What he wanted most was a tall glass of Oblivion, but rather than release his frustrated rage in drunkenness, he bathed quickly and began to prepare supper in order to face the dawn with a clear mind and nourished body. When he heard a light rap at his door, he couldn't imagine who still regarded him highly enough to pay him a call. When he found Zac on his doorstep, he gave him a cool greeting.

"I won't say I'm pleased to see you because I'm not. What is it you want?" Aidan demanded sharply.

Zac cast a furtive glance down the street before giving a reason for his visit. "I've got to talk with you," he explained in a conspiratorial whisper.

Not eager for company, Aidan nevertheless stepped aside to allow his former friend to enter. "I've not eaten all day, so I hope you don't mind talking while I cook."

"Is there enough for me, too?" Zac asked with a faint trace of his usual ready grin.

"Sure, if you don't mind eating with me now." Without realizing it, Aidan had made his portions generous enough to include Kara. The sudden realization that she would not be there to share the meal caused him a renewed burst of pain.

Zac closed the front door and threw the bolt with a dramatic clang. "She didn't even have the damn door locked. Why didn't you tell me about her, Aidan? I can understand how you would not want to tell everyone about her, but I thought we were close friends."

Aidan had prepared one of his favorite rice and squash dishes and he piled heaping servings on two plates, tossed Zac a fork and, after his friend had taken a place at the table, took a seat opposite him. He took several bites before looking up to respond. "Maybe that was a mistake, but I never considered helping Kara an act of treason. She's not seven feet tall, by the way, but just six feet. She's slender, but her figure is lovely and nothing like a reed," he scoffed sarcastically. "Her hair is the glorious color of flames, and nothing like blood."

"My God, you've fallen in love with the bitch, haven't you?" Zac cried out in an incredulous gasp.

With the speed of a striking cobra, Aidan reached across the table to grab his friend around the neck with a stranglehold that threatened to snap his neck like a brittle twig. "Don't you ever insult her again!" he warned dramatically before releasing him. The force of his bone-crushing grip had left bruises which showed plainly even on Zac's deeply tanned skin, and he was as shocked as his friend that he had lost control of his temper so totally. But he had been sorely provoked and he would not apologize for it.

When he had finally caught his breath, Zac rose to get himself a glass of water and then returned to the table. "Look, I'm the only friend you've got left, and I came here tonight because I want to help you. Nobody believed that tale about wanting information from the pilot, but if you had said you had fallen in love with her, well, that would have been different."

Aidan shook his head. "Like hell it would." He continued to eat his meal with a hearty appetite, but his mind was focused on the coming dawn when he hoped he would be able to find Kara safe and sound.

Still not understanding his friend's actions, Zac made another attempt to draw him into a more revealing conversation. "You're in an awful mess, Aidan. Don't you even care?"

He had not once considered his own problems; he had been too concerned about Kara. But when asked that question, he wasn't surprised to find he didn't care in the slightest. "No. Until I'm certain Kara's safe, I'll be far too busy to worry about myself."

"She's got to be dead," Zac reminded him softly. "You didn't see the bloodstains, Aidan, but they were splattered all over the rocks."

"So what? You have no proof it was her blood."

"No, but—"

"Will you take me there in the morning? Can you recall the exact spot where you saw the blood?"

Zac leaned back, uncertain how deeply he wanted to become involved in his friend's plight, but Aidan seemed so convinced his cause was just that he reluctantly agreed. "I guess so, yeah. I could take you there if seeing that awful mess will make you realize she's dead."

"She's not dead, Zac. Don't ask me how I know, but believe me, she's still very much alive."

"All right, fine. She's alive and well. You can't bring her back into the city, though. Damn it all, Aidan, you know the evil Alado created here—how could you have fallen in love with one of their kind?"

Aidan was still unwilling to admit to the others that Kara had been sent by Alado since she would never be considered on her own merit then, so he took a different tack. "She's a delight in every respect, Zac: bright, beautiful and incredibly loving. If you fell in love with such a splendid woman would you let anyone tell you you couldn't have her? Well, would you?"

That question struck uncomfortably close to home, and Zac found it difficult to look his friend in the eye as he replied, "I would try to remember where my duty lay and not pursue such a female."

"Wonderful. Such devotion to duty is truly inspiring, but would you stand idly by and watch as the woman you loved was torn to bits by people too ignorant to even know how to read?"

"What's that?" Zac asked innocently.

"You see what I mean?" Aidan threw up his hands in disgust. "We have forgotten more than our great-grandparents ever knew. Kara's knowledge is the key to so many things. To condemn her to death without reason makes no sense at all!"

"But there *is* a reason!" Zac protested immediately. "If we allow even one of Alado's troops to reside here, our city will soon be overrun with the sadistic rogues!"

"That's not going to happen," Aidan assured him confidently. "Kara's been unable to contact her base ship, so no one else is coming here."

"How can you be so certain?" the dark-eyed young man asked suspiciously.

"I know how much she wants to leave, and she hasn't been able to do it, that's how. No one has cared about what happens on 329 for so long that I doubt many recall it even exists."

"That fact I don't doubt, but still—" Zac argued.

"Stop worrying and finish eating. I want you back here at dawn to go with me to the mountains. If we can find Kara as I hope to, then you'll see for yourself she's no threat to anyone here."

Zac nodded thoughtfully. There were many who regarded him as a hero for tracking down the spaceship's pilot. That adulation was exactly what he had craved when he began the search, but now he felt so sorry for Aidan that he was robbed of all his previous joy.

"If only you had told me about her," he began apologetically, "I'd never have caused you this embarrassment. You know how much everyone envies your prowess as a warrior. In many men that envy borders so closely on jealousy that those mixed feelings will swiftly become hatred. Then there are other men who know their wives love you. They'll be only too glad to see you suffer whatever disgrace this incident warrants. What will become of you if by some miracle you do find your Kara alive? You can not live as an outcast in the mountains, and I know you'd never take up residence with the moles."

Aidan frowned slightly, for the problems his friend had just described were most definitely real and would have to be faced immediately. "I'll simply have to find a way to convince everyone that Kara is an asset to the city rather than a liability, but I meant what I said: I'll fight every man on this planet if I have to, because I have no intention of allowing her to be harmed."

Certain the young woman was already dead, Zac did not

press the issue. They finished eating in companionable silence, and he departed with a promise to return at dawn.

It was after midnight when Kara came to. Her head ached even more painfully than it had the morning after she had taken the liberal samples of the deceptively innocent-tasting Nectar of Oblivion, so she lay very still, trying to recall what stupid blunder she had made this time.

She was lying on a narrow ledge in a room barely large enough to turn around in. There was no door that she could see, just an arch which opened onto a dark corridor. Three candles sputtering in a wall sconce lit the small chamber with an eerie glow and cast flickering shadows up the rocky surface of the walls. This was no ordinary room, she realized with a start, but a somber cell with a high, domed ceiling whose tiny central opening revealed a bright patch of stars. Thoroughly confused, several moments passed before she realized her wrists were encased in smooth metal bands that were attached to a ring beneath the ledge by a length of sturdy chain. Had she fallen through time to awaken in some ghastly medieval prison? Even knowing such a disaster was impossible did not raise her spirits. At least she could see the sky, but as it began to lighten she feared the dawn might bring a fate even worse than the one she had already suffered. Seeing light reflected on the walls of the outer corridor, she knew someone was approaching and she tensed apprehensively.

Serafina entered Kara's cell with a light, dancing step and placed her lantern near the prisoner's feet. When she saw that Kara had awakened, the pretty visitor raised a fingertip to her lips. "Hush, do not cry out. My name is Serafina, and I don't want anyone to catch me here."

"Where are we?" Kara whispered with a painfully dry throat.

"At the back of Mine Eleven," the friendly girl explained. "I've brought some water. Are you thirsty?"

"Yes, desperately." Kara watched as Serafina removed a small golden flask from the pocket of her short smock and handed it to her. Kara gulped down the entire contents. She had not once wondered what the women of 329 wore, but apparently it was little more than the shorts preferred by the men. "Thank you, that was wonderful. Do you know why I was brought here? Why I'm being kept in chains?"

Seating herself by Kara's feet, Serafina hoped they would have a long while to chat since she was so very curious about the stranger. "Cruz found you trespassing on the ridge and the clumsy ox hit you much too hard. I'll bet your head hurts something awful, doesn't it?"

"Yes," Kara admitted readily, "it certainly does. I didn't realize I was trespassing though. Do you live down here in the mines?"

"They call us moles in the city, but I don't mind that. It's much cooler down here, and we have everything we need to make us happy."

"That's good, but I still don't understand why I'm being kept in chains. If you'll just call the person in charge, I'll apologize for trespassing on your territory and be on my way."

Serafina laughed as though Kara had just told the most amusing joke. "You'll never leave us now. Cruz wants to take you for his wife, but too many of the other men want you also, and the challenges will all have to be fought."

Though the excruciating pain tearing up the inside of her head nearly blinded her, Kara knew she didn't want to remain there as some mole's wife. "I thought women were always given a choice in the selection of a husband. Am I to be given none?"

"Oh, you'll be given a choice," Serafina revealed quickly. "You're from Alado, aren't you? That means you have no rights unless you agree to live here with us. Otherwise—" rather than complete her sentence she drew her index finger slowly across her throat.

Kara licked her parched lips, again desperately thirsty despite the drink she had just taken. "That's the choice? To take one of your men as my husband or die?"

Serafina nodded. "Yes, but you'll like it here with us, I'm sure you will."

The girl had a charming sweetness that not even the grim

topic of their conversation could dim, but Kara was appalled by the prospect of taking a mole as a husband. She lay back and closed her eyes knowing she would do whatever she had to to survive, but if that meant taking some stranger for a husband, she would escape at her first opportunity.

"Miss?" Serafina called softly. "Did you fly that craft all by yourself? Was there no man with you?"

Thinking the moles lived in a society as chauvinistic as Aidan's, Kara phrased her reply carefully. "My ship needs only one person to operate it, and that person can be male or female."

"Really? How can that possibly be true?" Serafina asked with innocent wonder. "Women can do so few things here."

"Is there something you wish to do?"

"Oh yes," Serafina confided easily. "I'd like to learn how to make jewelry from my grandfather, but he tells me only men have the skill to do such delicate work."

"You don't believe that, do you?" Kara asked sweetly, knowing she was sowing the seeds of rebellion in the pretty girl's mind.

"No, I don't. I have watched him since I was a child and I'm certain I could do it if only he'd give me a chance."

"Of course you could. How are children taught here? Do boys and girls attend school together?"

"What is school?"

"A place where children are taught all sorts of interesting things." Since Aidan hadn't been taught to read, she doubted the moles excelled in that art, either. "They're given lessons in art, music, history, and math among other things."

"Oh no, we have no need for that here," Serafina explained with another pretty smile. "Girls are taught by their mothers and boys by their fathers. It usually works very well."

"Until someone like you wants to learn what is wrongly considered a man's trade?" Kara inquired softly.

Serafina sighed sadly as she smoothed out her smock. "Yes. That must sound very strange to you if the Alado women are allowed to pilot spaceships. That would never be allowed here."

Before Kara could answer she knew she was going to be sick, and Serafina hurriedly brought her a battered bucket from the far corner. "Oh, I knew Cruz hit you much too hard!" she cried out in alarm. "I better go now. You rest and someone will come for you in the morning."

The helpful girl was gone before Kara could thank her for her kindness. She felt utterly wretched, but her head hurt too badly to cry. What would happen in the morning she could barely imagine. Maybe she would be forced to watch the men fight for the privilege of marrying her. It would be difficult to reason with some battered brute who had just risked his life to win her hand, but once alone with him she knew she could control him with her mind, so she wasn't worried about being raped. All she cared about was getting away. She hoped Aidan wasn't in too much trouble. That she had been found in his house certainly must have been incriminating, but she prayed he had been able to talk his way out of whatever problems she had caused him. She hoped he would not forget what she had taught him, but as she fell into an exhausted sleep, she feared Mother might never answer her constant pleas for rescue.

Two women dressed in long, flowing gowns came for Kara at dawn. They offered nothing to eat or drink, but released her from her chains and led her down a long torchlit corridor to another small chamber which held a dark and forbidding pool. When they shoved her toward it, Kara recoiled with a shudder of disgust.

"You can't possibly expect me to bathe in that!" she insisted defiantly, certain the water had to be filled with all manner of loathsome creatures.

The pair seemed frightened when she did not immediately obey them, and one went back to the arched entrance to make certain no one had overheard their captive's remark. The other held up a simple cream-colored gown which was identical to her own. "You must bathe and dress in this. Do it willingly or you will be beaten, half-drowned and then dressed by one of the men!"

Since she already felt as though she'd been beaten and half-drowned, Kara hoped to avoid receiving those punishments. "This isn't where you bathe, is it?" she asked with an inviting smile.

Confused by that question, the woman replied hesitantly, "No, but we were told this would be good enough for you."

"Well, you were misinformed," Kara stated simply as she attempted to influence her with her mind. That effort brought only a staggering pain, and she had to reach out for the damp wall for support or she would surely have fallen to her knees. The fact that she had been injured too severely to summon the strength for such mental manipulation frightened her badly, for she had not thought she would be left defenseless when she had to face the man who had won the right to call her his wife. She closed her eyes, let the pain roll on through her head, and in a moment it began to subside.

Alarmed by Kara's obvious distress, the two women conferred briefly, then after again checking the passageway to make certain there were no others about, they led her to another chamber which was as beautifully tiled as Aidan's bath. The well-lit room had a high, vaulted ceiling and contained a tub the size of a small swimming pool. The water had a sparkling clarity which was wonderfully inviting.

"You must hurry," the two women warned in frantic whispers. "We'll all be punished if we're caught here."

"But why?" Believing their fright was genuine, Kara began to peel off her suit as she questioned them. "Why shouldn't I be allowed to bathe in this delightful pool rather than that stagnant pond?"

"You will understand in time," the taller of the two insisted. Seeing the graceful tattoo which swirled up Kara's leg, she pointed an accusing finger. "What is that? Will it wash off?"

"No, it's permanent," Kara explained. But when she stripped away her teddy and revealed the lush garden of blossoms that adorned her breasts, her two guards backed away in horror. "Oh come now, this type of body decoration is considered very beautiful in my home. I'm sorry you don't like it." Since they seemed too appalled to reply, Kara turned away, but she took great care not to move too fast as she slipped into the delightfully warm water of the pool. She tried to shampoo her hair, but as she touched the right side of her head her fingers became sticky with blood. Knowing that washing might only cause her to lose more blood, she abandoned the idea of shampooing.

She had been on the mountain. She could remember that clearly now, but she had not seen the man who had hit her. Feeling another wave of nausea coming over her, she sat down on the steps to rest until it passed before getting out to dress. "What do you wear under your dresses?" she asked as the woman again held out the gown they had brought for her to wear.

The women exchanged startled glances and then shrugged. "Why, nothing. Now put this on, it will cover those hideous flowers. Then come. We are already late."

Kara slipped on her own lingerie before donning the filmy garment. Unwilling to leave her suit and boots behind she quickly rolled them up and carried them under her arm. "I'm ready." She was then led through a seemingly endless labyrinth of narrow tunnels. She tried to keep track of the turns, but there were so many she knew she would never be able to retrace her steps successfully. They were moving up a slight incline, steadily climbing toward the surface, and with each step the approaching hum of voices grew louder until they at last entered a huge cavern filled with more people than she could count in one glance. The ceiling of the vast underground room was higher than any cathedral. Bathed in bright sunlight from more than a dozen circular skylights, the enormous cave filled the slender redhead with an equal mixture of awe and dread.

Again overcome with the strange sensation of being lost in the dim reaches of Earth's medieval past, Kara gazed about the assembled crowd and took note of a group of giggling children running about playing tag. Their laughter and antics were largely ignored by the huddled groups of adults, all seemingly engrossed in excited discussions of what was to come. The noise was deafening, for the multitude of lively conversations bounced off the stone walls and then echoed time and again off the high rounded ceiling.

The more talkative of the two women who had been with her rushed off to inform a small gathering of men in the center of the room of Kara's arrival. Just as the scout had feared, the glances that were then turned toward her were filled with the dark glow of lust rather than bright sparks of curiosity or admiration. After conferring briefly with the woman, a heavyset man with a bushy brown beard that blended into his heavily furred chest left the others to come toward her, but what she could make out of his expression bore no trace of a welcoming smile as he greeted her.

"Teresa says your skin is marred by ugly paintings. Is that true?"

"No, it isn't," Kara replied proudly. "I have a tattoo, but it's quite a beautiful design."

Before she could offer a single word of protest the burly man pulled a wicked-looking dagger from a sheath at his belt and slit her gown from neckline to hem. His lecherous gaze followed the slender trail of the curling vine as it traversed her calf and encircled her thigh but, his curiosity still far from satisfied, he reached out to tear away her pale lavender teddy.

Kara braced herself as she raised her right arm to block that move, knowing she lacked the strength to put up much of a fight but still determined to resist being stripped nude for as long as she possibly could. From what she had seen, the female moles were docile creatures, and this man had made a grave error in expecting that same submissiveness from her.

Brushing her hand aside with a brutal slap that nearly cracked the delicate bones of her wrist, the man's taunting laughter came to an abrupt end when a deep voice rang out over the noisy crowd.

"Take your hands off my wife, Kyle, or I'll slit your throat twice!"

The bearded man was as astonished by Aidan's arrival as the rest of his kind, but he paused only long enough to give the blond warrior a disgusted sneer before he pulled Kara into his arms. "Are you his wife?" he asked in a tone that clearly conveyed his disbelief.

Kara had no idea what the moles' customs might be, but she knew if Aidan were there he had come to help her, so she readily backed up his claim. "Yes, I am his," she declared.

Since he had walked so brazenly into the moles' meeting hall, Aidan knew he would have to continue to display the courage that had brought him there. "She's coming home with me, Kyle. Let her go now and I'll not harm you."

"Not harm me?" the surly fellow replied with a deeply sarcastic chuckle. "You never saw the day you could harm me, and I say this woman belongs to us."

"She is my wife," Aidan repeated as he drew his knife and stepped forward, "and you're not man enough to make her a widow."

Kara knew Aidan was either the bravest man she had ever known or a damn fool, and at the moment she couldn't decide which. She was terrified he would be hurt while she stood by powerless to help him. The problem was she had no way to let him know that, and she was afraid he would expect her help when her head ached far too painfully to allow her to give it.

The bearded man seemed amused by Aidan's challenge and turned away from Kara to face him. "She is the pilot from the spacecraft. How can such a woman be your wife?"

"It was a case of love at first sight. Surely you've heard of it," Aidan boasted with a broad grin. "Or perhaps not, since none of your kind is handsome enough to impress a woman with his looks."

That he would use such bold humor made Kara smile despite the dire nature of their situation. She wondered which man was Cruz, for if any of the moles deserved to die that day, surely it was the brute who had clubbed her from behind. Seized by a sudden inspiration, she called out to Aidan, "When you've finished with Kyle, please kill Cruz, too, as a favor to me. He hit me in the head so hard I can barely think."

There had not been nearly so much blood spattered about as Aidan had been led to believe, but now knowing it had been Kara's, he was quite willing to provide whatever revenge she desired. "He is a dead man," he replied with an engaging wink. "Well, which of you wishes to be first?"

Kara feared Aidan hadn't understood her message at all. She gripped her bundle of clothes in a nervous grasp, then wrapped the torn gown across her breasts to restore a degree of modesty to her appearance. When a ruggedly built individual with a lumbering gait left the group standing in the center of the room and came forward to talk with Kyle, she knew he must be Cruz. Clad only in shorts as the rest of the men in the cavern were, Kara noticed that his back, chest and arms were covered with a thick growth of dark hair. Aidan looked like a god compared to Cruz and Kyle, and she prayed he was half as good a warrior as he believed himself to be. Surely if he were the best of the city dwellers, he would easily defeat these two hairy beasts.

Cruz drew his knife as he took a step toward Aidan. "If this woman is your wife, then why did she run away from you?"

Aidan shrugged off that question as unimportant. "We'd had a lovers' quarrel. Since no woman could ever love you, you'll have to take my word that they happen. Now quit wasting my time. If neither of you has the guts to fight me, then I'll just take my wife and go home."

Again Cruz and Kyle conferred briefly, then Cruz returned to the center of the large room and gestured for everyone to step back to create a sizable clearing. "I'll take you on first since I captured the slut," he barked hoarsely. "Come down here. I want to get this over with quickly so I can bed her."

"The only woman who would willingly lie in your bed would be a dead one," Aidan taunted as he entered the makeshift arena. He had already emptied his mind of the crowded room's many distractions and was as eager as his opponent to begin the fray. "Then again, you probably sleep fairly often with your mother, don't you?"

Kara was delighted to see how infuriated Cruz had become under Aidan's barrage of insults. He was obviously very strong, but his anger made him careless. He began the fight with wide swinging motions which ended in a series of awkward and ineffective jabs. Aidan fought back with the

ease of a highly disciplined master. Fascinated by the agility
with which he moved, Kara watched in rapt silence as all
around her the boisterous crowd cheered for Cruz, who had
made the mistake of believing brute strength would make up
for his total lack of style. When in desperation he threw all
his weight into a wild lunge at Aidan, he left his broad belly
unprotected. The blond warrior simply sidestepped the savage blow and with a powerful upward thrust plunged his
weapon into the man's hairy chest. When he withdrew his
knife, Cruz dropped to his knees, coughed up a puddle of
blood and fell face forward into the gore, then was as still as
a stone.

Aidan raised his blood-drenched weapon and gestured toward Kara. "Release my wife to me now, Kyle, and I'll let
you live."

Shaken by the speed with which his comrade had died,
Kyle grabbed the red-haired woman by the arm and shoved
her ahead of him as he approached Aidan. Lifting his knife
to her throat, he offered a challenge of his own. "No! Leave
us and I will let her live! Stay and I'll kill her before I face
you!"

With the villain's blade pressed against Kara's lovely
golden skin, Aidan dared take no action, but he didn't understand why she didn't render the man helpless herself.

Kara saw Aidan's confusion and readily understood its
cause. At that precise moment two of the children who had
been playing tag pushed their way to the front of the crowd
and, seeing their bright eyes widen at the sight of Cruz's
body, had an idea how to help. Even if she were too weak to
influence an adult, she knew she could frighten a child.
When their sweet little faces turned toward her, Kara smiled
as she filled her mind with the most sinister collection of
screeching, howling, flesh-ripping vultures she could possibly imagine. Terrified by the projection of those horrible
mental images, the children began a chorus of such ear-
piercing shrieks that all those standing nearby began to
search about wildly for the cause of their fright.

Distracted by the noise of the sudden disturbance, Kyle's
grip slackened on her arm and Kara slammed her elbow into

his solar plexus with such brutal force the man's knife flew from his hand. All around her confusion reigned. Grateful her ploy had worked, she reached out to take Aidan's arm, and they made a furious dash for the bright rays of sunlight she prayed marked an exit to the outside world.

CHAPTER
◊ X ◊

When he saw Aidan and Kara come hurtling down the mountainside toward him, Zac knew instantly they would have no time to answer questions. Grabbing his own spear as well as the one Aidan had left in his care, he followed as his friend turned down the trail which led away from the city. Understanding that if the moles gave pursuit they would naturally assume they had made a run for their home and go the wrong way, he followed when Aidan left the path which skirted the desert and began to climb up the rocky face of the mountain toward the summit. By the time the blond warrior was satisfied they had gone far enough to be safe and called a halt to rest, they were well beyond the moles' cave and far enough above it to keep any activity near the entrance under surveillance. Protected by a wall of rock, the three then attempted to make themselves as comfortable as possible while they took a much-needed rest. Zac had brought his canteen and quickly passed it around.

Aidan wiped his bloodstained knife in the sandy soil between the rocks before replacing it in its sheath. "I had to kill one of them, a big, burly fellow named Cruz. Do you know which one he was?"

Zac shook his head as he swallowed a gulp of water. "All

the bearded oafs look alike to me. I've heard the name, but I don't know which man he was." He then turned to look at Kara who was seated at Aidan's right, afraid she would again try to cast some mysterious spell on him as she had done the previous morning; but he was horrified by the sight of the blood trickling in a steady stream from behind her right ear. It had begun to drip down on the bodice of the gown he could not help but notice had been ripped all the way down the front. "The woman's badly hurt, Aidan, just look at her."

Kara tried to smile, but she really didn't understand why Aidan would have brought this particular man with him. He looked terrified of her and she had done him no harm. "Don't worry," she assured him breathlessly, "the gash in my scalp must be fairly deep, but if it didn't kill me yesterday it won't prove fatal today."

"Let me see." Aidan got up and knelt in front of her, then quickly issued an order. "Take off that gown. I'll rip it up to bind the wound, or you just might bleed to death before I can take care of you properly."

Unworried by that grisly prospect, Kara continued to recline languidly against the rocks. "Give me a moment to rest first. I'm sorry I couldn't do more to help you. I managed to summon the mental energy to scare those poor children out of their wits, but I couldn't concentrate deeply enough to reach Kyle or any of the other adults."

At the mention of that name, Zac grew even more alarmed. "Now there's a man I know. He's one of their worst," he revealed apprehensively. "Did you have to go up against him, too?"

"No, although I was actually looking forward to it until he made Kara's death a prerequisite for the fight." Unwilling to wait for her to disrobe, Aidan pulled the sheer garment off her shoulders and with a couple of insistent tugs removed it completely. He then tore several long strips from the cream-colored fabric and wound them tightly around her head to stem the flow of blood still oozing from the deep gash.

"Please forgive my lack of manners. I should have introduced Zac to you immediately. He's a bit impulsive, as you must haved noted from his surprise visit yesterday, but I usually consider him my best friend. The fact that he came with me today after the fright you gave him shows you he's a man of great courage."

"How do you do, Zac?" Kara inquired politely as she extended her hand. Her suit and boots made a small bundle in her lap, only partially hiding the revealing lines of her teddy, and she apologized for her appearance. "I'll get dressed in just a minute. I don't usually converse with men in no more than my lingerie. I hope you'll forgive me."

That she had such elegant manners and rare natural charm under what were clearly the worst of circumstances impressed him most favorably, but Zac was fascinated not only by the warmth of her personality, but also by the neatly drawn, pale green vine which curled lazily up her right leg then reappeared to drape gracefully over her left shoulder, teasing his senses with curiosity about what lay hidden. Totally amazed to find her such a unique beauty, he found it impossible not to stare.

"I'm sorry, but do you always go around with your body painted like that, or did the moles do it?"

"It's a permanent design called a tattoo, Zac," Aidan answered crossly. "I happen to like it very much, so if you don't care for it yourself, just be quiet about it."

Not knowing exactly what to say about the redhead's looks since her vibrant coloring was so unusual, to say nothing of the sensuously appealing tattoo, Zac quickly agreed. "I like it, too."

Kara closed her eyes in an unsuccessful attempt to fight away the jarring pain that still pounded in her head before she spoke. "Thank you, gentlemen, but my appearance isn't really the problem here, is it? Even if you've managed to convince the moles I belong to you, what's going to happen when we reach your city?"

Now that he had the opportunity to study her features closely, Zac knew he had done Kara little justice with his description. People would be expecting a near monster, not this delicate beauty. Looking over at Aidan's worried frown, he felt horribly guilty that he had no way to undo the harm he had caused them. "What *do* you plan to do now? You know no matter what you decide I'll stand by you."

"What choices do you have, Aidan?" Kara asked softly. "If you'll tell me all the possibilities, perhaps I can help you decide which one is best for us both."

Aidan knew he had to be careful not to sound impossibly arrogant to her, so he began with a choice he had no intention of using. "Right now, most of my people believe you are dead, so if we could keep you hidden you'd be safe. Unfortunately, as you can see, nothing grows up here in this rocky soil. If you were to remain here until I can contact Mother and arrange for your rescue, then I'd have to bring food and water to you daily. That would be a small chore, but I'd surely be followed and then you'd face the same danger you did with the moles."

"Somehow I thought the danger with your people was much worse than being forced into marriage."

Aidan exchanged a worried glance with Zac before continuing. "Yes, they are so frightened we will soon be overrun with Alado's forces that they can't accept you as an individual."

Kara looked away to gaze out over the desert, but the sight of the endless expanse of sparkling white sand was far from reassuring. Alado had not sent her there to make maps for no reason. She was certain Aidan knew that, too, so she would not be so foolish as to promise 329's isolation would continue when in all probability it was drawing to a close. "Perhaps we can think of some way for you to bring me supplies only once a week," she suggested helpfully.

"I thought I'd just explained why I'll not have you living up here all alone like some wretched old hermit," Aidan insisted emphatically, sorry she had missed his point so completely.

Kara shrugged. "I would not be old, even if I was living like a hermit," she pointed out with a wistful smile. "Besides, you could put the provisions in a good hiding place and leave. Then when I was satisfied you had not been followed, I could go and get them. That should minimize the danger to us both."

She was quite pale, admittedly feeling too weak to use the mental defenses he had found so utterly disabling. That she would even consider trying to survive alone was heartwrenching and upset Aidan so badly he refused to discuss it any further. "No, I won't ask you to hide up here. The chances that your presence would be discovered or that you'd be hurt are simply too great. The desert's out too since it presents even greater hazards."

Now it was Kara's turn to frown. "If you don't consider these mountains or the desert safe for me, what's left?"

"I want to take you home where you'll be not only comfortable, but also safe," Aidan announced confidently. "It's ridiculous for us to hide and sneak around like cowards. I want to take you back to my house and I'll be only too glad to fight anyone who objects to your presence in the city."

Kara glanced over at Zac, thinking he would object, but he didn't seem shocked by Aidan's plan. "You've already killed one man today. Isn't that enough bloodshed for you?"

"It is a matter of principle, Kara. I'll not question anyone's right to despise Alado, but I'll simply not allow them to turn that hatred on you. Now, since it looks like the moles are too disorganized to make any attempt to follow us, let's go home."

"No!" Kara argued immediately. "I've caused far too much trouble for you already. If you're forced to fight for me, you might be seriously hurt or even killed. Rather than risk that, I'll stay right here."

Exasperated with her ridiculous decision, Aidan grew far more stern. "I wish you could see how battered you look; then maybe you'd realize why it's impossible for me to leave you here. Maybe this is the one day in your entire life when you can't cloud my thinking with the power of your mind, but if you'll not come willingly, then I'll toss you over my shoulder and take you along screaming. Do you understand me?"

"No, I do not understand," Kara insisted. "Since I'll soon be gone, why put your life in jeopardy? Let them continue to think I'm dead." She crossed her arms over the lush swell of her breasts and stared at him with all the defiance she could muster.

Aidan grabbed her silvery suit and boots from her lap and leapt to his feet. "Without clothing, shelter and provisions you'll die of exposure and dehydration within hours, and I refuse to lie and trek back and forth up here to care for you. Now stand up and put these on or Zac and I will stuff your luscious body into them as best we can!"

Kara watched Aidan's expression harden into a mask of fury and replied in a shocked whisper, "Why, you're no better than the moles!"

"Make your choice," the blond warrior offered generously. "Come with me or I'll escort you back to them. Kyle can consider himself your husband by default if no one else cares to challenge him for you."

That disgusting threat made Kara feel sick through and through. She drew up her right knee, rested her elbow on it and shaded her eyes with her hand as she tried to decide what to do. Landing on 329 had been like falling into a vast pool of quicksand, and with each step she took she became more entangled in its strangulating grip, but she refused to drag Aidan down with her.

"Well, get up!" Aidan ordered once again.

"Just a minute, I'm still trying to decide what I want to do," Kara murmured softly.

Aidan looked at Zac, then raised his eyes to the clear blue sky overhead. "Dear God, you have to think about the choice I've given you?"

"Yes, of course. I consider all of my choices carefully, don't you?"

"Not when the result is as obvious as this!" Aidan taunted her loudly, then noticed she had grown even more pale. He knelt beside her and lowered his voice to an enticing whisper. "Kara, you must trust me. I want only what is best for you."

"How can it possibly be the best thing for me when it will bring so much torment for you?" the scout inquired with her usual show of concern for him.

Zac could only marvel that the slender young woman had

so little fear for her own fate. Neither she nor Aidan had spoken of love, but clearly it existed between them. Thinking there was one angle his friend had not considered, he proposed it.

"Demanding that Kara be allowed to live amongst us might be seen by some as no more than insufferable arrogance on your part and would generate no sympathy. On the other hand, were you to take her as your wife, her defense would be a noble cause. Every man has the right to protect his bride from harm. Marry her now, Aidan, and she can't be turned away from the city. Simply repeat the words, and I'll be your witness."

Since he knew the scout had no intention of remaining on 329, marriage was a subject he had not thought they would discuss until she had given up all hope of being rescued. He knew Zac was right though; he could not simply demand that Kara be given the respect she deserved when everyone in the city feared her presence would bring a return of Alado's barbaric domination.

"Zac's right, Kara, a marriage between us would add a valuable weapon to use in your defense. It would end all question of your loyalty." The look that filled the disheveled young woman's golden gaze at that suggestion was one of stark terror, however, not the quiet acceptance for which he'd hoped. "Kara, what's wrong? You and I get along very well together. Why would marriage change that?"

The mere mention of marriage overwhelmed Kara with memories of nearly unbearable sorrow. "No! I'll not marry you! You can't force me to do it, either!" She was trembling all over and on the mountaintop the air was far too thin for her to breathe deeply enough to induce a calm meditative state, so she did not even attempt it. "It's impossible! I refuse even to consider marriage! I just won't do it!" she vowed in a voice choked with tears.

Aidan had never before proposed to a woman, and while he knew his words had lacked all hint of romance, he feared Kara's reaction was the most hostile a man could possibly receive. Well, he had given her a choice and she had made the wrong one, so now he would no longer provide her with any options other than those he would insist she take.

He had said he had befriended her as part of a clever ruse to gain information. Perhaps no one had believed that tale when he first told it, but they most certainly would now. Laying her boots aside, he grabbed her left ankle, planning to get her clothed even if she proved uncooperative, but the sight of her badly bruised foot shocked him. "I should never have had you running barefoot over these rocks. Why didn't you stop me and put on your boots?"

Kara's head ached so badly she hadn't even felt the sharp edges of the stones as she had crossed over them. "Did I hurt myself?" she asked with a puzzled frown. "I didn't feel it."

Aidan took a scrap of her discarded gown, dampened it with the water remaining in the canteen and washed her feet with tender care. He then helped her don her suit and boots. "I'm certain you'll feel it later and I'm sorry." While he would not speak his thoughts aloud, he hoped the pathetic state of her appearance would aid their cause. "We'll go back over the mountains. It's a longer route, but there will be less danger of running into any moles bent on exacting revenge." He helped Kara to her feet, then took a firm grip on her arm and, after making certain Zac was ready to go, started to climb higher still.

By the time they reached the bluff overlooking the city, Aidan had had plenty of time to elaborate his plan. Kara hadn't said a word as they traveled, and Zac had never been given to needless chatter, so they made the trip with no more than occasional warnings issued to one another to watch out for the dangers of the trail. The cliff protected the city from invasion, so rather than go over it they would have to climb down the side to the trail and approach the gate in the usual manner.

Hoping Kara had also had time to do some serious contemplation, Aidan drew her aside and sent Zac on ahead. "I know my proposal was a very ill-timed and clumsy one. Please forgive me for that. Nothing would make me happier than to take you as my wife, and you couldn't have understood that." Though his smile was a most engaging grin, he felt the lithe redhead recoil from his touch and was badly disappointed and deeply hurt by that unspoken rejection.

Kara shook her head emphatically. "There is nothing for me to forgive, Aidan. Your offer was very generous, and I know my refusal sounded most ungracious—but please, do not press me for such an alliance. It's impossible."

Curious, Aidan pressed her to explain. "If I hadn't come for you today, what would you have done to protect yourself from the moles? You must have seen enough of them to know they are hairy brutes with lustful appetites. How did you plan to avoid marrying one of them? Surely you didn't just hope they would kill each other off fighting over you."

The few men she had had an opportunity to observe in the city had been tall and well built, like Aidan and his friend Zac, so she could readily understand why he would make fun of the heavyset moles who apparently preferred to grow beards clear to their waists than be clean-shaven like the far more attractive city dwellers. Despite the warning she had received from her late-night visitor, the moles had not threatened her life, but had planned to welcome her into their midst as a wife. "I didn't relish the idea of having to take a man like Kyle as my husband, but knowing I'll be rescued soon, I could have done it."

"What?" Aidan asked sharply, releasing her with a forceful shove. "A mole is good enough to be your husband, but I am not?"

Knowing her point was difficult to explain, if not impossible, Kara attempted to make him understand. "That's not what I said. There is a world of difference between making the sacrifices necessary to survive in a hostile environment and marrying you."

Clearly disgusted, Aidan took several steps away before wheeling around to face her. "No, the choice is exactly the same. You'd have had to marry a mole to remain with them, and marrying me will insure your survival in the city. You may be one of Alado's most proficient scouts, but here on 329 your only value is as a beautiful woman!"

Rejecting that insult as demeaning, Kara clenched her fists at her sides as she straightened proudly. "You've refused to help me hide in the mountains, and I've refused to try and win acceptance from your people by marrying you. That brings us to another choice. Since everything is settled by challenges here, I'll fight my own battles rather than rely on you to do it for me!"

"Don't be ridiculous. There's not a man in the city who would raise his hand to a woman," Aidan informed her in a voice so deep it was close to a ferocious growl.

"Not even you?" Kara asked with an inquisitive glance which swept slowly over his muscular frame. "According to you, justice is considered done no matter who wins a fight. I've been taught a dozen ways to defend myself. I can beat you or anyone else who dares to challenge my right to exist here. You can tell that to your friends. If they don't want me in their city, then they can just try and throw me out!"

Not since the morning she had awakened after drinking the Oblivion had he seen Kara so furious, but he knew were she to go around issuing such fiery challenges she would only make everyone more determined to be rid of her. That was a risk he would not take. His expression grew thoughtful as he moved close. "There is, of course, one other choice," he offered in an offhand manner.

Kara was far too curious not to want to know exactly what he had in mind. "What other choice could there possibly be?" she asked without altering her hostile stance.

"This one," Aidan offered with a wide smile to allay her suspicions. Before she understood what he meant to do and could lunge out of the way, he bent down, grabbed her around the knees and tossed her over his shoulder. "If you'll not be my wife, then you'll be my prisoner!" he announced with a triumphant shout of glee.

Kara grabbed the waistband of his shorts to steady herself and then began to pound on his back. "Put me down!" she screamed, but upside down she quickly became exhausted while his only response to her frantic pleas was a devilish chuckle, and he did not break his stride as he carried her down the mountainside.

Dangling limply over his shoulder, Kara could not fight

Aidan as well as the blinding pain which filled her head as the blood rushed to her brain. She could feel the cut opening up again and the sticky warmth of her blood as it soaked through the makeshift bandage. When it began to drip down the back of his shorts she watched it in rapt fascination as the bright red stain grew larger. Just as he had warned, she thought hazily, she really was going to bleed to death. "Aidan," she called softly, but he kept walking down the steep trail, each bone-jarring bounce bringing forth another large drop of blood.

Kara's silence pleased him so greatly that Aidan did not even stop to look at her before he strode through the gate. The guard was clearly shocked to see him since everyone knew he had been confined to his quarters, but the warrior made no excuses for disregarding that command since he knew Fermin had had no real authority to give it. "I've recaptured the woman," he stated matter-of-factly. "As you can see, she put up a bit of a fight, but I've got her well under control now. Should anyone wish to speak with me or her, we'll be at my home."

As Aidan passed through the gate, Zac stepped from the shadows to join him. Not wanting to believe his own eyes, he fell in by his friend's side as he called back over his shoulder to the astonished guard, "I'll give Aidan an escort to his house to make certain he gets there safely." He then grabbed his friend by the arm and pushed him into a deserted alley rather than let him walk down the main street. "My God, how many times did you hit her?" he asked in a frantic gasp.

When Aidan lowered Kara into his arms, he was horrified by the sight of her blood-soaked bandage and cursed his own stupidity for not remembering how badly she had been hurt. "I didn't hit her at all!" he explained hurriedly, "not even once!"

Zac reached out to touch her throat and after an anxious moment nodded. "She's still alive, but we better get her home and sew up that wound before she loses more blood.

The excitement of the last two days can't have done her much good either."

"That's where you're wrong, Zac. This woman thrives on adventure." Cradling her tenderly in his arms, Aidan carried his unconscious prisoner the short distance to his home. Since they had taken the back way, they passed no one, but when they reached his door he was annoyed to find it standing ajar.

"I know this apartment belongs to the Captain of the Guard, but I did not expect to be evicted so soon.'

Zac shoved open the door and Aidan carried Kara over the threshold, but he had no time to waste arguing with Fermin, Duke and the five others awaiting his arrival.

"I don't have to ask to what I owe this wonderful honor. Unfortunately, I'm far too busy to entertain this afternoon, so you'll have to be on your way."

Not amused by that greeting, Duke stepped forward to respond, "For the time being, I've taken over as Captain of the Guard, and this is now my home rather than yours; so you're the one who'll be leaving. The woman looks half-dead already. Either you carry her to the square and finish her off or I'll do it for you."

Aidan shook his head slowly. Duke was an unusual choice to take over his position. The man was his near equal in height, a handsome brute with coal black hair and pale green eyes, but while he clearly had the strength to be a warrior, he had never shown the slightest inclination to become one. "There's no room for sheep here, Duke, and I know that unlike your wife, you never neglect your sweet little ewes."

Infuriated that Aidan would insult him so brazenly, Duke drew his knife. "You will leave my wife out of this discussion. Since you clearly haven't the stomach for it, give me the woman now and I'll slit her throat myself."

"This woman," Aidan explained through clenched teeth, "has agreed to become my wife. The moles, who are far more clever than you men, realized instantly—as I did—that her value as a woman far outweighs the peculiar circumstances of her arrival here. It's high time I had a mate, and I mean to make her mine. Since you already have a wife, although I doubt she recalls your name, you'll not be able to challenge me for her, Duke, but I'll accept any other challenges offered."

Awakened by the sound of angry voices, Kara pretended to be unconsious still. She peered surreptitiously through her thick lashes, wanting to assess the situation fully before she spoke. She recognized the interior of Aidan's home, but none of the hostile group surrounding them. Aidan was holding her so tightly his fingertips were digging painfully into the smooth flesh of her arm and thigh, but she did not think it a good time to complain. Her attention was drawn instantly to the dark-haired man gesturing with a knife. He was snarling at Aidan in a menacing whisper, but before she could grasp the meaning of his words, the gray-haired man at his side interrupted.

"This joke has gone far enough, Aidan. It would be lunacy to marry this—this creature. Hand her over to us now and we'll make an example of her that Alado won't soon forget."

"Never," Aidan replied without the slightest trace of fear, "since that's a message Alado will never receive. I told you before she is far too valuable to execute. She's not only a priceless resource on Alado's tactics, she's also a female who'll make an excellent breeder of intelligent children. I'll not let superstitious fools sacrifice the woman I've claimed as my wife. She's been with me since the last storm and, believe me, her talents in bed make her well worth keeping."

Fermin's eyes narrowed slightly, for despite the fervor of Aidan's comments, he had simply provided proof that the accusations against him were correct. "You'll have to win the right to wed her, Aidan, and I think you'll have challenges aplenty. You'll probably win the first few, but you can't possibly win them all," he promised with a satisfied smirk. "You've gotten far too much power, but you're going to lose it all. And for what? Some alien bitch whose kiss can't possibly be any better than that of our women."

"Her kiss is as exquisite as the rest of her, Fermin. Since

you're a widower, are you certain you would not like to challenge me for her yourself?"

Without bothering to reply to that taunt, Fermin reminded Aidan of the conditions for the challenges. "You have until dawn on Saturday to change your mind. As you well know, once the challenges begin, they can not be stopped."

"Not until all are ready to admit I am the victor." Aidan nodded toward the door. "Since Kara wouldn't be safe anywhere else in the city, she'll stay right here with me until then. Now good-bye."

As he passed by, Duke couldn't resist offering one last insult. "Guard her well, Aidan, or her life will soon have as little value as your own."

Zac slammed the door behind the last of Aidan's uninvited guests, then swore a long string of bitter oaths. "Do you believe the nerve of that jackass? Duke's never fought anything but a defenseless sheep and now he's talking like he owns the city!"

Certain they were now alone, Kara looked up at Aidan. "I meant what I said. I will fight the challenges, not you."

Delighted to find the beauty in her usual feisty mood, the warrior gave an ecstatic whoop of joy. "Nonsense, you can't fight prospective husbands. Now come sit down on the counter so I can finally sew up that gash in your head."

"You will not!" Kara insisted with equal conviction. "Just look at my finger. There's not even the slightest scar. All you need do is apply some of the same medicine."

Aidan had already noticed how rapidly her hand had healed, but the wound in her scalp was far worse. "Bring me the bottle of Oblivion from the bedroom, Zac. I'll pour it down her throat since that's the only way I'll be able to get her to shut up."

"You wouldn't dare!" Kara turned her body with such a violent twist that she was able to slip from his arms. "I won't swallow a drop of that vile liquid and I won't let you touch me. I heard what you said. The only reason you helped me was because I am a woman and you need a mate.

Well, you've wasted your time because I will never agree to marry you!"

Aidan took a deep breath and let it out slowly. "I didn't mean that the way it sounded, Kara. I was only trying to confuse them, not insult you." But even though he would not admit it to her, he knew what he had said had been the truth. What had intrigued him most about her from the very beginning had been the fact that she was a female and an extraordinarily lovely one at that.

Kara backed away, feeling dizzy and weak. She was so terribly disillusioned by the comments she had overheard that she didn't know what to do to regain control of her life. She had come to depend on Aidan because he had given his help so willingly, or at least she had thought he had. Now she knew it had all been a ploy to win her affection in hopes she would become his wife. "The very last thing I will ever need is a husband!" she shouted hoarsely.

When Zac walked back into the room, Aidan moved forward with a cautious step. "I know you're frightened. So am I. If you don't want the Oblivion, then I'll drink it myself."

"I'll join you," Zac called out with a hearty laugh. "Hell, there's not a woman in the city who wouldn't leap at the chance to be your wife, and the only one you want doesn't want to get married. Even if I tried to tell this story no one would ever believe it."

"This is one story you won't dare repeat, Zac. It would ruin my reputation completely," Aidan advised with a charming chuckle.

The two men continued to exchange teasing jokes as they inched toward her from opposite directions. Looking first at one and then the other, Kara found it increasingly difficult to stand. She reached out for the counter to steady herself, but her fingers were too weak to get a firm grasp, and with a graceful sway she sank to the shiny gold and white floor. She saw Aidan's face clearly for only a split second as he once again lifted her into his arms, then his mocking smile disappeared in the mists of a deep and dreamless sleep.

CHAPTER
◇ XI ◇

Aidan watched Altair's brilliant late afternoon rays dance upon Kara's glossy curls and attempted unsuccessfully to force back the urge to cross the room and pull her into his arms. It had been a long and uncomfortable week. They had had a windstorm to rival the one in which she had nearly perished, but with the challenges only one day away the weather had grown calm. He was desperately sorry he had not kept Kara drunk on Oblivion since the day he'd brought her home. He still recalled fondly what a delightful imp she had been under the potent liqueur's influence.

Laying his newly sharpened knife aside, he left the low cushions at the table and went to sit beside her on the garden wall to satisfy at least part of his desire. She had been picking strawberries with such meticulous care she had gathered no more than a dozen in half an hour. "Kara?" he called her name softly when her attention remained focused on her task rather than broadening to include him.

"Hmm?" The preoccupied scout raised her right hand to brush a stray curl off her forehead. Her hair was becoming too long, but she had scant interest in trimming it herself and had simply let it go.

Now that she had glanced toward him, her sweet expression lit with a hint of curiosity, Aidan could think of nothing he truly wanted to say that she would want to hear. Then he thought of the Banshee and began to smile. "After tomorrow, you'll be recognized as my wife and treated with respect. We can go to the square, and you can work with Sonia yourself. I've done my best, but I know you've taught me only a portion of all you know. I'm sure you'll have much better results than I have had."

Kara now found it difficult to listen to anything Aidan said without wondering whether or not he had some ulterior motive. He had continued to tell her he was going to the square each day to check her Banshee for incoming messages from Mother. Yet since she had overheard him extolling her value as a "breeder," she no longer believed that was where he had actually gone. "Perhaps," she replied suspiciously, thinking she would be fortunate not to find her ship's computer damaged beyond repair.

Such a downcast mood provided a sharp contrast with her vibrant coloring, and annoyed that no matter what he tried he could no longer reach her, Aidan's voice grew stern. "I know your stay on 329 has been anything but enjoyable thus far, but everything will change after tomorrow. You'll be able to meet people and—"

"I'd rather not meet people who wish me dead, thank you," Kara replied coldly.

Frustrated that she had again refused to make plans with him, Aidan's frown deepened to a dark, miserable scowl. "How can you still not understand what it is I'm trying to do for you? As my wife you'll be expected to be loyal to us, not Alado, so there will be no reason for anyone to fear or dislike you. It will be recognized by everyone that you belong to me, not to our enemies."

Kara set the small basket of strawberries aside and reached out to take his hand. "That's an interesting view, but you must know it will be a totally incorrect one. No matter what you and your people choose to call me, I will still be a scout with the Fifth Squadron of Alado's Expeditionary Force. I will always be my own person, not merely an adjunct to you. A marriage between us would be pointless because I'd be the worst of wives for you."

Aidan brought her fingertips to his lips and kissed each one tenderly before replying. "We make up our own marriage contracts here, Kara. You may ask me to promise you anything you like, including the freedom to continue being a scout. Isn't that all you've ever really wanted from a man?"

Amazed by that offer, Kara didn't believe he could possibly mean it. "How can you want to make me your wife knowing the instant Mother comes for me I'll be gone?" the redhead asked with a puzzled frown.

"I know, such a bargain makes no sense at all to me, either," Aidan agreed with a disarming grin, "but I hope you'll always want to come home to me as often as you can." His offer was not nearly as selfless as it seemed, however, for he was counting on the fact that Mother's disappearance would continue to be as permanent as it now seemed.

Kara shook her head emphatically. "No, I can not accept those terms, Aidan, for they give me a great advantage and would provide nothing but disgrace to you. Surely you'd be the laughingstock of the whole city were you to wed me and then have to spend most of your life alone. I'd not ask that of any man."

Aidan took a deep breath so he could speak his mind in one fluid thought. "You are going to marry me, Kara, and I do not care how many men I have to fight tomorrow to win that privilege. I'm going to beat them all, and then you'll become my bride. Nothing will change that. I am merely offering you the most generous terms possible because I know you don't share my enthusiasm for the match. Since it's our custom that the bride sets the conditions for the marriage, it will be to your advantage to ask for the freedom you truly want." He released her hands as he rose to his feet, so anxious to win her consent he couldn't abide this new failure to do so.

Rather than allow him to storm out of the house as he had done frequently during the last week, Kara rose to face him. "Wait, we might not have another chance to discuss tomorrow's challenges, and I want to know how they will be run."

Aidan swore under his breath. She wanted to be positive he would survive them all before she promised him anything! Her cleverness never ceased to amaze him, for there was no one like her on 329. "The challenges are very straightforward, Kara. A small area is roped off in the square. The two participants must agree on the choice of weapons or to fight hand-to-hand. Someone acts as referee, and—"

"A man, I presume?" Kara interjected with a sharply raised brow.

"Of course!" Aidan responded immediately. "Only the men fight, so who is better qualified to judge if the fight is a fair one?"

Kara nodded agreeably, dismissing that bias as unworthy of debate for the moment. "Is there a weapon you'd rather not use?" she asked instead.

"You've seen me fight with a knife, but I'm every bit as good with a spear or my fists."

"The problem will lie with the referee then. How is he selected?"

That the bright young woman wished to analyze that question so thoroughly puzzled him. "Each man brings a friend to referee, and the choice is made by the toss of a coin."

Since Kara knew how easily that could be rigged, she made a mental note to insist a coin be chosen at random and tossed by someone in the crowd. "You understand now that I don't want you to do this. I think it's senseless to base any decision on a contest of brute strength, and—"

"It is not merely 'brute strength'," Aidan denied heatedly, "it is a matter of superior skill."

"Whatever." Kara brushed aside his objection with a careless wave. "It would make far more sense for me to be given the opportunity to speak with your people. I could at least try to convince them that neither I nor Alado means them any harm. That would prevent you from suffering any injury while at the same time allowing me to show them I am a resourceful young woman who does not require the protection of a husband to survive here."

That she clearly thought him incapable of defending himself, and therefore her as well, infuriated Aidan. "I have served as Captain of the Guard for the last four years because everyone considers my skills to be far superior to the others'. It does not matter who Fermin, Duke and their crowd intimidate into fighting me, there's no way I can possibly lose!"

"On the contrary, there are several ways, Aidan, but from what I overheard, they plan simply to overwhelm you with so many challenges you can't possibly win them all."

"They can't raise those numbers, Kara, it's impossible. We don't fight to the death, but no one would be so eager to take the beating I'm sure to give him to volunteer for it without good cause."

"Then they'll be provided with that inspiration, I'm sure, whether it be in the form of money, sexual favors or perhaps the privilege of being the new Captain of the Guard," she observed astutely.

"You're forgetting the primary motivation, aren't you? The man who beats me would win you for his wife."

"You already know how swiftly he'd learn I'll not be treated as a trophy," Kara informed him coolly.

"Look, we've gotten completely off the subject, as usual," Aidan remarked with more than a trace of annoyance. "Zac and I have our plans made." He had not intended to disclose them, but since she had displayed such unexpected interest, he decided to explain. "Have you ever wondered why I'm so deeply tanned if my primary responsibility is to guard the city at night?"

Kara was chagrined to realize she had not once asked herself that question. "No, but now that you've aroused my curiosity you must satisfy it."

"I intend to," the handsome warrior assured her. "We all train in the afternoons. It's not an organized event, but each afternoon someone can be found practicing his skills in the athletic field near the gate. Since your arrival, I've been too busy to go there often, but I know precisely what each man's weakness is because at one time or another I've been asked for advice by everyone. Only bachelors can challenge me tomorrow, and despite what Fermin may think, few of my friends will desert my side to join his. Zac and I have a fairly good idea of who'll show up to challenge me, and there can't be more than half a dozen at best."

"That's still too many," Kara mused with a frown. "Even

if you insist each man choose the weapon you know puts him at a disadvantage, you can't help but become exhausted."

"You've shared my bed too often to believe I exhaust so easily, Kara." Aidan could not help but toss out that boast, although the fact she had not shared his bed all week had been a deep disappointment.

"Don't be ridiculous, Aidan," the redhead responded with cool disdain. "Sex is relaxing while physical combat most assuredly is not."

"That's true. I'll have to beat each man as swiftly as possible in order to conserve my energy. My opponents will begin with a tentative jab or punch, but I'll come back with everything I have and they won't even see it coming. I don't have to cripple a man to hurt him badly enough to make him withdraw swiftly from the challenge."

Kara shuddered in disgust as her vivid imagination painted that brutal scene in gruesome detail. "That's a good plan, but you still may need help. Will they allow me to be there?"

"Why, so you can frighten the children?" Aidan asked with a cocky grin.

The headaches she still had were now faint, and Kara was certain she could again frighten whoever she chose. "I realize for a warrior of your strength and skill to consider calling upon a mere woman for help is absurd, but still, I might be able to be of some assistance. Now, will I be allowed to be there or not?"

Aidan paused a long moment before he replied. "Everyone will want to see you. I should have thought of this before now, but you'll need a gown like the women here wear rather than your uniform. It will make you appear less foreign."

"You may dress me up in flowing sheets and call me your devoted wife, but I'll be Alado's scout, Aidan. No disguise will change that."

That was it. The woman was impossible. Aidan shook his head regretfully and turned away. "Think of it this way: if you wrap yourself in a flowing sheet and call yourself my

wife, you will at least be alive when Mother finally shows
up to get you!"

Kara made no effort to stop him as he strode out the door.
The first time he had left her she had been terrified someone
would attempt to kidnap her, but apparently no one felt inspired to attempt such a plot. She carried the basket of bright
red strawberries into the ktichen, rinsed them off thoroughly
and set them aside for dinner. She was certain the handsome
warrior's enormous self-confidence inspired awe in nearly
everyone, but she wished she had been able to make him
face the fact that there existed the possibility, even if it were
extremely remote, that he could be beaten. She leaned back
against the counter and folded her arms across her chest,
determined that whether or not he wanted her help, she
would readily give it rather than allow him to lose.

In an attempt to win Kara's respect for his prowess, Aidan
regaled her throughout dinner with tales of the many challenges he had fought and won. "It did not occur to me until
this afternoon, that while the men who've lost to me might
wish to see me beaten tomorrow, everyone who's ever hired
me to fight for them should be on my side."

"Let's hope they outnumber the others then. What was
that remark you made about Duke's wife? Were you just
trying to insult him, or was there more to it?"

Aidan chewed the piece of stew meat in his mouth at least
three dozen times before he thought of a way to answer that
question. "Do you remember what I told you about men in
the early days sharing their wives with friends?"

Kara's eyes opened wide at that memory. "Wait a minute.
Are you trying to warn me that even if I do consent to marry
you, other men will expect to share our bed? Or are you
telling me that you and this man Duke have shared the same
woman? Is that why he hates you?"

"That was three questions, Kara. Can you be still long
enough for me to answer them all?"

"Of course!" she replied crossly, but the fire in her golden
glance made that promise seem doubtful.

"First, no, you need not expect other men to try to share

in my good fortune where you are concerned. I'd kill anyone who even dared to suggest such a thing to you. Your second question is far more difficult to answer. Because of the initial shortage of women, adultery has never been considered a crime here. I doubt there's a man under the age of fifty who hasn't at one time or another slept with Brina since she's such a friendly and affectionate woman, but that's Duke's problem and not ours."

"A simple yes or no will do, Aidan. Have you slept with the man's wife or not?" Kara asked insistently.

"You promised not to interrupt, but I knew you couldn't do it." Aidan got up and carried his plate over to the stove to get a second helping of the savory stew. "Would you like some more?"

Kara had as little appetite for the meal as she did for the subject of their conversation. "No, thank you. The answer's yes, then, isn't it?" she called to him.

Aidan waited until he had returned to his place to reply. "I know many of our customs may strike you as unusual, but—"

"Unusual does not even begin to describe what I consider them, but that's not the point. It sounds like Duke has hated you for years and now he sees a way to get even with you for sleeping with his wife. Has he nothing but sheep, or does he have influence as well?"

That she would not criticize his behavior, but simply analyze it as it applied to the coming challenges, amazed Aidan. "Wait a minute. You mean you don't care about Brina and me?"

"Why should I care?" Kara asked with feigned indifference. She dared not ask if he was in love with the woman because she didn't want to hear the answer.

"You are a proud woman. I know you would not want people whispering about me behind your back, but you needn't worry. I will always be faithful to you."

"How could you be when I will be away so often?" Kara asked pointedly, seizing yet another opportunity to emphasize how greatly her independence would affect their marriage.

"All right, let me put it another way. I would be as faithful to you as you were to me. Does that sound like a more workable arrangement?" When Kara only responded with a disgusted glance, Aidan knew that if by some miracle he could claim her for his wife, she would remain faithful to him. That was a more exciting prospect than he had thought possible and he broke into a broad grin.

"As to your third question, Duke hates me because I am everything he is not. He might be a wealthy shepherd, but he's a shepherd all the same. That Brina likes me only adds to his jealousy, it didn't create it."

The more he had told her about the challenges, the more Kara had come to· realize her presence in his life had only served to compound the problems he had already had before her arrival. That fact failed to make her feel any better, however. "Well as I see it, there are far too many people who either despise what I represent or who are jealous of you to make the outcome of tomorrow's challenges all that certain. I promise you one thing though: If this heroic attempt of yours to protect me fails, I'll not marry someone else. I'll not leave you if you lose. Unlike the women here, I know I could never fall in love with a man simply because he'd beaten you in a fight."

"That's a comforting thought," Aidan teased, still certain he had nothing to fear. He drummed his fingertips on the table top as he continued to smile. "You've not screamed at me once for sewing up the gash in your head. Even if my handiwork leaves a scar, it won't be seen with all your curls."

Somehow Kara thought that would be the least of the marks he would leave on her. "I'll get the dishes," she volunteered suddenly. Leaping to her feet, she carried her plate over to the sink. When she returned for his, he caught her wrist and pulled her down to his lap where he kept her confined in a playful embrace.

"You're well now, aren't you? Your mind is as bright as ever. Are the headaches gone?" He nuzzled her ear with sweet kisses, then leaned back to await her reply.

While it was nice of him to inquire about her health, Kara

knew that was not what he really wanted to know. He wanted to make love to her; the desire lighting his blue eyes with a smoldering fire was unmistakable. But he wanted a wife and she wanted freedom—how could they make love and forget the enormity of that difference?

The cause of Kara's confusion was so readily apparent that Aidan decided he would be wise not to press the issue of where she would spend the night just yet. "I want you to try on the gown I bought in case you need to adjust the hem. We'll have to be at the square before dawn, so if you need to alter it you'll want to do it now."

"I'd still rather wear my own clothes."

"You know it's not just a question of clothes," Aidan reminded her softly.

Kara swallowed hard, aware that he knew all her objections to the coming day's events without her repeating them. "Yes, I know, and I understand why you want them to see only a young woman rather than one of Alado's scouts."

"Good. That's the most encouraging thing you've said to me all week." He eased her off his lap, got to his feet, then gave her a hand. "Come on, I want to see you in that dress."

Reluctant to try it on, Kara hesitated a long moment before following him into the bedroom, where he swiftly unwrapped a long, sleeveless sheath. It was woven of a lightweight, white wool jersey shot through with bright gold threads which became a glittering border at the hem. It was so elegant and beautiful she was simply speechless.

"You don't like it?" Aidan asked apprehensively.

Kara reached out to feel the delicate fabric with an admiring touch and found it even softer than his comfortable robe. "I love it, Aidan, but do the women here dress in such beautiful clothes every day?"

Delighted to have pleased her, Aidan gave her a charming smile. "The wealthy ones do. Now let me help you try it on."

Kara quickly slipped out of her suit and boots, then pulled the lovely white gown on over her head. The garment was so well tailored that the graceful lines complemented her slender figure most attractively. She adjusted the draped neckline at the shoulders and then turned toward him. "Well, what do you think?"

He handed her a pair of gold sandals, waited for her to put them on and then stepped back a bit. "You look like an angel. The length is perfect, and I'm glad you like the dress. I've never bought presents for a woman, but I really enjoyed buying that gown. I'll see you have plenty more."

"I've caused you far too much trouble as it is, Aidan. I'll not have you going into debt to clothe me," Kara advised him seriously.

Her comment amused the warrior enormously. "I have more money than you could ever spend. I told you fighting challenges for others pays very well. Don't you believe me?"

Kara gestured toward his scant attire. "Then why don't you wear more clothes yourself if you can afford them?"

Aidan looked down at his shorts and boots and shrugged slightly. "I do wear a vest when I fight, but like most warriors I consider other clothes unnecessary. I'll have to introduce you to Barret, our banker. His calling naturally requires a more impressive wardrobe, but mine does not."

While Kara was certain the economics of 329 must be a fascinating subject in itself, she was in no mood to hear about it that night and her expression clearly showed it.

Noting her distress, Aidan pulled Kara into his arms and gave her a warm hug. "I am the strongest man in the city, my love. I can force everyone to accept you, or anything else I want, but I've no wish to become such a brutal dictator. I know you haven't got the slightest interest in marrying me, but believe me, it's the best possible way to dissolve the fear everyone has of you. Once my friends get to know you, they'll be able to separate you and Alado in their minds and they'll come to love you as I do, regardless of what their feelings still might be for your corporation."

Kara closed her eyes as she rested her cheek against the warrior's bare shoulder. She wrapped her arms around his slim hips to return his embrace as she inquired softly, "That's the first time you've ever said you love me. Do you mean it?"

Aidan had been so intent on convincing her of the benefits of their marriage that he had not even realized he had used the word "love." He had never been the type to make careless promises, but he knew she was unlike anyone he had ever known and his feelings for her were also unique. "Yes, I do love you," he admitted frankly. "I love you very much."

Standing in his arms, Kara felt the delicious warmth of desire mixed with the most tender concern. Yet she dared not speak of love, for surely it should bring a bright glow of happiness rather than the icy dread that filled her heart. Knowing she owed Aidan an explanation for her reserve, she stepped out of his arms, took his hand and led him over to the foot of the bed. "There's something I want to tell you. Will you sit here with me for a minute?"

"I will gladly spend the entire night with you, but if you have waited this long to confess you already have a husband, it won't matter. After tomorrow you'll simply have two," he teased as he sat down by her side.

"No," Kara replied very seriously. "I have never been married, so you needn't fear that. You've never mentioned your parents. Are they living?"

As always, Aidan was amazed by the unpredictability of Kara's questions, but he gave her a prompt reply. "My mother died giving birth to me, and my father was killed in a rock slide on the mountains when I was four, so I never really knew either of them. My grandfather raised me, but he died three years ago." Recalling that the one time he had asked about her childhood it brought disastrous results, he hoped he had not sounded flippant. "He was a great man, and I'll always miss him. You would have liked him. He believed that strength was not nearly as important as intelligence."

"Really? I would have liked him then," Kara agreed.

She looked so thoroughly miserable that Aidan did not know whether or not to encourage her to tell him what was on her mind. Deciding she needed to release her feelings, he slipped his arm around her shoulders in a protective embrace. "I will be happy to listen to all you have to say, Kara. Now what is it?"

As Kara relaxed against him, her golden eyes filled with huge tears she couldn't force away. They spilled over her thick lashes, rolled down her flushed cheeks and splashed soundlessly on the bodice of her snowy white dress. "You asked me one time to tell you something about myself, but I couldn't do it then."

"Are you certain you want to tell me now?" Aidan could readily see the tale would be painful to recall, and he could not bear to see her suffer for any reason.

"Oh yes, I must," Kara assured him, but she needed several minutes to grow calm enough to begin. "I look exactly like my mother, Aidan, so much so that her old friends are often startled when we meet unexpectedly. She was a scout, too, and a very fine one. My father was Alado's most talented architect. He designed imaginative environments so perfect they were mistaken for God's own creations. He built resorts for Alado as well as elegant private estates."

"You all lived together on Mother?" Aidan inquired softly.

"Yes. It is a wonderfully exciting place for a child, and most of us who grew up together chose not to leave."

Aidan was becoming more apprehensive by the second, for nothing she had said so far was in the least bit sad, and he knew there had to have been some terrible tragedy to account for the depth of her depression. "Are your parents still on board?"

"No," Kara disclosed tearfully. "They were an ideal couple. My father was dark like Zac, very handsome and dashing. Both he and my mother were devoted to their careers, but they simply adored each other and spent every spare minute they could together. It was as though their honeymoon had never ended. Their love for each other was so plain everyone could see it."

Since it was obvious Kara had loved her parents dearly but could not speak of them without becoming nearly hysterical, Aidan was afraid he already knew how her story would end. "What happened to them?" he whispered hoarsely.

"My mother was a superb pilot, but she was killed on a

training mission when another scout's ship collided with hers. It was entirely his fault, but placing blame on someone didn't bring her back. My father had always encouraged her to fly because she loved it so, but he blamed himself for giving her that freedom since it led to her death. The burden of that guilt simply destroyed him. I was twelve, old enough to understand the agony of his grief, but although I tried my best, there was nothing I could do to relieve it. He lived only a month without her. His doctor called it a heart attack, but I knew better. He had taken great care to make his death appear natural so I would not be suspected of coming from an unstable background. But he died by his own hand."

Aidan was overwhelmed by the emotional impact of her story, but rather than compassion, he felt the darkest rage. "Your father may have been a miserable coward who couldn't face life without the woman he loved, but I'm not nearly so weak! Didn't the bastard realize what he would be doing to you? All he taught you was that love brings unbearable pain. That's just not true!"

"Oh, but it is true, Aidan, it really is," Kara argued as she wiped away the last of her tears. "I decided never to marry rather than risk causing a man the inconsolable anguish my mother caused my father."

Life on 329 had made Aidan a very practical man, and he drew on that good sense now. "Since we've no fuel to get your Banshee into the air, the only death you're likely to face is from old age."

"If your people don't kill me first," the redhead reminded him with a touch of her usual defiance.

"The fact that you have so little faith in me is appalling!" Aidan shouted right back. "How many times must I tell you that I will not lose tomorrow before you'll believe me?"

"I believe you," Kara admitted hesitantly, "but that doesn't stop me from worrying about you."

"Why you'd waste your time worrying about me I'll never know, but you'll see tomorrow just how pointless it has been." Aidan started to rise, but Kara reached out and lay her palm on his thigh to stop him. He knew exactly what she was going to do, but before he could push her hand away the pulsating waves of pleasure had already begun. "Kara," he moaned. She moved her hand slightly higher and the warmth spreading within his loins was so delicious he could not even recall why he had been so angry. Then he fell back on the bed in a careless heap.

"You don't understand anything about me, do you?" Kara purred softly as she unbuttoned his shorts. "At least you are remarkably easy to undress." To make love to him while at the same time using her mind to give him pleasure was a most appealing challenge at the moment. She and Aidan would have but a brief time together, she was positive of that even if he was not, and she wanted his memories of her to be sweet.

She removed his boots and then his shorts before rising to kick off her sandals and pull off the lovely white gown. She stepped out of her teddy and tossed them both on the carved chest which contained his clothing before joining him on the wide bed. She had always enjoyed the sight of his body since he was so handsomely built, but she knew her compliments only amused him so she did not offer any more. She concentrated instead on arousing him with teasing kisses on his eyelids before moving to his ears. As she leaned down to kiss his lips, the tips of her breasts caressed his chest. He wrapped his arms around her waist, but his touch was so gentle it provided little in the way of restraint and she easily eluded him. She nuzzled the hollow of his throat with a playful kiss that left a heart-shaped purple mark she knew would still be visible in the morning.

She watched a slow smile spread across Aidan's face and knew he would not be angry with her for taking advantage of him in such a fiendishly loving manner. Were it possible for her to take a husband, she would want a man exactly like him. He had the wit and courage to match her own, and far more charm, but their lives were woven of strands so different she knew they could never truly become one. It would only be at precious times like this, when nothing else existed, that they could share the same dream.

Her lips traced an enticing spiral down the center of his broad chest and over the flat, hard muscles of his stomach as her nails moved slowly up his inner thighs. She could feel each quiver of excitement she created within him and waited until she sensed he could stand no more to bring him the tranquility of pleasure's most perfect release.

Aidan felt his blood ignite with flames of desire as Kara's generous kisses grew still more deeply erotic. Her hands gave him no respite from the molten rapture which seared his veins, and he could no longer lie still while the soft swirl of her tongue drew him ever closer to the edge of abandon. The fiery heat of her mouth enveloped him then, drawing forth the last ounce of his reason. He wound his fingers in her glorious curls to hold her fast as the ecstasy erupted from deep within his powerfully muscled body in a dazzling climax that left him more drained than if he had fought a thousand men. When at last he had the strength to open his eyes, he found her curled languidly beside him with a maddeningly superior smirk gracing her lovely features. "You're really proud of yourself, aren't you?"

"Shouldn't I be?" Kara inquired with a teasing innocence.

Aidan lunged for her, tossing her on her back and imprisoning her beneath him as he held her wrists locked in a powerful grip. "Does the word bitch mean anything to you?" he murmured as he lowered his mouth to her throat, intent on leaving his own mark upon her creamy smooth skin.

His teasing kiss tickled so terribly that Kara began to laugh. "The last time you called me that we ended up making love in your tub. Do you want to do that again?"

"Later," Aidan promised softly, too entranced by the welcoming warmth of her slender body to want to move off the bed.

Kara snuggled against him. "I love you," she stated simply. "That's why I'm so worried about you. Didn't you understand that?"

Aidan leaned back slightly to look down at her. "No, but I certainly do now."

"Good," Kara purred sweetly. "Now please let go of my hands so I can hug you."

"You'll have to promise to do lots more than that," Aidan replied with a devilish chuckle. To his great delight, she did.

CHAPTER
◊ XII ◊

Kara knelt on the bed behind Aidan while she braided his hair into a single plait. After she had tied the end with the leather thong he had provided, she leaned over to kiss his shoulder with a loving nibble. "There, it's finished." She watched as he donned a well-worn brown leather vest and lightweight brown gloves which, along with his usual pair of tan shorts and boots, completed his battle attire. "It's no wonder you have so many scars if that's all you wear for protection," she mused apprehensively.

Aidan gave his gloves a final yank and scoffed at her concern. "Most of my scars are due to scrapes I got into as a kid, not fighting challenges. I don't usually get touched, let alone hurt, so I don't need a lot of heavy padding."

His confident reassurance failed to lift his lover's somber mood, however. She moved off his bed and shook the folds out of the soft fabric of her new gown. The close-fitting sheath was wonderfully comfortable, the classical style exquisite, but she felt as though she were dressed for a masquerade ball. She felt so little like a bride. She didn't want to think about the upcoming challenges or dwell on the impossibility of becoming Aidan's wife, and so she chose a completely different topic to fill the last minutes before they left his home.

"The mole women were barefooted, or at least the ones I saw up close were," she remarked as she slipped on the gold sandals. "I don't understand how they can stand living underground as they do. It was like being held prisoner in the dungeon of some medieval castle, and I didn't like that creepy sensation one bit."

"Then it's a damn good thing I showed up when I did, isn't it?" Aidan teased her playfully. They'd gotten little rest during the night, but he felt elated still, rather than tired, because he had appreciated her generous loving so greatly. "Castles had handsome knights as well as dank dungeons, don't forget that."

"Ah yes, knights." Kara fluffed out her still damp curls with her fingers, then decided she was as ready as she would ever be and turned toward him. "I can see why you would like knights since they were a superb class of warrior. They rode fine stallions, wore magnificent suits of armor, fought glorious battles for their kings and in their spare time rescued damsels in distress. You would have made a wonderful knight, Aidan."

Amused by her compliment, he chuckled slyly. "Thank you, but you've forgotten the dragons. Surely every ambitious knight got to slay a dragon or two on his way to rescuing one of those pretty damsels."

"Not really," Kara explained with a touch of regret. "The knights were a very real part of Earth's history, but dragons never existed outside the pages of fanciful medieval tales."

"Who knows? Maybe one day you'll discover a world whose skies are filled with dragons. Until then, I have one I'll give you." Aidan went to his chest and rummaged around in the bottom for a small cloth bag he then carried back to her. "This is a good luck charm my grandfather gave me, but I think maybe you're the one who'll need it today."

Curious, Kara loosened the drawstring and after a gentle shake, a fine gold chain with an intricate charm in the shape of a ferocious dragon crouched in a defiant pose fell out into her palm. The proud little beast was no more than an inch in height, but so perfectly detailed she could see the scales on his tail and wings, the fierce gleam in his eyes and each of his tiny claws. "Oh Aidan, this is marvelous, but surely you don't want to give it away."

"I most certainly do," the brawny blond insisted as he took the chain from her hands. He had to remove his right glove momentarily to drape the exotic necklace around her neck and fasten the clasp. "It's perfect for you. Every sorceress should have her own dragon to help her cast spells."

Kara knew exactly to what sort of magical spells he was referring. She held the remarkable charm in her fingers for a long moment, uncertain whether or not she should accept it. "I'll not argue with you again that I don't do magic tricks or cast spells, since I know you are only teasing me. If you usually wear this yourself, though, I would rather you wore it today."

"No, I can't. The chain is stronger than it looks and an opponent might try to use it to choke me. I have always considered the fact that I own it to bring me luck enough to win any contest. Now wear it for me today, and I don't want to hear another whisper of worry from your lips."

Kara knew that would be a difficult promise to keep, but she nodded in agreement. "I love this little dragon, and you too. I'm certain you'll win all the challenges swiftly, but should you need my help, I'll be there to give it."

Aidan rested his hands on his hips as he shook his head emphatically. "Oh, no you won't. I intend to fight the men on my own terms, Kara, without any help from your magic."

That was an even more difficult promise to honor, and Kara knew there was no way she could keep it if he appeared to be in any great danger of losing a match. She smiled sweetly, knowing he would not trust her word if she gave it too readily. "I'll not do a thing unless you're flat on your back screaming my name. How's that?"

Aidan threw back his head and howled with laughter because that image was so hilarious. "No one has ever knocked me off my feet, Kara, so it is agreed. If the situation looks that desperate then by all means work all the magic you can."

Impatient to be going, he placed his newly honed dagger in its sheath and picked up his spear. Taking Kara's hand, he escorted her through the house and out to the street. Although it was quite early, the air was warm, flowing gently with the last hint of the brutal desert wind, and there was no need for him to offer her his cloak. Before they had reached the first corner, Zac came running to meet them followed by Juno, a strapping teenager who fancied himself a warrior although he had never done anything requiring more bravery than standing guard at the gate.

The two took a moment to catch their breath, then Zac blurted out their news. "Duke let some moles in. That big ugly brute, Kyle, and two others came to demand satisfaction from you for killing Cruz, and Duke just let them walk right in through the gate! He told them they could find you at the square and issue a challenge with the others."

Since Zac and his youthful companion seemed so greatly alarmed, Kara knew the situation was every bit as desperate as it sounded. "How could they have known to come here today unless someone invited them?" she asked in a hushed whisper.

Aidan wasn't surprised she was so quick, only that he had not thought of the moles himself. "It's obvious they're here simply to cause me grief, but we've never accepted challenges from moles and I'll not break with that tradition now."

"How will you be able to avoid it?" Kara asked perceptively, knowing he was far too proud to let anyone call him a coward, especially a mole!

The blond warrior replied with a wicked grin, "Have you forgotten? I can do whatever I damn well please here unless someone has the muscle to stop me. We will approach this problem one step at a time. I'll beat whoever dares to challenge me for you, then I'll toss the moles over the wall, and then I'll ask if Duke wants to fight me for the position of Captain of the Guard. If he does not, then the job will again be mine. Hell, even if by some miracle he does gather the courage to fight me, the job will still be mine."

While Zac and Juno enthusiastically cheered that boast, Kara could not. "This has got to be some sort of a trap, Aidan, and I don't think you should just swagger right into it!"

Aidan responded by wrapping his hand firmly around her arm and propelling the flame-haired beauty along by his side as he led his small party toward the square. "Of course it's a trap. I am not so stupid I missed such an obvious point, but until we arrive at the square and see just exactly whom I'm expected to fight, I won't be able to formulate a more detailed plan. All you need do is look as though you actually believe I'll live through the day!"

The prospect of having to watch him fight his own kind had been bad enough. She had no idea how she could look at the despicable Kyle again without becoming physically ill. She clutched the dragon charm tightly in her hand, hoping it was not the only source of Aidan's luck. When they reached the square, she was astonished to find that not only men had been curious enough to rise at such an early hour, but also women and children. It appeared the whole city was present, and counting quickly, she discovered they numbered close to one thousand.

As dawn approached, the lively banter of the crowd increased in volume until it rivaled that of the boisterous scene in the moles' cavern. Latecomers continued to join those waiting in the crowded square while people living nearby were seated on their rooftops in order to have the best view. That everyone was so eager to witness the challenges simply disgusted her, and when she heard a man shout a question about odds, she grabbed Aidan's arm in a frantic clutch. "Your people don't actually bet on these barbaric contests, do they?"

The way she had phrased her question made the warrior wince, but he told her the truth. "Yes, gambling provides a large part of the crowd's enjoyment since not everyone can appreciate the challenges simply as sporting events. Don't they allow betting on Mother?"

"Never!" Kara advised him sternly. "Gambling is considered the very antithesis of sport!"

"The what?" Aidan asked with a befuddled frown.

"The exact opposite, a complete contradiction," Kara explained unhappily as she continued to hang on to his arm. She was so appalled by his customs she shuddered with revulsion. All of life on 329 was the antithesis of the sophisticated world in which she had lived aboard Mother, she thought absently as she continued to search the crowd for any hint of a friendly face. To her immense relief she did see more openly curious glances than outright hostile ones, but she still couldn't wait for the day to be over.

Since no one would have a better understanding of the odds, Aidan guided Kara over to the banker and introduced him to her. He was grateful when she did no more than give the man a shy smile, but Aidan quickly began to pump him for information. A jovial fellow only a few years his senior, Barret was of medium height with a trim build. His wavy blond hair was lightly flecked with gray while his eyes were the same vivid blue since the two men were not only good friends but also cousins.

"This is a very strange morning in many ways," Barret confided in a conspiratorial whisper. "It's assumed you can take any of us, but we've never had moles at a challenge before, and they've thrown everything into confusion."

"Your thinking is usually far clearer than that," Aidan advised in a voice loud enough to be readily overheard. "The moles are here because I killed one of their miserable number. If I killed one, then I can kill others just as easily since they have far more bulk than brains."

Barret gave the confident warrior a sly wink. "Now you and I may believe that, Aidan, but the fact that not everyone does is what will make the day so interesting and profitable for us both."

While Aidan seemed more concerned with discussing odds than knowing who planned to challenge him, Kara strained to learn something from the conversation taking place all around them, but the open courtyard was so noisy she could make out little she could understand. All too frequently the words she heard were most uncomplimentary terms used to describe her as Aidan's alien mistress, although she did not understand how anyone could possibly consider her an alien when all their ancestors came from the same small planet. After a short while she forgot that complaint when she realized "alien" was the kindest thing anyone called her. Looking over at Aidan, she wished he were paying closer attention to the coming bouts than how much the banker had already taken in in bets.

Finally, when she could stand no more of the horrible suspense, she interrupted the two men. "Please forgive me, but who is in charge here? I thought the challenges were to be fought closer to dawn than noon."

"You see what a delight she is?" Aidan remarked casually to Barret. "She's not the least bit worried about me. She's simply growing bored. Well, my love, I am in charge since I'm the one who must accept the challenges, and you're right, it is growing late. Let's begin."

Kara had not dreamed her question would bring such a quick response and she clung to Aidan's hand as he led her toward the enclosure in the center of the square. To her dismay there were two dozen men standing with Zac, but from the tone of their laughter she swiftly grasped they had come to cheer for Aidan rather than fight him.

Taking Kara along with him, the agile warrior continued past the roped-off ring and stepped up the side of an attractive circular fountain to gain the crowd's attention. Then he explained the purpose of the day's events matter-of-factly.

"As most of you know, I wish to take this woman for my wife. If any man objects to our marriage, or wishes to wed her himself, then this is the time for him to declare it."

A hushed silence fell over the crowd as all strained to see who would come forward. A long moment passed before Kyle began to rudely thrust people aside as he made his way to the front of the crowd with a ponderous, swaggering gait. "None of your cowardly kind wants that yellow-eyed she-devil for a wife, Aidan, but I'll gladly make her the prize in a fight between us," he snarled belligerently.

"We do not give our women to moles," the blond warrior

reminded him proudly. "You've no business being at this challenge. Now take your friends and go home, or you'll swiftly wish you'd run all the way there when you had the chance."

"That's not one of your women, Aidan," Kyle pointed out with a deep rumbling chuckle. "She is Alado's and neither yours nor mine until after the challenge is fought."

"He is right, Aidan!" Fermin shouted promptly, and his words were echoed by Duke and a chorus of others of similar prejudice. "We were born depising Alado, and that includes her as well. Give her to Kyle and be done with the bitch!"

Kara had absolutely no experience dealing with hostile crowds, but she lifted her chin proudly and remained by Aidan's side as though she were already his wife and supremely confident of his skills. She had not the slightest doubt he would protect her with his life, and she realized she had not once thanked him for being so willing to defend her. She could not help but be impressed by how clever Fermin and Duke had been, however, for she could see people glancing toward them for approval before they spoke out against her. Stationed throughout the crowd, they made it appear the opposition to her presence in the city was widespread, when without such badgering she doubted the majority would have sided with the loudmouthed mole.

Aidan was so thoroughly disgusted that he had not foreseen such a conspiracy he wasn't in the least bit reluctant to accept Kyle's challenge. He raised his hand for silence. "I never thought we had such cowardly men residing here. Men have spoken out against Kara, and yet they will not step forward to fight me themselves. If you have hired this wretched mole to fight in your places, then I will gladly face him; but it must be agreed upon by everyone now that I will fight only him to settle this question and no others. Is that understood?"

"You know the rules! You must accept all challenges!" Duke cried out, for he had convinced several men to fight Aidan if he survived the bout with Kyle, thinking the warrior would be so exhausted he would have little of his usual strength and an easy victory would be theirs.

Aidan was ready for that objection and swiftly silenced it. "As you were so eager to agree that the rule prohibiting moles from competing will not be enforced today, therefore neither will any of the others. There will be only this one bout. There will be no referee, no weapons, no holds barred, nor any type of blow considered a foul. Now, is there anyone here with the courage to object to my terms with his fists? If not, then let's get the challenge over with promptly and go home!"

Zac and his friends had now had sufficient time to study Fermin and Duke's tactics, and this time broke into a rousing cheer before the hecklers planted around them could interfere.

As the crowd parted for them to approach the ring, Kara could not escape the horrible feeling that both she and Aidan were about to be sacrificed to satisfy the unruly mob's lust for blood. It was all too obvious now that she truly was an alien; but in a city where decisions were made in such a brutal manner while the gleeful spectators bet on the outcome, she was glad to be considered an outsider. She had not expected anything like this where the unique abilities she possessed would be so difficult to use. Her skills in hand-to-hand combat were excellent, but of little value here where she was so badly outnumbered. As with everyone else she could use her mind to influence Kyle only if he looked directly at her and she thought the chances slim that he would allow his attention to wander from Aidan. No, the only time he would glance toward her would be to gloat, but she vowed to seize that opportunity swiftly should it arise.

Her fingers strayed again to the tiny dragon resting between her breasts on its delicate gold chain. Yes, she thought with a satisfied smile, she would conjure up a gigantic fire-breathing dragon who would swoop down from the sky, lift Kyle right out of the ring and carry him high above the mountains. It was the perfect monster to terrorize the hairy brute, since she doubted a flock of vultures would frighten him when he probably ate chickens without bothering to pluck out their feathers first. Quite pleased with her imaginative idea, her smile grew wider still.

As Aidan handed his dagger and spear to Zac to hold, he caught sight of Kara's mystical glance and knew instantly she would not leave the outcome of the bout to chance. Pulling her close so he would not be overheard, he reminded her of their bargain. "I can handle this slobbering idiot on my own, Kara, without any of your tricks."

Kara gave the handsome warrior a quick kiss on the cheek. "Yes, I know," she agreed confidently. "I could never have a more able champion than you."

He still felt as though she were up to something, but Aidan had no time to argue with her. "They've played right into our hands by agreeing to allow me to fight only this one bout. They've outsmarted themselves, and I'll not lose the advantage that is already mine." He returned her kiss, then gave her a jaunty wink and stepped into the ring.

That Aidan was even more highly skilled at hand-to-hand combat than she had thought possible became apparent, for he began by adopting a series of clever moves which kept the lumbering Kyle constantly moving and yet always facing directly into Altair's blazing rays. The openly hostile mole was not nearly as tall as Aidan, although he outweighed him by at least thirty pounds. His actions were clumsy, his steps slow, his reach not nearly as long as Aidan's, but what he lacked in physical grace he obviously had in strength, for his massive chest and arms were very muscular, as were his back and solidly built legs. That Aidan had vowed to toss him over the wall clearly seemed an impossibility, but Kara began to wish he could really accomplish such a feat.

Rather than using spoken insults, in this match Aidan merely reached out at will to punch the heavyset mole squarely in the face; his step was so light he easily avoided any blow Kyle tried to mete out in return. After a few minutes of such playful tactics, the hairy brute's dark beard was red with the blood dripping from his broken nose. Apparently considering such a wound minor, the man ignored it and began to quicken his methodical pace.

The fact that Aidan was still handsome after having

fought so many challenges simply infuriated Kyle, and he swore to himself the blond would not leave the ring that day unscarred; yet each time he swung at him, he missed his mark by a wide margin. Finally realizing he could not hope to beat Aidan while fighting a bout more suited to the city dweller's lightning-fast style of combat than his own brutish pace, he moved in close, tucked his head against his shoulder and slammed into the blond's chest to force him back against the ropes. Using his considerable weight to keep his opponent pinned, Kyle fastened his stubby fingers around Aidan's throat with a crushing grip, but the agile warrior made a fast grab for the mole's groin and lifted him clear off his feet with a grasp so agonizing the brute released his throat at the same time he let out a piercing howl of pain.

Since he had stated no moves would be considered foul, Aidan had used the swiftest manner possible to disable his opponent. As Kyle continued to stumble backward yelping in pain, he pursued him; then, with a nimble leap, Aidan struck him full in the mouth with the heel of his right boot and dislodged several of the mole's badly stained front teeth. The outcome of the challenge was easily predictable then, for while Kyle proved to have enormous endurance and a high tolerance for pain, he was so slow that each of Aidan's punishing blows and kicks did additional damage. Soon Kyle was too dazed to remain on his feet and sank to his knees, nearly unconscious. Rather than deliver a final crippling blow to the disabled man, Aidan turned his back on him and walked to the far corner, his expression one of complete boredom. He had hardly worked up a sweat and, except for a ring of pale bruises encircling his neck, there wasn't a mark on him.

Aidan waited patiently for Kyle's gaze to clear enough to recognize him before he shouted at the man, "Will you concede the challenge now?"

After a long moment, Kyle staggered to his feet, struggled to take a step forward and then two more. He raised his hand shakily to his forehead, as if to massage away the pain, but with uncharacteristic speed he lashed out at Aidan's jaw. Only the blond's natural wariness and agile reflexes prevented him from being knocked flat by the mole's furious blow.

Kara turned away when, clearly disgusted by his opponent's deceit, Aidan began to give the already blood-drenched mole an unmerciful beating. She would have left the crowded square but his cousin, Barret, who had taken a place at her side, swiftly blocked that move.

"Since you will be the winner's prize, my dear, you may not leave before the challenge is over."

Just as Aidan had mentioned, the banker was dressed differently than the warriors. The seams of his tailored white shirt were enhanced with gold thread, his cream-colored shorts neatly pressed with a crisp crease and his hands adorned with an impressive collection of gold rings. Since he was obviously wealthy, it sickened Kara all the more that he would wish to make money off such a disgusting spectacle. "Why does Aidan refer to you as a banker when your business is clearly gambling?"

Barret glanced toward the ring to make certain Aidan still held the upper hand before replying with a philosophic shrug, "All of life is a gamble, Kara. Allowing you to marry Aidan is a gamble for us all. I wonder if we'll come to regret it before he does?"

The man's blatant insult shocked Kara badly, but she had no time to reply or step away before the ropes were lowered and Aidan half-carried, half-dragged Kyle over to the fountain. He held the man's head under the water to revive him sufficiently to concede the match, but when the mole proved to be too stubborn to speak the words, he pushed his head under again. When Kyle finally realized just how eager Aidan was to drown him, he nodded frantically.

"You have won!" he admitted through a series of sputtering coughs after Aidan hauled his head out of the water.

The challenge decisively won, Aidan stepped up on the side of the fountain to make certain Kyle and his two friends made a hasty retreat. When they had left the square, their heads bowed in disgrace, he pointed to Duke. "We have one more thing to settle today. If you wish to be Captain of the Guard, then you must fight me now for that right."

The curious crowd had not expected to see another match and, eager to hear Duke's reply, pressed close. The shepherd glanced quickly at Fermin, who was standing beside him, hoping for some way to escape such a humiliating confrontation. Knowing they had been beaten, the gray-haired man turned away and walked off through the crowd, leaving Duke on his own.

"Well?" Aidan called loudly. "Do you want the job enough to fight for it?"

"No!" Duke finally had the presence of mind to reply. "It is yours."

Aidan leapt down off the fountain, pulled off his gloves, then rinsed his hands and face in the water before walking back to Kara. He raised his right hand and whispered a soft command. "Place your left hand against mine."

"But why?" the redhead asked with her usual curiosity.

"Because I won the match," Aidan stated simply.

His grin was too enticing for her to resist his request for more than a few seconds, and she quickly lifted her hand to his. The resulting shout that went up from the crowd was a deafening roar. Afraid they had suddenly turned against her, she clung so tightly to him that Aidan began to laugh. "Do not be frightened, beloved, the noise is meant to wish us well. You've just become my wife."

What Kara had expected she didn't really know, but taking a man's hand in public did not seem like any kind of a marriage ceremony.

"What?" she asked in dismay as she quickly withdrew her hand, but it was obviously too late.

Aidan could not help but laugh at her stricken expression. Hugging her tightly to his side, he waved to the swarm of friends who had crowded around them. "We'll join you after I've changed my clothes," he promised. Surrounded by the boisterous well-wishers, he guided Kara protectively toward his street. Invitations for food and drink were numerous as they made their way through the town, but he declined them all graciously. When at last Zac and the rest of his friends turned off to enter Dodge's Tavern, they were finally alone.

Aidan had cast numerous sidelong glances in Kara's direction, but the ferocity of the scout's dark scowl had failed to lessen since they had left the square. While he was tremendously pleased by the way the morning had ended, she clearly was not. "Did you really want to see me land on my ass so you could rescue me?" he finally asked accusingly.

"Of course not!" Kara responded immediately, saddened that he would consider her shallow enough to be jealous of his victory. "I didn't want to see you hurt. It's only that, well . . ."

Having never before seen the young woman at a loss for words, Aidan tried again to confront her and bring her complaints out into the open. "You're obviously disappointed about something. If it isn't the challenge, then what is it?"

As they moved along through the now deserted street, Kara kept a watchful eye out for someone who might wish her harm. She couldn't understand how Aidan could be unsure of the cause of her despair and told him so in terms she thought he would readily understand.

"A wedding is supposed to be a joyously celebrated occasion, Aidan, not a brief gesture at the end of a ghastly brawl," she pointed out sarcastically. Again on the verge of tears, she was too proud to give in to them.

"Then you're not sorry I had no reason to call upon your help?" Aidan asked with a deep chuckle.

That he would be in a teasing mood when she had given him a serious reply to his question did nothing to raise Kara's spirits. "I am sorry about a great many things that have happened here, but not that you defeated Kyle so soundly when the bastard deserved no better!"

Startled by her burst of anger, Aidan accompanied her in silence for several paces before making what he considered a generous offer. "If you would like a different type of ceremony, we can have another or as many as you'd like. There's no set pattern here. As with everything else, we do as we please. I've already promised you complete freedom, so I did not think you would object to becoming my wife without any vows being exchanged."

"It would have been thoughtful to warn me what putting

my hand to yours meant, Aidan. Is a divorce arranged with similar ease?"

Coming to an abrupt halt, the warrior grabbed Kara's arm to wheel her around to face him. "We have no divorce here, so you needn't worry that any careless gesture will make you a single woman again."

Kara returned his furious stare, feeling another of 329's endless perils closing in on her. "That's another thing you should have had the courtesy to discuss with me!"

In truth, the word divorce had not once crossed his mind, but Aidan had no wish to discuss the issue on the street corner. He moved his hand to her elbow to guide her toward his home. "I realize ours was an unusual courtship in many respects, but—"

"Unusual!" Kara gasped, shocked by such an understatement.

"Highly unusual?" the warrior restated with a quizzical glance.

Kara clamped her mouth shut to force back the furious response she was so sorely tempted to shriek. Then, recalling that all the man's actions had been inspired by a desire to save her life, she felt deeply ashamed for criticizing his methods. Taking a deep breath, she attempted to be far more gracious about their marriage. "I doubt I would be alive today were it not for all the help you've given me. I don't want you ever to think I'm not grateful for it because I truly am. I can only thank you now and hope that someday I can repay your kindness in full measure."

Aidan did no more than seethe silently until he had closed his door behind them. Then he leaned back against it and barked hoarsely, "Gratitude is the very last thing I'd ever want from you! Now, I fully intend to spend the afternoon celebrating our marriage with my friends. Do whatever you like until I am ready to go."

Kara stood mute as he strode into his bedroom, uncertain why her polite words of gratitude had been rejected so forcefully. Aidan had always been extremely polite while she knew she tended to be far too blunt. She had made the effort to be polite this time, however, and look what it had gotten her. All she had succeeded in doing was infuriating the proud man who clearly intended to call himself her husband, although she felt anything but married to him.

She got a drink of water and spent a long while pacing restlessly; when Aidan had still not reappeared, she ventured to the door of the bath. He was seated on the steps of the tub, water from his hair trickling down his back. He appeared to be in absolutely no hurry to finish his bath despite his insistence that they join his friends.

Wondering whether something was wrong, Kara called out to him softly. "Aidan? I couldn't bear to watch all of that beastly match, but I saw enough. I doubt you'll ever need my help to win a challenge, but you would tell me if you were hurt, wouldn't you? I would never tell anyone else."

Aidan gave her a sheepish glance as he called over his shoulder, "How many bones are there in a hand?"

"There are eight in the wrist, five in the palm, and fourteen in the fingers, which makes twenty-seven altogether." Kara supplied the brief anatomy lesson and then, realizing the full import of his question, rushed over to the tub and knelt by his side. "Do you think you've broken your hand?"

Aidan held up his badly swollen right hand and attempted to wiggle his fingers without much success. "Whether or not every last bone is shattered I don't really know, but it sure feels like they are."

"Should I call someone?" Kara inquired sympathetically. "Do you have physicians here?"

Feeling very foolish, Aidan hesitated a long moment, then climbed out of the tub and reached for a towel which Kara quickly helped him wrap around his hips. "Yes, we have physicians, but I can't let anyone know I've been hurt, Kara. If Duke and that malicious crowd found out I broke my hand they'd be back as soon as they could to issue a challenge."

"Yet you must have known you had been hurt when you dared him to challenge you."

"Of course, but I knew he would not accept it," the handsome man explained with a sly grin.

His continued confidence was maddening, but Kara could not help but feel responsible for what had happened to him.

"Come sit down at the table. Maybe you've just bruised your hand and not broken it." She took great care not to touch his badly scraped knuckles and began by examining his wrist carefully. That caused no discomfort, but as soon as she moved on to trace the outline of the bones in the back of his hand, Aidan winced in pain and she had to ease the pressure. After giving him a moment to catch his breath she tried again and could clearly discern breaks in two of the five long bones, but she scarcely needed to point them out to him since he cringed so readily at her touch. "We're both going to pass out if I try to set the broken bones for you. I think I better go get Zac, or someone else you trust."

Aidan objected strenuously to that suggestion. "No, it's far too dangerous for us both." He felt his hand carefully. Deciding her diagnosis was as accurate as any he could make, he looked up at her. "We'll have to take care of this ourselves."

Kara closed her eyes tightly, sick with fear and certain they would never be able to do it right. Then she remembered Mother's fine staff of surgeons. "Look, let's just wait until Mother arrives. We have doctors who could repair the damage in minutes," she assured him with a smile.

Aidan did no more than shake his head slowly before giving his injured hand a fierce enough tug to bring the two broken bones into alignment. The excruciating pain that tore through his palm shot clear up his arm and was more than enough to cause him to pass out, but he had something important to prove to the redhead and stubbornly refused to display such weakness in front of her. It took him a moment to catch his breath so he could speak, but then he made a polite request. "Now, if you'll please get some cloth to bind this up it will be fine," he prayed aloud, but his skin was still very pale despite his deep tan.

Horrified, Kara raised her hands to cover her mouth as she fled the room so she would not be sick in front of him; but the sight of Aidan setting his own broken bones had been just one gruesome shock too many.

CHAPTER
◇ XIII ◇

The boisterous revelry at Dodge's crowded tavern was so unbridled that a riot would have gone unnoticed. Aidan's resounding defeat of not only a hated mole but also the conservative forces that had attempted to remove him from a position of power in the city was considered cause for celebration by every man who prided himself on being a warrior as well as most of those who trembled in fear each time it was their turn to take a shift at guard duty.

Just as Aidan had assured Kara, not another mention was made of a charge of treason, nor did anyone show the open contempt for her they all still felt for Alado. His victory that morning had been so decisive it was unlikely anyone would challenge him for a good long while for any reason. That he had taken a wife, even such an extraordinary one, simply added to the exuberance of the merrymaking and provided an additional excuse to order round after round of ale so that everyone present could take a turn proposing a toast to the newlyweds.

Nearly everyone wished them a large and healthy family which did not strike Kara as unusual—but it embarrassed her all the same. Remembering Aidan's boast that she would have bright children made her realize that was another important subject they had not discussed but certainly should have.

While she was no stranger to wild parties and lively taverns, since scouts were very fond of both, Kara felt more like an imposter than ever as she sat beside Aidan in the popular bar's most spacious booth. Concealed by the badly scarred table top, his right hand lay on her left knee and her fingertips rested lightly on his whenever she felt him grow tense; she knew the sweetness of her touch would ease his pain. No one had guessed his injury was anything more serious than bruised knuckles, nor had anyone remarked on the fact that he used only his left hand to lift the tankards of pale golden ale Dodge kept sending over to their booth. She had been pleased to find their friendly host also stocked a generous supply of a lightly fragrant strawberry wine, but she had sipped no more than two goblets of it by late afternoon.

There were eight of them crowded into the semicircular enclosure, and while Kara had made an attempt to follow the teasing conversation at the table, she found herself lost within minutes of their arrival. Zac and Eric had each come alone, although the latter made his fondness for the barmaid so plain that the petite woman spent far more time at their table than at any of the others. As soon as Tory had been introduced, Kara realized she was the young woman whose charms had almost prevented her from reprogramming Sonia.

The vivacious girl was dressed in a pale blue knit sheath similar to hers, but the barmaid's was slit up the right side to expose the entire length of her shapely leg. Were she to adopt such a revealing style, Kara knew her tattoo would cause a sensation. But Aidan certainly wouldn't appreciate it, and she had no desire to draw more attention to herself. The other women she had seen that day had been attired in gowns as conservative as her own, so she thought perhaps Tory's style of dress was simply one the flirtatious young woman preferred for work since the more daring hemline obviously added to the male patrons' enjoyment of her attentions.

In addition to the two handsome bachelors and Tory's almost constant presence, two married couples had joined them in the booth. Seated nearest to her was a gregarious man named Bram and his wife, May. He was sandy-haired, brown-eyed and never missed an opportunity to make a teasing comment, while she was a slender young woman with luminous green eyes and long chestnut curls who seldom spoke but never stopped giggling at her husband's jokes.

The other couple was equally charming. The husband, Jarl, was a good-looking man almost as blond as Aidan, but green-eyed while his wife, Eden, was dark and petite with such an impish personality she reminded Kara instantly of a pixie.

There had been a futile attempt to explain to her how each was related to the other either by blood or marriage, but when that had left them all teary-eyed from laughter they had swiftly turned to animated accounts of the challenges each man had won. From that subject the conversation had drifted to the strong probability of a battle with the moles coming within the next few weeks. Such an alarming prospect caught Kara's interest immediately and prompted her to at last join in the lively discussion.

"Do they strike without any provocation?" she inquired apprehensively, hoping they would not choose that night when so many of the city's men were well on their way to becoming quite drunk.

"That we exist is provocation enough to a mole," Jarl responded with a disgusted sneer. "They are incapable of any deeper reasoning than that."

Kara saw a momentary frown cross Zac's expression. He appeared to be on the verge of arguing with that derogatory opinion, but remained silent. "Does no one ever try to bring about a lasting accord with them? If they can behave peacefully during market day, why can't that monthly truce be extended throughout the year?"

Aidan chuckled as his friends turned to gape at his bride, for her politely worded question had astounded them all. "I should think you, better than anyone else at this table, would understand why we have no interest in making peace with the moles. The first thing they would want would be our women, and that would be the end of the truce right there."

"From what I saw the moles have attractive women of their own. Why would they want yours?" Kara responded with her usual penchant for pursuing a subject to its end.

"Because they are greedy bastards who want everything

we have. They would not exclude our women from their selfish desires. No, it is impossible to trust a mole. If they're not watched closely on market day, they steal everything they can. There are many people who think allowing them into the city once a month is too often. Peace negotiations are out of the question between us," Aidan assured her with a confidence that met with ready agreement all around the table.

Intrigued by the mention of the moles, Eden leaned forward slightly. Her voice was high and so breathless that everyone had to strain to hear her above the noise of the crowded room. "Just think how horrible it would have been for you had Aidan lost the challenge to Kyle! You'd be surrounded by those hateful brutes right now rather than being here having such a wonderful time with us. Weren't you very frightened that might happen?"

Kara shrugged innocently. "Why no, it never even occurred to me that Aidan might lose." She glanced toward him and was pleased by the width of his smile. He looked very proud to know she had such confidence in him when in fact she had meant to take the measures herself to insure he did not lose. That such a precaution had been unnecessary had been a delightful surprise. She touched the dragon charm with a fond caress and returned his smile with a wonderfully warm one of her own. She still thought engaging in intermittent skirmishes with the moles ridiculous since it had to be costly to both sides, but she knew a noisy bar wasn't the place to debate the possibility of a permanent truce.

They were all distracted then as a raucous shout went up from the group of young men leaning against the bar. As she glanced around the large hall, Kara noted there were but a few men dressed in more tailored clothes as Barret, the banker, had been, while most wore no more than the shorts and boots Aidan preferred. If being a warrior gave the men such pride, then she knew a proposal to eliminate war wouldn't be welcome, especially one coming from her, so she kept still.

"I can't stifle my curiosity any longer," Bram revealed

with a charming grin when everyone again quieted down around them. "How did you happen to land here?"

It both pleased and surprised Aidan that she glanced first at him before replying she had become separated from her base ship, but he nodded to encourage her to answer that question, which swiftly led to others. Zac had volunteered to take his shift and post the guards that night, and when he excused himself at dusk to handle that chore, Tory slid into his place beside Eric. She was as openly curious as the others about what Kara's life had been like, but they all had great difficulty imagining how she had spent her whole life on board a spaceship whose endless mission was the mapping of the universe.

"You mean each scout had his own quarters, not just a bunk in a barracks?" Jarl asked next, striving for more specific details.

"Yes, and while not nearly as large as Aidan's home, our apartments are very nice," Kara assured him. "Mother is like the most interesting city, except she travels constantly through space." She paused there, unwilling to describe more of her world when theirs would sound so backward by comparison. "We have homes and families, dear friends, good times together, just as you do here," she explained instead, choosing to stress the likenesses between them rather than the differences.

Eric gave her a skeptical glance. "Why has this marvelous ship never come here?"

"I'm sure you know that answer as well as I do, Eric. Alado declared Mining Colony 329 closed at the time of the revolt, and all interest in what occurs here ceased at that time," Kara reminded him softly, sorry she had had to mention the corporation's policies since she could no longer defend them in good conscience.

"Well, it sure looks like they have forgotten about you as quickly as they forgot about us," Tory remarked sympathetically. "Now that you're married to Aidan, that won't matter though, will it?"

Kara felt the heat of Aidan's gaze even without turning toward him. He was obviously as eager to hear her answer

as the others, but she would not pledge to be a devoted wife
in front of his friends when he knew damn well she would
return to flying her Banshee the first chance she had. She
would also not announce she was positive she would be rescued soon, since that would only alarm his friends unnecessarily. "If everyone is as nice to me as you all are, then I'm
certain I will love it here," she replied graciously, knowing
full well she had failed to answer Tory's question, but the
little blond seemed not to notice and excused herself to wait
on the tavern's other customers.

Aidan winced inwardly, knowing as well as Kara that she
had just evaded a question whose answer was of vital impor-
tance to them both. He would not point that out, however,
since she was showing what he knew to be remarkable restraint in her conversation. She had answered each inquiry
tactfully when several times he had expected her to argue
with his friends as readily as he knew she would have disagreed with him had they been alone. Time and again Jarl
returned to the subject of Mother's mission, but Kara continued to reply sweetly it was simply to make maps, not war,
which was clearly his true question.

Aidan clung to the hope, which had grown stronger with
each passing day, that Mother would never come to 329. Jarl
seemed intent on finding out what they would have to face
when she did. Since he knew Kara's temperament to be quite
a volatile one, he decided they would be wise to leave before
her patience wore as thin as his own and she became upset.
"I'm sure it will take more hours than we have tonight to
satisfy your curiosity, Jarl, and Kara and I have a few other
things we'd much rather do."

Jarl laughed as loudly as the others at that joke, but still
asked one last question. "I'd like to know more about your
ship as I'm sure the other men here would, too. When can
you show us how it flies?"

Since Aidan had promised her one of the benefits of their
marriage would be the freedom to visit her Banshee frequently, Kara did not bother to glance at him before she
replied, "I'll be happy to show you my ship, Jarl, and as

many other people as have an interest in it too, women as well as men."

Bram found that idea so preposterous that he quickly turned to his wife and asked, "Do you know any women who would want to see how it works, May?"

The shy young woman needed only one glance at Kara's encouraging smile before she replied. "Well yes, I certainly would."

"So would I," Eden joined in quickly, her smile as always wide and bright.

Before Bram and Jarl could recover from the shock that their wives would have such an interest, Kara invited them all to meet the following day in the square. "I want to check out the ship thoroughly tomorrow and I'll be happy to have you all join me for as long as you can. Is noon all right, Aidan?"

The warrior slid out of the booth and helped his bride rise. "Of course. I'll wake you if you oversleep," he promised with a wicked grin which made his plans for keeping her busy the rest of the evening quite plain.

As they made their way through the crush of patrons on their way to the door, they were stopped so frequently by Aidan's friends who wished to propose another toast that nearly an hour passed before they at last reached the exit. As they stepped out to the walk, the silence of the dark deserted street was most welcome. Aidan slipped his arm around Kara's waist to draw her near now that he could speak without having to shout over the din of the crowd. "Everyone was obviously thrilled to meet you, but how could you have forgotten Alado forbids you to interfere in our way of life?"

Kara's posture stiffened instantly at what she perceived as unwarranted criticism. In her opinion, she had shown remarkable restraint all day and couldn't understand why he thought otherwise. "Just exactly what do you call interfering?" she asked pointedly.

Aidan sighed deeply, scarcely knowing where to begin. "The majority of the male population here are warriors, Kara. We have only two enemies, the moles and Alado. You have constantly told me Alado wishes us no harm, and now tonight you wanted to know why we couldn't make peace with the moles!"

"You're forgetting your system of justice by challenges," Kara reminded him with an icy stare. "You will still have each other to fight even if you make peace with the entire galaxy."

"I already know you find the challenges abhorrent. Let's see now, you would like us to make peace with the moles, to regard Alado as a corporation interested only in exploration and to completely revise our system of justice so it duplicates the despicable code of laws which exiled our ancestors here. Isn't that what you want? To say nothing of the trouble I can see you will stir up among the women!"

Struggling free of his light embrace, Kara wheeled around to face him. "Is it stirring up trouble merely to invite women to look at my Banshee?" she asked incredulously.

"No, it's not merely that," Aidan admitted regretfully, "but the description of a life where the opportunities open to women are equal to those given men could create problems. We have few enough choices here, Kara, without you interfering and making everyone miserable about those we do enjoy."

Intent on making her point, Kara continued to dance along in front of the perplexed warrior. "Change occurs every time two cultures come into contact. I realize the fact that I'm here reminds everyone of Alado, which they thoroughly despise, but that can scarcely be helped. I did not complain once that my life on board Mother was better than the one you live here. In fact, I've made no complaints at all the entire time I've been your guest, and—"

"My guest! Damn it all, Kara, you are my wife!" Aidan shouted in despair, not understanding how she could possibly have overlooked such an important point.

Kara raised her fingertips to his lips to silence any further protest. "Must we argue about this on the street?" she murmured softly. "We both know you do not expect me to be content merely tending your house and garden and being a companion to you." Before he could reply, she saw a flash of movement as someone darted into the shadows not twenty paces behind them and she lowered her voice to a frantic whisper. "We're being followed, Aidan!"

"What nonsense. This is a public street." But before he could turn to look back over his shoulder, she grabbed his arm to prevent such a hasty move.

"No, don't look! Let's just keep on walking. Say whatever you like, and I'll pretend to argue with you so he'll think we're too preoccupied to notice him."

"When have you ever had to 'pretend' to argue with me?" the warrior replied in a hostile snarl.

"Perfect!" Kara whispered, not realizing his question was a serious one. She moved slightly ahead of him, then turned back to respond so she could glance over his shoulder. This time she caught sight of not only one man, but two. "You know I can't cook. How do you expect me to prepare your meals?" she asked loudly for the pursuers' benefit. "I've never had to keep house either. Am I to have no servants?"

"Servants?" Aidan cried out incredulously. "What do you plan to do with your time, woman?"

"Amuse you, my darling, nothing more!" Kara confided playfully. She then moved close to whisper, "There are two of them, large men. Could they be moles?"

Knowing as a pilot Kara would be a skilled observer, Aidan realized he should take her word that they were being followed. He quickly used his left hand to hurry her along. "We're almost home. When it's within sight, run to the door and I'll take care of the men following us whether they're moles or not."

"You might be able to fight one man with a broken hand, but never two!" Kara insisted in a hushed plea. "I'll help you," she volunteered eagerly.

"You'll do as I say," Aidan ordered harshly, but Kara refused and shook her head emphatically. Rather than argue with his willful bride as they continued on, he pulled her around the next corner and pushed her into a dark doorway. Their sudden disappearance so surprised the men in pursuit that they hurriedly gave chase and came barreling around the corner at a dead run. The swifter of the two tripped over the toe of Aidan's boot and flipped high into the air. Despite a frantic attempt to catch himself, he came down on the stone walk head first, landing with a sickening thud. Having no time to slow his fierce pace, the second man then fell over his unconscious friend and went sprawling across the sandy stones, scraping away several layers of skin from his face and hands. When he began to shriek in pain, the tall warrior used his left hand to grab him by the scruff of the neck and hauled him to his feet. Recognizing him instantly, Aidan made a great show of solicitous concern.

"What a terrible accident! It's a good thing my wife and I happened along just now, Duke, or you and your friend might have lain here unattended for hours." Giving the unconscious man a savage kick to roll him over into the light, he recognized him as well. "Are you hurt, Mark? Your brother-in-law doesn't look good, Duke. I think you better get him home as fast as you can."

Aidan's bantering tone outraged Duke. He had meant to jump him from behind, hurt him badly and then flee without being recognized or caught. He realized too late that he would need several more men to get the better of Aidan and squirmed sheepishly under the powerfully built warrior's confining grasp. "I just want you to stay away from Brina!" he finally confessed in an anguished look. "Just stay away from my wife!"

Aidan released the disheveled fool with a disgusted shove. "Brina is a charming woman who deserves far better than the likes of you for a husband. Now take Mark and go home before I stop taking pity on you and give you both the beating you deserve."

Mark moaned pitifully as Duke helped him to his feet, but after a moment's pause to assess his injuries, he was able to stagger off with his help. Aidan stood with his hands on his hips as he watched them depart, waiting until he was certain he would have no more trouble with either of them before he turned to look at his bride. "Have I finally proven to you that I can take care of us both even if I have only one good hand to use?"

Kara brushed off her hands and stepped out into the light thrown by the lamp at the corner. "Do jealous husbands often follow you home?" she asked caustically, without first bothering to reply to his question.

"This is our wedding night, my love, let's not argue about someone else's problems."

"Our wedding night? Oh yes, so it is. How could I have forgotten?" She took hold of the skirt of her long gown to raise it slightly to accommodate the length of her stride and whipped around the corner to return to his street without him. "Wedding night!" she mumbled to herself. Apparently the man planned to play his part to the hilt, but she had no desire to continue their ridiculous charade a minute longer.

Aidan considered the fact that Kara had at least turned in the direction of his home such a good sign he did not race to catch up with her. When he found her patiently waiting for him at his door, he quickly reached out to turn the doorknob and ushered her inside. "We have a horrible aversion to locks here. I seldom remember to lock my door when I'm at home and I never bother to do it when I go out since carrying keys is such a nuisance."

"Yes, it is that," Kara agreed absently, knowing without having to ask that he would hunt down and punish anyone foolish enough to burglarize his home. Now that their privacy was assured she had no idea how to act, but not wanting to continue their argument when she had such a fragile grasp on her temper, she strode past Aidan into his bedroom. After hastily peeling off her clothes she entered the tub and prayed the melodic bubbling of the warm water would somehow ease her mind enough to allow her to think clearly. At last when Aidan came to join her, she asked him the question that weighed most heavily on her mind. "Our marriage will not be considered valid if we do not consummate it, will it?"

While unfamiliar with that term, Aidan nevertheless had a good idea what it meant. "You mean if we fail to make love?"

"Precisely."

Aidan chuckled slyly, thinking she must be teasing him in some strange way. "That would be a case of your word against mine since you're not a virgin, and I think you already know whose word would be accepted as the truth. Besides, why wouldn't we want to make love?" he asked in an enticing whisper.

"You said there was no divorce here, and I'd like to avoid making things difficult for you when I leave," Kara announced with the determined tilt to her chin he had learned to respect. The fact that she had not foreseen there would be no way to prove she had not slept with him maddened her thoroughly, but she hid that embarrassment well.

Her expression was now so completely devoid of humor that the courageous warrior readily sensed her serious mood. Rather than fly into a black rage, however, he forced himself to remain as calm as she was pretending to be. "What is it you're really mad about, the fact that I didn't need your help to beat up two men or the way I made you my wife?"

"I'm not mad about anything," Kara contradicted firmly. "But you and I both know I'll never fit in here, so why should we make ourselves miserable trying to pretend otherwise? It seems I can't open my mouth without disputing one of your traditions, but despite what you believe I've no desire to lead the women of 329 in a revolt against the men."

"No, of course not," Aidan agreed sarcastically, his temper beginning to flare. "All you want to do is go home to Mother, isn't that it?"

Kara found the churning patterns of the water that swirled around her shoulders far easier to view than his taunting smile. "That's all I've ever wanted," she replied softly, not daring to look him in the eye.

Regretting his taunt since it had done nothing to aid his cause, Aidan moved to her side then and raised his left hand to caress her cheek lightly. "This is no way to spend our wedding night, my love. I promised you your freedom. When Mother arrives, you may kiss me good-bye without the slightest trace of guilt, but since there's no sign of her tonight, I think we should simply lose ourselves in each other."

Kara raised a well-shaped brow quizzically. "Everything has its price, Aidan, and tonight will too. Will it be worth it to you?"

Aidan leaned close and answered that question with a deep, searching kiss, holding his breath until at long last Kara began to return his affection. As she moved to embrace him, he remained still, using only the light pressure of his lips and tongue to convince her no price would be too high to pay for a night of shared love. He was in no hurry. Endlessly patient, he continued to kiss her as though making love involved no more than that one sweet gesture that he would never tire of.

While she could have rejected Aidan's anger quite forcefully, his tenderness was impossible to refuse and Kara relaxed against him, for a long while dreamily wondering which of them tasted of strawberries before remembering it had to be the flavor of the wine she had sipped lazily all afternoon.

Although she could foresee a future fraught with problems, Kara forced her worries aside, preferring instead to be blissfully aware only of the beauty of the moment. While she enjoyed Aidan's loving kisses, she made no move to encourage him to give still more. Finally he wound his fingers in her curls to press her cheek against his shoulder as his lips moved to her eyelid and then down to tickle her ear.

"I've never loved another woman, Kara. Isn't that enough for you?" he asked in a voice husky with desire.

When she had nothing as sweet to pledge in return, Kara would make no demands upon this handsome man. She hugged him tightly as she whispered in his ear, "I love you, too, and tonight nothing else matters to me." Her breath caught in her throat then as he lifted her tenderly into his arms, pulling her hips slowly to his so that the fusion of their bodies would be as gentle and loving as their mood. One moment they were two lovers longing to share the same mind and soul, and in the next instant their hearts were beating in such perfect unison that their very spirits had become entwined. Kara thought Aidan was a joy to love, for he was not only handsome and strong, but also good and infinitely kind. That he was as lost in her charms as she was in his did not even occur to her until later when he carried her to his bed where their loving play continued with no threat of either of them drowning in warm soapy water rather than bliss.

Aidan let his fingertips trace a meandering path across Kara's delicately flowered breasts before sliding his hand down over her ribs to tease the firm flesh of her stomach. "Each time someone wished us many children you winced. None of my friends noticed, but I know you too well to miss such an obvious sign of distress. Since your mother had you without interrupting her career I know that's not what's bothering you, but does the thought that your children will also be mine disgust you?"

Not wanting him to misunderstand her answer, Kara first gave Aidan a reassuring kiss followed by a loving hug before she replied. "I had never planned to marry, Aidan, you know that, so the question of children is one I haven't considered."

"Don't you think you better start thinking about it?" Aidan teased softly. "Isn't there a good chance you're already pregnant with my child, or soon will be?"

Kara gave her head a reluctant shake. "No, Aidan, there's no chance at all."

"But why not?" The warrior sat up then, too intent on hearing her answer to recline by her side.

"What do the couples here do who do not wish to have children? You must have some means of birth control."

Drawing his well-defined features into a perplexed frown, Aidan replied tersely, "The women use intrauterine devices made of soft gold, but if you have such a device it can be removed."

Kara had never lied to him, not once. There may have been things she had taken great care not to describe like the aggressiveness of Álado's military division which actively suppressed all opposition to the corporation's policies, but she had never told him an out-and-out lie. She knew to return to Mother and still be his wife would be extremely difficult. It would be completely impossible to attempt such a feat were she also to be the mother of his children.

Thinking she could merely bend the truth slightly, she took a deep breath and explained quickly, "What I have is an implant which supplies a hormone to suppress ovulation. It can not be removed as easily as an IUD, and I doubt you have a surgeon here fine enough to guarantee he could remove it without gravely threatening my life." The truth was she did have an implant, but its removal was so simple she could easily do it herself. She was counting on the fact that 329 would have neither the physicians nor the facilities to prove her story a lie.

The heartbreaking news that the woman he had chosen as his wife could give him no children stunned Aidan so badly that his first impulse was to leave their bed and flee the house. The fact that he had nowhere to go to escape the pain she had just caused him was all that kept him seated by her side. Hoping for some way to change that unfortunate circumstance, he pressed her for more information. "How long do the implants last? Forever, or merely a few months or years?"

Since she was confident that she would be gone before she needed another implant, Kara told him the truth. "They are effective for a full year."

"One year? Is that all?" Overwhelmed with relief, Aidan's expression lit up with joy. "Well, how long have you had this one?"

His delight at the prospect of fathering a child she had no intention of conceiving created an even heavier burden of guilt in Kara. "Two months," she responded softly, knowing there was a world of difference between being capable of bearing his child and actually doing so.

Aidan raked his fingers through his flowing curls. "Then you could easily be pregnant by this time next year. God, how I wish you had told me that to begin with. You really scared me."

While he was ecstatic at the prospect of becoming a parent, she was now thoroughly depressed. She reached out to touch his arm, and he lay down beside her and pulled her into an enthusiastic embrace which only increased her torment. "Your cousin, Barret, told me all of life is a gamble. There's no way I can promise you a child, Aidan. It is only a dream of yours, and not all dreams come true."

Aidan leaned back slightly so he could study her expression more closely. "Is it only a dream of mine?" he asked incredulously. "You have no desire to have a child?"

Kara sifted through a dozen possible responses before she finally found one she thought would not insult him. "Not yet," she whispered tactfully. "Just not yet."

Her golden gaze held a sorrow so deep it told him far more than she wished to reveal, but Aidan kept that secret to himself. He understood it would take awhile before she came to accept what he considered an obvious fact: Mother was gone and she would never be able to leave 329. She was young; he could wait a year or two for a child. "I love you, Kara," he promised hoarsely, "and I will always love you whether or not you give me a child."

When she returned his sweet kiss with a far more passionate one, his response was immediate. He would spend no more time pondering the possibilities for their future when the night was still so new. He longed instead to caress every inch of her delectable body with searing kisses until she begged him to end her torment of desire. He was delighted, however, to discover she shared that very same goal. Her purpose plain in her bold caresses, he let her slip from his arms and lay back to enjoy her lavish affection. She was no innocent bride, but a temptress of extraordinary skill who moved over him with the slow, rhythmic ease of a serpent, and he vowed he would have a lifetime to savor her incredible array of erotic talents. Her enticing touch was cool, yet led him swiftly to the brink of rapture. Her kisses were afire with passion's heat, and with a low moan of surrender he was readily consumed by those wondrous flames.

Unwilling to rest until he had returned her generous loving and sent her senses reeling under the magic of his own exotic kiss and touch, a long while passed before Aidan was content to hold Kara cradled quietly in his arms. Sated with pleasure, he whispered a teasing promise in her ear. "Call me husband just once, and I'll let you go to sleep."

Kara snuggled against him, lazily enjoying the hard planes of his muscular body nestled against her supple curves. "What makes you think I'm ready to go to sleep?" she asked through a partially stifled yawn.

Aidan nuzzled her throat playfully. "You're so totally relaxed you couldn't get out of this bed if the sheets burst into flame. Now say it so we can both go to sleep."

"Would it please you so much?"

"Very much, my dear wife."

She had never found any word more difficult to say but, wanting to give him pleasure in every way she possibly could, Kara hesitantly complied with his request. "I love you, husband." She felt him relax then, and in a matter of seconds he was sound asleep. Kara lay awake for hours wondering how she would face the dawn when her life had changed so radically from the one she had always expected to live.

CHAPTER
◊ **XIV** ◊

When he awakened the next morning, Aidan found Kara already up and dressed in her shimmering flight suit. She was standing in his kitchen preparing tea. He strolled up behind her and wrapped his arms around her tiny waist to enfold her in a warm embrace. His lips tickled the nape of her neck as he began to tease her. "Were you still in my bed, I'd have a far more loving way to greet the day, but this will have to do."

Kara relaxed against him, too excited by the prospect of working with Sonia to regret she had gotten up first. "I thought you might sleep the whole day away and I've too many things to do to keep you company."

Aidan stepped back and turned her around to face him as he issued a word of caution. "I know you're anxious to visit your ship. Everyone is curious about it so you'll have plenty of questions to answer, but I would still like you to save some time to teach me how to fly it as you promised you would."

While his gaze was warm, Kara was hurt that he felt he had to remind her of her promise. "I know I am unused to having a husband, Aidan, but I will not shove you aside while I entertain your friends. You have barely begun to learn how to read, but we can use Sonia's keyboard now and you'll learn ever so much faster. What you already know is enough to begin learning how to fly though."

Aidan leaned forward slightly and rested his forehead against hers for a moment while he considered how best to handle his lessons. He then gave her a lingering kiss before making his request. "Please don't tell anyone about what you have taught me, or volunteer to teach anyone else."

Puzzled, Kara opened her mouth to argue, but he silenced that protest before she could make it with another lengthy kiss. "Aidan," she purred contentedly when he at last drew away, "how do you expect me to carry on my half of this conversation if you keep kissing me?"

The amorous warrior's only response was to kiss her deeply once again; he had never found any woman's taste as delicious as hers. "Tomorrow morning maybe you'll be smart enough to stay in bed. Then once we're up we'll be able to talk without any interruptions. Now promise me, not a word about our lessons to anyone."

Still perplexed by his request, Kara slipped her arms around his waist to pull him close and lay her cheek against his bare shoulder. "I am going to be safe here now, aren't I?"

"Yes, I promised you once you became my wife no one would harm you in any way. I'd rather not start people wondering about how much more you know than they do since it's only one step from that to worrying about Alado's power the way Jarl did last night."

"I understand," Kara agreed thoughtfully. "I'll give your friends a brief tour then say I need your help to do some routine maintenance. If we close the hatch, they'll just think we're making love, won't they?"

"Probably, but we can't use that excuse every day," he replied with a mischievous grin. "I think we better start making our visits late at night. That way no one will be walking about to notice what we're doing and become suspicious."

Seeking an alternative to that plan, Kara looked up at the opening in the roof and began to wonder if it would accommodate a ship of the Banshee's dimensions. If it would, that would solve several of their problems. "Could we bring my ship back here? I think we could lower it through the roof, and you've plenty of space in which to store it here."

That suggestion struck Aidan as being so bizarre that for a long moment he could do little but stare, first at Kara and then up at the ample opening above the garden. "You're not serious? Bring it here and lower it through the roof?" he asked in astonishment.

"Well, why not? Then we would not have to go creeping through the streets after midnight just to avoid drawing attention to the fact that I'm giving you reading and flying lessons. We could use Sonia as often and as long as we want and not worry about causing comment. That would be a big help to us both. There's plenty of light coming in so the solar panels can maintain the instruments at peak performance. I think it's just a question of whether or not the Banshee will fit through the opening."

Aidan walked over to his garden where he could better judge the long rectangular space through which they would have to lower the lightweight craft. He thought such a feat might be possible, but he wasn't altogether certain. "We'll have to measure the ship today to be positive it will fit, but I think we should wait until there's another storm and use that as an excuse to move it."

"You mean it's all right with you? You won't mind if I bring the Banshee here?" Kara could scarcely believe her ears, for she had not expected him to agree with her request without several hours—if not days—of intense argument.

"So what if it will take up half the front room? If you want the ship here, then I'll be happy to help you move it." When she ran over to give him an enthusiastic hug and cover his face with a flurry of tender kisses, Aidan was certain he had made the right choice. She was a wonderfully affectionate woman, and he decided right then that if there was any way he could possibly grant her requests, he would do it since she was so eager to show her appreciation.

"I understand though," Kara agreed as she gave him another loving squeeze. "We'll have to wait until it looks like foul weather might damage it before we bring it home. Now let's have some breakfast; it must be nearly noon, and I don't want to keep your friends waiting."

Aidan reached out to catch her hand as she turned away. "You did like them, didn't you? I mean, they did not seem silly or stupid to you?"

Kara hoped Aidan did not need her approval for himself, but rather for his choice of friends. "I thought your friends were very nice. It is remarkable that your people have managed not only to survive here, but also to build such an orderly society and prosper. I doubt any of you are stupid— except for Duke, of course. He doesn't strike me as being too bright," she added with a teasing smile.

"No, Duke doesn't have much in the way of brains, but I think he learned his lesson last night." Recalling the incident, he turned his right hand over to look at the bandage and decided it needed to be replaced. "Will you help me again with this after breakfast?"

Kara shuddered apprehensively. "Only if you promise to tell me exactly what it is you're going to do before you do it."

"I did that the last time!" he exclaimed. "Why should you complain anyway, since I'm the one who felt the pain?"

Several seconds passed before Kara spoke. "It's difficult to explain why, but I felt your pain, too," she admitted shyly.

Aidan pressed her to admit the obvious. "That's because you love me so much, isn't it?"

She had thought him handsome the first time she saw him; now that she knew him better, he was even more attractive.

He was wearing no more than his favorite pair of shorts, but she was used to his minimal attire now and did not think it immodest in the warm climate. He had saved her life more than once and wanted so badly for her to be his wife, but did she truly love him? She needed no more than a split second to reply. "Yes, I do love you even if you are dreadfully conceited, but I suppose that fault's impossible to avoid when a man is as handsome as you."

Aidan broke into a wide grin and gave her a playful swat on the fanny as he preceded her into the kitchen alcove. "And you're not the least bit conceited yourself?"

"Why no, not at all," Kara assured him sincerely. "Do you think I am?"

"Certainly not, I've seldom met a more modest woman," Aidan teased as he took the bowl of eggs from the refrigerator. He noticed that she had put on his dragon charm with her uniform, and while it pleased him very much, it also made him curious. "Are scouts permitted to wear jewelry like that necklace with their uniforms?"

"No, we're not, but because I have already broken so many of Alado's rules since I arrived here, I'm certain one more will not matter." Kara tried to stay out of his way as he got out the ingredients he would need to prepare an omelet for their breakfast. She watched closely, meaning to learn how to cook from his example without having to ask him for lessons. It was a useful skill, even if she had never had reason to practice it. Of course, she had never been a man's wife before, either. "Aidan?" she called sweetly.

"Yes, love?"

"I just this minute realized you have never told me your last name. If the women take their husband's names here, won't you expect me to use yours?" Kara thought her question a most natural one and was totally unprepared for the dark fury of Aidan's glance as he turned to reply.

"We don't use surnames here, Kara, for the obvious reason they would bring nothing but disgrace to our families. I have only one name, and you'll simply be known as my wife. I know you're bound to be curious about just who my great-grandfather was, but that's a secret I intend to keep."

Taken aback by such an unexpectedly defiant response, Kara needed a moment to formulate a coherent reply. "I'm sorry, Aidan, but I had simply forgotten how your people came to be here. Since I am your wife, I fail to see why you would be ashamed to tell me your name. I would certainly never blame you for your great-grandfather's crimes, nor would any other reasonable person."

"I will not give you his name, Kara. Don't bother asking me for it again because I won't change my mind," Aidan vowed with a determination he hoped would convince her; he had meant exactly what he said.

Kara licked her lips thoughtfully, wondering if the man would ever come to trust her completely. Then, recalling that she had not been all that truthful about having his child, she knew she would be wise not to bring up the matter of trust. "The list of prisoners' names is recorded in Mother's history files. I've read them, although I recall just a few. Certainly all of you living here must know whose descendants you are. Why should I be the only one who doesn't know my own husband's family name?"

Aidan wiped off his hands and approached her cautiously. "We do not use family names here. I've explained why. Now just let the matter drop."

Kara, however, didn't feel like giving in. "Zac is Joaquin Zacatón's great-grandson, isn't he?"

Aidan's eyes grew wide with alarm. "How could you possibly know that?" he gasped hoarsely.

"Oh come now, it's a simple matter to figure out, although I would never mention it to him. Zac isn't a common name, and he's dark, with the dashing good looks most Hispanics have. Alado was formed by the countries of North and South America, so we have plenty of men who share his heritage. I told you my father was dark. His name was León which is the Spanish word for lion. On board Mother, I am addressed as Lieutenant León, not Kara. Even if you'll not give me your name, I'll be happy to lend you mine. You may call yourself Aidan León if you like."

"You want me to take your name?" Aidan asked incredulously.

"Why not?" Kara replied with a shrug. "For a man to take his wife's name wasn't uncommon even in ancient times since not every family produced sons." She leaned back against the counter and folded her arms across her chest as she studied the rapid interplay of emotions that crossed his finely chiseled features. How she had gone from stubbornly resisting the prospect of becoming his wife to inviting him to use her name she didn't know, but she had no qualms about making such a generous offer now.

"Thank you," Aidan finally responded with a confused frown. "If ever I have need of a last name, I'll try and re-member to use yours." He turned away then to continue the preparations for breakfast, not certain why he felt he had just lost an important argument even though he had not revealed his great-grandfather's name. Kara had an amazing way of getting the better of him and she did it with such ease he had no idea how she managed the feat. "You'll have to help me," he admitted sheepishly. "I can't beat the damn eggs with my left hand."

Kara stepped to his side and took the fork and bowl. "I'll always be happy to help you, Aidan, all you need do is ask," she reminded him with a seductive smile which brought a ready grin to his lips. He knew as well as she that he spent most of his time refusing her help rather than requesting it.

When they reached the square, Kara and Aidan found Eric waiting with Jarl and Bram, but there was no sign of the two men's wives. Certain they had been left at home on purpose, the scout was deeply hurt by their absence. "I'm so sorry May and Eden aren't with you," she lamented softly. "I've had little opportunity to meet other women here and I had hoped we would become good friends."

Dressed in a long gown and seated in a booth beside Aidan in their favorite tavern, Kara had not appeared nearly as foreign to the young men as she did now. Today her im-pressive height and willowy figure were accented by her sleek, rainbow-hued suit which clearly identified her bold profession and declared instantly she was no docile house-wife. Her golden eyes held them fast with a disconcertingly perceptive stare and neither knew quite how to behave. The previous afternoon she had been Aidan's bride, and now she was clearly recognizable for what she truly was: one of Alado's finest scouts. Bram swallowed nervously before looking to Jarl for help. "There was something May forgot she had to do," he apologized nervously.

Grateful for any excuse, Jarl used the same one. "Yes, Eden will have to see you another time. Unfortunately, she was quite busy too."

"Will you please tell them how sorry I am to have missed seeing them today?" Kara replied, tactfully stifling the impulse to tell the two men what she thought of their transparent lies.

"Yes, of course," both men readily agreed.

"I told Zac to meet us," Eric interjected with a friendly smile, apparently unaware of how insulted Kara had been by the women's absence. "He should be here soon."

"Well since he's not here yet, let's just begin without him. I've already seen the ship on numerous occasions, so why don't you three go inside with Kara? She has a few minutes to spare to answer questions, then I'm going to help her check out all the instruments and that will take us the rest of the day."

Kara smiled at her husband, grateful he had stated she had little time to devote to giving lectures on the Banshee's capabilities. She gestured for the men to precede her, gave them a few minutes to look around by themselves and then provided a brief description of the task for which the ship was designed.

"My job is simply to fly the ship to the locale to be photographed and then monitor the robot cameras' performance to be certain the shots will provide the necessary detail for precise maps. My computer, Sonia, does all the navigational computation so I don't get lost. Would you like to hear her speak?" she offered graciously.

The three young men studied the broad array of twinkling lights, attempting to locate this fascinating talking machine, but none was certain exactly where she might be. Leaning over the keyboard at the navigational console, Kara typed in a greeting, then pressed the key to elicit a vocal response.

"Good afternoon, Kara," Sonia replied in her usual soft, soothing tone.

The men were so amazed they begged to hear more, and Kara asked Sonia for several other responses before she ushered them to the hatch. "I really do need to be certain all my instruments are working properly. I'll be happy to show you more on your next visit. Perhaps May and Eden will be able to join us then."

"Wait just a minute," Jarl said as he hesitated at the steps. "How do you fire the lasers?"

"My ship isn't armed, Jarl." Kara could see he didn't really believe her. "I've flown it for more than four years and I've never had a reason to use weapons. I certainly hope I'll have no need for them here." While she could see by his troubled expression that he still wasn't convinced, he left with his friend and she found Zac waiting outside with Aidan. "Do you want to come on board, Zac? I'll be happy to show you what I showed the others."

The dark-haired man readily accepted her invitation and was as fascinated as his friends by the advanced technology she described so easily. He listened carefully, then asked if he might sit down in the pilot's seat. When he had made himself comfortable, Kara knelt by his side to show him how to use the controls which folded down out of the way when the ship was not being flown. "Now I'd like you to tell me something, Zac," she explained in a conspiratorial whisper.

"What could I possibly tell you?" he asked with an embarrassed laugh.

"Yesterday when I mentioned making peace with the moles, you wanted to say something but didn't. Will you tell me what it was? I would really like to hear your opinion because I think it might be similar to mine."

Zac shook his head, reluctant to discuss his views with her, but her smile was so sympathetic and inviting that to his amazement he found he truly wanted to confide in her. "I have no lofty goals like creating a lasting peace," he admitted readily. "Over the years I've become friends with a mole who makes beautiful jewelry. His granddaughter is a lovely child. I have watched her grow up and, well, quite frankly, the thought of her becoming a mole's bride is more than I can bear."

"Is her name Serafina by any chance?" Kara inquired in an encouraging tone.

"You've met her?" Zac's blush was plain even under his deep tan.

Kara reached out to touch his hand lightly, not thinking her caress would affect him as deeply as it did Aidan until she saw the startled look in his eyes. She gave him only a sympathetic pat then and withdrew her hand. "I meant only to restore your calm, not seduce you," she assured him truthfully. "I met Serafina only briefly, but she seemed very sweet. If you like her so much, isn't there some way you can make her your bride?"

"Oh, no!" Zac exclaimed immediately. "We never marry moles."

"Why not, if she is as pretty as Serafina and you love her?"

"I did not say that I loved her," Zac pointed out quickly, obviously disgusted with himself for admitting so much.

"Your secret is safe with me, Zac, but I've seen Aidan fight two moles, and they certainly weren't invincible. If you want Serafina for your own, can't you challenge the moles for her?"

Zac gripped the padded arms of the pilot's seat tightly, his expression growing dark as he tried to make her understand the futility of such a hope. "I am not Aidan, Kara. He has more courage than a dozen of the rest of us. I know that if he had fallen in love with Serafina he would find a way to take her out of the caves, but I have neither his boldness nor his strength."

Perhaps it was simply his dark coloring that reminded her so much of her father, but Kara found Zac's predicament very touching. Rising to her feet, she gave his shoulder a quick squeeze. "There's got to be a way to arrange this, Zac.

I know for a fact Serafina isn't happy with her life. If you would talk with her—"

"No!" Zac rose quickly and hurried toward the hatch. "I've said too much. Please forget it."

He had not struck her as being a coward, but she did not try to detain him. She followed him to the hatch, where she found Aidan engaged in an animated conversation with his cousin, Barret. Not caring to speak with the banker again, she remained inside the Banshee and began to run the checks she had planned to do. She sat on the edge of her seat and typed the simple command she had taught Aidan to send the search beacons sweeping the skies for Mother, but there was still no response. Horribly discouraged, she sank back in the comfortable seat and closed her eyes. She was on the verge of sleep when Aidan entered and secured the hatch. "All set?" she inquired sleepily. "There really are tests I need to run and—"

Aidan flashed a predatory grin as he reached for the top button on his shorts. "You invited me in here to make love and that's exactly what we're going to do."

Certain he could not possibly be serious, Kara asked quickly about his cousin. "What about Barret? Didn't he want the tour, too?"

"No, he told me to give you his apology for what he said yesterday. He wouldn't admit what it was but said he has worried about it ever since. He can be rather tactless at times, but he didn't mean to insult you."

"That's a damn lie," Kara countered immediately. "He's no fool. He knew exactly what he was saying, and I doubt he has enough of a conscience to feel sorry about it now, either."

Aidan was shocked by the fervent hostility of her response to what he had considered an adequately conveyed apology. "I should have insisted he speak with you himself. He just stopped by to tell me that while few people bet on Kyle, those who did bet enormous sums, so my cut of his profit is a generous one."

"What? You mean when people bet on the challenges the winner receives a share?" That gambling was allowed was bad enough; that the winner was paid a portion of those ill-gotten gains thoroughly disgusted her.

"Not only the winner but the loser, too, except in this case because he won't give a cut to a mole. Now, I said we were going to make love, so I've no interest in arguing." He wore so little he needed no more than a few seconds to disrobe; then he knelt in front of her and leaned down to nibble the inside of her thighs with playful bites. "Take off your suit or I'll rip it off you," he ordered in a teasing snarl.

Kara put her hands on his shoulders to push him back slightly. "Aidan, you can't be serious. This Banshee is far too light for someone as athletic as you to make love in!"

"Nonsense," Aidan disagreed with a devilish chuckle. "It is perfectly balanced on its landing gear, and I'm not too wild. We won't move the ship at all. I promise the only thing trembling will be your heart."

Kara doubted that, but he was clearly determined to make love to her with or without her consent, and that was such a charming prospect she had no desire to refuse him. She swiftly began to peel off the suit. "You'll have to stand up so I can get out of my clothes," she insisted between giggles.

Aidan refused to budge from his pose between her knees. "No, you're a clever woman and I'll help you, but I'm not moving." While clearly she wasn't pleased by that challenge, after a moment's hesitation the redhead continued to wiggle out of her garments. "How do you usually make love in here?" he asked with a mocking grin, obviously very curious about it.

Kara couldn't help but laugh at that question. "I have never made love in here!" she insisted between convulsive bursts of laughter. "We fly alone and the ships are stored on end in Mother so it would be impossible to manage there."

"That makes this all the more exciting then, doesn't it?" Aidan remarked with a wicked grin as he held the end of her sleeves so she could pull her arms free. As soon as she had slipped the straps of her teddy off her shoulders, he leaned forward to free her breasts from the satiny smooth fabric and caressed the pale pink tips with tender kisses until they became firm peaks. He knew it was only the stunning beauty of her tattoo, but he would have sworn he could smell the blossoms' delicate fragrance as she wrapped her arms around his neck to draw him close. "Wait," he pleaded hoarsely, "I want all your clothes off first."

Being an agile young woman of considerable grace, Kara managed to completely disrobe with a minimum of awkward tugs, but she did it very slowly, with deliberate care in order to pay him back for making her remove her clothing in such a restricted position. When finally he tossed her flimsy garments over his shoulder to get them out of his way, his clear blue eyes were dark with smoldering desire. Their loving play had swiftly been overwhelmed by passion and she leaned forward to give him a lingering kiss rich in the incomparably sweet flavor of total surrender.

Aidan's hands moved over her with a possessive caress as his mouth left hers to follow slowly the path of the Love Vine as it curved down over her left shoulder before bursting into bloom. Now he could not even imagine savoring the fullness of her breasts without also enjoying the bewitching sight of their lush decoration. When at last he had had his fill of their enticing softness, he sat back for a moment and envied his dragon charm its place suspended above her heart. He held the gold creature in his hand briefly and then, preferring to continue their loving game, brushed it aside as he sent his tongue curling into her dimpled navel. She recoiled slightly as he continued to tickle her with playful kisses, but he knew she would never ask him to stop.

Her body was the most perfect one he had ever seen, smooth, sleek and yet graced with the most voluptuous womanly curves. He ran his hands up her slender thighs with an adoring touch before at last moving on to explore the triangle of bright red curls nestled between them. With a firm hold on her hips he drew her near, and she wrapped her legs around him, eagerly welcoming the caress of his lips and tongue until the pleasure he gave was so close to pain she begged him to stop in a tearful gasp. He moved swiftly to trade places with her and, once seated in the comfortably padded pilot's chair, he lowered her slowly on himself until the throbbing shaft of his manhood was buried deep within her hot, moist center. She placed her hands on his broad shoulders as she leaned forward and her tongue met his in a passion-drenched kiss that left them both breathless and yet still hungering for more. Without lifting her mouth from his she began to move with a subtle rhythm. The lightweight ship felt not the slightest motion while their hearts pounded with a furious tempo that rocked them to the very marrow.

Each time Kara felt Aidan about to lose control she remained motionless until the tidal wave of pleasure she had created within him subsided. Such respites were brief before she again began to tease him with rippling contractions which would have driven a weaker man mad. Finally even Aidan could take no more of her loving assault and forced her to be still while he brought her sensual torment to its natural end. The fiery heat of his release erupted within her and spread through them both as a delectable warmth that reached clear to their fingertips and toes. Kara relaxed in his arms, totally content, and whispered softly, "There's nothing I can teach you about flying, Aidan. You already know how to touch the clouds without ever leaving the ground."

"Why, thank you." Aidan would have liked nothing better than to stay here and hold her forever, but as his senses slowly recovered from the thrill of being with her, he realized they would have to be far more discreet. He ruffled her glossy curls as he regretfully put an end to their romantic interlude. "I think I've outsmarted only myself this time, because while I want to spend the rest of the day making love to you, I think we better run your tests and get out of here."

Kara gave him one more lavish kiss before she replied, "Are you never satisfied? First you wanted to make love here and now you don't?"

"I'd be happy to make love to you in the middle of the square, but I didn't realize we would get so carried away this afternoon. We're bound to make everyone suspicious if we don't reappear soon."

Kara eased off his lap, gathered up her clothes and moved behind him to dress. "When we're ready I'll open the hatch and you go outside. Measure the ship, pretend to check the landing gear, do anything that makes it look as if you're in the middle of some routine task. Then come back inside, we'll leave the hatch open, and I'll help you with some new words."

Aidan pulled on his shorts and boots, then combed his hair with his fingers. "I can't stop smiling, Kara. Everyone's going to know exactly what we've been doing in here no matter what I do outside."

Kara opened the hatch as she whispered, "So what? You're with your own wife this time. No one can complain about that."

Aidan started down the steps, then turned back to face her. "I didn't answer your question last night, but we will not be accosted by jealous husbands each time we leave the house. Please don't worry that I'll give anyone reason to be jealous, least of all you."

Kara had only been teasing him, but she could see he was completely serious and did not point her jest out. "Thank you," she replied instead. While he made himself busy outside, she sat down to work. Instead her mind kept wandering to how much more enjoyable it was to make love to him.

"You've really done it this time, Kara," she chided herself regretfully. She had loved other men, she had told him that, but never had the emotional bond between her and her lover been as strong as it was fast becoming with Aidan. His life had been very different from hers, but that only added to the excitement of their love rather than diminished it. As her fingertips moved over Sonia's keys, she remembered the vibrant warmth of his deeply bronzed skin and felt his disappointment that they couldn't continue to make love for hours. How she would ever be able to fly when memories of his affection distracted her so terribly she didn't know. She loved flying, but she loved him desperately, too, and dreaded the day when the inevitable choice between them would have to be made. Her eyes filled with tears she hastened to wipe away, not wanting to give in to sorrow while they were still together.

After Aidan had spoken with a sufficient number of people to be certain no one had noticed how long he had been inside, he dismissed the guards. Now that everyone knew the ship belonged to his wife, no one would dare to touch it. They would visit it frequently to keep their ownership in everyone's mind until it could be safely moved to his home. When he leaned in the hatch, he found Kara gazing at Sonia's screen with such an absent stare he knew her mind couldn't possibly be on work. He entered the compact craft and stepped behind her to look over her shoulder. "Is that how you spell 'love'?" he asked with considerable pride.

"Yes." Kara was delighted that he could read the message she had repeated over and over again.

"Just what sort of test are you running that requires you to inform your ship that you love me?" Aidan inquired slyly.

"A very important one, but I'm finished. Now what would you like to learn today?" Kara pressed the key to erase the screen and turned to look up at him, her golden gaze still alight with both unshed tears and love.

"I'm not going to be able to concentrate on anything but you this afternoon. Let's just go home, get in the tub and—"

Kara shut down Sonia and rose to her feet before he could finish his enticing invitation. "You're right. We've both been working much too hard. Let's go home."

Aidan thought of a hundred teasing replies but kept them all to himself rather than risk insulting her unintentionally. He was so delighted to find on at least one occasion she had preferred his company to working in her Banshee that he vowed to arrange many more such erotic diversions and provided her with a most attentive escort for the walk home.

CHAPTER
◇ **XV** ◇

Although she had never heard of another scout being stranded for an entire month without any contact from a base ship, after four weeks on 329 Kara's hopes for returning to Mother remained undimmed. Despite strong afternoon breezes, the weather remained clear, so Kara accepted Aidan's suggestion and went with him after midnight to work with Sonia. They had fallen into a comfortable if somewhat unusual routine since he had resumed his duties as Captain of the Guard. They slept late each morning, awakened to make love with a leisurely grace, prepared a lavish brunch, then spent the afternoons engaged in lively conversation with Aidan's large circle of friends in one of the city's many taverns. They would separate briefly while he made certain the city was secure for the night, then share a relaxing supper and another romantic interlude. As soon as he had posted the last shift of guards, they would go to the square and work with Sonia until they grew too sleepy to continue.

While Kara enjoyed participating in the lengthy discussions which were the chief form of recreation on 329, she found them horribly frustrating as well. She had soon discovered that while the other women's eyes danced with delight as they hung onto her every word, they never volunteered opinions of their own. She met many wives as charming as May and Eden, but none ever came to visit her nor invited her to their homes. After she had offered several invitations of her own only to be refused with a succession of pitiful excuses, she gave up the effort to get to know any of them better in a less inhibiting setting. The men presented a different but just as perplexing set of problems. They were either obnoxiously patronizing, or persisted as Jarl had in pestering her with questions about Alado's range of weapons, their only interest in her being as a source of information on their long-standing enemy.

In an attempt to follow local custom in at least one regard, during the day Kara wore one of the several attractive gowns Aidan had provided, but she slipped into her uniform at night for the trek through the city to her Banshee since she felt far more at home working on the ship in her flight suit. Certain that neither her style of dress nor manners would cause anyone to dislike her, she knew it had to be the far too liberal slant of her views which kept her from making any close friends among 329's residents. Since free exchange of thought had always been encouraged on Mother, she found it impossible to accept the way the closed society of the city dwellers stifled it. Had it not been for the constant loving reassurance of her handsome husband, she would have shunned all contact with the citizens of the desert planet and remained alone on her ship.

Although she saw him frequently, she had had no other private conversations with Zac. She understood why he was too embarrassed to approach her, but that didn't lessen her resolve that people should put love ahead of the destructive tradition that kept them apart. Since she had met Serafina, she planned to make a point of looking for her on the next market day, but until then Kara knew there was nothing she could do to help the young man win the woman he loved if he refused to help himself. It was that very reluctance to act that nearly drove her to distraction. So often she would enter a conversation and see by their expressions that there were others who were tired of despising Alado or hating the moles and would welcome change, but all were waiting for someone else to bring it about. Since she was clearly an outsider, and a female at that, her logical arguments did not sway anyone. Much to Aidan's chagrin, she stubbornly refused to keep quiet, however, and insisted she had an obligation to speak the truth since nobody else would.

It was near the end of another long day and Kara turned away to cover a wide yawn. She was standing behind Aidan as he sat in the pilot's seat using Sonia as she dictated simple sentences for him to type. He was such an enthusiastic student that she always waited until he suggested it was time to go home rather than interrupt his studies.

"You've become so proficient with reading and writing that I think tomorrow night we should begin compiling a history of 329. That would be far more interesting for us both, don't you think? You have so much valuable information and we can store it in Sonia's memory banks and then transfer it to Mother's history files later."

It was obvious to him that she would never see Mother again, and Aidan found it increasingly difficult to accept her frequent references to the base ship. While that difference in outlook made him rebel instantly at her suggestion, he refused to reveal his thoughts. "Since everyone here knows the story as well as I do, that seems like a completely useless project," he argued instead.

Kara was dismayed that he would object to such a noble enterprise and moved around the seat to face him. "It doesn't matter how much everyone here knows when people everywhere else know no more than the propaganda Alado circulated at the time of the revolt. It may seem like an immense undertaking, but it won't be if we write only a few paragraphs each day. I would especially like to detail the lives of the prisoners. I think it would generate a great deal of sympathy for your people."

Aidan's frown deepened as he continued to argue. "First, I'd rather not use my memories to influence people I've never met, and second, I doubt anyone will ever have the opportunity to read our history anyway; so there's just no point in writing it all down. You can teach me more about the Banshee's equipment if you're bored with giving reading lessons," he stated firmly.

Disappointed by his stubbornness, Kara knelt by his side

and rested her hand on his thigh. "What's wrong, Aidan? Your history is such a fascinating one, why don't you wish to share it? Are you afraid it will be used against you somehow?"

When she displayed such sympathetic concern, Aidan was ashamed by how greatly he had misled her. She waited so patiently for him to respond that he decided it was high time they faced the issue of Mother once and for all.

"Mother's gone, Kara. The sooner you accept that fact the better off we'll both be. Not a day goes by that you don't find some way to remind me your stay here is a temporary one. Can't you understand how much that hurts me? It's useless, too, since you know you're stranded here with the rest of us."

"So that's it," Kara mused regretfully as she rose to her feet. While stunned by his remarks she didn't bother to argue since his mind was obviously made up on the subject. "Think whatever you like—only time will tell which of us is correct. I know I'd soon lose my mind if I thought I would have to stay here forever. I'm sure you have plenty of friends who already think I have no mind to lose, since they consider every thought I have utterly ridiculous." Turning away, she paused only briefly at the hatch before descending the steps. "Stay as long as you like, I know the way home."

Aidan clamped his jaw shut tightly so he would not be tempted to shout the ugly string of obscenities that had leapt instantly to his mind. He had wanted her to face what he considered the truth, but she had been too proud to do it or simply too damn stubborn—he didn't know which. Her comment about his friends appalled him although he knew she had had a difficult time adjusting, if not to him, then most certainly to the ways of his people. She was not only beautiful and bright but also well educated and independent. While he loved her for it, he knew many of his friends could barely tolerate her presence since she had so much more spirit than their women.

Perhaps he had been wrong to take her to the taverns where her quick mind so easily antagonized the men and apparently left her feeling insulted and dreadfully out of place. Why hadn't he been smart enough to invite a few of his close friends to his home where they could have gotten to know her in a much more relaxed fashion? He was sadly afraid the truth was that his lovely bride was envied by most of the women and heartily disliked by the majority of the men, and he had been a great fool to think she would be accepted in time just because that was what he wanted. She had been right when she said only time would tell which of them had the correct view of the future, and he should have been wise enough to understand her unhappiness without burdening her with his own. If he hurried, he could catch up to her. He quickly shut off Sonia and sealed the Banshee's hatch for the night.

He had run only half the way across the square when the stones beneath his feet lurched so violently that he was thrown off balance. He tried to catch himself, then screamed in pain when the still-mending bones in his right hand refused to bear his weight. Unable to break his fall, he landed heavily on his right shoulder, tearing the skin and bruising the muscles badly. Wracked with pain, he lay sprawled in the open courtyard only to suffer the further indignity of being thoroughly drenched by the water sloshing over the side of the fountain when the angle of the stones shifted suddenly in the opposite direction. He slipped twice on the wet surface but finally managed to scramble to his feet. It took all his energy to keep his footing as he stared wide-eyed at the destruction taking place all around him.

The three-story buildings surrounding the square swayed back and forth as the ground beneath them writhed with a seemingly endless series of savage twists and jerks. Their ornate stone cornices were shaken loose and plummeted slowly to the walkways, shattering in an avalanche of jagged pieces. Added to that deafening roar was a hideous cackle as hundreds of panes of glass shattered simultaneously, followed by the terrified screams of the poor souls cut by those flying shards. Touched off by sparks, natural gas from a dozen ruptured pipes exploded like incendiary bombs, devastating buildings and sending flames leaping high into the air. Had Aidan been suddenly plunged into the most

wretched agony of hell the horror that surrounded him could
have been no worse. That he was powerless to do anything
but gape while he struggled simply to remain upright was
more than a man of his courage and strength could bear.

While the violent earthquake lasted less than a minute, it
seemed a lifetime to Aidan before the ground became level
enough for him to make any headway toward his home. The
people who lived in the apartments above the shops border-
ing the square were pouring out of their doorways now,
some carrying members of their families who had been hurt
while others stepped out into the night too dazed by fright to
comprehend fully what had happened.

He had taken only a few long strides across the wreckage-
strewn courtyard when the first aftershock hit, and he was
again knocked to the ground. The screaming began in ear-
nest then as many of those who had taken refuge in the open
courtyard were hit by falling debris. Determined to find his
wife before he gave aid to any of the quake's many victims,
Aidan struggled to his feet and made his way to the corner of
his street only to find that the second building on the left had
collapsed, blocking the road with an enormous pile of rubble. How many more of the neighboring stone buildings had
been shaken off their foundations he couldn't tell since the
only light was provided by the eerie glow of wildly blazing
fires, but clearly the quake had devastated much of the heart
of the city.

Knowing there had to be a way to reach the wall and
follow its curve to his home, he darted down the adjacent
street. When he found it blocked before the next corner, he
simply scrambled over the gigantic heap of stones and ran
on. All around him the noisy confusion continued to mount
as people gathered their families together and moved out
into the streets to fight the fires or to scream for help for
themselves or their loved ones. In the darkness he wasn't
recognized and ran on through the turmoil, pausing only
when he was forced to by another sudden aftershock.

He was drenched with sweat and breathing rapidly by the
time he finally reached his home, but while the structure had
sustained little damage, to his horror he found it deserted.

"Kara!" he screamed time and again but her name echoed away unanswered, and none of the people milling about near his home had seen her. He leaned back against his door, knowing hundreds of people might be trapped and he would be expected to organize the rescue efforts, but he wanted only to find his dear wife.

Ashamed to be so self-centered when all around him people were screaming in grief and pain, he summoned his resolve and refused to give credence to the possibility that Kara might have been severely injured or perhaps even killed. He concentrated instead on the capable young woman he knew her to be. She was agile and quick, so surely she had darted into a doorway where she had been protected from the quake's wrath, and at that very minute she would be rendering all of the assistance she could to his people. That image became so strong in his mind that he was certain he could do no less. Shrugging off his stupor of self-pity he began exploring the area near his home. He soon discovered that the damage had occurred at random, and not nearly as many buildings had been destroyed as he had first feared. The rubble from the few dwellings which had been left in ruins blocked the narrow streets completely and had given him the initial impression that the destruction had been more widespread. The orderly plan of the city streets had become an impassable maze choked with smoke and flames, but rather than spend another precious minute searching for Kara, he decided to let her find him instead. Since his first duty was the city's defense, he made his way to the wall and traveled the walkway to the gate.

To their credit, the men standing guard could all be found near their posts doing their best to fight fires, aid the injured or rescue survivors just as they would have had the city been under attack. Since the town was built of stone, the fires were quickly being contained before they could spread to wreak further damage.

With his right arm aching from shoulder to fingertips, Aidan swiftly realized he would be far more valuable coordinating the rescue efforts than using his one good arm for physical labor. He offered a word of encouragement to everyone he met, completed his inspection of the wall and, finding it badly damaged in a location inaccessible to attack, considered the city secure. He returned to the gate then to set up a command post so those most desperately in need of help would receive it first. Until dawn there would be no way to survey the damage accurately, and families who had become separated would only locate each other with difficulty, but he asked each person with whom he spoke if they had seen Kara. Unfortunately they had all been far too busy worrying about their own kin to recall having seen her.

Concentrating on the worst aspect of the disaster, Aidan made his priority the containment of the fires. Each time a blaze was put out, he shifted the crew to the next location, so the longer a fire burned the more people arrived to fight it. Swept along on that wave of success, the dedication of the volunteers remained high despite the backbreaking nature of their task.

Disregarding their usual division of labor by sex, Aidan assigned those not actively fighting the fires the job of moving the injured to the square, where they would receive medical attention so no one had survived the quake would die needlessly of their wounds. Older children were given the task of calming their younger brothers and sisters still sobbing in terror, while every man and woman who was not already on a crew was quickly put to work digging through the rubble for the people trapped beneath. As the first light of dawn broke over the ravaged city, cheers were frequently heard as grateful survivors crawled or were pulled out from under the heaps of scattered stones which had once been their homes.

After a night more strenuous than any he had ever faced in battle, Aidan was not satisfied to consider the emergency under control until the last of the fires had been extinguished. Then, no longer feeling guilty about searching for his wife, he turned his full attention to finding her. When he discovered that his house was still unoccupied, he thought she might have had an opportunity during the night to leave a message for him in her ship, and he made his way wearily to the square hoping with each step he took that he would meet her.

The large courtyard was filled with the injured, and he stepped carefully between the long rows of people resting on blankets spread on the uncomfortable stones. Grateful he had not found her there, he made his way slowly to the Banshee.

Releasing the lock on the hatch with one hand was difficult, but at last he managed to swing it open, lower the steps, and climb inside. There was no sign that anyone had entered the ship since he had left it, but he flipped Sonia on and sank back into the pilot's seat as he keyed in the standard request for messages. What appeared on the screen gave him a jolt every bit as severe as the one he had suffered during the quake. The message was concise and sliced through his heart with the ease of a white-hot blade: DELAY IN RESCUE UNAVOIDABLE. STAND BY. MOTHER.

Aidan read the seven words again and again, stunned to think Kara had taught him to read just so he would be able to relay such a message to her. Now all he wanted to do was smash Sonia's screen to bits. Placed out in the open, the Banshee had suffered no damage, although buildings had toppled nearby. Still, he cursed the fates that had left the ship unscathed. He pressed the key to erase the message, but it instantly reappeared and Sonia chided him softly.

"Mother's messages may not be erased. Wait for the signal before you reply."

"Damn you!" Aidan hissed. He shut down Sonia rather than stare at the long-awaited message from Mother. The blasted base ship was finally trying to contact Kara, and from what she had always said, it was imperative that she respond. But if she failed to send a reply, he had no idea what would happen. Would Mother send a rescue sled for her anyway or presume her dead?

"Aidan?" Kara called softly. Her curls were tangled, her face smudged with dirt, her suit splattered with blood, and while she looked as tired as he felt she was obviously unhurt as she entered the ship and came to his side. "You must have had the same idea I had. I was going to leave you a message. Did you already leave one for me?"

Rather than reply in words, Aidan pulled her down across his lap and kissed her with a passionate fury that left her so dizzy she could not see his terrified expression when at last he drew away. Exhausted, she did not complain about the enthusiasm of his welcome but instead snuggled against him and closed her eyes.

"I was about halfway home when the quake hit and the house I'd just passed collapsed with no more than a single shudder. I've been helping the neighbors search the rubble for survivors ever since then. We could hear two children crying all night, but we didn't reach them until a few minutes ago. I brought them to the square to rest and get something to eat and I was hoping to find you." She lay quietly in her husband's arms, certain the worst was over now, but knowing it might take several days to rescue all the survivors and months to rebuild the city. "I was so worried about you, but I knew how busy you would be, and since I had no idea where to find you, I decided just to make myself useful. I hope you haven't been worried about me."

"Worried does not even begin to describe the torture I've been through since we parted," Aidan admitted readily. "I'm sorry you've been so unhappy here. It's all my fault, I'm sure of it, but I'll see that things change from now on, I promise I will."

"Oh, Aidan, how can you still recall that silly argument after the night we've had? I'm the one who should apologize anyway. If only I could learn to keep my opinions to myself—"

"No! Say whatever you like!" the troubled warrior insisted. "We should all have that privilege since freedom is what we prize most here."

While she thought it a most unusual time to discuss 329's philosophy, Kara was grateful for his understanding. "I'm sorry I walked out on you. I shouldn't have done that. Will you forgive me?"

When she had so much more to forgive, Aidan dared not refuse. "Of course." He gave her another enthusiastic hug, wincing as the dull ache in his shoulder became a jarring pain.

"You've been hurt!" Thinking she had caused his discomfort, Kara tried to scramble off his lap, but Aidan held her fast.

"It's nothing but a few cuts and scrapes," he explained with an embarrassed shrug. "What about you? Is any of that blood on your uniform yours?"

"Not a drop," Kara assured him. "But I've never been so tired. Can we go home and rest for a while? If we worked in shifts, then not everyone would become exhausted at the same time."

"That's an excellent idea. Fortunately, we still have a house to call our own." Aidan made no move to leave the ship, however. He held her wrapped tightly in his arms, terrified he would lose her before the day was over. Mother's message had been burned indelibly in his mind, but only by keeping that transmission a secret could he hope to keep her with him. He was betraying her trust with a cruelty he had not suspected he possessed, but it was the only choice he had. He clung to the slender hope that if she failed to respond to Mother's message, the base ship would call off the rescue attempt. Dealing with the aftermath of the earthquake would keep them occupied for a long while, but could he keep her away from the Banshee long enough for Mother to give her up as lost? He had no idea how long that would be, but he knew he had to try.

Kara was too tired to analyze Aidan's apparent lack of ambition. She knew his stamina was greater than hers, but she didn't want him to drive himself so relentlessly that he would exceed the point of exhaustion and become ill. "We ought to go home and get some rest. Is there someone we can tell where to reach you?"

"I left word at the guard hut that I would be looking for you. They can find me at home if I'm needed." Aidan helped Kara to her feet and ushered her out into the courtyard, then waited while she secured the hatch. He was angry with himself now that he had not had sense enough to destroy Sonia while he had had the chance and could have placed the blame on the quake.

While the prospect of finally getting some rest was wonderfully appealing, Kara was worried by the fact that the people providing medical care to the rows of injured appeared to be doing little but dispensing liquids. "Can't all these people be taken somewhere else for treatment? Does the city have no hospital, or was it destroyed?"

"Alado made 329 disease-free and it still is. We have no need of a hospital since we are all blessed with good health. Babies are born at home and if a man gets injured during a challenge, then a physician sews him up right there. Sometimes a child breaks an arm playing, but that's not terribly serious. Horrible tragedies like this are so rare that a hospital would sit vacant for decades at a time. We've always brought our injured to the courtyard during attacks, so that's why we sent them here last night."

"You've had other earthquakes besides the one that destroyed the prison?" Kara asked in amazement.

"Yes, but none has ever been as violent as last night's." He could see by her sorrowful expression that she was reluctant to leave the square while so many of the injured still remained untended. "I thought you were too tired to work any longer. If in fact you'd rather stay here and help, then do so and I'll find a blanket somewhere and lie down for a while."

"Yes, I would like to stay for as long as I can. What are these people being given for pain? Do you have drugs here?"

"We have no need of drugs when Oblivion works so quickly and so well," Aidan informed her softly. She had a lovely profile, one he had studied on all too few occasions, he thought sadly. Overwhelmed with both fatigue and the fear he would soon lose her, he doubted he could remain standing much longer. "I'm certain the doctors will appreciate your help if you wish to give it, but I think I better find a place to rest before I collapse."

Kara nodded absently. "Yes, you rest and I'll do what I can. The medicines I brought with me would be useful for treating those who suffered burns, but I don't have nearly enough."

"Oh God." Aidan felt sick, for he knew Mother would have medicines aplenty, but he would rather his people got along with the herbal remedies they had always used than call for aid from Alado when the price would be the loss of his wife.

Thinking his sudden pallor was due to fatigue alone, Kara waved to a teenage boy carrying a stack of blankets and took the top one for her husband. "You're going to have to lie down right here before you fall down, Aidan. I'll join you when I can."

Beset by the problems caused both by nature and Mother, the prospect of losing himself in a few hours sleep was too inviting to delay. As soon as she had spread out the blanket he stretched out on it, cradled his cheek on his left arm and fell sound asleep.

Like every other ablebodied person, Zac had worked all night, first fighting fires and then digging through the rubble of homes under which occupants were known to be trapped. Some of the rescue attempts had met with success, sending workers into delirious exchanges of hugs and kisses, while the failures ended in the grim task of removing badly battered bodies. It was the persistent hope they would find more people alive than dead that had kept them all working, but finally they had all grown so weary they had to stop to rest or risk becoming casualties themselves.

Zac and Eric staggered off with Barret and spent several hours sleeping in the banker's front room, but when Zac awoke, his first thought was of Serafina. He had been working at such a frantic pace during the night that he had had no time to worry about anything other than the scorching heat of the fires or the enormous weight of the fallen stones they had struggled to lift, but now his mind was flooded with memories of the strikingly pretty girl. When the earthquake had caused such terrible destruction to the city, what must it have done down in the moles' dreary caves?

"Eric!" Zac punched his friend's shoulder but received only a faint moan in reply. "Wake up! We've got to go check on the moles!"

Astounded by the absurd suggestion, Eric reluctantly

opened one eye. "The moles? You're not serious," he asked
as he rolled over to get more comfortable.

"Yes, I am. We've got to go see what happened to the
moles!" Leaping to his feet, Zac rushed in to use the
bathroom and found his host lazily floating in his tub. "Barret, everyone has completely forgotten about the moles. I
want to go see what happened to them. Will you come with
me?"

Barret had assisted in the rescue work all night, too, and,
unused to such demanding physical exertion, was so sore he
had been unable to sleep. Since he considered himself quite
bright, he was appalled that he had not once wondered about
the cave dwellers himself. He got out of the water immediately and wrapped a towel around his waist. "You're welcome to use the tub. If we're going visiting, we should make
an effort to look presentable."

Relieved to find the man in a reasonable mood, Zac
slipped out of his shorts, sank down into the water and
began vigorously to wash off the sweat, dirt and ashes that
covered his body like a second skin. "If the roofs of the
caves collapsed, there might be hundreds of people trapped.
Do you think anyone could be convinced to help them when
we still have so much left to do for ourselves?"

Barret shaved quickly as they discussed the matter. "I like
the moles no better than anyone else, Zac, but they do a
great deal of the work none of us wants to do. Our whole
economy would suffer if our trade with them ceased."

Zac found it difficult to believe the man would consider
rescuing the moles as a necessity for their economy rather
than a humanitarian endeavor, then reminded himself that no
matter how peculiar the banker's thinking might be, he was
an influential man. Perhaps an economic argument would be
the most persuasive one to use since it would stir no emotional protests. "Yeah, they do make a lot of things it would
be difficult for us to make for ourselves. Why, I could no
more make a pair of boots than I could a gold bracelet."

The banker rinsed the lather from his face as he agreed.
"I'm glad you mentioned this to me, Zac, before you spoke
with anyone else. If we're the ones who reach the caves

first, the moles are bound to be grateful. Even if they suffered no damage at all, they are sure to be impressed that we were worried about them."

"And that will be good for business?" Zac asked politely, still horrified that the man cared nothing about saving lives.

"Precisely." Barret left the room, got dressed and then returned to the bathroom to bring Zac a pair of clean shorts. "Shave if you like, put these on, and I'll fix us something to eat. It will have to be cold, but I'm too hungry to care. Is Eric going with us?"

"If you can wake him, he will," Zac assured him. He finished his bath hurriedly and then was so anxious he could barely hold the razor steady in his hand; but if he was going to rescue Serafina, he wanted to look his best while doing it. When Eric insisted they tell Aidan where they were going, Barret swiftly agreed while Zac prayed Kara hadn't told her husband about his fondness for a pretty mole because that would make his motives all too clear.

A resourceful man, Barret took along a canteen of ale and half a dozen hearty sandwiches, so when they found Aidan they could provide him with ample refreshments while they enlisted his support for their cause. A few hours' sleep had improved the warrior's spirits greatly and he listened attentively as they explained what they wished to do. Since he knew his wife's views well, he quickly agreed, but with one stipulation.

"While your concern for the economy is probably commendable, Barret, I doubt I could raise much sympathy for the moles for any reason when so many of our citizens have suffered a loss. I think we should say we're going up on the mountain to get a better look at our own city. If while we're up there we notice the entrances to the moles' caves are blocked, then we certainly can't ignore their cries for help. Once we've begun the rescue effort, if it's needed, it can't be abandoned."

Kara had been sound asleep, too. Cuddled in her husband's arms she would have slept several more hours, but at first mention of the moles she was wide awake. While Barret's insistence that it was to their own advantage to check on the cave dwellers might have been true, she could not in good conscience refuse to go along once she learned they might be in need of help. The sandwich he had given her was so delicious she forgave him momentarily for being so mercenary and finished it quickly. Then she sat back to listen while Aidan and the men made their plans. When she caught Zac's eye, she smiled, but he blushed so deeply she knew there was only one mole he was hoping to save. "You told me you've had quakes before. Has anyone ever gone to get a damage report from the moles?"

"A damage report?" Aidan asked in surprise. "That's a wonderful phrase, and I think I just might use it. It will probably confuse the moles so badly they'll tell us whatever we want to know."

"All we need to know is if any were killed," Zac interjected impatiently. "There's still plenty of light to go today."

Aidan rose to his feet, then extended his left hand to help Kara rise. He wanted to take her with him to keep her away from Sonia, but he knew if he didn't appear to be reluctant to have her go along she would be suspicious of his motives. Since he had been a stranger to subterfuge until he had met her such a ploy was difficult for him, but he made the effort to carry it off well. "The mountain terrain's quite rugged, so I want you to stay here. We shouldn't be gone too long. Either the moles will be fine or they'll need more help than four men can provide; either way we shouldn't be gone more than an hour or two."

Kara chewed her lower lip nervously, not wanting to embarrass him by arguing with him in front of his friends, but not wanting to be left behind, either. Lifting her chin proudly, she simply offered her own suggestion. "I've already covered quite a bit of the mountainside, so I know I'll not find the hike too difficult for me. I promise I'll not slow you down or be in your way."

Aidan frowned pensively, hoping he looked undecided. "Well, I don't know, Kara, there's some danger involved in this and—"

To Kara's amazement, Barret interrupted and tried to influence her husband. "I'll watch out for her and see she comes to no harm." When Zac stepped forward to offer the same consideration, Eric joined the others. "We'll all look out for your wife, Aidan. Now let's get going so we can be back before dark."

Apparently overruled, Aidan broke into a teasing grin and reached for his wife's hand. "Oh, all right. With so many helpful escorts, you're sure to do fine." As they left the square he turned back briefly to look at the Banshee, but his glance as well as his heart was still filled with dread.

CHAPTER
◊ **XVI** ◊

Ryan Blake leaned over the shoulder of the technician seated at the bank of communications consoles and punched in Sonia's code himself. "God damn it! Her Banshee's at full power; why isn't Kara responding?"

New to her job, the small young woman trembled nervously as she hesitantly provided the most obvious answer. "We're receiving only the standard distress signal, sir. Lieutenant León must be away from her ship."

"That's impossible. She would never leave it unattended for so many hours at a time. She must be there. Keep requesting a response until you get one," he ordered curtly. Straightening up, he turned to look across the bridge at Mother's captain, Matthew Merrill, the man he held personally responsible for Kara's disappearance. Unable to contain the heat of his anger another second, he strode swiftly to Merrill's side and lowered his voice to a threatening whisper. "Kara's ship is undamaged, but there's still no reply from her. I don't want to waste another minute waiting for a report which she's clearly unable to send. I would like to take not only a rescue sled, but also an armed escort and go look for her myself."

Ryan was seven feet tall; everyone on board Mother, including the captain, had to look up when they spoke to him. "Permission denied," Merrill responded immediately. Since he was well aware of what little control Ryan had over his emotions and how deeply he cared for Kara, he hastened to disclose his own plan. "I'll not risk your life needlessly. If there is no response by nightfall on 329, Mother will pay them a visit herself. That should be a sufficient show of force to convince those bandits we expect Lieutenant León to be returned to us unharmed. I may have had no say in how this despicable operation was begun, but I have every intention of overseeing its successful conclusion," he vowed confidently.

Ryan knew that no matter how frequently he was promoted he would never command a base ship for he lacked the cool, logical temperament always displayed by their captain. Barely out of his thirties, Merrill's auburn hair was thick and wavy, his features ruggedly handsome and his gray eyes capable of a gaze so piercing that his crew carried out his orders with lightning speed. The man's trim yet muscular build was handsomely displayed in his close-fitting red uniform, but he scarcely needed the distinctive garment when he had such a commanding presence and personality.

Ryan smiled with relief. Base ships usually remained in orbit around a planet, but he had recently had the rare privilege of seeing Merrill take Mother down through the clouds to pick up a scout, and that was a thrill he would never forget. He knew unless the captain found Kara alive and well, the population of 329 would swiftly cease to exist. "Yes, sir," he acknowledged crisply, certain if there was anything left of Kara to rescue, Merrill would soon do it.

While Zac had feared the earthquake might have damaged the moles' caves, he wasn't prepared for the horrible devastation they found. The main entrance to the subterranean world through which Aidan had walked to rescue Kara was sealed off by a massive rock slide. Even more frightening was the discovery that the entire mountainside where the huge meeting hall had been was now a deeply sunken crater. "Oh dear God," he moaned. "They must all have been crushed to death in an instant."

While the three other men appeared only mildly dismayed, Zac was obviously grief-stricken. Kara stepped quickly to his side and gave him a sympathetic hug. "The tunnels and side chambers go far back into the mountain, Zac. I doubt anyone was in the main hall when the quake struck since it happened so late at night. There must be other entrances. Weren't the moles smart enough to have a rear exit?"

"Yes," Zac replied, hurriedly grasping onto that hope and wanting to check each one, believing that not all of them would be blocked. "I know of one not far from here, do any of you know of others?"

Aidan turned to confer with Eric and Barret. "As far as I know, there is only the one other entrance on this side, but there are at least three facing the western desert." When the other men could name no more, they quickly divided up. Barret went with Zac to check the other entrance on their side while Eric and Kara accompanied Aidan to the far side of the mountain. Before the larger group had visited all three sites, Zac and the banker rejoined them.

Zac could barely report what they had found, he was so badly shaken. "The second entrance is buried under more rubble than the first. What are we going to do?"

While Aidan was surprised to find Zac so deeply concerned, he did not ridicule him for it. "The first tunnel we found had caved in. The second is just over the next rise. Let's hope it isn't blocked, too." They found it impassable as well, however, and when they saw that the last entrance had also collapsed, they sat down beside it to rest and formulate a plan.

Since she was the only one who had been through the mole's underground domain, Kara spoke up quickly to volunteer what information she had. "There couldn't have been anyone in the hall behind the main entrance, so I think it would be a waste of effort to try and tunnel in there. I saw several skylights—if we can find one still open, we might be able to call down to them and see where they are digging out and begin working opposite them until we meet in the middle."

Aidan looked away to hide his smile, for while his friends were clearly amazed by Kara's suggestion, he thought it excellent. "Well, are there any other ideas?"

"I don't care where we dig, but I think we should get started," Zac stated firmly. "We can use torches to provide light and work all night. There's no point worrying about being outside the walls after dark since none of us can possibly be captured when the moles are all trapped in their caves."

Barret frowned. He couldn't envision such a large-scale rescue attempt being mounted within the few hours remaining before dark. "I hadn't imagined such a terrible catastrophe as we've found, but I think Kara's idea is a good one. If there are any moles left alive, then we ought to work cooperatively to save them."

"Just tell me what the skylights look like, and I'll start searching for one," Eric offered as he got to his feet and brushed off the seat of his shorts.

"Someone ought to go back to the city." Kara gave her husband a quizzical glance and waited for him to decide who to send. "I would go, but since no one pays the slightest attention to what I say, I think I should stay here with Eric."

"I want to stay here, too," Zac declared immediately.

Aidan nodded thoughtfully, pleased that Kara wanted to stay on the mountain since her decision fit into his plans to keep her away from Sonia so nicely. "All right, why don't Barret and I go back and see what equipment and volunteers we can find? I'll give the order to leave the gates open all night and then we'll start back. With luck maybe you'll have been able to contact the moles by then. If by any chance you find they've dug themselves out, don't bother to congratulate them. Just come on back down the trail as quickly as you can."

Impatient to get started, Zac helped Kara to her feet. "We'll take no unnecessary chances. I promise you that. Just hurry back."

Aidan led the way, but he paused several times to look back at Kara while she and his friends were still in view. "We'll need to bring food, ropes and shovels. What else, Barret?"

"Blankets so we can stop and rest, and Oblivion for the injured," the banker suggested helpfully. "Perhaps we should arrange for someone to escort your wife to your home as the work is sure to be too strenuous for her."

Aidan winked at his cousin. "I won't ask her to work, but I would still like to have her with me."

"I didn't think you would ever fall in love," Barret teased with a hearty chuckle, "let alone be so devoted to your bride."

"Nor did I," Aidan was swift to admit, but he prayed Kara would never learn just what the limits of his devotion truly were.

Captain Merrill requested the infrared filters for the scanners, then projected the images being received on all of Mother's viewing screens so the scenes of 329 could be seen by his entire crew as he analyzed them. "As usual I'll welcome any additional interpretation anyone wants to share. It appears the planet has a single community located on the site of the prison facility. The colony has suffered extensive damage, and though I have no clues as to the cause or the time frame, it appears to have been recent. Lieutenant León's Banshee is located in an open area adjacent to the mountains, but she has not responded to our replies to her distress call. I want the scanners set for the sensors in her suit and see if they can pinpoint her location."

He turned to see that his order was carried out before again focusing his attention on the screen which dominated the forward section of the bridge. The multiple lenses of the robot scanners began a systematic sweep of 329's terrain and, after only a few seconds' delay, focused in on the activity in the mountains. A small triangle began to flash on the giant screen, indicating that the beams had homed in on the unique weave of an Alado flight suit.

"Well, we have something here. Let's hope it's Lieutenant León rather than some rogue wearing her suit as a turban." After boosting the magnification of the scanners he studied the flurry of activity on the screen before again addressing his crew on the intercom. "I need ideas on this. We've got torches and lots of people. There's no snow so they're not out for night skiing. What else could they be doing?"

From the bridge to the docking bays, the attention of Mother's entire twenty-five-hundred-man crew was focused on the overhead communication screens. Several moments passed before the silence was broken by a feminine voice. "Sir, do you think it's a religious ceremony of some sort?" There were half a dozen other suggestions ranging from the logical to the bizarre before Captain Merrill gave the order for Mother to move in closer and then hover in place.

"All right, at my signal we'll turn on the running lights. The people we're watching will either scatter like roaches or they'll give us the polite welcome Alado deserves. One, two, three." He pointed to his first officer who threw a switch, instantly illuminating Mother so that she shone with the brilliance of a spectacularly decorated Christmas tree.

Suddenly bathed in bright light, Kara turned with the others to look up at the sky, but she alone cried out in delight. She threw her arms around her husband's neck and jumped up and down excitedly as she shouted in his ear, "I told you Mother would come for me! I told you so!"

She had said Mother was large, but Aidan had never dreamed the base ship would be so monstrous in size or incredibly beautiful. The structural framework of the six-tiered spaceship was made of the same strong but lightweight alloy as the Banshee and was a gigantic replica of the scout vessel's basic wedge design, but with the addition of a rectangular tail portion which gave it the remarkable appearance of an arrowhead when viewed from below. Built in a grid of interconnected triangular forms, its broad base narrowed with each successive layer so that from the side the ship resembled a flat-topped pyramid. The top four levels were liberally accented with panels of a clear acrylic with the hardness of diamonds. Like fine crystals, the beveled edges of the panels reflected the brilliance of the running lights in a thousand sparkling beams. No star had ever graced the heavens with a more compelling glow, but Aidan's immediate reaction was to step behind his wife and wrap his arms tightly around her waist to hold her fast. "No!" he screamed in a voice that shattered the silence of the awestruck crowd. "No!"

Matthew Merrill clasped his hands behind his back as he continued to study the perplexing scene on the mountainside. A puzzled frown graced his features as he scanned the faces of the men and women staring up at Mother. While obviously astonished by the sudden appearance of the base ship, not a single soul had turned tail and run. "The men are armed with knives and what look like picks and shovels, which I suppose isn't surprising for descendants of a mining colony. I haven't got a clear shot of the man holding Lieutenant León, so let's hope he's amenable to persuasion. Transmit my comments to him." He hesitated a moment as the exterior speakers were activated, then issued what he hoped would be an effective greeting in a deep and resonant tone. "This is Captain Matthew Merrill of Alado Base Ship mtr-14. Our mission in space is exploration and discovery, and we have come to 329 only to rescue Lieutenant Kara León. Once she and her aircraft are on board we will continue our voyage. If you release her unharmed, none of your people will suffer the slightest injury."

Aidan held her in the same frantic clasp with which he had embraced her that morning, and Kara was afraid she now understood the real reason for his earlier desperation. Knowing the time was poor for confrontation of any sort, when he made no move to release her she used her mind to project the loving waves of peace and tranquility to which she knew he would have to respond.

"Do not be frightened, Aidan," she coaxed softly. She had always known this day would come, but after an initial burst of joy, she found her husband's sorrow far outweighed her pleasure. When he dropped his hands to his sides, she waved cheerfully, knowing all her friends on board Mother would be watching her. "Captain, we have people trapped by an earthquake and need heavy equipment and personnel to help rescue them, please."

Matthew shook his head wearily, then turned to the members of his crew standing on the bridge and turned off his microphone momentarily to speak with them. "Is there any reason why I should be surprised by that request? Of course, she was forbidden to contact these people she now refers to as 'we'!"

"She can hardly be faulted for aiding in a rescue attempt after an earthquake, sir," Ryan spoke forcefully in Kara's behalf, his relief that they had found her immense.

Again addressing the crowd below, the captain spoke calmly. "The need is critical?"

"Yes, extremely so!" Kara insisted.

Aidan was slow to grasp the fact that Kara had thought first of the trapped moles rather than a swift return to Mother. Now he grabbed her arm to remind her Alado was unwelcome there. "We can do without their help, Kara."

Standing nearby, Zac half ran, half slid down the hillside to join in the discussion. "For the love of God, if they're willing to provide help, let them do it!"

"He's right, you know," Kara insisted persuasively. Turning to look up at Mother, she asked again, "Will you please send help, Captain?"

"What's going on down there?" Ryan was staring intently at the images on the screen. "Are they actually arguing about it?"

"As Kara knows quite well, it is Alado's policy to respond with aid whenever it is requested. We are forbidden to refuse it under normal circumstances, but this is an unusual case since it comes from a planet not under our control. In this instance, whether or not we send aid is up to me."

"Do you suppose it's a trap?" Ryan proposed suspiciously.

"If you're afraid of being hit with a shovel, then stay on board," the captain replied with more than a slight touch of sarcasm. He was a naturally cautious man, however, and revealed that in his next request. "I will send an excavation team when you and your Banshee are on board, Lieutenant. I am dispatching a rescue sled immediately. Be at your ship to meet it."

Kara sighed in frustration, then reached for Aidan's hand. "Come on, we'll meet the sled, then go home and get cleaned up. We can't go on board looking like we've been up for two nights in a row even if we have."

"You want to take me on board Mother?" Aidan asked incredulously.

Kara attempted to analyze the intent of that question from his befuddled expression, but still didn't understand his reluctance to join her. "Yes, of course. Not only are you my husband, but you are in charge of the rescue operation and should be the one to describe just what sort of help we'll need."

Her reply was so reasonable that Aidan simply nodded, but as he looked up at Mother, he couldn't believe what he had just agreed to do. "I am going to go up into that ship and tell the captain what I need?"

"Yes. Don't be frightened. I'll fly us up in my Banshee as soon as we're ready to go."

"Well, go!" Zac encouraged with a frantic wave. "We'll keep working until you get back with help."

Aidan paused for a moment to look at the tired and dirty faces of his friends. The rescuers were either leaning wearily on their shovels or had slumped to the ground for a few moments of rest. "Is it agreed by everyone then—we'll ask for help from one of Alado's ships?"

When that started a heated discussion, Kara quickly spoke up. "Not only can my ship supply help to rescue the moles, but they will also provide excellent medical care for the people who were burned or injured yesterday. Nothing will be asked of you in return. Please believe me."

Because Kara had set such an admirable example herself, no one present doubted her word, and a consensus was quickly reached to accept Alado's aid.

"We better hurry or the sled will reach my ship before we do." Kara again grabbed Aidan's left hand in an attempt to pull him along.

"We are going to accept Alado's help to rescue the moles." Aidan could not believe the irony of that prospect. "Do you realize what you've accomplished here in just a few weeks' time?" he asked his bride as they swiftly covered the rocky terrain with agile steps.

"The impossible?" she asked with a lilting laugh.

"Exactly." Aidan turned frequently to look up at the imposing spectacle Mother presented in the nighttime sky. "What does MTR-14 mean?"

"It means the ship is a major tactical and reconnaissance vessel. The nickname Mother is just an affectionate slang term for an MTR. It was the fourteenth vessel commissioned by Alado, so that's why it has that number." Its many lights did not reach them after they passed the crest of the mountain and began their descent, however, and she had to slow down to take more care not to slip and fall.

"Tactical means it's designed for warfare, doesn't it?" Aidan was growing more apprehensive with each pasing second. The crew of the monstrous ship might well offer aid and then exact a terrible price regardless of Kara's reassurance otherwise. "Kara, if this is some terrible trick Alado uses frequently to land without opposition on unsuspecting planets, please tell me now."

They were quite alone, approaching the path that led to the gate, and the ground was almost level. Stopping to turn and face him, Kara chose her words carefully. "Just because you play tricks on unsuspecting people does not mean it is Alado's policy to do the same!" she challenged defiantly.

"What are you talking about?" But even as he asked that

question, he knew she must suspect, even if she couldn't prove, what he had done.

"When you got to the Banshee first this morning there was a message for me from Mother, wasn't there?" she asked accusingly. "Captain Merrill would never have brought her in without first trying to contact me to complete the usual rescue procedures."

Aidan took a deep breath and let it out slowly. His failure to reveal Mother's effort to contact her had caused him the most guilt-ridden day of his entire life. He had always prided himself on being a man of honor, but he had betrayed the trust of the woman he loved with the same ease he had betrayed the people of his city to protect her. He saw no point in arguing about her accusation. "You know why I did it," was all he offered in his own defense.

Kara turned away, too angry and hurt to care what excuse he had. "I haven't time to discuss it with you now." Not waiting for him, she rushed on ahead. Confronting the maze of rubble-strewn streets, she turned back to call to him, "They can clean up this mess, too!"

Aidan broke into a run to catch up with her and act as guide. "This way is best now," he assured her, meaning to see that she reached her Banshee with no unnecessary delay. The people in the city could see Mother clearly but had not been able to hear the captain's conversation with Kara, and Aidan found himself besieged with questions. "Come to the square and I'll need to explain only once!" he called out time and again. Soon they had a sizable crowd following in their wake. To his utter dismay, Aidan found himself confidently reassuring his friends that Alado had offered help they would be foolish to refuse since it would benefit them all. There wasn't a person listening who had not had a member of his family injured, his home damaged or his street rendered difficult if not impossible to traverse, and the offer of assistance from such an unlikely and heartily disliked source wasn't refused. Not knowing how much space the rescue sled would require to land, he waved them all back to clear a large area near the Banshee.

While he was speaking to the crowd, Kara opened the hatch, climbed in and flipped the switch to activate Sonia. She sent a brief message to Mother informing her she had reached her ship and was awaiting the arrival of the rescue sled. When Aidan came to the door, she purposely didn't look up at him. "This won't work unless we're truthful with each other, Aidan. That means we'll have to tell the truth even when it hurts."

"Do you still want me to go with you?"

Kara turned toward him then. "Yes, I'd like them to see that Mining Colony 329 produced some fine men despite the horror of its inception."

Without responding, Aidan turned around and sat down on the top step. He didn't understand how she could consider him a fine man after what he had tried to do to her. He had behaved selfishly, so clearly he loved himself more than he loved her and he knew that wasn't how love was supposed to be. "I've never been in love before, Kara, and I guess I'm not very good at it."

"Well, Lord knows neither am I," the distraught redhead admitted readily, but before they could continue their conversation she heard the rescue sled approaching and slipped past him to go out to meet it.

While Mother made not the slightest whisper of sound, the rescue sled was a noisy contraption consisting of a platform with a large, high-powered engine capable of towing damaged Banshees rigged below and a small crew compartment and reserve tanks of fuel mounted on the top. It hovered above the square for a moment, then settled down in front of Kara's ship. Not knowing what to expect, Aidan watched closely as three men climbed out. The first two were mechanics who were dressed in bright yellow coveralls and white helmets with reflecting visors that made them appear more like robots than humans. They were followed by the tallest man Aidan had ever seen. He seemed simply to unfold as he stepped out of the sled and just kept straightening up until he towered above his two companions. Spotting Kara, he greeted her with an enthusiastic whoop of joy, scooped her up into his arms, kissed her soundly, then swung her completely around in a circle before replacing her on her feet.

When he finally stepped back, Aidan called out to his wife. "I'd like to meet your friend, although I can do without the hug and kisses."

As Aidan rose and took a step toward him, Ryan reached out to take Kara's hand and pulled her back toward the sled. "Kara is to return to Mother," he reminded the powerfully built stranger.

The man was dressed in a shimmering silver suit like Kara's, but the cut was slightly different to accommodate the masculine physique and proved to be not nearly as revealing as Aidan had feared a man's suit would be. While the man gripping Kara's hand was tall, his build was lean rather than muscular. He was unarmed and, while he appeared fiercely determined to protect Kara, Aidan doubted he had any reason to fear him.

As she watched the two men slowly sizing up one another, Kara thought only of how uneven a match it would be; despite Ryan's remarkable height, he was no fighter. "Ryan, I'd like you to meet Aidan." She paused briefly, undecided whether or not to explain why last names were not used on 329, then decided she had far more relevant information to impart. "He is my husband," she added matter-of-factly, as though she had already introduced him a hundred times that day.

Astonished to find that Kara had married what he regarded a filthy, half-clothed, muscle-bound, long-haired brute, Ryan dropped her hand as though the touch of her skin suddenly revolted him. "How can that possibly be true? You've been here only a few weeks and you knew we would be coming for you as soon as we could! Why would you marry this . . . well . . . this creature?"

"Loathsome creature is a nice phrase," Aidan supplied with a wicked grin, though he did not offer his hand.

Ignoring her friend's lack of manners and her husband's witty response, Kara continued the introductions. "Aidan, this is Ryan Blake, another of Mother's scouts. We fly with the same squadron, so naturally he was very worried about me."

"Naturally," Aidan agreed snidely.

Fearing the men might soon come to blows regardless of Ryan's more civilized upbringing, Kara stepped between them. "Would you do me a favor, Ryan, and help the mechanics check out my ship? I think all it needs is fuel. You can go back with them, and Aidan and I will follow as soon as we've had a chance to change our clothes."

"Does he actually have others?" Ryan asked with a sneer.

"Stop it, Ryan!" Kara demanded immediately. "We've both been working almost nonstop since yesterday's earthquake and I know we look like hell, but it can't be helped." She took Aidan's arm then and turned away. "Thanks for staying with my ship. I'll see you on board Mother later."

Ryan put his hands on his hips and swore bitterly when the mechanics began to chuckle. "You heard her, all the blasted ship requires is fuel!"

"That may be true, but Captain Merrill requires a complete assessment before we allow the ship in the air," the senior mechanic informed him.

"Well, get busy then!" Ryan ordered impatiently. "I don't want to be stuck here all night." He paced up and down as they worked through their checklist of maintenance procedures, trying valiantly to ignore the curious stares of the people still lingering in the square.

Aidan waited until they had reached his home to speak. The doors of the kitchen cabinets stood open and dishes and foodstuffs had fallen out on the floor. Seeing Kara's anxious glance, he shook his head. "A few plates got broken and the water from the tub got splashed about a bit, but we've no time to clean up anything but ourselves now." He followed her into the bedroom, leaned back against the doorjamb and folded his arms across his chest. "Is Ryan a fair sample of Alado's manpower?"

"Why do you ask?" Kara inquired flippantly. "Are you planning an attack?"

"No," Aidan readily confessed, "I wondered if you and he had been lovers."

Kara sat down on the foot of the bed to pull off her boots and gave him a withering glance. "No, Ryan's far too intense for my tastes. I think it was obvious he's overly fond of me though. Now come on, let's hurry."

There was no way Aidan was going to hurry what he planned to do, but he wanted to be clean first. After stripping off his boots and shorts he went to soak in the tub. The hot springs still provided warm water, but he would need gas to cook. "Can Alado fix the gas lines, too, while they're here?"

Kara moved to the doorway of the bathroom to reply. She was wearing only her lavender teddy, displaying her pale golden arms and legs while her face and hands were still stained with the dirt of the mountainside. "All the damage can be repaired. Just make certain your initial request for assistance includes everything that needs to be done so the work can be completed simultaneously."

"I will," he assured her. "Aren't you going to join me?"

Completely unaware of his amorous intentions, Kara shook her head. "No, I need to wash out my uniform first. I'll have to wear one of the gowns you gave me back to Mother and put on a clean uniform there before I meet with Captain Merrill." She grabbed a towel but stepped back into the bedroom to remove her teddy. When she reappeared and went to the sink to rinse out her clothes, she had the towel wrapped discreetly around herself.

Since her chilly mood wasn't conducive to passion, Aidan finished bathing, wrapped a towel around his hips and, when Kara finished her wash, stepped up to the sink to shave. While pretending to pay close attention to his task, he was in fact observing his wife's reflection in the mirror to keep an eye on her while she bathed. She had seemed infuriated by his deceit when she had first accused him of it, but now her mood, while subdued, didn't alarm him. At least she wanted to introduce him to the captain of Mother, and he considered that a very good sign. He drew his razor up his throat slowly, taking his time so that he completed his grooming at the same time she left the tub and returned to the bedroom. He followed her quickly then and, stepping up behind her, unfastened her towel and pulled it away before she could raise her hands to stop him.

"Aidan! Stop playing, we've got to hurry," she scolded him, but she couldn't stop laughing long enough to give her command a serious ring.

"I'm not playing," Aidan replied in a seductive whisper. He remained behind her, nuzzling her nape with tender kisses while his hands caressed the fullness of her breasts.

"Aidan." Growing wary, Kara tried once again, but he had pulled her back against him, and there was no mistaking the sincerity of his affection. She was startled that he would pick such an inopportune time to make love, then realized he wanted the fact that she was his wife firmly imprinted in her mind, as if she could possibly forget. Relaxing against him, she lay her hands over his, content to let him have whatever reassurance he would claim was rightfully his. When he leaned down to lift her knee slightly to give him the room to enter her where they stood she was taken completely by surprise, but the resulting sensation was so wildly pleasurable she lost herself in that beauty and gave no more thought to his motives or choice of position. He was so strong he held her easily in an embrace every bit as passionate as it was primitive. When at last the final shudders of ecstasy which had blessed their sudden union became the soft, warm tremors that would heat their blood for hours, he lay her down on his bed and cradled her in a tender embrace.

"Let's stay here just a little while longer," he invited as his lips sought the flushed peaks of her breasts.

Kara slid her fingers through his long, damp curls to press his face close, too content to argue about how he wished to spend what could so easily prove to be their last hours together. Their love had been an impossible one from the very beginning. She reminded herself of that sorry fact again and again as she returned his passion-filled kisses, but it made the pain of their imminent parting no less acute.

CHAPTER
◇ **XVII** ◇

Kara could not help but laugh as Aidan sorted through the entire contents of his clothing chest, tossing one garment after another over his shoulder until the floor of the bedroom was littered with discarded apparel. She was already dressed in the first of the close-fitting sheath dresses he had given her since it was her favorite, but she knew they were already so late another few minutes would make no difference.

"Aidan, it really doesn't matter what you wear, my love."

Finally reaching the end of his wardrobe, the apprehensive man straightened up and turned around slowly to face her. "I've waited all my life for Alado to return and I don't want anyone else referring to me as a 'creature'!"

Attempting to be of help, Kara bent down to pick up a pair of cream-colored shorts. "The temperature is controlled at a constant sixty-eight degrees on Mother. That must be more than thirty degrees cooler than the average temperature of 329. You have a wardrobe suitable for the desert climate and you needn't apologize for it. Ryan was not only shocked but jealous to learn I had married you and he was deliberately trying to be insulting—so don't waste another minute worrying about his remarks. Now, why don't you wear these? Don't you have a shirt here somewhere?" Handing him the shorts she had chosen, she began rummaging about for a shirt, but each garment she picked up was a pair of short pants.

"I never bother with shirts," Aidan explained sullenly.
"I've never needed one until now."

"Well, then, why don't you wear that leather vest you
wear for challenges if you feel you need more clothes?"
When he was obviously reluctant to accept that suggestion,
Kara tried another tack. "The only purpose of this visit is to
meet Captain Merrill and request his help with the rescue
attempt. Surely that doesn't require elaborate formal dress."

"The point is we don't even have any formal clothes
here!" Aidan shouted angrily, losing all control of his
temper.

Sensing his problem wasn't really clothing, but was far
more likely his hatred for Alado, Kara made the only other
suggestion she could. "If you'd like, I'll go and report in,
describe the moles' situation to the captain and then meet
you back at the site where we've already begun digging.
That way you needn't go on board Mother, nor meet anyone
else. I know you're tired—I am, too—but I don't mind
going alone."

The muscles tensed along Aidan's jaw as he considered
her proposal thoughtfully before rejecting it. He wasn't
about to let her out of his sight when he didn't trust the
bastards of Alado not to move swiftly to keep them apart.
That was not a fear he cared to share with her, however.
"I'm not afraid of them, Kara, I never have been. But I
don't want anyone laughing at either you or me."

Relieved to find his problem was no greater than that,
Kara smiled lovingly. "You are a very handsome man,
Aidan. No one is going to laugh at you for any reason. They
will undoubtedly envy me. In fact, I'm sure of it."

Not convinced, Aidan nevertheless tossed away the towel
he had been wearing and pulled on the shorts she had chosen. Thinking perhaps his vest was appropriate, he pulled it
on and instantly the smooth leather against his skin reminded
him that he was a warrior and a very fine one at that. Kara
was right, there were a dozen reasons why he didn't want to
go on board Mother, but what did his clothes matter? He
pulled on his boots, ran his fingers through his hair and
stood up, ready to go. His expression was too serious to give

his wife the mistaken impression he was looking forward to the visit, however.

Kara had picked up most of his clothing and left the rest for later. While she had done her best to sound confident about their reception, she knew she was in for not only a stern lecture but a long one. That thought was so depressing that she said little as they returned to the square. The rescue sled was gone, but there were still people milling about, apparently hoping they would have the chance to see the Banshee fly.

As soon as they were inside, Kara locked the hatch. Opening a compartment beside it, she pulled down the seat which was neatly stored inside. "This seat is used when mechanics fly with pilots to check the ship's performance. It's not all that comfortable, but this flight will be a short one. I'll just take her up, circle Mother in a wide arc and enter the docking bay at the rear."

"Why don't we just use your seat and you can sit on my lap?" Aidan offered with a teasing grin.

Kara placed her hands on his chest, gave him a light kiss, then followed it with a gentle push to force him down into the jump seat. "Don't tempt me while we're in the air, Aidan, or you're liable to get us both killed. Now buckle the seat belt and keep quiet until we arrive."

She took her own seat then, put on her helmet, quickly completed the standard preflight checklist, then began the final sequence of procedures which would take the lightweight Banshee aloft. When the hum of the engines reached the right pitch, she turned to wink at her husband, then with a light hand on the controls she coaxed her sleek craft into the air. With the ease of a hummingbird it rose straight up, and when she had cleared the city Kara turned out toward the desert with a graceful swoop. She looked over at Aidan and was pleased when he returned her happy grin.

"I'll take you the long way!" she pledged with a laugh and, increasing her speed to the maximum she sped out over the desert, climbing steadily until she had gained sufficient altitude to complete a complicated series of aerobatic loops and turns before setting her course for Mother and signaling she was coming in. An expert pilot, she coasted into the docking bay, cut her engines, pulled off her helmet and ruffled her curls with her fingertips. "Welcome to Mother!" she called happily as she turned to face Aidan.

"Just a minute," Aidan whispered hoarsely, his face as pale as the fabric of his shorts. "I think I'm going to be sick."

"Oh no! I'm so sorry. I never should have shown off like that when you've never been up in a spaceship. Just put your head down and take a few deep breaths and you'll be fine." Kara was angry with herself for not having been more thoughtful. She had just wanted to have some fun—she had not dreamed she would make him airsick. "You won't get sick on Mother, Aidan, there's no sensation of movement at all on her."

Aidan followed her directions and when he was certain he would not faint, he reached for the buckle of his seat belt, fumbling clumsily with it before finding the release. He then rose shakily to his feet, certain he would never feel completely well again. Giving her a lopsided grin, he apologized. "I think I should have let you come alone."

"You'll be fine in a few minutes, really you will," she reassured him again. The hatch swung open then and to her dismay Kara found not one of the docking bay's crew, but Captain Merrill himself. "Good evening, sir," she greeted him self-consciously.

Merrill had taken the precaution of strapping on a sidearm after hearing Ryan's description of Kara's husband, but rather than the ruffian he had expected, he found the blond young man quite handsome and did not feel the least bit threatened. He stepped aside while they climbed out of the Banshee and then responded politely to Kara's introduction.

"Welcome aboard, Aidan. As far as we know, 329 has as sterile an environment today as it did the day Alado left it, but as a precaution to us both, I must insist that one of our medical staff make certain neither of us will infect the other. The procedure only takes a few minutes and is neither painful nor embarrassing." Gesturing to his left, he indicated a man dressed in the white uniform of a laboratory technician.

"Roger will take you up to the medical unit. In the meantime, Lieutenant León and I will discuss her mission, and you will join us when your exam is completed."

Aidan was as surprised as Kara that the captain had met them himself, but he rebelled instantly at the man's efforts to separate them no matter what the excuse. "Since Kara has been on 329 for so long, shouldn't she be examined? After all, if I am carrying any sort of disease, then she will be, too."

Merrill looked down to hide his smile, for the man was correct, and he knew he would have to find some other way to speak with Kara alone. "Excellent suggestion, Aidan. Go with him to the medical unit, Lieutenant, and then bring him up to my quarters."

Glancing down at her flowing gown, Kara was embarrassed she had not had time to don a uniform before he saw her. "I'll need a minute to change my clothes."

"That's not necessary, don't bother," the captain informed her curtly.

"Yes, sir." Kara's heart fell as she watched him walk briskly toward the bank of elevators. He had been far too friendly in her opinion, and she was certain the lecture he planned to deliver was going to be even more stern than she had feared. She didn't want Aidan to have to suffer through it with her, though. "I'm certain he wishes to speak with me privately. When we go up to his cabin, let me go in alone first."

"No, I won't," Aidan insisted as he took her arm and started after Roger, who had also turned toward the elevators. Aidan tried not to appear overly curious, but he was deeply impressed by the wide range of equipment stored in the docking bay. The immense staging area occupied the rear half of Mother's fifth level, providing an enormous amount of space with an extremely high ceiling. Not only were there more Banshees suspended vertically from overhead than he could count without his purpose being obvious, but also there were half a dozen rescue sleds and other craft whose functions he couldn't begin to guess parked beneath them. Even at that late hour the cavernous room was brightly illuminated and filled with mechanics working on the repair and maintenance of the various craft.

While the captain stepped into the first elevator, Roger led them into the second. Aidan saw Kara reach for the rail to steady herself and swiftly did the same. There were no longer any functioning elevators in his city, but he knew what their purpose was and tried to appear thoroughly bored as they traveled from the fifth level to the third. Roger then led them down a long corridor, opened a door on the left and stepped aside so they could precede him into one of the medical unit's many treatment rooms.

"I'll go first," Kara quickly volunteered. She stepped into a large glass booth in the corner and waved to Aidan as Roger closed the sliding doors. He then punched in a code on the control panel and watched the readings closely as the lights in the booth changed in rapid succession from red to violet to white, denoting a sweep for contamination which had yielded no positive results.

"You're clean," he announced as he opened the door. He turned then and gestured for Aidan to enter. "Next."

Kara gave her husband's arm a loving squeeze as she passed him. "Don't worry, if Merrill had had the slightest suspicion that there's any disease on 329 he would not have let us out of the Banshee without clearance. They already know we're both clean."

Since the booth had caused Kara no obvious discomfort, Aidan stepped inside and turned around to face her. He tensed slightly, half expecting poison gas to come seeping in, but other than the lights changing colors nothing happened. The second Roger opened the door Aidan stepped out, grateful the puzzling process was over. "You said they could fix my hand," he reminded Kara, thinking if he needed to fight his way out of the captain's quarters he would need both hands to do it.

"I haven't forgotten. It will only take a minute. Is Trey on duty now?"

Roger shrugged. "Could be, let me go check."

A nondescript man of medium height, weight and coloring, Roger, Aidan was certain, couldn't possibly have been one of Kara's lovers. Wanting to make good use of the time they had alone, the warrior pulled his wife into a reassuring hug. "I know the captain might have a few complaints, but since they're all unjustified, let me stay with you so I can back you up if need be."

"Thank you, but I doubt he would say anything in front of you. That's probably just as well since I know you would argue even more heatedly than I will." She kissed him, thankful for his concern, but then jumped back when the door slid open suddenly. "Hi, Trey!" she greeted the physician warmly, embarrassed he had caught her in her husband's arms. She quickly introduced him and explained Aidan's injury, but not how he had received it.

Trey's name was actually Randolf T. Whitman III. He had always been known by his nickname, however, and insisted Aidan use it rather than his last name and his professional title. "If it's possible, I would like to visit your city and meet some of your physicians to see just what sort of treatment they provide. Naturally I would be happy to give them a tour of our facilities in return."

"The only things I recognize here are the table and the sink," Aidan admitted truthfully. A gleaming metal counter ran along one wall of the room and the space above it was filled with shelves containing devices of all shapes and sizes, but he could not even begin to guess their function. "Our physicians are used to treating injuries due to accidents, but there are only a few of them and a great many people were injured in the earthquake."

"I hope we can be of assistance." Trey removed the tight wrapping from Aidan's hand and tossed the long strips of fabric into the waste chute. "Now, if you'll just step over here to the counter and place your hand on this glass panel, I'll take a look at the break."

Aidan followed the man's directions and watched in rapt fascination as the bones of his hand were displayed on an overhead screen. He could see the break clearly, but the bones were correctly aligned, not out of place, and he was quite pleased with his handiwork. Trey, however, was studying the projected image far more intently, giving Aidan an opportunity to observe him closely. He judged the man to be a few years older than himself. His hair was dark brown, his eyes were a pale blue-gray and his features were so fine they had almost a feminine delicacy, though there was no trace of anything other than a masculine temperament in his manner. Aidan looked over at Kara, his glance suspicious. Understanding his unspoken question, she shook her head slightly.

Trey frowned as he pointed out several old injuries which he had noted even if Aidan had not. "You've broken your hand several times. This is not the sort of injury that usually occurs in an earthquake either. How did it happen?"

While Kara tried to signal him with a frantic glance, Aidan disregarded her warning and told the truth. "I was doing my best to hurt a man so badly that he couldn't hurt me. It's something I've done fairly often, too."

Trey pressed a button to make the image of Aidan's hand permanent in their files and then asked to see his left. While having no broken bones now, it too showed the signs of previous injuries. Using a strictly professional tone, he gave his patient some advice. "I can fuse the break, but I want you to promise me you won't expect me to do it too often. You might live like a gladiator on 329, but physical violence is unheard of here on Mother. It's simply not tolerated, and I don't want to see either you or Kara suffer just because your ways are different from ours."

"Just please fix my hand," Aidan requested firmly. His shoulder was still a bit stiff, but not so painful he couldn't live with it. "All I'm planning to do is help with the rescue efforts to save people still trapped by the quake."

Apparently satisfied with that response, Trey opened one of the drawers beneath the long counter and took out a slender instrument which he used to shine a soft, warm light on the back of Aidan's injured hand. The battered warrior felt only a slight tingling sensation, but when the doctor asked him to make a fist he found he could do so without feeling any pain. "That's it? You just shine a light on broken bones and they're healed?"

Trey put the remarkable instrument away before he gave a brief explanation of its function. "Actually, the light has nothing to do with it. It merely shows the physician where the beam of energy is focused. It does no more than speed the body's own natural healing process. That's how most of our procedures work."

Intrigued, Aidan flexed his hand several times to be certain he would feel no pain. "Can you repair broken arms and legs as easily?"

"Yes, but it takes a matter of hours or days rather than seconds. It all depends upon which bone was broken, of course, and whether or not it was a clean break."

Kara could see by Aidan's expression that he had many more questions, but all she could think of was Captain Merrill pacing his cabin and growing more furious by the minute when they failed to appear. "You'll find Aidan absorbs knowledge like a sponge, Trey. Can he come and talk with you another time? Merrill is waiting for us now."

"You've no more complaints?" Trey asked routinely, but he doubted a man in as superb physical condition as Aidan appeared to be could have many.

"None that I can think of, but I hope you really will be willing to help us with the earthquake victims," Aidan reminded him.

"As soon as Merrill gives the order," Trey assured him graciously.

"Well, he won't ever give the order if we don't meet with him." Kara grabbed Aidan's elbow and pulled him toward the door. "Thanks, Trey." The doctor waved as they went through the door, but Kara didn't have the time to waste to wave back. "Oh God, I am in so much trouble I will never get out, but once you get Trey talking he'll never stop."

"Is he your doctor?"

"Yes, but not my lover," she insisted emphatically. As they reached the elevators, Kara hit the call button with a furious slap and was delighted when the double doors at their right promptly slid open. Thirty seconds later they were standing in front of the captain's cabin on the second level and all desire for haste had deserted her, but she squared her shoulders and placed her right hand on an opaque panel beside the door and held it still the few seconds required to identify her fingerprints. The door then slid open and Kara reached for Aidan's hand, gripping it tightly as they stepped over the threshold into the captain's quarters. The door had also opened at the end of the small entryway, and they walked through it into the spacious chamber located on Mother's starboard side which served as the captain's office.

The acrylic panels along the exterior wall and overhead gave the room a spectacular view equaled only on the bridge. The dark blue carpeting and soft lighting enhanced the effect of an open terrace. Brightly lit to provide an atmosphere conducive to work during the day, it was now quite late and its owner was ready to relax. He came forward to greet them, his manner far more charming than Kara had thought she had any right to expect.

"I'm sorry we're so late," she began, but then realizing she could scarcely say they had been making love, she kept still and waited for him to respond.

"It is I who owe you an apology, Lieutenant. Let's make ourselves comfortable while I explain why your rescue was so long delayed, and then you can tell me what you'll need in the way of assistance, Aidan." Merrill waited until the bewildered couple had settled themselves on one of the deeply cushioned sofas placed for maximum enjoyment of the view before serving them each a small silver tumbler of an exquisitely flavorful melon liqueur. Rather than sit behind his desk, he moved his chair opposite them. Molded of the same clear acrylic as the rest of the cabin's furnishings, the chair had been specifically designed to fit his proportions and was as elegantly styled as a piece of freestanding sculpture.

"As you said, it's very late and I'm quite tired, but I'll do my best to explain what happened. Your whole squadron was engaged in missions the day we received orders to conduct an immediate drill at full battle conditions."

Astonished, Kara set her tumbler aside on the adjacent acrylic cube. Lit from within with a soft amber glow, it served as both a table and a lamp. "But why?" she asked in dismay. "Alado is a peace-loving corporation."

Merrill pursed his lips thoughtfully as he glanced first at

Kara and then at the powerfully built man at her side. "Excuse me a moment before I answer that, Lieutenant. Just what is your position on 329, Aidan? You definitely look like a man who knows how to take care of himself. Do you have some responsibility for the lives of others as well?"

Aidan didn't know if it was the strangely seductive setting or the captain's bloodred uniform, but he was instantly suspicious of the man's intentions. "I am Captain of the Guard. I am responsible for our city's defense."

"I see. Do you plan strategies for battle and have an opportunity to carry them out?"

"Yes," Aidan assured him confidently.

"Good, then you will understand my predicament perhaps better than Kara would." He paused to refill their glasses with more of the flavorful pale orange liqueur before continuing. "We have drills quite often in order to simulate disasters of one sort or another to allow the crew to practice for a real emergency."

"I understand," Aidan assured him, for he was no stranger to such a practice.

"The order to conduct a battle drill is highly unusual and this one was even more unique. Three months ago Mother was fully reconditioned, and at that time she was outfitted with a device that can create a force field surrounding the ship so that all scanner beams are deflected. The genius who created the mechanism was positive it would render a base ship invisible to detection, but it had yet to be tested under battle conditions. We were forbidden to recall our scouts in flight and instructed to activate the device and see if they would be able to penetrate it and return."

"What?" Kara cried out in an astonished gasp, unable to believe she could possibly have understood him. "You mean when I tried to track Mother's location but found only a void it was merely an electronic smoke screen? I could have followed my own calculations and returned safely even though nothing appeared on my ship's scanners?"

His expression devoid of emotion, Merrill nodded. "Yes. The experiment was twofold in that regard. First we wished to ascertain if the device would successfully deflect the Banshee's scanner beams, and we also wanted to see if any of our scouts would trust their own instincts rather than their guidance equipment and come home regardless of the fact that their scanners couldn't detect Mother's location."

Since a base ship's mission was exploration and its primary responsibility was to safeguard the lives of scouts, not to put them at risk so needlessly, Kara was infuriated to learn she'd been used in such a dangerous and unprincipled experiment. She wanted to shriek every filthy curse she knew, but she realized throwing such a tantrum wouldn't lessen the fury of her temper one bit. Instead she asked a question in the most reasonable tone she could manage, but the icy tone of her voice made her true feelings clear. "Well, how many scouts proved to be a lot smarter than I was? How many made it back on schedule?"

"None," the captain admitted solemnly. "Not one."

While the captain might have thought he had understood why Alado had risked the scouts' lives so recklessly, Aidan did not. He could tell by his wife's horrified expression that she didn't, either. He was glad Trey had been able to mend the bones in his hand, and he doubled both hands into fists as he rose to his feet. "No commander worthy of the name risks his troops' lives in a drill. You could have sent the scouts out knowing exactly what to expect on their return and tested this stupid device without any risk to anyone."

While she agreed with him, Kara rose and grasped Aidan's arm in the hope he would be still. "Wait! I want to know what happened to my squadron. Are Ryan and I the only ones who survived this outrageous experiment?"

Merrill struggled to rise to his feet, his day having been as long and tiring as theirs. "There were six of you out that day, and I have spent every hour since then attempting to rescue you all. You had gone the farthest, and that's why it has taken so long for us to reach you."

"Then you did find all the others?" Kara asked breathlessly, hardly daring hope that they had.

"Thomas Hart and Nicole Perlier are on board along with you and Ryan, but we were unable to find any trace of Cheryl and Ramon or their ships. Whether they are alive or dead we can't be certain. The search is being continued by Fleet Command's rescue teams, so I still have hope they will be found alive."

Stricken by that grim report, Kara swayed slightly and Aidan put his arm around her waist to steady her. "Knowing Alado, I'm certain you consider the test a success since you were able not only to prove this experimental device works, but also rescued the majority of the scouts you betrayed to do it."

"Aidan," Kara spoke his name softly, her request for restraint a mild one since she considered his temperamental outburst justified.

"No, he is right," Merrill admitted readily. "Alado does consider the drill an unqualified success. I, however, have refused to conduct another and will undoubtedly soon be replaced as captain by someone with far more ambition and far less scruples."

"Isn't it a little late for you to be concerned with ethics?" Aidan pointed out snidely.

"Perhaps not," the weary captain mused. "Since the past can not be changed, I suggest you two sit back down while we decide how your planet can best be served by the equipment at my disposal. There may be far more you can do to influence Alado's course, but that will have to wait until the rescue operation is completed to be discussed."

Kara frowned slightly as she looked at Aidan. She had no idea to what the captain was referring, but she was sufficiently intrigued to want to hear it. "I think we should put our personal feelings aside for the moment and request the help needed to free the—" rather than call them moles and spark the captain's curiosity, she quickly chose a less offensive term, "the cave dwellers who are trapped." She pressed Aidan's hand firmly, silently beseeching him to agree rather than create an even more troubling scene.

Aidan wanted to get off the blasted base ship as swiftly as possible. He had been as deeply shocked as his wife by the captain's explanation of the outrageous experiment which had nearly cost her her life, but the man had still not answered the most obvious question: Why did Alado want to mask the location of a base ship? The implication was obvious: to protect the giant vessels in time of war. Aidan had no idea which of the corporations Alado considered potential enemies, but the mere fact that Mother was hovering above 329 made the prospect of war an extremely dangerous one for his people should the hostilities erupt soon.

He saw none of those worries in Kara's glance, only a deep sorrow for the loss of her two friends. While he would have much preferred to refuse Alado's help now that his low opinion of their tactics had been confirmed, he knew he had far too much to learn to be vindictive. He nodded to Kara and when she was seated, he took his place at her side and explained in concise terms what their requirements were.

"You are certain some of these people trapped in the caves are still alive?" Merrill asked first, wanting to be certain his crew wouldn't waste valuable time and effort digging up corpses who would be better off left buried.

"Positive," Aidan assured him. "We've spoken with them through skylights they used to supply both light and air. We have been enlarging one of the skylights in order to pull the people up on ropes, but there is a danger we'll collapse the whole mountainside in on them so we've been working very cautiously."

Understanding the rescue operation was complicated by the unstable nature of the hillside, Merrill excused himself to go to his desk where he first turned on the overhead screen, then used the intercom to request that equipment and personnel be dispatched immediately to the surface of 329. Looking up, he spoke to them again. "Do you wish to spend the night here, or return to the disaster site?"

Kara was clearly too tired to go back, so Aidan made his own decision quickly. "Can I use your speaker to give directions to my men? If so, I'll wait until morning to return."

"Of course, come to my desk and you may do so from here." Merrill first gave the command to activate the exterior speakers, then stepped back. "Just speak as you normally do. You'll be heard and can hear and see the responses."

Since he knew Zac wouldn't leave until all the moles had been rescued, Aidan addressed him by name and was pleased when his friend promptly moved into view of the screen. He winked at Kara as he explained briefly that help would soon arrive and that he would return at dawn. When Zac acknowledged his message, Aidan walked back to his wife, took her hands and lifted her easily to her feet.

"Just a minute, Lieutenant," Merrill called before she could leave. "Clearly you've disobeyed several of Alado's standing orders while on 329, but as far as I'm concerned the fact you've survived is all that matters. That's the only piece of information which will be placed in your file."

"Thank you, sir," Kara replied gratefully, for she knew only too well what a disgrace the truth would create. It would make her appear completely undisciplined, and no scout could afford to have such a reputation.

Aidan, however, reacted far differently. "The conditions under which she was allowed to become lost ought to be mentioned as well as the fact that she was rescued and protected by the man who became her husband," he pointed out swiftly.

"You are a very clever young man, Aidan. As I said, we will have more to discuss after the rescue mission is complete. Good night."

Since they had been clearly dismissed and were getting away without the reprimand for impertinence she thought Merrill had every right to give, Kara again took Aidan's hand and emphatically tugged him toward the door. She didn't draw a deep breath until they were out in the hallway. "The captain is the only one who has quarters on the second level. We'll have to take the elevator again to go to the fourth level, where the rest of us live."

"Is your cabin as nice as his?"

Kara gave Aidan a skeptical glance as she shook her head. "Not quite, but I do have a choice location and therefore a nice view. Are you hungry? We could get something to eat."

"No, I'm too tired to eat." Aidan rested his hand on her waist as they left the elevator and walked to her cabin. As it had in the captain's quarters, the door opened after her fingerprints had been identified as belonging to a person authorized to enter. "What if I were by myself, how would I get into your room?"

"We'll put your prints into the master computer in the morning, and then you'll have no problem moving about at will," Kara informed him through a wide yawn. "I'm sorry, but I'm so tired I can scarcely keep my eyes open."

As soon as Aidan had stepped into her well-designed and neatly kept quarters, the door slid shut behind him. The far wall and a portion of the ceiling above it were acrylic, providing the double bed below with the impressive canopy of the nighttime sky. To his right was an acrylic chair and desk with built-in shelves above. Adjacent to that was a large viewing screen and the communications equipment provided in all rooms. Two thickly padded lounge chairs placed opposite the screen were the room's only other furnishings. The left wall was taken up with closets for storage of Kara's clothing and possessions. A door at the end of the closets led into the bathroom.

Dismayed to find her quarters no larger than his bedroom, Aidan first checked to be certain there was no door leading to another room before he spoke. "Is this all you have to call home?"

Kara switched on the screen so he could watch the rescue mission taking place below while she prepared for bed. "This is considered more than adequate space for a single person. Married couples and families are entitled to more, of course." She slid open the closet doors and removed a flimsy pink garment from a hook.

"What's that?" Aidan asked with a chuckle as he reached out to catch the hem.

"It is a nightgown," Kara informed him sweetly as she entered the bathroom. "I'll be just a minute."

As he waited for her, Aidan stood close to the screen where he could recognize his friends easily as they scurried about lugging heavy buckets of dirt and cumbersome coils of rope. They had yet to begin bringing up moles, but he was certain with the equipment the captain had promised they would have rescued quite a few by dawn. When Kara came out of the bathroom wearing the gown of feather-soft pink silk, she moved into his arms and he gave her a loving hug. "You look very lovely, but I thought you were tired."

"I am, but I don't often invite a man to spend the night here with me, and I don't want to waste a minute of it."

Aidan slipped his fingers through her flame-red curls to tilt her lips up to his. "I'll try not to disappoint you then," he whispered softly just before their lips met in a lingering kiss.

He had never expected to be a guest aboard one of Alado's ships or share a bed crowned with a halo of stars, but the prospect was most inviting with Kara as his companion. Destiny had given him a remarkable bride, and as he carried her to the bed he had a moment to wonder what further adventures fate might have in store before he was too lost in her loving to think at all.

CHAPTER
◇ **XVIII** ◇

As the rescue sleds from Mother began to arrive, Zac found the situation every bit as ironic as Aidan, for he had never expected either to work cooperatively with Alado or to have such a high regard for a mole. Dressed in yellow overalls and white helmets, the rescue crew from Alado were both male and female and spent only a few minutes observing the terrain and discussing what had already been done before setting up their equipment. Since the skylight had been enlarged successfully to provide access to the chamber where the survivors of the quake were huddled, they lowered an expansion ladder suspended from a crane down through it. Mounted on the back of one of the rescue sleds, the apparatus added no additional weight to the mountainside above the cavern and therefore posed no threat to the lives of those trapped below.

As the first of the moles scrambled up the ladder, Zac held his breath and prayed Serafina would be among them, but they were all small children. As soon as they emerged, their attention became riveted on Mother, and they stood staring up at the colossal ship with gaping mouths and wide, terror-filled eyes. Worn out by their ordeal, the youngsters clung tightly to one another, their circle widening with each new arrival until the more compassionate of the city dwellers drew them aside where they would be out of the way and gave them something warm to eat and a soothing spiced herb beverage to drink.

Zac was already standing as close as he dared, but the second group to traverse the ladder proved only to be slightly older children and again did not include Serafina. No longer able to hide his anxiety, he asked one of the boys if he had seen the young woman.

"No, I've not seen her," the frightened lad replied, but as Zac turned away to ask another, he reached out to grab his hand. "I heard someone say she would not leave her grandfather. He is an old man and too badly injured to move."

"What? Are you certain?" He knew from Kara's description that the mountain was a vast network of tunnels, like an anthill, and Zac feared Serafina's loyalty to the elderly man might cost her her life. He waited as more children appeared, followed by several women carrying infants. Those emerging were all adults now, but the overwhelming majority were women followed by a few men well up in years. When he saw no young men coming up the ladder, he approached an elderly man he had seen on market days and made an offer he knew would be honored. "Your men needn't fear we'll attack them at such a time. Please call down to them to come up, too."

The horrible strain of the hours since the quake showing plainly in the man's slumped posture and weary expression, he was nonetheless reluctant to admit the truth. "There are no more of our men left alive," he mumbled numbly.

Zac scanned the large crowd of moles, unable to believe

the man's words. "Only women, children and a few elderly men survived the quake? That makes no sense. How could all the warriors have perished without their women or families being harmed?"

The old man remained silent, shuffling his feet nervously, but when Zac proved to be relentless in questioning about the circumstances surrounding the men's deaths, he finally spoke again. "The warriors were in the great hall," he began hesitantly. "They were talking of things that concern only men. When the quake collapsed the roof, they were all buried alive."

"All of them? Kyle, too? Oh, I know only a few of your names, but all were killed? All of them?" Zac could scarcely believe the old man's tale was true, yet his voice and expression were as mournful as his words.

"Yes, we have lost them all," he insisted tearfully.

Zac gave the grief-stricken man a sympathetic pat on the shoulder but took the precaution of verifying his story through conversations with several others before he began to believe it. If the adult male mole population had all been together, they could have been doing only one thing: preparing to attack the city. Was it simply a trick of fate that had led them to plot an assault on the night that would prove to be their last? For their war council to end in a mass burial was exactly what he believed the hairy bastards deserved, but he also realized such a terrible tragedy for the moles would have a profound effect on his city as well.

When no one had appeared at the top of the ladder for several minutes, the crane operator prepared to lift it, but Zac called out for him to wait. "Just a minute, I think there may be injured who'll need help climbing up. I want to go down and see what assistance is needed."

"I think you better hurry," a lanky engineer who had introduced himself as Tweed advised as he pulled off his helmet to wipe the sweat from his brow. "From what I've overheard, the tunnels are all unsafe now. I'm going to ask Captain Merrill for permission to use explosives to seal them."

Outraged that the man thought he had such authority on

329, Zac waved him back. "You are here at our invitation. No explosives will be set unless we give that order."

"If one of those tunnels falls in on you, everyone will agree the order wasn't given soon enough," Tweed threatened harshly.

Ignoring that sarcastic comment, Zac quickly called out to the moles gathered nearby. "I know Domingo is injured and his granddaughter stayed with him. Does anyone know where they are or if there are others still in the caves?" He waited while his question was discussed, but each time someone thought a family might be missing, they were located elsewhere in the crowd. Finally he was satisfied that everyone was accounted for except Serafina and her grandfather. "All right then, where are they? I'll go down and get them myself." That offer was met with considerable skepticism at first, then several teenage boys volunteered to accompany him, but Zac refused to accept their help, thinking that the lives of the few males who had survived ought not to be risked. He listened carefully to the directions to Domingo's apartments, then repeated them aloud to be certain he understood.

"You'll never be able to remember all that," the engineer from Mother exclaimed, not realizing how greatly the people of 329 relied on their excellent memories. "Wait a minute." He walked around to the front of his sled and returned carrying a clipboard holding a pad of paper with a pen conveniently attached by a thin cord. Standing next to the mole who had supplied the directions, he began to sketch a map with her help. "Here's the room where we lowered the ladder; four corridors lead from it and—"

Zac was as fascinated as the mole as the tall stranger created a map to the precise specifications he was given. When it was complete, he tore the sheet of paper from the pad and handed it to him.

"Thank you. I'm sure this will be helpful." Zac didn't care to admit he had never before seen a map, but the drawing of the passageways was so easy to understand he was certain he could put it to good use.

"I just don't want three people lost," Tweed responded gruffly. "Here, take this light and hurry."

Zac had planned to take a lantern, but the device the suddenly helpful volunteer had provided was a thin cylinder that produced a broad beam of light and was far easier to carry. "Thanks again. I'll be back." He was surprised then as the moles called out to wish him luck. Of course, he was hoping to rescue two of their number, but still, the thoughtful gesture was strangely touching coming from them.

Having no idea what to expect, Zac made his way down the ladder, then paused at the bottom to look around the spacious room the survivors had occupied. A few blankets had been left behind as well as a canteen or two. The air was filled with the scent of some peculiar incense making him wonder if perhaps he was standing in their church. He had no idea if any of the moles were particularly religious, but rather than tarry to analyze the room's function, he looked at his map and headed down the tunnel which led off to the right.

As soon as he had entered the narrow passage, he felt as though the walls were closing in around him, suffocating him with an oppressive silence, and he immediately broke out in a cold sweat. All his life he had heard tales of the horrors of the mines, but this was his first experience in one and he knew he would never have survived such a dark, dismal world for more than a few days. His respect for his great-grandparents increased tenfold. He had never considered himself a coward, but had it not been his precious Serafina who needed him, he knew he would have swiftly turned back. Thinking only of how badly he wanted to find her, he continued through the subterranean maze clutching the light tightly in one hand and the map which had grown damp from his sweaty palm in the other. He prayed the woman who had provided the directions had not forgotten the placement of one of the tunnels, for if she had not remembered their location correctly then he might wander around for hours without even coming close to Serafina and Domingo.

The dank air was laden with dust, and the path under his feet was strewn with rubble. In some places Zac had to get down on his hands and knees to crawl through the tunnels since they had become almost impassable. He stopped to rest briefly each time he came to a large chamber and tried to force away the terror the close confines of the passage-ways evoked, but he could only struggle valiantly to suppress it and never overcame it completely.

Finally Zac reached the point where he thought Domingo had lived.

"Serafina!" he called out with what he hoped would pass for confidence rather than the scream of fright it truly was. When he heard her answer his heart filled with joy, but he took several deep breaths to steady himself before he dared face her. He followed the path to his left until it opened out into a room which had been spacious and attractively furnished before a third of its ceiling had collapsed. He found Serafina sitting cross-legged on the rug, her grandfather's head cradled in her lap. The elderly man's pale skin looked ashen, and even without feeling his pulse Zac knew Domingo was dead. He sat down beside the girl he adored, gave her a reassuring smile and tried to think of some sympathetic words that wouldn't sound trite.

At first Serafina was certain she was dreaming, but when his shoulder brushed hers, she knew Zac was really there. But that was impossible. "Zac, what are you doing here?" she asked in a startled gasp.

The trails of her tears were clearly visible on her rosy cheeks and there were shadows under her bright blue eyes, but even if not overjoyed, she didn't seem displeased to see him. The dark-eyed young man decided the effort it had cost him to reach her had been well worth it. "We're evacuating the caves. You and Domingo weren't with the others, so I came to find you. I'm so sorry I got here too late to help him."

Serafina continued to hold her grandfather tightly as though he were merely sleeping and she did not wish to wake him. For a few splendid seconds she had hoped Zac might say he had come to find her because he loved her, but now she felt very foolish for having had such a dream and began to blush. "Did the city people really come to help us?" she asked softly.

"Well, of course!" Zac exclaimed. "Wouldn't your people have come to help us if the situation were reversed?"

Serafina thought such a generous gesture doubtful. "No, I don't think so," she admitted honestly.

"Well, we'll never know the true answer to that question, so let's not worry about it. The earthquake damaged our city, too, but not nearly as badly as yours." He wondered how much she knew and swiftly decided it wasn't a good time to give her the news of how many moles had been killed if she had not already heard it. "You'll all have to live in the city for a while until you can rebuild your homes, but I doubt anyone will want to return to the caves."

Serafina looked around the room, remembering how pretty it had once been, and hurriedly apologized for its present sorry state. "This was a very pleasant home, Zac. Perhaps it does not look that way to you now, but I was happy here."

She seemed so desperately sad that Zac was compelled to put his arm around her shoulders and give her a sympathetic squeeze. "You can't stay here much longer, little lady. It's far too dangerous now."

She had wrapped a blanket around her grandfather and he thought perhaps they might be able to use it to drag his body through the tunnels. Domingo had spent his whole life in the caves, though, and Zac could think of no more fitting place to bury him.

"You'll have to leave him, Serafina. Now we must go."

Before he could rise, she lay her hand on his knee to keep him at her side. "Oh, please, won't you let me stay with him just a little while longer?" she begged with a soft, pleading glance.

Zac knew they could not tarry because the danger of being trapped by additional cave-ins was too great. He shook his head and said, "We must go. Is there anything you would like to bring? I could start gathering it together," he offered helpfully.

Serafina thought a moment, then nodded toward her

grandfather's workbench in the corner. "I want to bring his tools. He refused to give me lessons, but I watched him make jewelry for so many years that I'm certain I can carry on his trade. I should have a trade, don't you think, now that I'm all alone?"

Zac reached out to brush away a strand of hair that had escaped her braid and smiled when she did not draw away. "I don't think you'll be all alone, Serafina. Don't you have other relatives?"

"Only a few cousins," she replied wistfully. "Or at least I did have some as of the day before yesterday. I'm not certain if I still do."

"Well, there must be someone who'll take you in." Zac held his breath, wishing with all his heart it could be he.

Serafina looked down at her grandfather, her thoughts on far happier days. "He was very good to me, Zac, and I will miss him terribly no matter where I go."

Zac could not imagine a less romantic setting, but his feelings were becoming much too difficult to hide. "Serafina, how old are you? I know that must sound silly when I've watched you grow up, but just what is your age?"

Thinking his purpose was merely to distract her from her sadness, the blond replied without hesitation. "I am seventeen."

"Seventeen?" Zac found that difficult to believe. "How can you possibly be seventeen years old?"

"It's a simple matter really," Serafina responded with a slight trace of her usually sunny smile. "I was born seventeen years ago."

"But I thought all the mole women—" He caught himself and, ashamed for having used the derogatory term to her face, apologized and began anew. "I'm sorry, what I meant is that I thought your girls still married at sixteen."

"Some of them do," Serafina replied, her expression growing troubled. "But my grandfather and I were not ready to accept challenges for me, and I have no idea what will happen to me now."

Even if she had loved one of the young men, he would now be dead. Zac simply nodded and fell silent as he rose to clean off Domingo's workbench. "Your grandfather was a wonderful craftsman. His pieces were always unique. I hope you can make such pretty things, too."

"To whom do you give all the things you've bought from us? Do you have many girlfriends or just one who wears it all?" Serafina asked shyly.

Domingo had worn a leather apron, and Zac continued to slip his tools into the pockets as he replied with a deceptively innocent answer. "There are many pretty women in the city and most are my friends. I enjoy giving them nice presents."

"You were always our favorite customer," Serafina confided sweetly. "You really appreciated the beauty of my grandfather's work while many people could not."

Zac barely heard her voice above the pounding of his heart. He might never have another chance to talk with her alone, and yet he couldn't bring himself to speak of love. Everything had changed since the earthquake, absolutely everything, and he clung to the hope that there would be many more changes to come.

Until that day, however, how could he offer marriage? If she refused even to consider it, his heart would never mend. Wouldn't it be better to hope she might have loved him than to hear her say she didn't? He envied his best friend, since Aidan had simply ignored the many barriers that might have prevented him from taking the wife of his choosing. Aidan never seemed to ponder his actions as thoughtfully as Zac knew he did, and yet when he chose to act, it was always decisively. Why couldn't he behave in the same confident manner? If it worked so well for Aidan, wouldn't it work equally well for him? Why couldn't he say "I love you" to the only girl he had ever really loved? "Serafina," he called as he turned, determined finally to end his tormenting silence before he lost his nerve.

The lovely girl had already slid her grandfather's head from her lap, raised the blanket to cover his face, and begun to rise. "I'm ready to go now. Thank you for giving me a few more minutes to tell him good-bye. That was very kind."

"Kind?" Zac mumbled absently. He wanted to be so much more than kind. "I'm so sorry about your grandfather. I know how much you loved him," was all he could manage to say, and it sounded hollow even in his own ears.

"Thank you. He knew it, too, and that's all that's important to me." She came to his side to fold up the apron in which Zac had stored the tools and gave the ruins of her home one last glance. "Did you have trouble finding me? If so, I better lead the way out. If you'll tell me which way, that is. I don't know which entrances were blocked."

The dear old man who had raised her was dead and Serafina was taking it calmly because they had enjoyed their love while he had been alive. That was a lesson Zac knew he had waited too long to learn. "I have a map. Can you understand it?"

Serafina turned the wrinkled paper several ways before she finally realized the pictures denoted the relative position of the underground city's many chambers. "Where did you get this, Zac? Who made it?"

"That story is too long to begin." He handed her the lantern which had lit the room and gestured for her to precede him. He glanced back at the old jeweler's body and shivered slightly. To speak of love now would be ghoulish, and he wanted only to get outside where he could breathe the fresh air in hungry gulps.

He was relieved to find Serafina moved so easily through the perplexing maze of corridors that even when they were forced to crawl a few yards, it did not slow them down. When they reached the entrance of the fragrant chamber where the ladder still stood waiting she stopped so abruptly that he bumped into her. Feeling very clumsy, he hastily apologized. "I'm sorry, I was looking at the ladder and I should have been watching you."

The pretty blond turned to face him, her grandfather's apron clutched tightly at her side. "You have been such a wonderful friend, Zac. Would you mind if I kissed you? I know your people do not like ours, but just this once, would you mind terribly?"

"I wouldn't mind at all," Zac confessed with the rakish

grin he usually reserved for other young women. There was plenty of light pouring through the opening overhead, so he laid the light he had been given aside with the map and waited while she put down the apron and lantern. They were already standing so close that it was a simple matter for him to slip his arms around her waist to draw her near. He moved cautiously then, hoping he would not frighten her, yet wanting to savor the moment forever as his lips began to caress hers softly. When she relaxed in his embrace and raised her arms to encircle his neck he was so delighted he hugged her tighter, then began to free her honey-blond hair from its confining braid. The glossy strands were far finer than his dark curls, and he wound his fingers in her flowing tresses as he whispered hungrily, "Open your mouth, Serafina, like this." She followed his directions shyly and then, finding the warmth of his tongue very pleasant, she began to tease him with sweet, deep kisses of her own.

Knowing both the time and place were horribly inappropriate didn't serve to cool his ardor even slightly, and Zac began to explore gently the smooth swells of Serafina's slender figure. At first it was only a gentle pressure from his thumbs to harden the tender crests of her nipples to delightful buds. When that brought a sweet sigh to her lips he traced the full contours of her high, firm breasts with his fingertips. Gradually he moved his hands around her, down her spine and over her hips to mold her body to his, then up again to stroke the soft fullness of her breasts. Her response to his lavish caresses was so loving that he could no longer resist the temptation to reach under her short smock to enjoy the luscious feel of her bare skin. His adoring touch grew ever more bold until she was swaying dizzily in his arms, calling his name in such an enticing whisper that nothing else mattered to him but pleasing her.

Serafina was certain that once they left the caves Zac would again become the friendly stranger he had always been, and she wanted to delay that horrible moment of separation for as long as she possibly could. She clung to him, wantonly encouraging his advances, and when he grabbed a discarded blanket and drew her back into the darkened corridor to peel away what few clothes she wore, her only concern was to shed her garments rapidly to speed the return to his arms. She loved being able to put her arms around him to hold him close, for she enjoyed the hardness of his chest pressing against the softness of her flesh, his taut, flat stomach, and the smooth curve of his hip. When she boldly began to explore the last of his marvelous body's secrets, she was thrilled rather than frightened to find him fully aroused. When he pushed his knee between her thighs to separate her legs, she rubbed against him, inviting him as she had each step of the way to make their few stolen moments of bliss a memory so wild and yet so pleasurable he would never be able to forget her.

She ran her fingers through his thick black curls to press his face close as he lowered his mouth to her breasts, teasing first one and then the other until the flushed pink tips were swollen with the rapture of his kisses. All the while his fingertips moved through the tangle of curls between her thighs, drawing her ever nearer the brink of ecstasy until her knees grew so weak they could no longer support her slight weight, and she slid slowly to the blanket he had dropped carelessly at their feet.

Drawn down beside her, Zac continued to kiss and caress the young beauty, eagerly feeding the fires of her desire until he was also consumed in the searing heat of passion's flames. His rational mind completely suppressed, he rode the crest of emotion sweeping through him, not once hesitating to consider how far he had led her until he felt her draw away in pain as his first possessive thrust drove deep within her. She didn't cry out or try to escape him, but suddenly she was so still beneath him that he came to his senses with a savage jolt. He had come to rescue the young woman, not rape her! Dear God, what had he done? He cradled her tenderly in his arms and lay still without withdrawing, knowing nothing he could say would undo the harm he had just inflicted. "I'm sorry," he whispered softly, longing to speak of love but fearing she would now consider such a declaration only a convenient lie.

Serafina felt him begin to move away then, but locked her

hands behind his back and refused to let him go. "Oh please don't be sorry. Please don't. This is all I'll ever know of love, and I can't bear to think you're sorry you made love to me. Lie if you must, but please don't say you're sorry, for I can't bear to think that you don't want to be with me." She began to sob silently, humiliated to think she had lured him into doing something he had come to regret so soon.

Zac was near tears himself by then, outraged that the customs of past generations made it so difficult for them to follow their hearts. No longer content to accept the mistaken notion that love between them was forbidden, he kissed away her tears and offered the words of reassurance that flooded his heart and soul.

"I love you, Serafina. This isn't all we'll have of love, it's only the beginning. I want you for my wife, from this minute on, for always. It tore my heart in two to see you only once each month and to know you would never be mine. I can think of no torture worse than the agony I've endured since the first day I saw you. I have wanted you so badly and for so very long."

His next words were lost as her mouth captured his in a searching kiss which clearly revealed her longing was every bit as deep as his own. Wanting only to complete what he had begun, he moved very slowly, tenderly striving to show her love's deepest pleasure rather than a renewed burst of pain. The sweetness of her kiss was so intoxicating, however, that he soon found it impossible to restrain the impulse to lose himself in the excitement of her love. With an abandon born of long, smoldering desire he carried her spirit aloft with his, thrilled to the very marrow with the depth of her response. She was even more captivating than he had dreamed she would be, and he had never felt so completely loved as he did lying locked in her fond embrace.

It was too dark in the tunnel for Serafina to see Zac's expression clearly, but she had heard each of his words. She wanted to stay with him always, to make love endlessly, but knew they dared not tarry another moment there. She smoothed his tangled curls off his forehead and kissed him one last time. "We must hurry," she whispered in a voice

still slurred with passion. "Someone else might come looking for us."

"No, no one else will come down here, but you're right.
We have too much to do to remain here all day." He leaned
down to nuzzle her breasts playfully, then rolled to his side.
"I'm going to take you home with me. Don't argue about it
either, because it's where you belong." He got up and hastily
pulled on his shorts. "Let me see if there's some water in
one of the canteens left behind so we can clean up properly."

Serafina responded with a throaty giggle. "Oh Zac, don't
you think it's too late to worry about being proper?"

Zac laughed with her, but he was very happy to find there
was enough water left in one of the canteens to rinse all
evidence of their passionate union from her supple young
body. As he helped her wash herself, she distracted him so
terribly with her teasing kisses and lilting giggles that a long
while passed before he was finally ready to escort her up the
ladder.

Aidan found the shower in Kara's quarters much too narrow for a man with his broad shoulders and washed hurriedly, eager to return to the rescue operation. She had
several foil-wrapped toothbrushes, so he helped himself to
one and borrowed one of the razors he found in a package. It
annoyed him to think she kept the items for impromptu visits
from male guests. Despite his best intentions not to do so,
when he woke her to say good-bye he could not keep his
curiosity to himself. "If Ryan is too intense, and Trey too
talkative, what about the captain? Have you and he—"

"Aidan!" Kara interrupted with an exaggerated show of
indignation. She sat up, glaring angrily. "Are you going to
interrogate me about every man we meet?"

"Probably," he admitted with a sheepish grin. He bent
down to retrieve her pink nightgown from the floor where it
had lain all night and replaced it on its hook in her closet. "I
know it's unforgivable, but I'm not used to having a reason
to be jealous."

"You have no reason to be jealous now. Captain Merrill

would never sleep with the women in his crew since that's the surest way to ruin two careers."

Puzzled by that statement, Aidan sat down on the foot of her bed. "You didn't worry about your career when you took lovers?"

"Never, because they always knew how much my career meant to me." Knowing she was making no sense at all, she reached out to take his hand. "I'm merely a scout, however, and that's entirely different from being the captain, since he evaluates our performances and gives out the assignments. Can't you see what a problem he'd have on his hands if it were known he'd been intimate with one of us? He'd be accused of being partial to one woman and she would be accused of using him to get the assignments or promotions she wanted. It would be disastrous for both of them."

"Why does it sound to me like you've given that speech before?"

Kara blushed deeply, embarrassed she had been so transparent. "I'm sorry. I've never been involved with Captain Merrill, but there was a first officer once, several years ago when I was much more naïve and had no idea how much dissension our affair would cause. He transferred to another base ship when I refused to marry him, and I learned my lesson very well from him."

"I didn't mean to pry," Aidan apologized sincerely. "It was merely the way Merrill looked at you that made me wonder."

Confused, Kara shrugged. "I never noticed anything unusual in his glance. He has always been very proper with me. I think you're imagining things, Aidan, and please don't look for problems where none exist." The warrior nodded, but he did not really look convinced, so she continued, "I've stayed on board Mother my whole career—my whole life, really—but many scouts like to move from ship to ship and request transfers frequently. There was only one scout still serving on Mother who might have given you a hard time about me, and that was Ramon. I'm very much afraid he's dead. That makes you the only man on board who can call himself my lover. Are you happy now?"

Aidan tried to smile, although he doubted he was very successful. "I'm sorry. This whole conversation should never have taken place, and I'll not interrogate you, as you put it, ever again. Now, I want to go back down to see what's happened with the moles. If you want to come with me, you'll have to hurry."

Kara replied with an impish grin. "Oh really? How did you plan to return to 329 if I'm not ready to fly you there?"

"You're not the only pilot on board."

"No, but I'm the only one where you're concerned," Kara warned him playfully.

"Don't tell me you're going to be jealous now."

"I hope not. Give me a minute and I'll get dressed. We need to stop and get something to eat, too, and that will give me the opportunity to introduce you to my friends."

Aidan's gaze was warmly appreciative as he watched her walk past him into the bathroom. He swore he would never tire of looking at her gorgeous body, even if she didn't have such marvelous tattoos. "Are you sure you want to introduce me to them?" he called loudly, hoping to be heard above the noise of the shower.

"Of course!" Kara replied. "You're my husband!"

"For the time being," he mused softly. He made the bed, then turned on the viewing screen in hopes the scanners would still be focused on the rescue site, but he found instead a recording of a symphony orchestra. Wondering if the musicians were on board, he moved close to observe the different instruments, few of which they had in his city.

When Kara left the bathroom to get a clean uniform and lingerie, she found Aidan's rapt interest in the concert so amusing that she walked up behind him and gave him a hug. "What sort of music do you have on 329? I never heard any."

"Drums, guitars, flutes, but people play them for their own enjoyment, not in groups like this one. These musicians are very good."

"Yes, they are very fine." She showed him how to switch the channels since Mother provided a large variety of program options when the screens weren't being used for the ship's business. Then she gathered up her clothes. "Watch whatever you like, I'll be just a few more minutes."

When she returned, he was still so fascinated with the musical program that he had not touched the control. "As soon as we have a free moment, I'll take you to the history files. You'll love it there. You can request any information you would like and it will be displayed for you on a viewing screen."

"What sort of information?" Aidan asked as he followed her to the door.

"Why, anything you could possibly name." She continued to encourage his interest as they approached the elevators. "I'm afraid we had little time for a tour last night, but the basic organization of the ship is a simple and logical one. At the top is the bridge which is the control center for flight. Access is restricted, so you will not be allowed up there without the captain's permission. The second level contains the main work area for our mission. That's where all the scouts' films and reports are organized and maps are made. Our training takes place there and that's also where the history files are located. It's a confusing place, so you better wait for me to go through it with you. As I told you last night, the captain's quarters are also there so he can reach the bridge swiftly in an emergency. The third level contains all the shops, dining halls, restaurants, entertainment centers, recreational facilities and the medical unit. It will take us days to visit it all, but I think you'll enjoy it. Half of the fourth level is reserved for housing while the other half is comprised of the laboratories that produce our food. I want you to see that. It's like a jungle."

"A jungle?" Aidan asked skeptically, having only the barest idea of what a jungle was like.

"Yes. We have gardens like yours, only the plants are grown in vats of chemicals rather than soil. Now that brings us to the fifth level which contains the docking bays and some space for storage of cargo while the sixth is where all the power for the ship is generated and the rest of the cargo is stored. That level is strictly off limits, so do not even consider going down there."

"Let's see, I'm to stay off the bridge and wait for you to show me the second and third levels. I guess it's all right for me to be on the fourth level but until I put my prints into the computer, I can't open the door to your room and I would certainly not risk getting lost in a jungle of any sort. I know I would only be in the way in the docking bays and I'm barred from entering the sixth level. Is that it? In other words, I'm to stick with you?"

She was startled by his sarcasm, but before Kara could reply the door of the elevator slid open, and they stepped out onto a flower-bordered concourse lined with staff dining rooms as well as a wide variety of restaurants ranging from snack bars to elegant establishments serving the finest cuisines. More than a city block in length, the sights and sounds represented home to Kara, but she could see by Aidan's startled expression that he was simply amazed. "What would you like for breakfast? Most of my friends eat in the officers' mess hall and they serve everything you could possibly want there."

The few people milling about at that hour were dressed in well-tailored uniforms similar in style to Kara's but in a wide variety of hues, some in brilliant colors and others cool pastels. He looked down at his shorts and boots, gave his vest a tug and then shook his head. "I don't know, maybe we should wait and eat later."

"No one will care in the slightest what you're wearing, Aidan. Besides, I'm too hungry to wait." She took his hand, shoved open the doors of the officers' mess and, finding several of her friends still lingering over morning tea, waved to them. While Ryan remained in his seat, the others leapt from their chairs and rushed over to surround her and greet her with excited hugs and kisses. "Oh, thank you! I've missed you all terribly, too!" Kara replied graciously, giving each an enthusiastic hug in return.

"Now why do I find that impossible to believe?" Thomas Hart exclaimed as he gave Aidan an enthusiastic handshake. A compactly built young man, he was short and stocky with curly reddish brown hair and hundreds of freckles. A friendly soul, he noted the pride with which Kara introduced her husband and saw to it that Aidan was swiftly drawn into the conversation so the handsome warrior did not merely become the subject of it. Thomas had been as shocked as the rest of them by Ryan's tale of the barbarian Kara had married, but he soon realized the scout's description of Aidan had obviously been colored by jealousy. "Come on, let's all sit down. You two must be hungry, and we'll keep you company while you eat."

As Aidan enjoyed his third helping of bacon and eggs, he marveled at what a congenial group Kara's friends were. He had never expected to be accepted with the warmth they had displayed. Perhaps it was merely the affection they felt for her, but they made him feel like a welcome addition to their close-knit group rather than an outsider. Their questions about his home were respectful, not taunting, and he liked them all very much despite the fact the uniforms they wore were Alado's. Ryan had left the room as soon as they had been seated, so Aidan knew it would be difficult to win his respect, but for the moment he was content to enjoy the good food and the lively friendship of those who had offered it willingly.

Zac led Serafina out into the large chamber, meaning to rebraid her hair where the light was good, but he stopped short when he saw Aidan seated on the bottom step of the ladder. "How long have you been sitting there?" he asked hoarsely, certain his friend hadn't been there when he had come for the canteen, though that had been some time ago.

"Long enough." Aidan raised his hand briefly to his mouth in a vain attempt to subdue the width of his grin. He rose to his feet and came forward, chuckling deeply as he wrapped his friend in a boisterous bear hug. "I don't want to hear another word from you about the fact that I failed to confide in you when I first met Kara. It's plain from your expression that you've kept an awful lot to yourself, too. Now why don't you introduce us?"

"Serafina, this is my best friend. His name is Aidan, and I hope you'll learn to like him, although I know it will take some time," Zac teased in return, relieved that his friend had chosen to be discreet.

Since she had seen the blond warrior rip his knife through Cruz's belly with the cool disregard for life a born killer displays, Serafina wasn't certain she wanted Aidan for a friend and moved closer to Zac. "How do you do?" she replied stiffly.

Thinking the sweet young woman was merely embarrassed, Aidan leaned down to give her cheek a light kiss. "My wife told me how kind you were to her. That's why I came down here to help Zac find you. I'm glad to see he doesn't need my help, though. Now let's get out of here before the roof caves in on us."

"Just a minute. I want to fix Serafina's hair," Zac insisted. He stepped behind her, divided her long straight hair into three sections and quickly fashioned a neat braid. "There, how does it look?"

"Beautiful," Aidan replied with a wink. The blond was extremely pretty, and the love which lit her eyes when she looked up at Zac made her lovelier still. "Now, before we go up the ladder, do you know what you're going to say when you get there?"

Zac broke into a wide grin. "Yes, I'm going to announce that I'm taking Serafina as my wife, and I'll fight any man foolish enough to argue about it."

"Perfect." Aidan stood aside to let them precede him up the ladder, laughing still that his often reticent friend had suddenly become such a man of action. Everything had changed, it seemed, and perhaps it was about time.

CHAPTER
◇ **XIX** ◇

"Use explosives to close the mines?" Barret shook his head. "No, that's neither Alado's decision to make nor ours, but the moles', or what's left of them."

Tweed was becoming more disgusted by the minute. "I was asked for advice and I gave it. If you don't block the tunnels now, people will keep going back for one thing or another until another quake knocks everything loose and buries a few more—except it will be women and children who are killed the next time. Blast them shut now and you'll save yourself a lot of grief later."

Aidan had relieved Zac who had, to the surviving moles' amazement, announced his plans to wed Serafina and then promptly left to take her to his home. Since he was again in charge, Aidan was not reluctant to state his opinion. "I agree with you both. Those cursed mines should be sealed for good, but it's not my decision to make. You would not appreciate it if I declared your home unfit to live in and blew it up, would you?"

"No, of course not," Tweed agreed impatiently. "I doubt they would listen to me, though. One of you will have to get the approval. Since it's not likely to come today, I'll take the crew and go on down the hill to the city." He turned away to shout orders to the workers who had come with him, and after the first rescue sled had started its engines nothing more could be heard.

Aidan waited until Kara's Banshee was the only piece of Alado's equipment left nearby before he spoke again.

"Whenever there has been a problem, I've solved it with my fists, but what are we going to do with all these homeless moles?" He glanced over to where Kara was playing with a group of small children and felt a pang of regret that it wouldn't be possible for her to conceive for several more months. Then a slow satisfied grin lit his expression with hope as he realized with Mother there, the risk of removing her implant couldn't be all that great. Knowing that was something he would have to take up with her privately, however, he hastily forced his mind back to the subject at hand. "Look, what I'm trying to say is that what we need here is someone to take on the responsibility to see all these widows, orphans and elderly men find homes. Someone bright and resourceful, someone who—"

Certain he knew what was coming, Barret raised his hands and started to back away. "Oh no you don't. I've got too much to do already."

With each step he took backward, Aidan took a step forward so the distance between them didn't widen despite the banker's attempt to escape. "Kara told me the moles had attractive women, but I didn't believe it until I saw them today. Have you noticed how pretty some of them are? Take the one with the two little blond boys over there, the strawberry blond? Do you see the woman I mean?"

While he had noticed her some time ago, since he considered her a good deal more than merely attractive, Barret was still reluctant to admit Aidan was right. "What do you expect me to do, marry the woman and adopt her two children?"

"Yes, that would do for a start," Aidan agreed slyly. "You have a nice home, and Lord knows if you had wanted one of our women you would have gotten married a long time ago. Did you plan to die a bachelor?"

"No!" Barret couldn't believe what was happening, but since Aidan's comments actually made sense, he knew he would feel like a fool arguing with him, so he didn't bother. "Look, that's the most pathetic group I've ever seen, but all I'll promise to do is escort them into the city and see if we can't inspire our people to take them in temporarily. With Mother here we ought to be able to borrow the equipment to get the city rebuilt in no time, and maybe we can build some apartments for the moles while we're at it. They've got so few men I doubt there will be anyone to fight a challenge should anyone wish to marry one of the widows, so marriage ought to absorb quite a few."

Aidan folded his arms across his chest, trying his best not to gloat over the success he was having with his cousin. "The challenges have served their purpose, Barret. Let's outlaw them now."

"What? How can you even suggest that?" the man cried in astonishment.

"I'm talking only about men having to fight to win a bride. I still think it's a damn good way to settle differences of opinion. I don't want to see the challenges abolished, just modified in purpose. That's all."

"Look, it's not that I'm afraid to fight for a wife. Is that what you're thinking? I'm no coward!" he insisted, totally exasperated at the imagined insult. "I've been working with everyone else since the quake, and there have been dangers aplenty."

"No one is calling you a coward," Aidan assured him calmly. "I think you've simply let yourself become so involved in your business interests that you've lost sight of what's really important." The persuasive warrior nodded again at the young woman he had pointed out. "I'll bet she's not a day over twenty and those are handsome little boys. If you were to ask her help in encouraging the others to enter the city, I'll bet she would be flattered that you singled her out. Naturally you'd be grateful for her cooperation and invite her to share your home—for what you can assure her will be a temporary stay, of course. You're the most charming man in the city, and it won't take her long to grow fond of you."

"You're absolutely shameless, Aidan!" But Barret was laughing at how neatly he had been cornered. "All I'll agree to do is help the women find places for themselves and their children to sleep for the next couple of weeks. The older gentlemen will need some help in that regard, too. I can at least do that for them."

"Thanks, Barret, I'm sure a building boom will be good for business. You could always look at it that way."

"I do think about other things besides business, at least once in a while." Thinking he would be wise to get the project he had somehow been fool enough to agree to rolling, he turned away and started off toward the pretty young woman with the two little boys. He was sorry there wasn't time to go home and clean up first, but he could tell as the shyness faded from the strawberry blond's smile that she would be happy to talk with him no matter how he might be dressed.

"What was all that about?" Kara asked as she joined her husband.

"Somehow I managed to talk Barret into seeing that the moles find places to go tonight."

"I think one tragedy is enough for those people." Kara's expression was grim as she watched the banker openly flirting with one of the younger widows. The mole women had taken the deaths of their husbands with admirable strength, but she hoped the man wasn't so tactless as to ask the woman for a date.

"I know you two don't get along, but if he's willing to help find homes for the moles and take charge of rebuilding the city, then those are two things I don't have to do. That means I can spend all my time with you. Do you want to go home or back to Mother?"

That was a difficult question to answer since she considered her quarters on Mother her home. "I'm sorry I snapped at you," she apologized quickly, thinking perhaps she had misjudged Barret's motives. "You know your cousin far better than I ever will and if he'll help the moles so you can spend your time with me, then I'm grateful."

"Would you like to tell him that?" Aidan teased, but his wife appeared not to notice the twinkle brightening his vivid blue eyes.

"No, let's not interrupt him. Why don't I take you back up to Mother and show you the history files? I know you'll love them as much as I do since you're such a curious person."

"You make it sound like a fault," Aidan responded, but

his smile was a slow, teasing one and he took her hand as they started back toward her ship.

"No, not at all. I think it's delightful that you're so eager to learn and I'm happy to help you."

She flew slowly over the mountains for a last look at the moles' former domain, then took care as she had earlier that morning to restrict her flight path to a wide, sweeping arc which brought her Banshee in line with the docking bay. She still felt like tracing fantastic patterns in the sky, but did no more than escort Aidan back to Mother by a route that wouldn't cause him any distress.

As soon as they arrived they rode the elevator up to the second level and made their way to the massive library where the history files were stored. While there was a wide selection of fiction which could be checked out and taken back to their quarters for pleasure reading, people doing research used the small screens set in cubicles along the outer walls to access data. Kara chose a secluded booth and motioned for her husband to take the chair beside hers while she showed him how to tap into the files.

"You use this keyboard exactly as you do Sonia's. When you turn it on, it's programmed to take your request, show you a list of what's available and, when you make your choice, present the information on the screen." As she glanced down at the keyboard, she caught a glimpse of the golden dragon she had worn with her uniform despite Alado's rule against the use of jewelry. "How about dragons? Let's see what we can learn about them."

Instantly wary, Aidan shook his head. "No, try something else."

"But why? I'm just showing you the procedure. We don't have to read all the material on dragons, for goodness sake." Before he could persuade her to do otherwise, she entered the word "dragon" and the message that a search was in progress flashed on the screen. "It takes no more than a few seconds. Yes, here we are now." She ran her finger down the listing. "You see? There's everything here from the dragon in Oriental art, to the constellation Draco, to plants of the arum family, to an Asiatic tree lizard. Oh, this is interesting!

A short musket was called a dragon and the soldiers who used it were dragoons. It goes on and on. If you want to read more about any particular item you just type in the word and the information will be supplied. Let me show you what Mother has on 329."

Aidan knew the louder he complained the more suspicious Kara would become, but he was desperately sorry he had not considered how much she could learn about him if she set her mind to it. Gripping the arms of his chair tightly, he watched as the file on his home planet appeared.

"Do you see what I mean? The history is very one-sided, and that's why I would like to add what you know to make the story complete." Kara was a perceptive woman, and while Aidan had leaned forward slightly to read Alado's blatantly slanted version of the revolt, he seemed so distracted that he did no more than frown as though he were annoyed it was so brief. Playing a hunch, she typed in the word "dragon" again. When the face of Cameron Burke appeared she was stunned, for the notorious hired assassin and Aidan resembled each other so closely they might have been twins.

"He didn't go so far as to leave calling cards with a dragon's silhouette, but that was what he liked to be called." Aidan spoke in a soft, soothing voice, but he could see Kara wasn't really listening. He waited until she turned toward him, her golden eyes bright with unshed tears before he spoke again. "Go ahead, read what it says about him. I can guarantee that none of it will be true."

"Not the truth?" Kara thought that highly unlikely. "It might be biased, but I'm sure it's accurate since the details of Cameron Burke's exploits were too well known for it to be otherwise. He was simply a hired killer. A man who would do anything for a price, and the more impossible the target appeared to be the better the fiend liked it. I doubt a more despicable human being has ever lived. It's no wonder you won't use his name." She slipped the gold chain off over her head and, regarding the dragon charm closely, asked him a direct question. "You said you got this from your grandfather, but it belonged first to Cameron, didn't it?"

"Yes, it is all I have that was his. It's very precious to me. That's why I gave it to you," he explained softly, his voice edged with tenderness.

Despite the high regard she knew he had for the man, she was simply appalled that she had unwittingly touched one of his cursed possessions. "I don't want it anymore." Kara shuddered with revulsion as she reached for his hand and pressed the gold necklace firmly into his palm. "I'm sure you know how to use the files now. Why don't you stay here for a while and look up whatever you like. I need to go next door and see if the film they removed from my Banshee's cameras were any good. After all I went through to get it, I certainly hope it was."

Aidan watched her lift her chin proudly and knew better than to try and talk some sense into her when she was in such an intractable mood. He knew better, but he tried anyway. "The man wasn't evil, Kara, and even if he had been, character traits aren't hereditary."

Kara leaned down to kiss him lightly, then turned away without replying since she didn't trust herself to speak. She tried to manage a sedate walk, but what she really wanted to do was sprint from the room at a dead run. It was no wonder Aidan had refused to reveal his great-grandfather's name, but she was devastated that he had not trusted her with that information when the villain was so well known. She would have kept his secret, hadn't he known that? She wondered who Cameron had married, thinking the woman couldn't possibly have possessed even a minute particle of good character herself. "God, what an awful lineage to give a child," she mumbled to herself, forgetting for the moment that she had not agreed to have one.

Seeing Lieutenant León approaching from the opposite end of the corridor, Matthew Merrill called out to her, "Lieutenant! Are you alone? I need to speak with you."

Here it comes, Kara thought to herself, knowing the captain must be aching to admonish her for her numerous rebellious deeds despite the kindness he had shown her the previous evening. "Yes, sir, I'm alone, at least for the moment," she responded when she reached him.

"Good, let's go up to my quarters. We have something important to discuss."

The man seemed to be in a great hurry and, as they entered the elevator, Kara took the opportunity to observe him more closely. He stood with his hands behind his back, in his usual proud military stance. She supposed he was handsome but, as she had told Aidan, she had never had any desire to be more to him than one of Mother's best scouts. She dug her nails into her palms, trying desperately to find the calm inner peace that so often eluded her in trying times.

"You needn't be so nervous, Lieutenant." Merrill smiled warmly as he led her into his office and again, rather than sit behind his desk, chose the place opposite hers on one of the room's comfortable couches. He leaned forward slightly, then spoke as though they were good friends rather than commander and subordinate. "I want you to tell me exactly what happened to you while you were on 329, but don't regard this as a formal debriefing. This is strictly off the record."

Kara took a deep breath, attempting once more to compose herself but having only partial success. She was deeply distressed to find herself related to Cameron Burke, even if it was only distantly through marriage. That was a secret she would never reveal, not to the captain or anyone else. Since Merrill already knew how she had become separated from Mother she described her meeting with Aidan, the events leading up to their marriage and the time before the earthquake in the briefest terms possible. While she gave her husband full credit for saving her life, she emphasized the fact that she had never stopped trying to contact her base ship and return home. Her delivery was unemotional, yet she had seldom undergone a more nerve-racking ordeal.

When she finished relating the four weeks she had spent on 329, Merrill waited a long moment before responding. "Is there anything else you would like to tell me?" he inquired with an encouraging smile.

"No," Kara insisted. "I've nothing more to say." The image of Cameron Burke was still all too vivid in her mind, but revealing that private torment would only increase her mental anguish. She wanted to keep the captain's respect, not lose it in an instant by revealing that dark secret from Aidan's past.

"On the contrary, there's a good deal more. Aidan saved your life, and you're obviously grateful to him. If that's all you feel, then I have the power to dissolve your marriage immediately since the circumstances surrounding it clearly involved duress."

"He didn't force me to marry him!" Kara denied vehemently. "There was simply no other way he could protect me."

"Perhaps duress is too strong a word, then, but would you have married him if you had been greeted on 329 with courtesy and respect rather than hatred and suspicion?"

Unable to look him directly in the eye as she replied, Kara focused her gaze on her hands which lay so tightly clasped in her lap that her knuckles were white. "Aidan is a man whose strength and courage are greatly admired by his people. What he did for me carried a high degree of risk to himself, so gratitude is the least I owe him." She hesitated momentarily as she searched for a diplomatic way to describe what had happened, then completed her reply to his question. "I'm certain I would have thought him very attractive despite the vast differences in our backgrounds, but no, I would not have married him had my life not depended on it."

"Then you don't wish to take him with us when we leave?" the captain inquired perceptively.

"I didn't say that!" Kara insisted too sharply, then instantly regretted it and apologized. "I'm sorry, what I mean is our plans were all tentative, and now that Mother is here . . . well, now I don't really know what he'll want to do."

Merrill had always thought Kara not only bright, but very beautiful as well, and he was far more fond of her than he dared reveal. "Lieutenant, I am merely trying to help you. If you wish to stay married to Aidan, then I have something I would like to discuss with him. If you would rather I refused him permission to travel on board, then I will. We'll not record your marriage in your file, and it will be as though it never took place. The decision is entirely up to you. Which will it be? What is it you really want to do?" When she remained silent, he realized she was hopelessly confused and offered another alternative. "Do you wish to resign your commission and stay here with him? I would hate to lose you, but if that's your choice then I'll arrange it."

Kara shook her head. "No, I'd be miserable here. I love being a scout far too much to give it up for any reason."

Thinking he was at last beginning to understand the source of her inner turmoil, Merrill grew even more sympathetic. "We can only remain here a few more days, Lieutenant. Why don't you discuss your options with Aidan? Then I'd like both of you to join me here tonight for supper at eight. As I said, if he comes with us, I have a job I think would be perfect for him."

Considering their conference over, Kara rose to her feet. While she thought his interest in Aidan very kind, she didn't wish to mislead him about her husband's abilities. "Aidan is very bright, but the educational opportunities on 329 have been extremely limited. He has only just begun to read and—"

Merrill interrupted to assuage her fears. "Don't worry, I'll not embarrass him by asking him to solve advanced mathematical equations. I have something entirely different in mind, but I won't discuss it with either of you until you've made the decisions you must about your marriage." As he walked her to the door, he had another thought and hesitated before allowing her to go. "If you and Aidan decide not to remain married, would it upset you if I invited him to come with us anyway?"

Kara tried not to gape, but she was simply flabbergasted by that question. Knowing that compared to 329 what Alado had to offer was infinitely better, Kara knew she could never be so selfish as to deny Aidan that opportunity. Emotionally it would be an impossible situation, but Mother was so large she knew they could avoid each other for weeks at a time with a little effort. "Make your offer to Aidan. I would not stand in his way for any reason."

The love that shone in her eyes was too bright to mistake

for simple generosity, but Merrill was far too wise to point that out to her since it was apparently something she had yet to discover for herself. He smiled warmly as he bid her good day, but he could not help wondering what the night might bring.

Since she had spent far more time with the captain than she had planned to spend checking on the progress of the maps of 329, Kara hurried back to the library. As she came through the door, one of the librarians waved her over to the main desk. "Yes, what is it?" she asked impatiently.

"Your husband told me to tell you he has gone home," the clerk informed her with a smile.

"Gone home? Thank you." Since she had no doubt at all what Aidan considered his home, she went down to the docking bay used by the Banshees. She had told the mechanics who kept her ship in service that she would probably make several trips while Mother remained stationed there and found the craft still sitting where she had landed it. She cruised out into the bright afternoon sky and indulged her passion for flying stunts for several minutes before bringing the easily maneuverable craft down at the base of the mountains. She trudged up the path, entered the gate without being challenged and swiftly found her way to Aidan's home.

He had cleaned up the mess in his kitchen, but she assumed he must have gone out and she had no idea where in the city he might be. Discouraged, she went into the bedroom intending to gather up the clothes and pair of boots she had left behind. Instead she found Aidan stretched out on the bed, and she immediately changed her plans as she hesitated at the door.

He had discarded his boots and vest and lay on his stomach with his cheek resting on his left forearm. His right hand hung limply over the side of the bed still clutching an overturned glass, and what he had done was all too plain. While she was tempted to lose herself in Oblivion's seductively innocent warmth, too, she knew she would have to stay sober or they would never make it back to Mother to have

dinner with the captain. Ignoring that obligation was unthinkable.

Certain that Aidan was as confused about their future as
she was, she slipped off her boots, removed the glass from
his hand and then crawled over him, agilely aligning her
supple contours to his so that when she relaxed, she fit perfectly on his back, her legs on top of his and her cheek
cradled on his shoulder. She smoothed aside his long curls
and nuzzled his nape with light kisses.

"What are we going to do, my love?" she purred softly,
knowing he would not hear a word she said. She had been
shocked to learn he was a descendant of Cameron Burke, but
that knowledge, while painful, had made her love no less
deep. "I care not at all who your people were. You're all
that's important to me and I should have said that before I
left you, but I was too hurt that you hadn't wanted to confide
in me. Why are we always parting when neither of us knows
what's in the other's heart? Why can't we find elsewhere the
same delicious accord we share in bed? Is there no way we
can ever fuse our separate lives into one that will please us
both?"

Aidan let Kara talk until she finally grew still, sorry she
would confess her doubts about their union in such a melancholy fashion while she mistakenly believed him to be
asleep. She never spoke her thoughts so freely when he was
able to respond. When her tears began to slide down his
back and drip over his shoulder, he could no longer pretend
to be asleep. "All I want to do is make love to you, but for
the life of me I can't figure out how to do it while we're in
this position. Can you?"

Horrified to find him so lucid, Kara scrambled off his
back, cuffing his ear as her feet hit the floor. "You snake!
You despicable reptile! How dare you let me think you had
passed out!" she screamed, her ravaged emotions erupting in
a furious fit of temper.

Aidan rolled over on his left side to face her and propped
his head on his hand. "Reptile? Please, you shouldn't
slander all reptiles simply because you're angry with me."
He patted the bed beside him. "Sit down. Pretend I'm still

asleep if it helps you confide in me, but we both know Mother won't remain here long, and I think we need to decide what we're going to do."

Knowing he was right, Kara tried to put aside her bitterness over the trick he had played on her despite her dreadful embarrassment. She sank down next to him, but she was dreading this conversation even more than she had the one with Captain Merrill. Everyone seemed to be pressuring her for the answers she couldn't bring herself to give, and that hurt badly. "That was a mean trick, Aidan. I thought you had had a glass of Oblivion and passed out."

"No, it was only a glass of water and I just fell asleep. I've never had a woman rest so comfortably on my back before and I was enjoying it too much to let on I was awake. Besides, look what happened when I spoke to you. Your loving mood was shattered instantly." He reached out to rub her back lightly, hoping to ease her obvious strain. "I think we should talk, Kara, or at least I think you should listen to me for a while now since I was polite enough to listen to you."

Kara gave him a fiercely accusing glance. "That wasn't being polite, Aidan, it was a farce to embarrass me."

The handsome warrior refused to reply in kind and spoke calmly. "You're the one who needs the Oblivion, Kara. Shall I pour you some?"

"No!" Kara was still mortified, uncertain exactly what she had said but positive it had been too revealing.

"All right then, compose yourself as best you can and just listen. I'm as guilty as you are, my love, for I've far more secrets to keep." He paused then to force away a pang of guilt as he realized he had no intention of being totally open with her now. "In some respects, you're right about Cameron. He was a paid assassin, but there is an important fact you don't know."

Kara frowned deeply, still skeptical that Aidan knew something she did not. "What is it?"

"Does Alado still have a board of directors that determines the corporation's policies?"

"Yes, there are nine of them, four women and five men at present. Why?"

"At one time the board had an elite private guard. The unit was small, with never more than half a dozen well-trained and highly disciplined members. Have you ever heard of it?" Aidan was positive she hadn't, but hoped to draw her into the story by asking the question.

Puzzled, Kara thought for a minute and then shrugged. "A private guard? Why no, if such a unit existed, I never heard of it. What did they do, just function as bodyguards?"

"No, nothing as respectable as that. The private guard was charged with the responsibility of representing the board when they thought their influence needed to be bolstered in some quarter."

"Public relations?" Kara asked incredulously, certain that wasn't what he meant.

Aidan couldn't help but laugh at her confusion. He reached out to clasp her hand tightly and brought it to his lips. "No, what they did was remove the troublesome leaders in the Confederation who in any way threatened Alado's power. Some were tyrants, drunk with their own power, who blatantly refused to follow policies which were for their own peoples' good. Others simply had philosophies of their own which put them in conflict with Alado."

Impatient for him to get to the point of his tale, Kara tried to hurry him along. "What has this got to do with your great-grandfather?"

That she didn't see his point frustrated Aidan, but he knew he would have to be patient if he wanted her to understand and tried again. "He was employed by Alado's board of directors as one of their private guards. The assassinations he carried out were at their request."

"But that's impossible!" Kara exclaimed in disbelief, terrified to think it could possibly be true.

"It's the truth, Kara. He worked for the board and he truly believed he was furthering Alado's ideal of peace by eliminating its enemies. But one day he realized they could never suppress all opposition to their policies and that some dissent was actually healthy. That's when he tried to resign."

Kara licked her lips thoughtfully as she studied her husband's expression. Clearly he was convinced his version of history was right, and after the ruthless way she had been treated just to test a new piece of equipment, she could no longer insist that he wasn't. "What happened then?" she whispered apprehensively.

"You already know what happened to him. Rather than accept his resignation, the board had him arrested and charged with the murders he had committed at their own insistence, plus the assassinations the rest of his unit had carried out. Then they threw in every other unsolved killing in the galaxy to make it appear the butcher of the century had been captured when his only crime had been believing in the leadership of Alado's board and accepting their assignments when he'd mistakenly thought them to be for the common good."

"But there was a trial. Why wasn't any of this brought out then?" Kara asked to allay her last trace of suspicion.

"The trial was closed to the public due to the massive publicity surrounding my great-grandfather's supposed crimes. He was guilty of some of the killings, you must remember, but there was no way the board would allow him to use the fact that he had been following their orders as a defense because they did not want their private guard to be unveiled, let alone have their deeds cataloged for the public. The trial was a sham, and he was given a life sentence on 329. From what Captain Merrill told us of how you scouts were used to test a new screening device, this board is as ruthless as that one. Nothing has changed in all these years."

Huge tears welled up in Kara's eyes, then spilled over her thick sweep of dark lashes and trickled down her cheeks. "Captain Merrill is a fair man despite what he did to us and you heard him swear he'd never do it again even if it costs him his command. So much of Alado is good, Aidan, so very much of it. But it must seem difficult to believe when you've seen a far different side." She knew then he would never agree to live with her on Mother and, heartbroken, she continued to weep.

Aidan had only wanted to share what he knew about the

man known as the dragon, Cameron Burke, but he had never expected to upset Kara as badly as he obviously had. When he pulled her down into his arms, her body again melted against his with a fluid grace that swiftly chased from his mind all thought of merely giving comfort. He wanted far more than simply to cuddle her while she wept and began to slowly peel away her flight suit.

He whispered the sweetest of endearments as he covered with lavish kisses each creamy smooth inch of skin he exposed. When at last he had pulled the shimmering suit off over her toes, he moved back across the bed to shower her face with kisses before his mouth eagerly covered hers. He found her lips so pliant and warm that her response heightened his desire. As he turned away for a moment to slip off his shorts, she stood to step out of a soft pink teddy, then returned to his bed and pulled him into her arms.

Kara was no longer crying visibly, but her sorrow was every bit as deep as she thought of how soon they would have to part. She loved him desperately and her kisses and caresses were filled with the affection that filled her heart. She wanted to hold him in her arms for hours, to memorize each plane of his superbly muscled body so that when she had to lie in her bed alone, she could instantly recall the memory of him. She wanted to taste and touch all of him, to kiss and caress him until the beat of his heart kept time with the wild pounding rhythm of her own. They had made love many times, but never with the fervor she displayed so readily now. She spoke not a word, but her devotion which fed the fires of her passion was unmistakably deep.

Aidan felt not only the love, but also the stark terror which made Kara's fingertips tremble as first her hands and then her lips moved down the taut muscles of his stomach. Knowing no man could ever have been blessed with a more affectionate wife, he decided it was far wiser to encourage her to express her emotions in making love rather than to demand the words she seemed to find it impossible to speak.

Throughout the time they had been together, her bright red curls had grown to a more softly feminine and flattering length and, as he slid his fingers through her hair to hold her close, he hoped she would never cut it again. He wanted to feel the sensuous softness of it as it brushed against his loins while her lips and tongue worked their unique brand of magic. He moaned softly then as the intoxicating pleasure she gave flooded his veins with a searing heat.

Basking in the most marvelous sensations, he surrendered himself completely, letting the silken smoothness of her loving lure him to the soaring heights of rapture and then far beyond until a shattering climax brought the exquisite torture of her deeply erotic kisses to a glorious end. Knowing she had satisfied him thoroughly, Kara rested her cheek on his stomach and cuddled close, content to wait for his reason to return before she spoke.

"We're to have dinner with the captain tonight. There's a question he wants to ask you, but I already know what your answer will be," she disclosed with a regretful sigh.

Aidan lay still, thinking it an odd time to continue their conversation, but not wanting to upset her again, he replied politely, "What is the question?"

Kara looked up at him then, thinking the blue of his eyes as strikingly handsome as she always had. "He would like you to come with us when we leave. He said he has a job that will interest you, but he didn't tell me what it is."

Aidan gave her a slow, sweet smile as he ruffled her curls. "Is the captain the only one who would like me to leave with Mother?"

Kara again lay her cheek on the warm hollow of his stomach as she tried frantically to find a coherent reply. "I want us to be together always, Aidan. You must know that, but it would be as unfair for me to ask you to leave your home as it would be for you to ask me to give up being a scout."

"I don't think so," Aidan confided softly. "I don't think it's the same thing at all."

"It isn't?" Kara raised up again to look at him and was surprised to see he seemed pleased when she still felt utterly miserable.

"No, it isn't. If you would like me to go with you, all you need do is ask." His heart nearly burst with pride then, for the joy that instantly lit Kara's face made her even more beautiful than when she had looked up and found Mother hovering overhead. With a squeal of delighted surprise she straddled his waist, threw her arms around his neck and gave him such an enthusiastic kiss that he had no doubt she wanted him on board Mother when the ship left 329.

The same stab of guilt he had felt before knifed through his heart, and he tightened his embrace. It was not only Kara's love that had influenced his decision, but also the suspicion that Alado was about to go to war, and as a warrior that was exactly where he wanted to be.

"I like the way you asked me, lady, and I promise you'll like the way I answer since you've just struck a pose I definitely know how to use." Channeling all his energies into pleasing her, he vowed she would never suspect any other thoughts save his love for her had ever entered his mind.

CHAPTER

◇ **XX** ◇

"Dragons are reptiles, aren't they?" Aidan displayed his usual curiosity as he slipped the gold necklace with the dragon charm over Kara's head knowing she would now have no objection to wearing it.

Kara had bathed and was dressed only in the lavender teddy she had rinsed out before leaving the previous evening, and she shivered as the charm brushed her bare skin. "I told you dragons don't really exist, but if they did, yes they'd be reptiles. The detail is so exact you can see the scales on this tiny beast." She gave her husband a light kiss and went back into the bathroom to fluff out her damp curls.

"Which gown do you think I should wear?" she called out to him.

Half a dozen long dresses lay across his bed, and he picked up first one and then another trying to make up his mind. Finally he chose the ivory gown with the golden thread, sat down on the clothes chest and used the tip of his knife to rip out the seam on the right side. He slit the gown nearly to the waist, hoping to show off the perfection of Kara's long shapely legs as well as her fascinatingly sensuous tattoo.

When he handed her the gown, she didn't notice what he had done until after she had put it on and smoothed it down over her hips. "Aidan!" she exclaimed with a throaty giggle. "What have you done to this? Do the respectable women of 329 wear their gowns slit up the side like this or only the barmaids?"

"What difference does it make? The captain won't know whether or not the cut of the gown is stylish or daring. Besides, I'd like to be able to catch a glimpse of your Love Vine as you walk."

Kara took a few steps and then made a sedate turn. "Well, I guess this isn't all that revealing and if you like it this way, then so do I."

Aidan broke into a charming grin, delighted she had not argued with him. He had borrowed a lightweight knit sweater from Zac and even though he had pushed up the sleeves, it did cover him more fully than his vest had. A rich cream color, it matched his shorts exactly and made his dark tan appear even deeper. "I'm going to have to get different clothes if I'm going with you. Will that be difficult to arrange?"

"No, not at all. There are all kinds of shops on the level where we had breakfast this morning, so you can find whatever you would like to wear."

"I'd like to dress as I always have, but somehow I don't think it will be considered appropriate." He had taken the time to polish his boots, for he didn't want to cause Kara any embarrassment about his appearance even though she had assured him repeatedly that he was more than handsome no matter what he chose to wear. When she was ready to go, he helped her gather up her belongings and carried them down the hill to her Banshee. He was getting used to flying, but he still didn't think he liked it all that much. Remembering how much Blair had wanted to go for a ride, he made a suggestion. "We ought to have a big party before we leave. Everyone has been working so hard to rebuild the city that it would be a welcome break. I know there are lots of people who would like to go for a ride with you. Would you agree to take them?"

Kara had already secured the hatch and begun her preflight checklist, but she paused to reply, "I'd love to, Aidan, but since a Banshee carries only two people at most, I'll have to use a shuttle. It seats twelve. Isn't that how you got back home today?"

"Nope, I flew down with Tweed on a rescue sled. He had come up for a piece of equipment and said he'd take me back with him. He seems to know how to repair almost anything. I didn't understand half of what he told me he planned to do this afternoon."

"Tweed's a character, all right. He's one of Mother's best engineers, but I don't pretend to understand him myself."

Reassured that he had not been the only one to find the man's technical jargon incomprehensible, Aidan leaned back and braced himself for the short flight up to Mother. He was getting used to it now; a sleek monster of metal and acrylic, it had a harmony of form and function as compelling as the Banshee, and he thought he might even learn to enjoy calling her home, for a while at least. When they reached the huge base ship, they went first to Kara's quarters to put away her clothes and then made their way to the captain's cabin.

"Does Merrill always dress in red?" Aidan inquired as they approached the man's door.

"Always. While all of Alado's employees wear uniforms of a similar style, the colors are unique to each group. Only the captain of a base ship wears red so his presence and authority on the bridge can be immediately recognized."

The door slid open before Aidan could respond and he followed his wife into Captain Merrill's office. A table set for three had been placed between the couches and the desk, and alongside it stood a covered serving cart. That the man had wanted to speak with them without being interrupted by a waiter piqued the warrior's curiosity even more, but he decided to let the captain do most of the talking that evening.

Encouraged by the opportunity to talk with Aidan again, Merrill made sure he and his bride were comfortably seated on the plush couch providing the most superb view and then offered cocktails. "Unfortunately, I must use my quarters not only for practical matters, but to entertain as well. I hope you'll not find the setting too forbidding, as I'd like to enjoy a relaxing meal and discuss business later. Is that acceptable to you both?"

"Of course," Kara replied, but she blushed as she realized she had not looked over at Aidan first to see if his opinion differed. She was relieved when he just nodded and smiled rather than complained that she had spoken for them both without his permission.

The captain was again so charming a host that Kara's embarrassment quickly faded. That she had to adjust her gown constantly so that the skirt would not fall open while she was seated proved annoying, but she finally solved that problem by crossing her legs and tucking the two loose sides of the skirt between her knees. When they rose to take their places at the table, she no longer had to worry that the cut of her gown would strike the captain as immodest and took her place, looking forward to enjoying some of the foods she had long been without.

Merrill rolled back the lid of the serving cart, ladled up three steaming bowls of a creamy beer cheese soup, offered them thick slabs of butter-drenched whole wheat bread, then took his place. "This is one of my favorites. I hope you'll like it, too."

"It's delicious," Kara purred, for truly she thought it was while Aidan, who had never before tasted it, took only a small sip. Finding its tangy taste unusual but quite good, he finished that bowl and then joined the captain in another.

"I wasn't certain what foods you would enjoy. I hope

those I selected are neither too bland nor too highly sea-
soned," Merrill said with a warm smile. "I'm glad I was
correct in the choice of soup at least."

"Since the production of food has always been a challenge
to us, you'll find we're extremely easy to please," Aidan
assured him. While none of the dishes the man served were
familiar to him, he found them all to his liking. The crisp
salad was made up of several thinly sliced greens of varying
shades and textures combined with diced peppers, mush-
rooms, chopped black olives and chunks of tangy cheese all
lightly coated with a zesty vinegar dressing. The unusual
salad was followed by succulent scampi bathed in a garlic-
flavored butter, and when the main course proved to be a
two-inch-thick steak garnished with vegetables steamed to a
crunchy perfection he couldn't believe his eyes. Having seldom eaten beef, and then only stews made from the male
calves born to the cows in their small herd of dairy cattle, he
had to ask what it was. "You have cattle on Mother?" he
exclaimed.

"No, a large portion of our diet is grown on board, but our
meats are all frozen," Merrill explained. "That way they can
be stored at peak flavor indefinitely and prepared in a matter
of minutes. The majority of the crew are vegetarians, but
while I try to adhere to that diet as much as possible, I've
never been able to overcome my craving for red meat." As if
to prove that point, he paused briefly to savor a bite of the
tender steak. "The amount of rations needed to feed a staff
of Mother's size is enormous, but we can travel for several
months without restocking, or indefinitely if we had to since
we generate so much of our own food."

Aidan found the taste of the charbroiled steak different
from lamb, the primary meat available on 329, but still he
enjoyed it. The captain continued to supply him with details
about the ship, all interesting even if not the subject he was
certain the man wanted to discuss. Dessert was a cream-and-
fruit-filled pastry so light it seemed to melt as his fork
reached his tongue. He knew he had never had a more elegant meal and wondered if the captain dined so well every
night. But Aidan was far too polite to ask that question.

When they returned to the couches for liqueurs, he was sorry he had not thought to bring the man some Oblivion. "We have a remarkable liqueur on 329. Its taste is delicious and its effect deadly. I will bring you some."

"I'm not certain you should," Merrill warned with a chuckle. "I have vices enough already."

"I will bring only a small bottle then," Aidan offered considerately, again making the captain laugh.

"Don't forget to bring the pears, too, since there is no other antidote," Kara suggested as she again crossed her legs to insure that her skirt fell in flattering folds rather than merely falling open.

"If your liqueur requires an antidote I don't think I dare even taste it." Merrill found the idea very amusing, however, and thought he just might give it a try. Now that the time had come to discuss his proposal, he wasn't certain where to begin. "Suppose you tell me your plans first, and then I'll see if they will fit into mine."

This time Kara remembered to glance first at Aidan, and when he reached over to give her hand a firm squeeze, she urged him to reply. "I think you should be the one to describe our plans," she encouraged warmly.

Aidan leaned back, totally relaxed as he spoke. "I find myself the Captain of the Guard in a city that no longer has enemies. That will leave me with far too much time on my hands, so if you can suggest some other employment, I'll be glad to consider it."

"You're not opposed to coming with us, then?" Merrill asked as a precaution before he explained his plan.

"I am not opposed to traveling anywhere Kara wishes to go," Aidan assured him. He had not released her hand and now laced his fingers in hers in an openly affectionate clasp.

While Aidan sat back, seemingly open to any idea, Merrill was on the edge of his seat, his gray eyes burning with the intensity of his emotions. "I have been with Alado since I was eighteen and first entered their academy. The corporation is immense. Much of it runs as autonomous units, but all are interconnected and ultimately accountable to the board of directors. They have called a meeting so that I may present the results of that cursed test in which Kara became stranded. It's to be held at the Fleet Command Base, which leads me to believe they've already decided to outfit the rest of the base ships with the force field device regardless of what I tell them."

"Doesn't the board usually meet there?" Aidan inquired, thinking that detail an important one to know.

"No, not in my memory they haven't. They meet in whatever location suits their purpose at the time. The board members usually prefer to emphasize the peace and prosperity of our corporation and avoid the installations which are chiefly military in function, as Fleet Command is. That is what has me so worried."

Seeing he had the full attention of both his guests, Merrill became more specific about his concerns. "I have a feeling they're going to tout the force field as the device which will eliminate any warfare between us and our competition. After all, it would be impossible for Europa to attack vessels it could not find. The problem is the device has not only defensive but also offensive capabilities in that it would allow us to attack from behind a screen of invisibility."

No longer able to keep still, Aidan interjected another pressing question. "Isn't war between the corporations still forbidden?"

"Of course, forgive me. The people of 329 would have no way of knowing how frequently Alado, and our primary competition, Europa, have come to the brink of war despite the fact that we are forbidden to seize territory by armed conquest. Usually what happens is that expeditionary teams from the two will arrive within a few days or perhaps hours of one another on some previously unexplored planet. Arguments are then inevitable as to who arrived first and that has upon several occasions led to armed conflict between them. It is no coincidence that out scouts are dispatched from a base ship rather than an intermediate vessel. Should there at any time be a question as to which corporation's claim is valid, my orders are to take whatever action necessary to insure Alado is the winner."

"Just what is meant by 'whatever action necessary'?"

Aidan responded suspiciously since the term struck him as rather vague.

Merrill shrugged. "Exactly what it sounds like it means. I may take whatever hostile and aggressive action I desire in pursuit of Alado's claim. At present, our firepower is approximately equal to Europa's. Armed conflict invariably ends in a stand-off or draw, so both sides try and avoid it."

"But if you were to approach one of Europa's base ships using the device that conceals Mother's position, you would be able to launch a first strike so devastating they'd be unable to return fire in time to save themselves." Cringing at the thought, Kara shuddered. "I agree with you. The force field is too cunning a weapon to have been designed for defense alone."

"I'm glad you see that, too. The only problem is that I can't prove that opinion to be a fact."

"And if you could?" Aidan prompted impatiently, feeling dreadfully ignorant and horribly uncomfortable about it. "What would happen then?"

"It would be banned because possession of such a weapon would be in clear violation of the Confederation's policies which are designed to insure peaceful exploration by the corporations." When Aidan nodded in understanding, Merrill waited a few seconds to allow the young man to ask any other questions he might have, but when his guest remained silent, he felt free to continue. "I'm sure you're wondering how any of this concerns you. The truth is, it needn't, unless you choose to become involved."

"I am a warrior," Aidan explained proudly. "If Alado wishes to declare war on Europa or anyone else, then quite naturally I would wish to become involved. But if war is forbidden, then I fail to see what value I would be to you."

"Your value is almost inestimable, Aidan, for you are totally unique. There is no record of your existence in any of Alado's files. That means you can move about as a courier without attracting any attention to yourself."

"A courier?" That was a word Aidan had never heard, but he was far too proud to admit that. "Just what is expected of such a person?"

"Only that you deliver messages. I have a friend on the board who is so totally committed to peace that I know she could not possibly sanction the use of the force field device as a weapon, nor the barbaric way I was required to test it. I am hoping there are others who share her views, either on the board or among the other captains of base ships."

"Anyone can pass messages," Aidan scoffed. "You don't need a man with my talents."

Sincere in his request, Merrill became more insistent. "You would make a discreet and trustworthy courier, Aidan, and I can not promise there won't be considerable danger in what I'm asking you to do. You may need to defend yourself, and often."

"Is it messages only you wish him to deliver?" Kara asked apprehensively. "Or is it something more?"

Merrill frowned, refusing to elaborate. Aidan's trustworthiness as a courier would have to be proven before he would involve him more deeply in his plans. "A courier is what I need now. If later I need Aidan to perform other duties, we'll discuss them at that time."

Aidan needed no more than a brief glance at his wife's skeptical expression to know her distrust was as great as his. Releasing her hand, he sat forward slightly. "I think you already know what it is you want me to do, and I also know exactly why you would single me out to do it. How did you find out who I am?"

Merrill made a brief attempt to deny Aidan's perceptive accusation, then spread his hands in a gesture of defeat. "I was merely familiarizing myself with 329's history when I came across the photograph of Cameron Burke. I will see that it's altered immediately so no one else will be able to recognize you, but quite honestly, my request had nothing to do with your heritage."

"Is the competition so keen for assassins that I can expect many offers of 'courier' work?" Aidan inquired sarcastically. Despite the captain's assurance, he was certain it was the fact that he was a descendant of Cameron Burke that had inspired the man to confide in him.

"It isn't an assassin I want!" Merrill countered sharply.

"What you mean is you don't need one just yet, but you soon may if the current board becomes any more militant. Isn't that the truth of the matter?"

To escape the defiant gleam of Aidan's accusing gaze, Merrill rose, turned away and focused his attention on the magnificent view. Nestled below, the lights of the warrior's city twinkled with a warm brightness that touched the captain's heart with a sharp pang of homesickness. After a moment's reflection, he apologized. "Perhaps I made a mistake in assuming you would have no loyalty to Alado and therefore would not object to helping me discover the board's motives. You have impressed me as an extremely capable man. As I told you, I've refused to put our scouts at risk for future tests of any sort. That stand may well put a quick end to my career, but I'll not go quietly. I believe there are others who share my views, but I can't approach them personally without arousing too much suspicion—not only about myself, but also about those I would visit. That would be unfair to them. That's why I need your help to discover the board's true intentions and, if need be, block them before the result becomes any more disastrous than it already is."

Kara studied her captain's rigidly proud posture and could find no fault with his plan. "Perhaps you're wrong," she suggested softly. "Perhaps the board won't fully understand how the force field can be used until after they hear your report."

Merrill turned slightly and smiled at her over his shoulder. "Now there's an idea I had not considered, and while it seems remote I suppose it is possible. Still, I can't help but believe there have got to be some members of the board who have known from the inception of the device what its capabilities for destruction are."

Aidan listened attentively as his wife and Matthew Merrill continued to debate the issue. Since he knew little about the board, he felt at too great a disadvantage to contribute anything until they at last fell silent. "Is any of this so-called 'courier' work to be carried out on board Mother?" he finally asked.

"No, why?" Merrill replied.

"Then I will give you my answer when we reach Fleet Command Base."

Clearly frustrated by the fact that he had failed to gain Aidan's confidence, Merrill tossed another question at him. "Why don't you trust me?"

"History," Aidan replied with a knowing chuckle, "the bitter lessons of history. I've spent all my life in one of Alado's most godforsaken prison facilities. I won't be sent to another."

"I can assure you I've no intention of being sent to one, either."

Fearing the two men might become even more openly hostile, Kara rose quickly and thanked the captain for his hospitality. "We'll say nothing about this to anyone, and not discuss it again with you until we reach Fleet Command Base. Aidan and I have a great deal to do so he'll be ready to leave with us. Will you please excuse us? The dinner was superb."

Aidan had risen with his wife and, after also thanking their host for the exquisite meal, he took Kara's hand and led her through the small entryway which led to the outer door. When they reached the elevator, he drew her aside before she could press the call button. "We've never put my prints into the computer so I can open your door. Can we do that now?"

Surprised that he would make such a request at such a late hour, Kara nonetheless agreed. "Of course. The master computer is manned around the clock. It's on this level, so it's not out of our way." She led him back down the corridor past the captain's quarters and then through a series of closed doors, all of which slid open silently as she placed her hand on the small panel conveniently positioned on the right side. Finally they entered a large room filled from floor to ceiling with an impressive array of equipment. While he could recognize the function of none of the monstrous machines, their twinkling lights reminded him instantly of the colorful display that had made Sonia so fascinating when he had first entered Kara's Banshee. He accompanied his wife as she approached the front desk to make their request, but it was promptly denied.

"I'm sorry, Lieutenant, but Captain Merrill left strict orders with all shifts that under no circumstances was any information about your husband to be entered into the computer."

"But—" Before Kara could even begin to argue, Aidan had taken her arm and led her away.

"I just wanted to see if he had already done it," the warrior confided in a low whisper. "I'll bet if we check the history files we'll find that the photograph of Cameron is gone, too."

Hoping to prove him wrong, Kara led the way through the maze of corridors to the library. Just as Aidan had predicted, the file on Cameron Burke now contained a photograph of a blond man who bore not the slightest resemblance to Aidan. Distressed, she quickly shut off the viewing screen. "I don't know what to say."

"You needn't make excuses for Merrill. He's only doing what any bright commander would: insuring the odds are in his favor before the battle begins. At least now I know he moves several steps ahead of what he says aloud. That's valuable information, so I don't consider the evening wasted."

Kara leaned against the back of one of the cubicle's two chairs, her nervous tension robbing her gestures of their usual grace. "Look, Merrill's tactics aren't really the issue. The problems are to discover the board's true purpose in sponsoring the development of the force field and to try and find some way to stop them if they plan to use it to wage war."

"How did such a noble cause become our responsibility?" Aidan asked incredulously.

"Well, I suppose because Merrill asked us to help him."

"You think I should help him, don't you?" Aidan pushed his fingers through his hair, sweeping the blond waves off his forehead as if that effort would clear his mind as well as his vision. "After what Alado did to my great-grandfather, how can you ask that of me?"

"It's not Alado who has asked for your help, but Merrill," Kara pointed out swiftly.

"Is there a difference?"

"Yes!" Kara stood up and laced her arm in his as they left the library. "There's a world of difference."

"The bastard didn't have to follow orders and let you think Mother was lost, Kara. That mistake appears to have cost him two scouts, and you might have been one of them. Maybe you can forgive him for that, but I sure as hell won't."

Kara knew better than to argue with the man when his expression was so stern, and she kept still. When they reached the privacy of her quarters, however, she reminded him of his promise. "You said you'd make up your mind after we reached Fleet Command Base and not before. Didn't you mean it?"

Unaccustomed to discussing strategy with a woman, Aidan moved swiftly to distract his wife. He stepped behind her and began to nuzzle the nape of her neck playfully. "Yes, I meant what I said, so don't waste your time trying to influence me when the decision is solely mine to make."

His soft lips sent chills of pleasure down her spine and Kara leaned back against him. "I love you," she declared fervently, "but all your decisions should be your own just as mine must be."

Her words had such an ominous ring that Aidan placed his hands on her shoulders to turn her toward him and ask, "What do you mean?"

Hoping her words would impress him, Kara chose them carefully. "I think the prospect of a war on as grand a scale as Alado and Europa would fight it excites you. I told you once Banshees could be armed and used as fighters. Just what do you think I would be doing if Mother went on combat status?"

That was a question Aidan had never once considered. He was chagrined to find she had discovered so easily that his passion for warfare was far more intense than his interest in supporting the commitment she and her captain had to preserving the peaceful coexistence between the corporations. "You would have to fight?" he asked hoarsely.

Kara nodded without speaking. She could almost see the conflicting streams of thought as they collided in a burst of painful awareness in Aidan's mind. "Your decision won't be such an easy one after all, will it?"

"Not one damn thing has been easy since the hour we met, lady, but it's far too late to start complaining that you make my life too complicated now." With a savage growl he swept her into his arms and, taking her hilarious burst of giggles for approval, carried her over to the bed. As he helped her out of the close-fitting sheath and lavender teddy underneath his tone softened. "When I used to stand guard at night I'd spend my time wondering about the worlds beyond the stars. I would hope and pray that someday I would be able to visit them, but I never expected to have a bride like you at my side. You're what matters most to me, Kara, and if protecting you means I'll have to prevent a war in which I would dearly love to fight, then prevent it is what I'll do."

Now reclining nude upon her bed, Kara's appreciative glance swept over Aidan as he tossed aside his clothes with his usual haste. "I didn't mean to influence your decision," she purred softly, but the width of her smile proved otherwise.

When her husband joined her in the bed, she pulled him close, as eager for his loving as he was to give it, and they each pushed aside the menacing specter of war in order to glory in the magnificent sensations of love. Lost in the sensual glories of taste and touch, nothing else mattered but sharing the gifts of love.

Hours later, with Kara snuggled sound asleep in his arms, Aidan looked up at the stars glowing brightly overhead and understood why he had always loved them so. Somehow he had known all those lonely years that their gleam was a promise of love that would one day be fulfilled. "I love you," he whispered tenderly. Warmed by that love he drifted lazily off to sleep where his lovely bride from beyond the stars filled not only his dreams but also his heart with contentment.

* * *

Aidan held Kara's hand tightly as they waited for Tweed to finish placing all the explosive charges in the caves. A sizable crowd had gathered, but not surprisingly it contained few of the surviving moles who had, after several days of debate, granted permission for the demolition of their homes. "Will it make a lot of noise?" he asked.

"I doubt it. The weight of the mountains should muffle the sound of the blasts. I think all we'll hear is a slight rumble, sort of like thunder as the tunnels collapse."

When at last Tweed detonated the carefully laid charges, Aidan felt the earth beneath his feet shudder. Fearing another earthquake he grew tense, but the vibration was slight and only momentary. "When I think of how many lives it cost to dig those mines, I'll never understand how the moles could call them home."

"Well, they are home to no one but ghosts now," Kara murmured solemnly, then shaking off that gloomy thought she turned the conversation to that night's party. "I'll be happy to fly the shuttle all afternoon so everyone who wants to go up in it can. What do you plan to do, come with me or stay in the square?"

Not wishing to insult her, Aidan tried to make his decision sound like the most reasonable one. "Since there's not all that much room in the square to maneuver the shuttle, I think I better stay on the ground to make certain the people waiting their turns stay out of the way."

"That's a good idea," Kara agreed, but she had known Aidan would rather do almost anything than fly. They had never really discussed it, but since the first time he had flown with her and nearly become ill, it had been clear he regarded the brief flights between 329 and Mother as gruesome ordeals. "I know you don't like to fly," she said graciously, "and I'm not insulted."

"You're not?"

"No, there are so many people hoping to be scouts as it is that I certainly don't need any more competition. Now let's get back to the square and get started. I want to have time to enjoy the party myself tonight." They returned to the shuttle she had left parked nearby. Kara flew it with the same ease she piloted her Banshee, and they soon landed in the square where the bravest of 329's citizens had already begun to gather.

Aidan watched with considerable pride as his lovely mate quickly allayed the fears of the curious group. She described the shuttle's ride as smooth as a magic carpet's and promised a pleasant experience no one would ever forget. When she returned with her first twelve passengers, their enthusiastic reports soon caused the waiting crowd to double in size, and before taking off again she gave Aidan a jaunty wave. Dressed in her uniform and helmet, he could not help but recall when he had first seen the gorgeous scout. Instantly he realized there was something important she had yet to teach him and when she again landed the shuttle, he stood by the hatch until she stepped out. "Can you teach me how to speak with my mind?"

Kara laughed, wondering what had made him suddenly want that skill. "I can try to teach you, but it is not nearly as easy as learning how to read." Glancing at the anxious faces of those waiting impatiently in line, she gestured for the next twelve to come forward. "I'm afraid we won't be able to begin today though," she apologized with a teasing smile.

"Tomorrow will be soon enough," Aidan agreed readily. On a sudden impulse, he gathered her into his arms for a lengthy kiss which inspired those waiting to burst into applause. When he released her, she was blushing brightly but didn't seem too displeased that he had kissed her so passionately in public. She scampered up the steps of the shuttle and was soon ready to begin another brief flight over the city and mountains.

After watching his cousin and his wife in amused silence, Barret walked forward to speak with Aidan. "Isela and her boys want to go up in the shuttle, but while they're keeping my place in line I want to talk with you a minute."

Aidan waved to the boys, again noting that their mother was remarkably pretty. "It's really good of you to take such an active interest in those three. How much longer will they be staying with you?" He made his expression merely curious rather than devilish, which was the one he was tempted to reveal.

Barret blushed slightly as he tried to explain. "The first few days Isela was with me we stayed up all night just talking."

"Just talking?" Aidan asked with a skeptically raised brow, for while he knew Barret enjoyed good conversation as much as any of them, that was not usually his interest in a woman, especially not when she was as pretty as Isela.

"Yes, just talking," Barret insisted emphatically. "Her husband was a drunkard who abused her and the children, so she's simply relieved rather than grief-stricken to find herself a widow. They own nothing more than the clothes on their backs and are so grateful for even the smallest gift that it brings tears to my eyes to give them presents. They won't ever be leaving my home, not if I have any say about it." He turned then to smile at Isela and her returning smile was so wonderfully sweet he knew Aidan would understand why he was taken with her. "I want you to tell Kara something for me."

"Why don't you tell her yourself?" Aidan suggested wisely.

"Because I'm too embarrassed to admit I was wrong, that's why. Will you tell her I'm sure none of us will have any regrets? Will you do that please?"

"If it means so much to you, I will," Aidan agreed.

"It does. What she and Alado have accomplished here is miraculous. We'll not be isolated any longer. Supply ships will visit us, we'll be able to go elsewhere. There's no end to what we can learn now that we'll have access to the rest of the worlds in the Confederation. Do you realize what that means?"

"Yes," Aidan replied with a broad grin. "It means we're not exiles any longer. We're finally free."

"I assume you're going with Kara. Will you ever come back?"

"This is my home. Of course I'll come back," Aidan assured him. He reached out to give his cousin a warm hug.

"And when I do, I'll expect you and Isela to have a few more little blond kids."

"Well, what about you? Don't you plan to become a father, too?" Barret teased playfully.

Aidan nodded. "Yes, I certainly do." He heard the shuttle circling overhead and had to draw their conversation to a close, but he was very glad that Barret and Isela had proved to be so compatible, for the man's attitude had become far more optimistic and that was a great improvement in his view.

By nightfall many of the city's inhabitants had had not one ride but two on the shuttle, and Kara could leave it parked in the square while she and Aidan went to the farewell party. Rather than being confined to one location, the whole city was ablaze with light as people moved in and out of homes and taverns. The crowds frequently spilled out into the streets where the merriment continued unhindered by any constraints.

Tweed had brought his whole crew; Trey and the other medical personnel who had treated the injured were there, as well as the many others from Mother's crew who had helped either with the rescue efforts or the rebuilding. It was quite the best party Aidan had ever attended and he took care to make certain his wife was always near at hand. It was late before he saw Zac walking toward him through the crowd, Serafina by his side.

"I wouldn't have left without telling you good-bye," he greeted his best friend loudly.

"You really are leaving when Mother goes?" Zac looked both envious and pained.

"I know you can handle things here," Aidan assured him. "The men all respect your judgment, and the fact that you've married a mole makes you the ideal person to manage the rebirth of 329. I know you'll do a fine job of it, too."

Zac was about to argue that he would be a poor substitute for Aidan when the beauty of his bride's adoring gaze made him swallow the words. He straightened up a bit, certain with Serafina at his side he could do a fine job of any task. "We'll all miss you."

Aidan glanced over at Kara, wondering just how frequently they would be able to return. "This is still my home, Zac, and I'll come back to see you." It was a poignant farewell scene they repeated frequently, until Aidan could no longer ignore the tears in his friends' eyes. As more and more old friends crowded around them, Aidan found he simply wanted to be alone with his wife. Finally seeing an opportunity to get away without their absence being noticed, he took her hand and led her hurriedly from the crowded streets using the deserted alleys to reach his home.

Since they had already removed his belongings, Kara didn't understand why they had returned to his house. "Did you forget something?"

"No." Aidan shut the door, threw the bolt and then pulled her into his arms. "I just want to spend the rest of my last night here alone with you. Do you mind?"

"Mind? Why, not at all," Kara responded as she relaxed in his embrace. "It's a wonderfully romantic thought. Where do you want to make love first, on the bed or in the tub?" she asked as she began to unbutton his shorts.

"Right here," Aidan replied with a devilish chuckle. He began to kiss her again and again until she could do no more than cling limply to his arms. He carried her over to the large cushions near the table and lowered her gently upon them. "Let's not just repeat our memories, let's make some new ones."

Kara's vision was blurred by passion, but she still thought his suggestion a most beautiful one and did her best to help him create a night well worth remembering.

CHAPTER
◊ XXI ◊

The view from the bridge was as spectacular as Kara had promised, and Aidan was grateful the captain had invited them to join him there for the departure from 329. As he watched the details of his city grow ever fainter as the desert planet receded in the distance, his elation over the coming trip was heavily tinged with sorrow. "I had no idea how lonely I was until I met you," he whispered softly in Kara's ear, not wanting anyone to overhear his words.

That her husband's mood had suddenly become so melancholy surprised the willowy redhead, and she slipped her arm around his waist to draw him close. "We will be able to go back, Aidan. You've not left your home forever."

The handsome warrior smiled sadly as he replied, "Everything will have changed by the time we return, including you and I."

Misinterpreting his mood, Kara frowned impatiently. "If you're sorry you agreed to come with me, just say so and I'll take you back right now."

Aidan flashed the charming grin he had always found so effective with other women, even if he had had no great success in using it with her. "I didn't say I was sorry to be leaving 329. This is what I've hoped for all my life. I know I'll miss my family and friends, but never 329 itself. It looks very small now, doesn't it? Very insignificant."

"You must never think that," Kara scolded. "Your people

sacrificed far too much to survive there for you to dismiss it so lightly."

"That's certainly true," Aidan agreed. "Oh, I almost forgot to tell you that Barret wanted me to say there would be no regrets. Does that make any sense to you?"

"Yes, it does," Kara replied, delighted to have finally received his cousin's blessing. "It means he's decided I'm the perfect wife for you after all."

Before Aidan could agree with that opinion, they were interrupted by Matthew Merrill. "I'm not going to press you for an answer to my proposition just yet, but I think we would be foolish to waste the time before we reach Fleet Command Base when we could be putting it to far better use."

"In what way?" Aidan asked absently, not revealing that his decision had already been made.

"Kara will naturally resume her usual schedule. When scouts are not flying actual missions, their time is divided between physical conditioning, training flights and assisting our regular staff of cartographers assemble maps from the data they provided. Since Kara had the opportunity to spend a prolonged visit on 329, she has a great deal of valuable information to record, and I don't want you to grow bored without her company."

Aidan knew better than to discuss the man's "proposition" on the bridge, and so he suggested another private conversation. "If you have suggestions on how I might keep myself occupied, perhaps we should discuss them in your quarters."

Merrill nodded to his first officer to take command, then gestured for Kara and Aidan to precede him. "Shall we go then?"

Knowing the captain had not recounted her schedule for no purpose, Kara excused herself as soon as they had reached the second level and made her way to the cartography unit. The film she had provided had been as excellent as her usual standard, and a variety of useful maps were being prepared from it. Seated atop a tall stool, she spent the rest of the morning with the staff of the map unit, admiring their attention to precise detail which allowed them to create maps unequaled for accuracy by any other base ship. When it came time for the noon meal, she was sorry she had not told Aidan where to meet her, but hoped he would go to the officers' mess, where most of the scouts preferred to eat, since she and Aidan had taken several meals there.

When Kara entered the room, most of her friends were already there and Ryan Blake waved her over to his table. "Merrill told me to tell you Aidan will probably be busy until tonight. What's he planning to do with him? Not turn him into a scout, I hope."

Rather than give Ryan another reason to be jealous of her husband, Kara merely shrugged as she took the chair next to his. "I believe each of them is curious about the other since they have led such different lives. They might even become good friends."

"Knowing Merrill's passion for duty, I doubt he allows time for friends who won't advance his career," Ryan remarked sarcastically. He then took a savage bite out of his sandwich and chewed it thoroughly before he spoke again. "I checked with the housing unit this morning. You have not requested larger quarters. Don't you plan to stay married long enough to make a move worthwhile? Not that there aren't plenty of other women on board who would invite Aidan to share their beds when you tire of him. . . ."

Infuriated by that insulting remark, Kara lowered her voice to keep their conversation strictly private. "What's gotten into you, Ryan? There was nothing between us but friendship, and now you're behaving like a jilted lover. That has got to stop."

"The only reason there was 'nothing' between us is because Ramon met you first, and you know it! I didn't crowd him because he was my best friend, but Aidan's nothing but a handsome rogue who'll revert to his criminal stock and disgrace you time and again. Get rid of him now!"

Kara struck Ryan across the face with the back of her hand with such force he nearly fell from his chair. He made a fast grab for the edge of the table to catch himself and knocked his plate onto the floor with a loud clatter. "My God, Kara!" he shouted in both shock and pain, horrified that she had struck him when he considered the advice he had given her to be sound.

"You stay away from me! A long way away, you understand?" Kara kicked her own chair aside and turned toward the exit, meaning to sprint from the room. Then she saw Captain Merrill and a tall blond surveyor standing at the door. She halted in mid-stride, took up a more sedate pace and prayed they had not witnessed all of the wretched scene, but she could tell from Merrill's fierce expression that he most certainly had seen it. When she reached his side, she whispered softly, "Forgive me, sir, but I was sorely provoked."

"Do you wish to press charges?" the captain asked through tightly clenched teeth.

"No, sir." Kara focused her attention on the tips of the man's highly polished boots, fearing he might think her far too temperamental to continue being a scout. She could hear Sonia's mellow voice in her mind, advising her as she always did to breathe deeply and grow calm, but she would be damned if she would let anyone insult Aidan and simply hold her tongue! "Lieutenant Blake and I merely had a difference of opinion."

"Well, it must have been an extremely violent one to come to blows," Merrill correctly surmised. "You know such behavior is not tolerated here. I usually advise men to settle their differences in the gym, but in this case—"

"I would volunteer to act as my wife's champion, but I think she has already put Blake in his place."

Kara gasped as she looked up at the surveyor. Aidan had had his hair cut in the short style preferred by most of the men on board Mother and, dressed in a surveyor's khaki uniform, she had not recognized him. Horribly embarrassed by the fact that she had not known her own husband when he had altered his appearance only slightly, her cheeks grew bright with a deep crimson blush. "If you've come to meet me for lunch, may we please go somewhere else?"

Aidan looked first at Merrill, who granted his permission with a slight nod before issuing directions for the afternoon. "When you've finished eating, have Kara take you to the gym. I'll leave instructions with Warren and he can arrange your training schedule."

Merrill left them then and strode straight toward Ryan Blake, whose right cheek was still throbbing painfully from Kara's brutal blow.

"Come on." Aidan took his wife's arm and urged her out the door. "I wish you had a kitchen so I could cook my own food. Or whatever else I'd like to have for lunch," he teased with a playful wink. "Is there some quiet place where we can eat while you tell me what happened with Blake?"

Kara had lost her appetite, but knowing Aidan was undoubtedly hungry she led him to a small cafeteria which served the hearty vegetarian fare she knew was similar to what he was accustomed to eating. She took only a small dish of yogurt for herself and sprinkled the top with chopped nuts while he took a heaping plate of steamed vegetables and rice. "I'm sorry I didn't recognize you, but you look completely different with your hair cut short and—"

"Only different, not better?" Aidan had consented to having his hair cut only after the captain had explained that the present length would make him too conspicuous. He had insisted the barber leave untrimmed a long strand at the back of his head that ran down the nape of his neck, however, explaining the style was a tradition among warriors.

Considering that a serious question, Kara studied his appearance thoughtfully for a moment before she replied, "I didn't think it was possible for you to be any more handsome, but with your hair brushed away from your face your features are far easier to appreciate. I think you truly are better looking. Why did you pick the surveyor's garb? Do you plan to study to be one?"

"No, but we tried each of Alado's uniforms and with my fair coloring, I'm damn near invisible in khaki. Hell, you didn't even notice me and you're my wife!"

Kara couldn't let that remark go unchallenged. "It's not that I didn't notice you. I did. I just didn't recognize you, that's all, and it's no wonder. I'm lucky to have escaped with no more than a dirty look from Merrill. He could have charged me with assault if he had wanted to."

Thinking her worry absurd, Aidan disagreed. "All you did was belt the guy once, and he must have deserved it. Why would Merrill want to punish you for that?"

"I told you violence of any sort is forbidden on Mother. We live together too closely and for long stretches at a time to make such displays of temper permissible. It was a stupid thing for me to do, especially in a room full of witnesses."

Aidan reached across the table to take her hand in a soothing clasp. "Look, if Merrill criticizes you in any way, I'll tell him I won't consider working for him for any price. If you would like me to, I'll take Blake to the gym and have it out with him, too. Might as well get it over with now as later."

Kara shook her head emphatically. "Absolutely not. He's just jealous and behaving stupidly. I'll not drag you into it."

"I have a feeling I'm in it already. He must have said something about me, didn't he?"

Stalling for time, Kara stirred the chopped nuts into her yogurt as she tried to think of some way to divert the direction of their conversation. "It's really a problem Ryan has created for himself. He and Ramon were close friends and—"

"Ramon?" Aidan knew he had heard that name before, but it took him a few seconds to place it. "Oh yes, Ramon. There's still no word on what happened to him?"

"Absolutely none." Kara finally brought a spoonful of yogurt to her mouth. It was delicious, a smooth and creamy vanilla enhanced by the crunchy nuts, but she still wasn't hungry. "Would you like this? It's really good."

"Sure, I'll finish it if you don't want it."

"I don't." Kara pushed the dish across the table and leaned back in her chair. "What did you and Merrill talk about this morning?"

"Not much," Aidan admitted between bites. "He wants me to put my version of 329's history into the files, same as you did. I'm to keep in shape, learn all I can about the board of directors and practice firing a variety of weapons so if I need to be armed when I deliver his messages I'll have the necessary skills to defend myself."

"But you didn't tell him for sure that you would do it?"

"Not yet, and it's better this way. I don't want to lose my bargaining power should I need it to get you out of trouble."

His teasing grin made Kara blush again. "I'll stay out of trouble. I promise."

When they reached the gym, Kara introduced Aidan to Warren Kerr, a fitness expert who had been on Mother's staff for almost two years. He was nice-looking with curly brown hair and green eyes and had the well-muscled build the men of his profession all shared. While his manner was pleasant enough, she considered him much too impressed with himself. He tended to show off and flirt with her first and offer advice on exercise second. She had seen him repeat that pattern with many other women and knew he was apparently attracted to any pretty female. Having lived all her life on board Mother, she knew the gym's facilities well and simply avoided the man when she went there. Since the captain had directed her to leave Aidan in Warren's care, she hoped the two men would get along better than she and Warren did. "I think it's obvious my husband is used to working out, but he has not had the advantage of using any of our equipment."

Warren sent Aidan into the locker room to put on a pair of shorts, and when the young man returned he studied his powerful build with admiration. "Well, regardless of what form of training you're accustomed to, it's obviously highly effective. Would you like the job of being my assistant?"

Aidan laughed at that offer. "If I have any spare time, I'll come down here, how's that?"

"All I can hope for, I guess," Warren replied regretfully. "I'm sure you know how to do the basic exercises, push-ups, sit-ups, that sort of thing."

"Sure," Aidan assured him. "They're good for warming up."

"Fine. What I'd like to do is get an idea of your strength now, then we can work out a program to increase it. How many push-ups can you do?"

Aidan shrugged. "As many as I want to. Why don't you show me how many you can do, and then I'll double that?"

Warren glanced over at Kara, who was trying without success to hide her smile. "The object isn't to compete against me, or anyone else, but only against yourself, Aidan. How many push-ups I can do doesn't really matter."

"If you can't set an example, keep up with your students, how do you expect to earn their respect?" Aidan inquired seriously.

"I didn't say I couldn't keep up with everyone else, only that it isn't necessary." Seeing the warrior's glance take on a decidedly mocking gleam, Warren realized this was one man who would not accept his guidance without a practical demonstration to prove he had the authority to give it. "All right, I'm not too busy this afternoon, so I'll be happy to show you some acceptable levels of performance, but I don't expect you to double them."

"I can do it," Aidan vowed confidently. "You needn't try and make it easy for me."

Warren was fast learning to dislike Aidan immensely. Determined to put a stop to what he hoped was merely the man's reckless bravado meant to impress his wife, he asked Kara to count while he dropped to the padded floor and completed four hundred push-ups. When he got up, he reached quickly for a towel to wipe the sweat from his face and also to hide the fact that he had to take several deep breaths before he could speak. "You needn't double that, Aidan, just match it."

"That won't be any trouble to match. I'll still double it." Aidan winked at Kara and then made Warren another offer. "If you're so certain I can't do it, would you like to put some money on it?"

Warren was so shocked that he dropped his towel and leaned down quickly to pick it up. "I will assume you don't know wagering isn't permitted on board Mother and pretend I didn't hear that."

"I'm not talking about opening a casino, merely having a friendly bet." Aidan's smile was so innocently charming it would have been difficult for anyone to imagine he had earned a good portion of his livelihood by taking a cut of the money bet on him in athletic contests.

Warren could see by Kara's startled expression that she

was as surprised by her husband's outlandish suggestion as he, but he was positive Aidan couldn't possibly do eight hundred push-ups, so he knew he had nothing to lose. Besides, he could use a little extra cash. "I don't mind making a small wager. How does fifty dollars sound to you?"

Aidan shook his head. "No, that's not enough to make it worth my trouble." In truth, he had no idea what the current value of Alado's dollar was since meals were furnished without charge to Mother's crew, and he and Kara hadn't gone shopping in any of the base ship's stores yet. Assuming the coach hadn't wanted to risk much, he made a counter-offer. "Make it one hundred instead," he suggested as if the amount were a trifle.

Warren wiped off his perspiring brow, and certain Aidan had more conceit than talent, he agreed. "You're on, but if anyone ever hears about this it didn't happen, you understand?"

"Far be it from me to break any of Alado's laws." Aidan leaned over to kiss Kara lightly for luck and to silence the loud objection he was certain she was about to make, then dropped to the mat and proceeded to do eight hundred push-ups without even working up a sweat. When he rose, he made Warren a generous offer. "Want to go double or nothing that I can beat you at sit-ups now?"

Kara knew exactly what was going to happen. Aidan would undoubtedly challenge every man on board who thought himself in good shape until he found someone who could beat him. As far as she knew, if Warren couldn't do it, then no one could. "I'd advise you to pay up and stop this stupid game right now, Warren, before Aidan ends up owning every possession you treasure."

Warren, however, was too angry to take that advice. Certain he could do better with weights, he offered a challenge of his own. "Let's not waste any more time warming up. Let's go over to the weight training area and continue our sport there."

"Fine, but the rules have to change. I won't lift double what you can, but I'm sure I can better any record you set."

"You're on!" Warren exclaimed ambitiously, and he broke

into a jog as he headed for the far end of the gym where the weights were kept.

"I don't believe you're doing this to him," Kara disclosed with a disapproving frown. "There's no point in it, for one thing. The man's job is to assist you in your own personal growth, not provide you with an opponent."

Aidan sighed wearily. "I seem to recall Merrill saying you would be too busy to keep me company. Don't you have something else to do this afternoon? Just tell me where to meet you for dinner and I'll be there."

Having been clearly dismissed, Kara refused to make any kind of a date for dinner. "I'll be in my room later this afternoon. Just meet me there and please don't try and disgrace Warren just to make yourself look good!"

"Is that all you think I'm trying to do?" Aidan asked with a sullen scowl.

"Well, isn't it? How do you think he's going to feel if you beat him at every skill he's trying to teach the rest of us? He would scarcely feel good about it."

"All he'll learn is that I like competition," Aidan vowed hoarsely. "Most men do."

Exasperated, Kara tried one last suggestion. "Stop the bets before someone overhears what you're doing."

"Why? Merrill can't toss me overboard," the wily warrior pointed out with a rakish grin.

Kara clenched her fists tightly at her sides, "Look, if you don't want to give everyone the mistaken impression that the residents of 329 are indeed rogues who ought to be left in exile, then you better start thinking of something other than yourself for a change!" She stormed off then, not giving him a chance to get in the last word, but she was both worried and frightened that either she had never really known him or he was fast becoming someone she didn't want to know.

To force her personal problems aside, Kara spent the afternoon working in the library going over the files on the board of directors. She was embarrassed to realize that other than their names, she knew little about the nine people who determined Alado's policies. After several hours she requested a printout of the most current information as well as photographs. Kara placed the material in a file folder and carried it back to her room, planning to study it later with Aidan. When she found him standing in the bathroom shaving, she wanted to know how he had entered her quarters. "I'm sorry, I thought I'd be back before you finished in the gym. How did you get in?"

"Merrill gave me a security pass. I can go anywhere I like, although it's damn handy to be able to get in here when I need to."

"He gave you a pass?" Kara couldn't believe the man had actually done that since such a card provided unrestricted access to all levels of Mother. She leaned against the open door of the bathroom, still trying to get used to the difference in her husband's appearance. "What prompted him to do that?"

"He's hoping I'll agree to do his dirty work for him, that's what. The security pass is only a sample of the privileges he can provide. I'm supposed to be impressed."

"It doesn't sound as though you are," Kara mused thoughtfully.

Aidan rinsed off his razor, then wiped the last traces of lather from his face. "Frankly, as long as I can get your door open, I'll be happy. I'm sorry about this afternoon, but I just didn't like the way Warren Kerr looked at you and—"

"Oh that," Kara remarked with a disgusted frown. "He looks at all the attractive women the same way. His business is creating healthy bodies and he enjoys looking at them. I don't take it personally."

"Well, I do. It was a pleasure to take his money, believe me, and it was better than breaking his nose since you told me violence wouldn't be tolerated here. That was my first choice, though. Do you really think I'm going to give 329 a worse reputation than it already has?"

Kara shook her head and apologized. "No, I shouldn't have said that. It's just that you're used to settling things differently than we are, and I wish you'd stop to think before you do something you might soon regret."

"Merrill said he usually tells men to settle differences in

the gym," Aidan reminded her with a sly smile. "That's how I'm used to settling things. That's all I did today."

"You're impossible. You know that, don't you?" But Kara couldn't help laughing. "I guess if you settle arguments in the gym and are discreet about the bets, you'll do all right. Now where would you like to eat dinner?"

"The officers' mess, of course. I don't want Blake to think we're afraid to face him."

After a moment's reflection Kara agreed, but she was relieved when Ryan didn't appear while they were dining. When they returned to her quarters, she showed Aidan the materials she had gotten on the board. "Are you too tired to go over this now? I think we should study just a little bit each day. Then, by the time we reach Fleet Command Base, you'll know these people better than they know themselves."

"Sure, let's see what you have." Aidan pulled off his boots and stretched out on the bed. "Come curl up here beside me," he invited with an enticing smile.

Kara doubted they would study the information about the board for too long in such relaxed poses, but Aidan proved to have more interest in the subject than she had dared hope. "Political analysts usually divide the board into three factions. The first group are pacifists, while the second is nearly the complete opposite and can be counted on to take an aggressive stand on every issue. Then there's a more or less fluid middle group which can lean toward either side depending on the issue. They might vote with the pacifists when it comes to preserving a planet's natural environment, but with the militants when it comes to setting prices for commodities." She stopped then to make certain he understood her. "Does that make sense to you?"

"Of course. I'm sure it's the same everywhere. Very few people are consistently committed to a particular set of ideals. Most can be swayed one way or another depending on what's at stake and whether or not they'll be personally affected by a particular decision."

Kara was delighted to find her husband not only understood what she had said, but also had seen it in practice. "Yes, that's exactly it. Too many people don't care at all about decisions unless it directly concerns them and then they start screaming, but often by then it's too late." She sorted through the photos and accompanying biographies in order to present the board members in a logical order. "I'll begin with the most idealistic member of the board, Daya Crane. You would like her. She's a lovely blond with an IQ in the 200's who positively radiates tranquility. She's in her early forties, and this is her second term on the board."

Aidan picked up the color photograph the computer had provided and found Kara's description easy to believe, for the blue-eyed blond had the most angelic expression he had ever seen. "She would be unlikely to order a base ship to abandon her scouts, wouldn't she?"

Kara nodded thoughtfully. "Yes, that's precisely the question we should ask about each board member. Daya would never put anyone's life at risk for any reason, I'm certain of it. Now, Emerson Thatcher is next. He's an eloquent speaker, but not nearly as bright as Daya. He usually votes with her, though. He's sixty and has been on the board for nearly eighteen years. His gray hair gives him the appearance of wisdom and, from all reports, that's an image he tries hard to cultivate. I think he's too calm and steady to want to risk war, so I'll put his photo with Daya's." Kara shuffled through the biographies for a moment, then began with the leading militant.

"This is Cipriano Acuña. He's cut from the same revolutionary mold as Zac's great-grandfather, Joaquin Zacatón. He has a huge following in South America, but he's not highly regarded elsewhere. He's fifty-three and is in his second six-year term. He prides himself on being a weapons expert and he would not have any qualms about sacrificing a few insignificant scouts to test something with the potential of the force field."

Aidan studied the man's photograph for a long moment before beginning a new stack. "He has Zac's dark coloring, but from the evil gleam in his eyes, I'd say that's where the similiarity ends."

"No, they're nothing alike. I've never met the man, but in his news briefs he's just as intense as he appears in that still photo. He's so dedicated to the goal of expansion that he might be more at home on Europa's board." She paused for a few seconds to again sort through the sheets of information and photographs she held.

"This man is Jess Hudak. He's new, thirty-eight years old, and since his election has been Cipriano's shadow." She tossed the sandy-haired man's photo on top of the South American's and then began to describe the only militant woman. "At forty-five, Arla Keyes is in her second term. She's far more intellectual in her approach than Cipriano, but there's little difference in their views."

Aidan regarded the dark-eyed woman's severe features with a shudder. "Looks like a real witch to me. Is she married?"

"I think so, but she's not the type to allow anyone much access to her private life." Kara scanned the woman's biography hurriedly, then shook her head. "No, it says she's a widow. Well, those three—Cipriano, Jess and Arla—are the most vocal and aggressive members of the board."

Aidan laid their pictures side by side, then studied Daya and Emerson's photos again. "Already I don't like the sound of this, Kara. These two look too sweet to have any real power, while these three look like they would go for the throat in an instant."

"Don't forget the board has four other members though, so there's really a buffer between the two extremes." She laid out the remaining pictures between the ones Aidan had arranged. "Pearn Leland is a very practical person. Her main interest is in keeping costs down, and that philosophy has gotten her reelected three times. Herald Hyson is new. He's only thirty-four, an attorney who seems more interested in following the precedents of the previous boards than setting new ones. Burl Elliott is the oldest member of the board at sixty-three, and although he's the current chairman, he's more a moderator of the group than a true leader. Delia Holguin is also new. She's thirty-nine, a physician whose specialty is genetics. I don't think there's been time to see which way she might go."

"As you might expect, Alado's board was never the topic

of conversation on 329. Does a simple majority win any vote?"

"Yes, five votes are needed to change any existing policy or to pass a new one."

"That means if our fierce three are backing the force field, they would have to win the support of at least two others. If Daya and Emerson are longtime pacifists, they would not waste their time on them, so I'll move them over here out of the running. Pearn has been around too long to be easily swayed, so let's toss her out. Burl has no real clout, so he goes, too." Aidan rearranged the photographs of the remaining members.

"That leaves us with the two new board members: Herald Hyson, whom you say is an attorney with little imagination, and the doctor, Delia Holguin. If I were Cipriano, I would do my damnedest to pull those two into my camp with whatever leverage I had to use, money, sex, drugs, prestige, you name it."

Deeply impressed, Kara stared at the neat arrangement of photographs her husband had made. "That's not only logical, Aidan, it's positively brilliant! Let's go tell Merrill your theory and see what he thinks of it!" she suggested excitedly.

Aidan picked up the papers and photographs carefully, then tossed them off the bed onto the floor. "It will keep until morning. Besides, for all we know, all nine board members voted to test the device. Until Merrill gives his report and can get some idea of the group's reaction, we won't know if we're on the right track or not." He was confident they were, however.

"Well perhaps not, but—"

Aidan leaned across Kara then, forcing her gently back upon the pillows to interrupt her argument with a slow, deep kiss he did not end until he felt her initial resistance melt away. He liked to surprise her, to feel her reaction go from startled to the seductive warmth of acceptance. He had helped her remove her flight suit so frequently that he could now do it without lifting his mouth from hers. But he was shocked at how swiftly she managed to strip the surveyor's khaki suit from him. All the men's uniforms had a similar cut, but the thought of her undressing other men who must have been every bit as eager to possess her as he was provided a severe jolt. He drew back for just an instant; then wound his fingers in the straps of her teddy to pull them off her shoulders. "I'm sorry you don't recall the first time we slept together as vividly as I do. I'll never forget it as long as I live."

Intrigued by that thought, Kara propped herself up on her elbows. "Why don't you just do what you did then? But rather than smearing Oblivion all over me, there's a small bottle of honey-flavored brandy in the bottom drawer of my desk. Use that instead, and this time I'll remember the evening well."

Aidan couldn't help but laugh at that idea. "You really want me to do it?"

"Yes, of course." Kara smiled sweetly, but her golden eyes were alight with mischief. "Since I can't share the memory of our first romantic interlude, I want you to re-create it for me."

On his way to the desk Aidan tossed the clothes they had discarded across the nearest lounge chair. He found the bottle of brandy, broke open the seal and took a sip. "This is a bit too sweet, but still good. Not as good as Oblivion, certainly, but good enough."

Kara slipped off her teddy and let it drop to the rug. "Let's have soft lights and sweet music, too." She reached over to the control panel beside the bed to dim the lights to a subtle glow and then selected a tape of romantic melodies performed by a string ensemble for lush musical accompaniment. "Should I pretend to be asleep?"

"No, you were wide awake. Just lie back, and I promise you'll enjoy this." He poured a tiny amount of the brandy into his left palm and using his right thumb began to trace her Love Vine from her instep. "I had never seen a tattoo and I was as fascinated with it as I was with you." He leaned down then to lick off the light trail of brandy with the tip of his tongue. "You couldn't remember if you had ever made love before or not, but that didn't bother me in the slightest."

While Aidan's touch was so light it tickled, Kara dared not laugh for fear she would break his loving mood. "I'm sorry if you were disappointed to find you weren't the first man in my life."

Aidan paused a moment to reflect. "No, I wasn't disappointed. We were having far too much fun for that." He scooted up a bit and rubbed a generous amount of the fragrant brandy over her kneecap. "I like the way the vine swirls around your leg. It is as alive as your skin."

Kara was still propped up on her elbows, trying to imagine how she could ever have been so drunk that she would have allowed him to take such liberties when they had just met. Now it was wonderfully erotic, but had it been then as well? "Aidan," she whispered softly, "you're not just making this all up, are you?"

"Making what up?" the warrior inquired as he shifted his position again to focus his attention on her slender thigh. He rubbed his thumb up slowly from her knee, around her thigh and then let his fingertips stray to the soft red curls that lured him toward a warm sweetness all her own. "Isn't this exactly as I described it to you the next day?"

But in his own mind his memories began to blur and he knew it didn't really matter whether he repeated the exact same moves when he could make others which would be as enjoyable. He tilted the bottle then to pour a thick stream of the rich brandy into her navel. The golden brown liquid swiftly overflowed that small indentation, spilled over the flat plane of her stomach and trickled down between her legs. With the abandon of a fat cat savoring cream, he leaned down to lap up the brandy slowly from her satin-smooth skin. "What is this delicious stuff called?" he asked between swallows.

"*Beso de la Abeja,*" Kara replied breathlessly. "Kiss of the Bee."

"That is a marvelous name." Aidan looked up and smiled widely. He licked his lips, then gently spread her thighs. "I don't want to waste a single drop of it."

Kara reached out to touch his newly shorn curls. His hair was thick, but not nearly as blond now that the long sun-bleached tresses had been trimmed away. He was handsome, bright and so very loving. Relaxing completely, she lay back to enjoy the tender kisses he was bestowing so generously on the firm flesh of her inner thighs. He was as gentle as a warm desert wind, teasing her senses as he drew slowly toward the most exquisitely sensitive part of her graceful body. To remain deeply relaxed, to float peacefully on the rise and fall of the music and the swell and ebb of sensations rather than writhe in anticipation of its climax was one of the many skills she had been carefully taught, and it was well worth the effort to practice, for it made the pleasure he gave her all the more luscious when at last he reached his goal.

Aidan paused briefly to look up at his beloved's blissful smile before allowing his tongue to trace the path of the honey-flavored brandy until it mingled with the exotic taste of her own unique essence. "I like your taste even better," he murmured hungrily, so entranced with the languid ease of her surrender that he was as lost as she in the ecstasy he had created. The lilting strains of the music swirled within his mind, blending with the soft lights to form one of the most perfect moments he had ever lived, and he did not draw away until he was certain the pleasure he had given her could not be more complete.

With a charming insouciance Kara welcomed Aidan's kiss as his mouth returned to hers, but she wrapped him in a warm embrace only briefly, then slid from his arms. "Wait a minute. Don't I get to drip the brandy over you now?"

"Later," Aidan suggested anxiously, his voice husky with desire.

"Oh no," Kara insisted. "Now, but rather than your toes, I want to start here." She leaned down to get the bottle of brandy, poured no more than a drop on a fingertip, then traced the outline of his lips before kissing him again. "You have very nice ears, too, very tasty."

Aidan moaned softly, certain he wasn't going to be able to stand much of her sweetly worded teasing. Her touch was light as it traveled over his broad chest, but when he reached up to caress her breasts she pushed his hands away.

"It's my turn now, beloved, not yours," she cautioned.

She continued to slide her fingertips over him, outlining each muscle and rib with the brandy before she lowered her lips to his warm bronze skin to torment him with slow kisses which led down the contours of his splendid physique.

Unlike Kara, Aidan had little in the way of mental discipline and he couldn't simply lie back and enjoy her tantalizing touch when she was driving him so wild with desire that the stars overhead had taken on a bloodred glow. With the low growl of a fiercely determined predator he made a sudden lunge, captured her in his arms, then rolled over to pin her beneath him. "Your turn is over," he insisted firmly. "It's my turn again."

Kara gave a delighted giggle as she wrapped her arms around his neck to bring his lips down to hers. She loved him far too much to accuse him of not playing fair. It made no difference to her whose turn it was as long as the pleasure they created was so deeply shared.

"I love you," she whispered as she moved beneath him in an invitation he was quick to accept. Lost in the rapture of her lavish affection, Aidan didn't reply with words, but the depth of his passion was stunning proof of his devotion and more than enough evidence of his love to please her.

CHAPTER
◇ **XXII** ◇

Kara was not only amazed, but also deeply impressed by the ease with which Aidan adapted to life on board Mother. Despite her initial fears, he had not gone out of his way to humiliate the other men with demonstrations of his superb physical prowess. He still enjoyed what he regarded as friendly competition, but refrained from making bets with the men who had begun joining him each morning when he worked out in the gym.

When Captain Merrill had suggested he study martial arts with the first officer, Jason Macleod, who was widely respected in the field, he had proven to be the man's equal. While he hadn't known the specific names for all the moves he had been taught by his grandfather, Aidan knew how to use the actions themselves with remarkable precision. With his own unique strategies, he quickly defeated Jason's other students, including Ryan Blake. While Aidan found that match greatly amusing, Ryan did not, and his own furious anger contributed to his swift defeat.

Aidan devoted as much time to intellectual pursuits as physical ones. He picked up the basic skills required of a surveyor to justify his use of that uniform and keep anyone from becoming overly suspicious of how he spent his time. Having tended a garden all his life, he frequently spent part of his afternoons in the fourth level's hydroponic gardens. He enjoyed talking with the technicians and observing their constant experiments to boost production by adjusting the levels of nutrients in the vats containing the high-yield plants that kept Mother's crew well supplied with fresh fruits and vegetables. At other times he could be found in the library looking up the answers to the questions that had puzzled him all his life or surreptitiously gathering still more information about the diverse group that made up Alado's board of directors.

Having never seen a film or heard much music, he liked to spend the evenings with Kara viewing her favorites, or listening to something from Mother's vast musical library. They never listened passively, however, but always used the selections to create a harmoniously romantic environment in which to make love. They talked about moving to larger quarters, but since they spent little time in their one room, neither saw any reason to request more space. With the one exception of Ryan Blake, Aidan was well liked. Kara was happier than she had ever been. Her husband placed no restrictions on her, and in return she had given none to him.

They were living what she considered an ideal life until the afternoon Aidan paid Trey a visit.

Kara had just stepped out of the shower when she heard the door to the outer corridor slide open and closed. She wrapped a towel around herself and leaned around the corner to greet her husband. "I'm glad you're back early," she called out happily, but the fury of his deep scowl was so frightening she quickly stepped out into the room. "What's wrong? What's happened?" she asked anxiously, unable to imagine what could possibly have upset him so badly.

"Why don't you tell me what's wrong!" Aidan countered bitterly. "Because that's exactly what I want to know. Just what the hell is wrong with you?"

Completely confused, Kara regarded her husband with a befuddled stare. "I'm sorry, but I have no idea what you're talking about. Maybe if you went out and came in again it would help."

Aidan put his hands on his hips, his pose as well as the tone of his voice deliberately hostile. "I had an extremely interesting talk with Trey just now. Does that give you a clue as to why I'm so damn angry with you?"

Kara shook her head, sending a fine spray flying from her damp curls. "No, I've no idea why Trey's opinions would infuriate you so. The man's talkative, but his ideas usually aren't even remotely controversial. What did he say?"

Aidan found it difficult to believe that the young woman who was regarding him with such wide-eyed innocence could possibly be so dense when he had always considered her quite bright. "It isn't his opinions that disgust me, but yours. I thought you and I were as close as a man and woman could ever be, and all the while you've been lying to me. Didn't you think I would ever be curious enough about your implant to ask Trey about it?"

Kara could feel the heat of a bright blush as it flooded her cheeks with brilliant color, for it was plain he would accept no excuse for the fabrication she had told him. He obviously regarded what she had said as the most despicable of lies when it had seemed her only choice at the time. "I'm sorry if you were surprised or embarrassed by what Trey told you. Give me a few minutes to get dressed and then we'll talk about it."

"Talk about it!" Aidan shouted hoarsely. "What's the point when you'll probably just lie to me again? I don't want to talk to you. I don't even want to look at you!" With that angry farewell he turned his back on her and walked out.

Kara waited up long past midnight, but Aidan didn't return to their quarters. The next morning she was too distraught to face her friends, let alone try and concentrate on any sort of work. Going to the gym was out of the question, too, since Aidan might be there and she didn't want to risk another angry confrontation in front of others. She felt so utterly depressed and lost that she reported out sick and spent the day in bed trying to catch up on the sleep she had missed. When Trey came to see her in mid-afternoon, she was horribly embarrassed to be in her nightgown still. She opened the door only a fraction of an inch and apologized hurriedly. "I'm sorry you were worried about me, Trey, but I'm not sick. I just got too tired."

The usually lovely redhead had dark circles beneath her eyes and her expression was one of such hopeless distress that he felt fully justified in pushing his way inside. "You are one of Mother's healthiest females, and I'd like to see you stay that way. It doesn't matter whether your problem is physical or mental, you've clearly got one. Now, what can I do to help?"

The handsome physician's offer was too sincere to be rejected rudely, and Kara let the door slide closed rather than demand that he leave. "I'm just tired," she insisted once again.

"Well, I saw Aidan alone last night and again at breakfast and he certainly looked fine. Does he know you haven't left your quarters in almost a day?"

Kara turned toward the bed to avoid Trey's perceptive gaze. "I didn't want to bother him," she responded softly as she crossed the room. Hoping he would soon leave, she perched on the side of the unmade bed and folded her hands in her lap.

"He came to talk with me yesterday, but I don't think I answered his questions the way I should have." Trey followed her across the room and sat down on the foot of the lounge chair nearest the bed. "Do you want me to talk with him again?"

Kara shook her head, sorry he had figured out what was wrong on his own. "You mustn't think this has anything to do with you. It's entirely my fault."

Trey disagreed. "The decision to have a child is a very serious one, Kara. It's not something a couple should make without considerable discussion. I don't think Aidan realizes that while he's made many friends and seems to be fitting in rather well on Mother, there are still many differences between our beliefs and his. Our discussion yesterday was purely technical in nature, and I can see now that that was a grave error on my part. The married couples we know usually don't wish to have children for a number of years, but apparently on 329 men and women expect to have a baby before they celebrate their first anniversary. It has been centuries since we've regarded procreation as the primary focus of a marriage, and I didn't even touch upon that point with him."

Kara sighed sadly, realizing their problem was even more complex than she had first thought. Perhaps the issue was more than whether or not she had lied to Aidan. It also involved conflicting views on the very nature of marriage itself. Rather than improving her mood, Trey had only succeeded in making her feel all the more confused. "Thanks for wanting to help, Trey, but this is something Aidan and I will have to work out for ourselves as best we can."

"Not by crying yourself to sleep, you won't," Trey advised sympathetically. "Tears provide only a momentary release. They solve nothing in and of themselves."

Kara found it impossible to argue with the logic of that remark since she did not feel any better than she had when

Aidan had stormed out the door. "What do you prescribe instead?"

Trey flashed a disarming grin. "I think we should teach Aidan how to solve conflicts more constructively. What time do you two usually go to dinner?"

"Around seven, why?"

"If he's not here by seven-fifteen, then I'll take you to dinner myself," Trey offered graciously.

While Kara understood what he was trying to do, she didn't think it was wise. "No, making Aidan jealous isn't a good idea, Trey. It will just make him all the more furious with me."

The physician rose as he disagreed. "This has nothing to do with anything as juvenile as attempting to make your husband jealous. It is strictly a matter of nutrition. If Aidan doesn't come for you, would you go to dinner alone?"

"No," Kara admitted reluctantly, knowing she would be much too embarrassed to face her friends when they would all ask where Aidan was and she didn't even know. "No, I'd just stay right here."

"It is settled then. I will stop by at seven-fifteen. If you have gone to dinner with your husband, fine. If not, then you will accompany me in the interest of good health," he invited with a sly wink.

Surprised to find the unexpected option of having a charming dinner companion remarkably attractive, Kara walked him to the door. "You're being very sweet to do this, Trey. I'll repay the favor as soon as I can."

"Think nothing of it," the friendly physician replied. "I'm only sorry I didn't invite you to dinner years ago."

As the door slid closed behind him, Kara wondered if he was serious. Well, if he had had any romantic interest in her he should have pursued it long before now. There was a lesson to be learned from that, she was certain. Surely it would be better to take some action, any action at all, rather than mope around her quarters hoping that by some miracle Aidan would return home with a more reasonable attitude.

Encouraged by that thought, she dried the last of her tears and began to look forward to the evening.

Kara had left their quarters by the time Aidan arrived to shower and change his clothes for the evening. He saw the necklace he had given her lying on the desk and slipped it into his pocket. He had spent the day with Matthew Merrill qualifying with a number of weapons, but his preoccupation had been so obvious that he had finally been forced to admit he and Kara had had an argument which weighed heavily on his mind. The captain had been surprisingly sympathetic, but Aidan had not described the nature of their disagreement since it would have been far too painful to reveal.

Now he didn't know what to do. He had thought avoiding his wife for a day or two would help him control his temper, but his anger hadn't even begun to abate, and he doubted the feeling of betrayal would ever ease. Had he discovered she had been unfaithful to him he would have felt no less abused. Unable to remain in her quarters where her presence surrounded him even when she was away, he left hoping to find something among Mother's many diversions which would help him pass what he knew would be another sleepless night.

Trey had carried most of the conversation and Kara had eaten little, but she still thanked him for an enjoyable evening when he walked her to her door. The whole time she had been with the helpful physician she had hoped to catch a glimpse of Aidan, but there had been no sign of him. When they reached her quarters she tried to conceal her disappointment at finding them empty, but she didn't fool her friend.

"Whether or not your husband comes home tonight, I want you to promise me you'll get some sleep and report for duty in the morning. Alado's policies are very generous when it comes to keeping families together, but if Merrill suspects you and Aidan are having problems, my guess is that he'll put him off Mother when we reach Fleet Command Base. If I see him, I'll tell him that's what he's risking, too."

Kara knew the captain regarded Aidan far too highly to bar him from the base ship, but she didn't confide her reasons for that opinion. "He can't keep avoiding me much longer," she said instead. "Thanks again for taking me to dinner. I'll heed your advice and be back to work in the morning." She knew she should extend an invitation for him to remain with her awhile longer, but after a whole evening of his company she wanted to be alone and bid him a hurried farewell before closing her door.

Initially she found no sign to indicate her husband had returned to their quarters during her absence, but when she entered the bathroom and saw he had discarded his clothes with her laundry she was pleased to think he apparently still lived there. That was little comfort, however, and despite her promise, it was a long while before she fell asleep.

True to her word, Kara not only reported for duty the following morning, but she also took out her Banshee for one of the routine training flights scouts were required to make between missions. As always, she found flying so absorbing and exhilarating that she was able to forget her problems completely for the better part of the day.

When she returned to her room in the late afternoon she was both astonished and delighted to find Aidan stretched out sound asleep in the lounge chair nearest the bed. He had taken a shower before sitting down to rest. His towel was carelessly draped across his lap, but it was the elaborate tattoo gracing his right arm and shoulder with lavish decoration that surprised her even more than his sudden reappearance. A fire-breathing dragon was clawing his way up and over her husband's shoulder as though he were bent upon reaching his heart. The beast's long spiked tail was coiled around the warrior's upper arm while his wings spread from the lizardlike body so one curved down over his shoulder blade in back while the other unfurled near the creature's head which was magnificently detailed upon Aidan's chest. The mythical creature was complete to the last detail. His color was the same pale shade of green she had chosen for her Love Vine while his scales and features were outlined with a shimmering gold and accented in scarlet. It was a terrifying image, and yet at the same time drawn with such incredible artistry that it was exquisitely beautiful—the perfect symbol for the man she loved.

Kara was studying the marvelous dragon so intently she did not realize for several seconds that Aidan had awakened and was observing her with an equally appreciative glance. "Do you like it?" he finally asked.

"I love it. Risa did my tattoo, and I'd say from the precision of yours that she did it, too. Am I right?"

"Yes, and it took all night. I didn't realize it would hurt so badly, but whatever she gave me to drink for the pain knocked me out for most of the day."

When he reached out to pull her down on his lap, Kara was careful to rest her head upon his left shoulder so she would not put any pressure on his skin while it was still sensitive. She waited for him to say something about where he had been the rest of the time since she had last seen him, but when he offered no explanation she didn't dare ask for one. "Aidan," she began hesitantly.

"Hush." Aidan's left hand combed lazily through her soft tangle of curls before his finger moved lower to caress her cheek. "You could talk forever and I'd still never understand why you did it. Just promise me you won't lie to me again."

While he had stated that request in reasonable terms, Kara couldn't agree when he had no understanding of her motives for misleading him. She snuggled even closer as she attempted to explain. "Everything happened so quickly, Aidan. When I had to make an emergency landing on 329 I expected to be stranded for no more than a few hours. I never dreamed I'd meet you or have such an incredible adventure. The prospect of having a child was simply too much for me to accept when my whole life had been turned completely upside down, so I told you it was far too dangerous to remove the implant. I deceived you only to protect myself, but I never meant to hurt you."

Aidan had always known she had wanted to return to Mother while he had hoped to keep her with him. Now they both had their wish, but he still wanted her to have his child.

"So what happens now, Kara? Can I hope we'll have a child someday, or will you give me excuses forever?"

Kara sat up slightly so she could look directly at him as she replied, "Isn't our love enough for you for now?"

The two days he had spent without her had been the longest of his life, and even with her cradled in his arms he still felt depressed. "It's the very fact that I love you so much that makes me want to have a family with you. You can have a baby and still fly. If your mother did it, so can you."

The instant he spoke those words he regretted it, for Kara's golden eyes filled with huge tears. He pulled her back into his arms, nearly crushing her with the power of his embrace. "That's the real problem, isn't it? All the word family means to you is the painful memory of your parents' deaths. I didn't mean to remind you of that awful time and I won't do it again. We'll have a child when you want to and not before. Surprise me if you like. I'll be happy no matter when you choose to make me a father."

Kara could not help but cry then because she had never expected him to be so wonderfully understanding. She clung to him and wept until she fell asleep in his arms, exhausted by her sorrow.

Even after his wife's tears finally stopped splashing on his chest, Aidan continued to hold her tenderly. He didn't understand how she could have grown up to be so fiercely independent when her spirit was so terribly fragile. Her personality was a mass of contradictions, and yet everything about her fascinated him and he knew it always would. She was right, he decided. They still had so much to learn about each other that it was much too soon to complicate their relationship with children.

He rested his chin atop her curls as the last of his doubts melted away. He never wanted to be separated from her ever again, and he promised himself no matter how heated their arguments became he would never walk out on her again. He had to stifle a laugh at that thought, for he knew that, despite the depth of their love, their life was never going to be placid.

CHAPTER
◇ **XXIII** ◇

Fleet Command Base was a gigantic rotating space station which completed a revolution every sixty seconds so its gravity equaled that of Earth. Built in the shape of a wheel, the outer ring housed docking bays large enough to accommodate base ships while the spokes contained transport tubes in which shuttle cars provided immediate service to the command center located in the domed hub. It was as remarkable a feat of engineering as Mother was herself, and Aidan was as eager to explore the facility as he was to attend the meeting of the board of directors. The captain had provided him with the dove gray uniform of Mother's security police for the occasion, insuring that the warrior would be mistaken for his personal bodyguard and not noticed for himself. Merrill had also insisted that Kara attend, hoping he could present her as one of the surviving scouts so those who had risked her life so recklessly could see exactly what they had done. Since the board was meeting in executive session, there were no other spectators.

A keen observer, Aidan watched and listened closely as each of the board members spoke. There were half a dozen items of routine business to be acted upon before Matthew Merrill was scheduled to present his report, but by then the tension among the nine members of the board had been clearly demonstrated. It seemed to matter little what topic was under discussion, for Cipriano Acuña interrupted constantly. With a belligerent combination of ridicule and disdain, it was he who managed the flow of business rather than the ineffectual chairman, Burl Elliott.

Aidan leaned over to whisper in his wife's ear, "I don't like Acuña. It's clear he has the makings of a tyrant rather than a statesman."

Kara nodded in agreement, for Cipriano showed no interest in striving for a cooperative accord with the others. Rather than the cohesive unit the board ideally should have been, what she saw that day was a deeply divided group. Repeatedly Cipriano cut the discussion short by calling for a vote in which Jess Hudak, Arla Keyes, Delia Holguin and Herald Hyson would vote with him. When Matthew Merrill was at last called to come forward and present the results of the test of the force field, it swiftly became apparent by their confused expressions that the majority of the board had no idea what the device was.

Daya Crane, the gentle blond, was the first to speak. "I am sorry, Captain Merrill, but upon whose authority was this test made? I don't recall any discussion of such a device at any of our previous meetings."

"The test was ordered in a message transmitted in the board's own top secret code," Merrill replied with an accusing stare which swept Alado's leaders. "I did not question its source."

"Well then, I will," Daya responded in a voice that carried surprisingly well for being so soft and sweet. The board was seated around a semicircular table so each member could see the others. "You are chairman of the committee that supervises the Expeditionary Force, Cipriano. Did your group make this decision without the full consent of the board?"

The dark-eyed man chuckled as though her question were quite amusing. "It is still in its experimental stage, Daya, so full consent isn't required. The reason we have committees is to spare the group the burden of deciding insignificant issues, but you know that as well as I do."

Aidan clamped his hand over Kara's wrist as he felt her start to rise from her chair. "Hold on!" he whispered. "Screaming at the man won't help us." The redhead shot him a murderous glance, but slumped back down in her seat as ordered.

"You can not possibly consider such a test 'insignificant'," Daya countered firmly. "Captain Merrill has just explained that two of his scouts are still missing and that the four who were eventually rescued had all suffered greatly from their ordeal."

"Daya, please," Cipriano chided in a patronizing tone. "The force field proved to be far too promising a defense to waste our time lamenting the loss of two scouts. Besides, we can't be certain they are dead. It's possible they were picked up by ships belonging to other corporations and will be returned to us safely at a future date. The only reasonable conclusion is that the device appears promising as a defense system, but of course it will require further testing before we discuss installing it not only in all our base ships but in all our intermediate vessels as well."

Pearn Leland began tapping her fingernails on the table in a furious staccato rhythm to draw Cipriano's attention. "There was no authorization for funding this project," she objected strongly.

The handsome South American replied with a charming smile, then said, "The device was furnished by the inventor at no cost to us, so no funding was required."

Merrill glanced back over his shoulder at Aidan and Kara, as disturbed by the cavalier manner in which Cipriano manipulated the discussion as they were. Fearing there would be no more questions, he promptly interjected his own opinion. "The device clearly has such a great offensive potential it would be banned by the Confederation. The prototype should be destroyed and no further tests of any similar device ever be made."

Finally asserting the leadership he had allowed to fall to Cipriano Acuña by default, Burl Elliott responded sternly, "That is a matter for the board to decide, Captain Merrill. Thank you for your informative report. I know I need not remind you that you are not at liberty to discuss what has transpired here with anyone. You may go."

Merrill grabbed up the notes he had barely begun to use

and left the conference room. The extent of his fury was plain for all to see in the length of his stride, and without delay Aidan and Kara rose and followed him out the door. The captain didn't slacken his pace until they reached the shuttle station. Rather than take one of the small, high-speed cars for the return to Mother, he took them to the outer ring of the space station through a tunnel used by maintenance personal. When they finally emerged, they were in a docking bay occupied by a sleek vessel emblazoned with Alado's winged crest, signifying that it belonged to a member of the board. Here again Merrill chose to use the hatch open for service personnel, and they saw no one on their way to the owner's private quarters.

The luxurious cabin was decorated in a soft robin's egg blue. The deeply cushioned couches were upholstered in a handwoven fabric whose muted colors matched the blues and greens of the decorative tapestries which adorned the walls. Obviously at home there, Merrill went straight to the bar, where he began to prepare tall fruit drinks heavily laced with alcohol. "The situation is even worse than I feared," he remarked as he handed them the soothing beverage. Swiftly downing his, he returned to the bar and this time began to mix a pitcher of the exotic pink brew. "I hope these aren't too sweet for your tastes, but they are what our hostess prefers and I know her mood will be even worse than mine by the time she arrives."

Wondering just who their hostess might be, Aidan glanced at Kara, but she raised her finger to her lips to still that question. "I realize the board transacts a great deal of its business in committees, but shouldn't Cipriano have informed everyone he wished to test the force field under battle conditions?" he asked instead.

"Yes, of course, but you've gotten a fair sample of his style. He simply dismisses all objections to his actions as trivial complaints and regards any criticism as petty. None of the other board members seem able to gather the support to oppose him effectively. Each of the nine individuals is an expert in a different field. They are supposed to combine their wisdom to provide Alado with the excellent leadership it deserves, but obviously Cipriano Acuña's lust for power has thrown the process dangerously out of balance."

Aidan gave his drink a tentative sip and while it was indeed too sweet for his liking, he decided in the interest of being a polite guest to drink it anyway. "Was it wise to make that comment about the use of the force field as a weapon?"

"Probably not, but I was too angry to keep quiet about it. Even as powerful as Acuña has become, it will take him some time to relieve me of my command, so I'll use every opportunity I have to speak out against him." He turned then as the door to the cabin slid open with a slight hiss.

In a flowing gown of pale mauve, Daya Crane seemed to float rather than walk as she stepped across the threshold. She had freed her hair from the confining braid which had held it in place during the board meeting, and the shimmering tresses now spilled about her shoulders with the grace of a golden veil. She went first to Merrill and, moving very close, kissed him lightly before turning to greet her other guests. "Welcome," she stated with a distracted smile. "I am sorry we have not met under better circumstances."

Merrill quickly introduced Aidan and Kara as trusted members of his crew, but he gave her no more information than that about them. "Was there any more discussion about the force field after I left?"

Daya accepted a drink, sat down on the couch opposite the one her guests had chosen and waited for Merrill to take his place by her side. "Yes, of course there was, but it swiftly deteriorated into an argument over whether or not experimental devices must be cleared through the whole board before they are tested. It is one of Cipriano's favorite tactics. He'll divert the topic under discussion to a strictly procedural dispute when the question in this case is clearly the strong probability that he plans to use the force field as a weapon."

"In your opinion, what is the most likely target?" Aidan probed curiously, beginning the vital series of questions he hoped she would answer.

Daya glanced first at Merrill, and when he gave her an encouraging nod, she set her drink aside and began to explain her concerns in more depth. "Any and all of our competition," she readily replied. "Alado has traditionally operated with an extremely effective pattern whereby our energies are focused first on exploration followed by efforts to colonize our new acquisitions." The slender blond gestured almost constantly as she spoke. Her motions were subtle, yet her hands were never still as she used them to emphasize her words. "It is a natural process of growth as we expand our influence in the universe. For the last year, however, the Expeditionary Force has been dispatched on an increasing number of missions, but plans to establish colonies, which is my interest, have not kept pace. We have begun simply to seize territory, survey it and then move on. Our whole emphasis has shifted from exploration and colonization to simple exploration to lay a claim for its own sake. Your last voyage was a good example of what's been happening. 329 was once considered off limits, but now it is being remapped because it will be useful as a staging area for further exploration."

Aidan thought it strange that neither Kara nor Merrill had ever mentioned Alado's plans for his home. "What would that mean to the people residing there now?"

Daya frowned slightly. "I didn't realize there were any survivors of the mining colony."

"How could you not have known that?" Merrill asked accusingly. "My report on the planet was complete down to the last head of sheep."

"Not the one I was given," Daya explained as she reached out to take his hand in a gentle clasp which clearly showed their relationship was far deeper than friendship. "It was a brief description of the desert terrain only with a notation that maps were being processed."

"All of your reports come directly here to Fleet Command Base, don't they?" Kara asked the captain.

"Then they are reviewed by the Expeditionary Committee

before they are made public," Merrill quickly explained. "Who's on the committee now besides Cipriano?"

"Jess Hudak and Arla Keyes," Daya explained regretfully, "his puppets."

Merrill thought himself very stupid for not seeing what had happened himself. "Of course, and Mother is probably not the only base ship whose reports are being edited."

While his companions sat in stunned silence, Aidan was sifting through the most likely possibilities why Cipriano Acuña would alter reports, and time and again he came up with the same premise. "The man's using his influence to seize territory but not following up with colonies. He's manipulating reports and testing weapons. It's doubtful he'd go to such lengths merely to keep himself amused. I think he's planning on starting a war."

Daya's clear blue eyes filled with horror at that grisly thought. "Oh no, that can't possibly be true. He would have to be insane even to consider that."

"What makes you think he isn't?" Aidan inquired calmly. "From what I saw of him today it's clear he has no regard for human life and no respect for any of the opinions of the other board members. That makes him a very dangerous man."

Merrill swiftly agreed. "I had hoped I would be able to influence the board myself or, failing that, to organize the officers at Fleet Command Base to stop whatever faction had sponsored the development of the force field. Now I don't even know where to begin. I'm afraid if we tried to warn people what Cipriano Acuña is doing, our fears would sound absurd until it was too late."

While Kara's expression showed she was as upset as the others, Aidan felt not the slightest bit of distress. He had volunteered to serve as the captain's courier, but he had never believed he would be asked to do no more than carry messages. "It seems what you need is an assassin after all, Merrill."

"A what?" Daya gasped, her fair skin turning deathly pale.

Merrill slipped his arm around her shoulders and gave her a comforting hug. "Aidan has a devilish sense of humor, my love, but he meant nothing by it." He gave the warrior a warning stare to silence him, but at the same time his almost imperceptible nod showed he agreed.

While Daya Crane was an ethereal beauty, she was also highly intelligent and extremely perceptive. Aidan puzzled her. He was not only remarkably handsome, but he also had the commanding self-assurance of the graduates of Alado's academy. Since he wasn't wearing the academy's distinctive gold ring, however, she was curious as to how he had become a member of Matthew's crew and inquired about his background.

Aidan made no attempt to conceal the truth. "I'm not part of the crew. I'm from 329 and I'm traveling on board Mother because that's where my wife is assigned." He watched as the attractive blond's posture stiffened slightly. She had recoiled inwardly when he had mentioned his home, and although that reaction wasn't unexpected, it disappointed him all the same. "Captain Merrill told me he was worried about the direction the board's been taking and hoped my help would prove useful. If you want to make some plans in that direction, then we'll stay. If not, then I'm sure you two would rather be alone just as Kara and I would."

Daya licked her lips thoughtfully, her choice obviously a difficult one. "No, please stay. I have always thought it possible for one person to make a difference in any situation. I have been frustrated by my inability to provide alternative leadership to the board, but I'm afraid my personal style is simply perceived as soft compared to Cipriano's arrogantly manipulative tactics. I know he has met with the others even when the board isn't in session, and that has apparently helped him deepen his influence over them. He has never invited me to his estate, but I've heard it's most impressive. It's located on Alado's resort planet in the Capella System, Alegría. He's a compelling man in public, and I imagine he's even more persuasive in a luxurious private setting."

Intrigued, Kara asked for more detail. "Does his estate have a name?"

"Why yes, although it doesn't really suit him. It's *La Casa Contenta,* the house of contentment. Have you heard of it?"

Kara smiled knowingly. "Why yes, I've been there. My father was the architect, and I remember the estate very well. It was always one of my favorites. Is it generally known that Cipriano entertains his fellow board members there?"

"No," Daya assured her. "That's the last thing he would want known since we are all supposed to remain independent in our thinking. At one time we were, too."

"When did Acuña begin extending these invitations?" Aidan asked pointedly.

Daya hesitated a moment, trying to recall when she had first learned of it. "He and Jess became close friends. I believe he was the first one to go there. That must have been a couple of years ago when Jess first joined the board. From time to time someone else will mention they've been there. I never really paid any attention to the comments since I wasn't eager to go myself. Now I'm sorry I don't remember more."

Merrill and Aidan exchanged knowing glances before the captain spoke. "Would you be willing to visit him now? I imagine he would be surprised if you showed an interest in seeing his home, but no man could possibly embark upon the path he's apparently chosen without having plans of some sort."

"And there would surely be some evidence of them there," Aidan agreed.

Daya stared at her three smartly uniformed guests. They were a determined trio, but her response was one of complete dismay. "You expect me to somehow inspire Cipriano to invite me to his home, go there and then spy on the man? Is that what you're suggesting?" she asked incredulously.

"No, of course not," Aidan assured her. "You would just

be the distraction, and I would do the spying."

"The man has a large cadre of bodyguards; it would not be an easy task. What if you were caught?" Daya was trembling in fear.

"I won't get caught," Aidan vowed confidently. "I think the man's ego is so inflated that he would believe any line you gave him. You're a stunning woman and he's an attractive man. What about that angle? Does he know about you and Matthew?"

"That's a secret no one knows," the captain quickly informed him. "We would have married long ago if it weren't for the obvious conflict of interest between our careers."

"Well, I'm sadly afraid your career is already on the line, Matt, and it would be very selfish of me to consider only my own with something as important as maintaining the peaceful exploration of space at stake." In an attempt to steady her nerves, Daya took a deep breath and let it out slowly. "I don't think it was merely your sense of humor that prompted you to mention assassination, Aidan. Such a drastic action must be ruled out now because I'll have no part of it. I can't believe Cipriano is deliberately planning to incite a confrontation which might lead to war, but his actions are too suspicious to ignore. If we can discover just what he does hope to do, then we can use that evidence to stop him through legal means and he'll be removed from the board immediately. I would never sleep with the man, but I will show enough interest in him to win an invitation to his home in hopes we can learn more of his plans. If the fool doesn't invite me, well then I'll just pay him a call anyway."

Kara and Aidan laughed as readily as Matthew Merrill at the fragile blond's sudden show of daring. The captain pulled her into his arms and gave her a boisterous hug. "That's my girl. Now let's have something to eat. I find it far easier to think on a full stomach."

"You don't mean think, you mean plot," the delicate beauty corrected, but in the course of the evening she grew as committed to their plan as her companions.

CHAPTER
◇ **XXIV** ◇

The board met for three more days at Fleet Command Base and when the members prepared to depart, Daya had indeed succeeded in winning an invitation to visit Cipriano's home. Again meeting on board her ship, she described the circumstances to her coconspirators.

"We had an elaborate luncheon today at the close of our last session, and I managed to take the seat beside Acuña before Arla could. As soon as he sat down, I told him I wished there were some way for us to reconcile our differences but that the board's schedule was so demanding there's little free time in which to share our opinions in an informal setting. He did not doubt my sincerity for an instant and asked if I would consider visiting his home." She smiled impishly then. "I'm embarrassed to admit I appeared so reluctant to accept his invitation that he had to coax me for the better part of the meal before I agreed to follow him to Alegría."

Aidan complimented her on her newfound talent as an actress, then turned the conversation toward more practical concerns. "We could travel with you, but I would rather have my own ship so no one will be able to tie our actions to yours, Daya."

Matthew agreed. "We'll not just have a ship, Aidan, we're taking Mother. With the force field activated we can remain within range as we track Cipriano, but our presence will be undetected. Once we reach Alegría, Kara's Banshee will be indistinguishable from the other air traffic. She can put you down on Cipriano's property and wait to pick you up. Alegría's lush vegetation will make it a simple matter to camouflage the Banshee for a few hours. I don't think you should plan to spend more time than that searching his home for evidence, do you?"

"No, with Kara's help I'll have the layout memorized, but I think we should have some way for Daya to contact us so I can arrive within hours of her departure."

"I can wear a transmitter concealed in my jewelry so you can hear every word I say if you like," Daya volunteered.

"No," Merrill objected instantly. "That's far too dangerous."

Daya shook her head, sending her flowing hair billowing about her shoulders. "I do it all the time, Matt. You know I travel almost constantly visiting our colonies. I don't like to have my security personnel surround me too closely because then people are afraid to approach me. But it's imperative that I be able to summon them in an instant if I need them."

"No," Merrill insisted again. "We'll make the plans right now so your visit will be brief. You'll spend no more than two days with Cipriano and depart the morning of the third. Then if anything goes wrong, he'll not suspect you were part of our plan and you'll be able to continue to fight him."

"This is going to be dangerous, isn't it?" Daya asked apprehensively.

"Very," Aidan admitted. "But as I said before, you'll be no more than a diversion and you'll come to no harm. Not even Cipriano would dare harm a board member visiting his home."

"Let's hope not," Daya prayed aloud, but she didn't look nearly as confident as she had earlier.

"There's only one thing more I need to know about him," Aidan confided. "My wife can not only transmit messages with her thoughts, but pleasure and pain as well. We've never had time for her to teach me that skill. Can Cipriano or any of his men do that type of mental manipulation?"

"You mean this?" Daya asked sweetly.

Aidan recognized the wistful melody of Alado's greeting

before she had begun the words. "Yes. That's precisely what I mean. Can he do it?"

"Cipriano is not a man given to reflection of any sort, and to send messages with thoughts requires years of practice. Many people believe that if the training is not begun in early childhood, the ability is lost and the skill is impossible to attain. He's in his fifties so he was an adult before the practice gained wide recognition. I'm almost positive he can't do it. As for his bodyguards, no, they'd have no such talent either. He employs the brutes for their strength, not their mental capacity."

"Good," Aidan responded with a smile, thinking the odds in his favor were getting better all the time.

Cipriano Acuña's ship left for Alegría the following morning with Daya Crane's traveling behind it. Matthew Merrill then reported a fire in the forward compartment of the fifth level cargo hold and was immediately ordered to remove Mother from the Fleet Command Base facility while fighting it. The emergency did not actually exist, however, but Tweed had not questioned his captain's orders when asked to simulate it. He tripped the sensors sounding the fire alarms, then congratulated the on-board crews arriving to fight the blaze for responding so promptly to the drill. Mother did not report the end of the mythical emergency for several hours, then Merrill activated the force field and the base ship disappeared from Fleet Command's screens.

"We have already reported the fire as being out so they'll assume they can't track us due to residual technical problems and not be overly concerned for the time being. I'll bounce messages off satellites to them frequently enough to keep them from sending out any pursuit. If all goes well, I'll not be charged with piracy."

Aidan chuckled at that thought. "If this is piracy, it was too damn easy."

"Don't become overconfident," Kara warned. "Things will be far more complicated once we reach Acuña's estate." While she was worried, it was plain her husband wasn't. He was going to do what he did best and clearly he was elated by the thought. His mood remained high while he memorized the plans of the spacious home and, since he had absolutely no idea what challenges a tropical terrain presented, they viewed every film in Mother's library with such a setting. By the time they reached Alegría, he was more than ready to deal with the assignment, but a dangerous complication they had not foreseen swiftly presented a new dilemma.

Merrill located Aidan in the gym and Kara in the library and summoned them immediately to his quarters. "I don't know what possessed Daya to do it, but she's wearing a transmitter. It's set for the frequency she and I use, and we're getting every word Cipriano speaks to her."

The captain was so obviously distressed that Kara hastened to reassure him. "He would still not harm her even if he found it. Perhaps he'll say something that will provide us with some valuable clues. May we hear it too?"

Merrill hesitated a moment, then walked over to his desk. "Daya and I have been lovers for a number of years. It's still a secret because we've been so diligent in our efforts to keep our relationship from becoming public knowledge. We've always sent messages to each other in codes or on frequencies not generally in use. I don't even know why I turned the receiver on, but I did."

Kara came forward to lean against the captain's desk. "Do you think we would criticize you when you had every reason to be discreet? If Daya took the risk of wearing a transmitter, then we ought to at least listen to what's being said."

Convinced she was right and afraid he was being very foolish, Merrill pulled open the right-hand drawer of his desk and flipped several switches to broadcast Daya's transmission over the desk-top speaker. "They were just strolling around the gardens, talking about flowers when I sent for you."

Aidan sank down on a couch and gestured for Kara to join him while they listened to the rambling conversation taking place at *La Casa Contenta*. Daya responded with no more than casual comments as her host provided what seemed to be a well-rehearsed tour of his estate. The man's manner was so charming that Matthew began to interject sarcastic comments. "Do you believe that? He's suggesting flowering plants for the colonies he never votes the appropriations to found. He must think Daya is very stupid."

"He couldn't possibly think that," Kara argued. "She's regarded as brilliant by everyone." The redhead leaned forward slightly. "Maybe he's leading up to something. Let's keep listening."

The trio took turns pacing as the hours passed. They ate cold sandwiches for dinner, unwilling to miss a second of the conversation between Daya and Cipriano, and finally their patience paid off.

"Oh, dear God," Merrill gasped when he heard the man mention his name. "He's going to try and blackmail her!"

Aidan held up his hand in a request for silence, straining to hear Daya's response. "Damn it, we should have foreseen this and told her to agree to anything. I can handle the guards, but we were counting on her to keep Cipriano occupied so I could search for evidence. She's going to refuse to even listen to him and leave. Come on, Kara, we've got to go down there tonight!"

"Keep listening!" Kara shouted over her shoulder to Merrill as she dashed after her husband. They had gone over their plan dozens of times, but now that the moment to implement it had arrived it seemed wildly improbable to her. Her Banshee had been outfitted with lasers and she knew how to fire them, but as she pulled on her helmet, she prayed she would not have to use them. Aidan had changed into the shorts, leather vest and boots he had worn for challenges, and the dragon tattooed so vividly on his golden brown flesh added a further touch of wildness to his image. As soon as he had fastened his seat belt he flashed a wicked grin and gave her the thumbs-up sign.

"I love you," she responded, and taking the pilot's seat she guided the lightweight ship out into the night and set the course for Alegría and the sprawling estate she had once visited as a child.

She approached the small planet developed solely as a resort, deliberately avoiding the landing strip used by

Alado's commercial flights. She swept down below the level
of the scanners to approach Cipriano's estate without being
tracked. The property was surrounded by a high stone wall
which was well lit to discourage intruders, but Kara found a
desolate stretch well inside that boundary and eased the
Banshee down behind a natural screen created by a row of
imperial palms. She cut the engines and turned to look at her
husband. "Are you all right?"

Aidan nodded. He felt a bit queasy, but had no time to
waste giving in to it. "If I'm not back by the first light of
dawn, return to Mother without me. No arguments, just do
it."

"I know the plan," Kara insisted, but she had no intention
of leaving Aidan there alone. She would fire the Banshee's
lasers into the house and land on the roof to drag him out
before she would leave him. He had his knife at his belt and
the laser pistol Merrill had insisted he take strapped to his
hip. He held a machete to slash through the underbrush, and
she knew he would make short work of any guard he happened to meet. "I won't ask you not to take any unnecessary
risks because I know you'll do as you please."

Aidan didn't argue with that opinion since it was correct.
He gave her a slow, sweet kiss and then, after no more than
a momentary pause at the hatch, stepped out. The coarse
grass that blanketed the ground was wet and clung to his legs
with every stride, but it was simply annoying and didn't
impede his progress.

The humidity created by Alegría's tropical climate and
lush vegetation was oppressive, but he found the foliage
provided such good cover that he did not curse the heat
which encouraged such abundant growth. He used the machete only when he could not clear a path by hand, for he
dared not constantly swing the long-bladed knife or the noise
would have swiftly attracted a great deal of notice. As it
was, he used it with such stealth that he soon reached the
border of the gardens surrounding the house and having no
further use for the machete dropped it into a hedge. He remained in the shadows, for they had not known how often
the grounds were patrolled on foot.

As he waited, Aidan decided the plan they had made on board Mother had served its purpose and he discarded it now in favor of a far bolder one of his own. It was almost diabolically simple and he was certain it would appeal to Cipriano Acuña. He had to admit the man had an impressive home. Built of a pale green stone native to the planet, it had the timeless beauty of its jungle setting, as though it were a monument to a long forgotten civilization. Thinking it a fair sample of Kara's father's work, he decided the man had indeed been a genius.

He heard someone whistling as he approached then, a decidedly careless habit for a man employed as a guard. As soon as the fool had passed him by, Aidan used the heel of his hand to give him a vicious chop across the back of his neck. The man went limp and Aidan caught him before he fell to the ground. He dragged him back into the bushes, tore off the guard's shirt, ripped it into two-inch strips, then used them to tie and gag the man securely. The guard had also been armed with a laser pistol, and Aidan tossed that well out of reach. Knowing then that the grounds were protected by a poorly trained force, he moved forward again and waited for the next man to appear.

Perhaps worried about his missing companion, the next guard was jogging. Aidan stuck out his foot and watched as the hapless individual tripped and slammed into the ground where he lay for a moment gasping to regain the breath which had been knocked out of him. The agile warrior sprang on the man's back before he could rise, grabbed his hair and pushed his face into the dirt. "How many guards are on duty tonight?" he asked in a fierce whisper. When the man didn't reply, Aidan drew his knife and pressed it against his captive's throat. "If you would rather I simply count bodies, I will begin with yours!"

"Six! There are six of us!" The guard was pinned so tightly to the ground he could barely draw enough breath to speak.

Aidan made this man rip up his own shirt, then left him bound and gagged a good distance from his first victim. He kept moving, and spotting a tree with a sturdy branch over-

hanging the path the first two guards had been on, he
climbed up and waited for the third. He was merely playing
with these men and saving his energy for more important
game. When he finally decided it was time to move on to the
house, he left six tightly bound guards behind.

Aidan circled around to the back of the mansion and
waited by the pool for a few moments to make certain his
approach hadn't been observed. The water was lit from
below with cool green lights which sent eerie shadows up
the magnificent dwelling's stone walls. There was one light
showing in the servants' wing, but seeing only an elderly
couple already clad in their nightclothes chatting at the
kitchen table, Aidan dismissed them as posing no threat to
his mission. Since they might sound an alarm, however, he
would not leave them free to roam the house. Three pairs of
doors opened off the patio and, finding the second set un-
locked, he stepped through them into a comfortable den. He
quickly made his way to the kitchen, introduced himself politely to the pair of astonished servants, then left them neatly
bound and gagged in the pantry.

Keeping in mind the drawing of the floor plan Kara had
made, he moved cautiously to the wide wooden staircase.
Staying close to the wall, he mounted each step carefully to
avoid making them creak, then turned to his right when he
reached the landing. The master bedroom was at the far end
of the hall and as he worked his way there he took the precaution of making certain each of the other rooms was
empty. When he reached the last door, he drew the laser
pistol and flipped the power switch to the lethal range. He
then kicked open the door and with a triumphant shout leapt
into the center of the room and leveled the weapon at the
man in the oversized bed.

Cipriano Acuña was so astounded by the sudden appearance of an armed man in his bedroom that he had no time to
reach for the pistol he kept in his bedside table before the
intruder had fired a blast dangerously close to his head. Not
recognizing the powerfully built blond as the security guard
who had been with Matthew Merrill at the board meeting, he
raised his hands and began to shout with the authoritative

tone of a man used to giving orders. "Don't shoot! Whatever it is you want, you can have it!"

Aidan kicked the door closed behind him and approached the bed with a confident swagger. He had not expected to find Daya in it, but the pretty woman had not even blinked when he had entered and appeared to be so dazed she still hadn't noticed him. "She drunk?" he asked insolently, but he kept his weapon trained upon Cipriano's heart.

"My God, man, have you no idea who I am?" the South American demanded in a belligerent tone.

"You're Cipriano Acuña and that's Daya Crane," Aidan replied with a sneer. "That's easy. The real question is who I am."

"Look, just get out and I'll forget this ever happened," Acuña offered bravely as he glanced about the room, desperately seeking something to use as a weapon. But he saw only the glowing light signaling that the camera concealed in the ceiling was still operating.

Aidan raised his sights slightly and fired again, this time singeing the man's thick black hair. "I hope you like wearing your hair parted in the middle. Now I insist you give it a try. You'll never guess my first name, so I suggest you try for the last."

The pungent aroma of burning hair was enough to inspire Acuña to regard his visitor with new respect, but he had no idea why the man's name was of any consequence. "Call yourself whatever you like. I'll pay any ransom you name, but you'll not get a penny if you harm either of us."

Daya still hadn't moved. She was propped against the pillows, apparently nude beneath the filmy sheets, but she might have been a decorative cushion for all she was contributing to the conversation. Aidan shook his head as though he were greatly disappointed. He gestured toward his tattoo, which was barely covered by his open vest. "The dragon should have given you a hint. My name's Burke. I've decided to pursue an old family tradition and I'm starting with you."

What was left of Acuña's deep tan faded when he realized

Aidan was a hired killer and not merely a flamboyant robber. "No wait! No matter what you've been paid, I'll double it!"

"You don't have that much," Aidan replied regretfully. "Sorry."

"But I soon will!" Acuña insisted with his usual arrogant bravado.

Apparently intrigued, Aidan put his right foot on the end of the bed and rested his arm across his knee, but he didn't lower the laser. "How?"

"It would take me hours to explain!" the angry man replied hoarsely.

"You have five minutes," Aidan responded with an evil chuckle.

Cipriano Acuña wasn't used to taking orders and clearly disliked it. "Alado is now the most powerful corporation exploring space, but what if it were the *only* corporation? What if our competition ceased to exist?"

"That would never happen," Aidan replied disdainfully.

"Oh yes it will, and soon," Acuña vowed confidently. "It will begin with warfare between Europa and the Asian Alliance. Their base ships will be attacked and destroyed by ships their scanners can't find to return the fire! We've accelerated our rate of acquisition. Competition between the corporations has never been more fierce. Disputes over territory are becoming more frequent, but while our competition will destroy each other, our ships will be invincible! Think of the possibilities, man!"

Aidan appeared to ponder them thoughtfully, but then he shook his head. "When any enterprising thief can walk right into your bedroom, you'll never be able to pull off anything that grandiose."

Insulted as well as embarrassed by the breach in his security, Acuña unwittingly took Aidan's bait. "You're obviously a clever man. I could use you on my staff. Put that laser away. Let's go downstairs to my study and talk. I'm certain I can make you a far better proposition than the one that brought you here."

Aidan stared at him a long while, letting the man's tension mount to a nearly unbearable level before he agreed. "I've been a mercenary all my life and I always work for the highest bidder. If you can actually do what you say, then I'd be a fool not to listen—and I'm no fool. I'll decide when to put the laser away, though. Now get out of bed slowly." He scooped up the robe lying across the foot of the bed, patted it down to be certain the pockets held no weapons and then threw it to the man. "Daya won't even know we're gone. I thought she had more class than that."

"Class? What an archaic term," Acuña thought aloud. "She proved surprisingly stubborn, and I had to use a drug to change her mind. She'll recall nothing when she wakes but she'll be far more receptive to my views in the future."

"If you have one." Aidan gestured with the laser. "Get moving."

Kara watched the sky gradually begin to lighten. Terrified that Aidan wouldn't return before dawn, she left her ship and began to pace distractedly beside it. All his arguments seemed ridiculous now. He was undoubtedly stronger and perhaps far more cunning, but she should have gone with him anyway since she possessed a wide range of skills herself. If anything happened to him when she should have been there to prevent it, she would never forgive herself. Unable to wait any longer, she started down the path Aidan had blazed for himself.

Despite the manner in which they had met, Cipriano Acuña found Aidan's confidence and obvious strength assets he definitely wanted in his employ. When they reached his study, the blond didn't let him near his desk until after he had searched it. "You're very thorough, aren't you?" he asked with clear admiration.

"I would have been dead long ago if I weren't. I'm surprised you've survived this long with the fools you had for security."

"Did you kill them all?"

"What do you think?" Aidan replied noncommittally.

"It's no loss since, as you say, they were worthless," Acuña said, dismissing the men from his mind. "It has taken me years to establish, but I have a network of informants in the other corporations. They provide me with plans for their explorations, and it is a simple matter to see to it that Alado's ships are the first to reach any targets which look promising."

"That must be expensive. Are you sure you can afford my services, too?" Aidan asked with a sly grin.

"Of course. Getting money has never been a problem for me. Take Daya Crane for instance. She was about to star in a film with me when you arrived. Perhaps you would like to co-star; a threesome would be all the more interesting. She's widely respected, but she certainly won't be after what I intend to make her do. She won't want her lover to see that film, nor will she want him to lose the base ship he's so proud to command. He loves that ship more than her anyway. I have her in the palm of my hand along with several others on Alado's board."

Aidan appeared puzzled. "You can't be blackmailing them all with compromising films."

Acuña chuckled at his own cleverness. "Of course not. Daya's reputation is above reproach so she's most susceptible to embarrassments of a sexual nature. The others have different flaws. One needed the money to cover poor investments, another has a daughter whose lover died under mysterious circumstances and he didn't want her prosecuted for murder. It's not really blackmail. I merely do favors and then ask for repayment at a later date."

"You ought to expand that beyond the board," Aidan suggested helpfully. "I'll bet a man with your influence is asked for favors all the time."

"Oh yes, of course I am. I keep very detailed records so I never forget an outstanding debt."

Before Aidan could reply, a burly man appeared at the door with Kara slung carelessly over his shoulder. "I found this scout out in the garden but I didn't see anyone else. What shall I do with her?"

"That's my pilot," Aidan admitted readily, disgusted to see there were more than six guards prowling the grounds.

"Just leave her in a heap by the door and I'll handle her later. Well go on, get out. We're busy."

The guard's eyes widened in dismay. "Mr. Acuña?"

He nodded. "Yes, do as he says. Leave her here and go." When the man had left, he made what he thought was a clever observation. "To dress your pilot as a scout is a bizarre touch. Doesn't that draw too much attention?"

"Not on Alegría it doesn't. The place is swarming with Alado personnel on vacation. It's the best disguise there is." Apparently ignoring the unconscious woman, Aidan finally placed his laser pistol in its holster, crossed his arms over his chest and returned their conversation to its former topic. "I still think your plan to put the other corporations out of business is farfetched. As for working for you, well, let's just take it one job at a time. My first assignment ought to be to take care of the man who sent me here. What's that worth to you?"

Acuña was enjoying their discussion and was disappointed to find his visitor's main interest was money. "Mineral rights usually prove very lucrative. I can arrange for you to get such a contract."

Aidan swore with the filthiest expression he knew. "What I want is cash, up front, right now, or I'll finish the job I came here to do and collect for it."

Kara opened one eye cautiously, uncertain how she had reached the house when her last memory was of the gardens. When she saw Aidan casually conversing with Cipriano Acuña while she lay sprawled on the floor, she knew she couldn't possibly be awake. When she realized they were arguing over how much he would be paid for a murder, she knew it was a nightmare, not merely a dream. Her head ached badly and as she reached up to touch the lump at the nape of her neck, Acuña recognized her.

"That's the scout Merrill brought with him to our meeting. There's no way I'll let her leave here alive."

"The little bitch is in love with me. She'll do whatever I say, so don't worry about her," Aidan explained offhandedly, apparently caring little for the young woman.

"Merrill's the one who sent you here, isn't he?" Acuña asked accusingly. "The bastard. Who does he think he is?"

"He's already dead," Aidan assured him. "But I want to see half the cash now."

"Aidan!" Kara gasped, horrified by the bargain her husband had struck.

The warrior simply laughed at her distress. "You know I've always worked for the man who can pay me the most, sweetheart, and that's all I'm doing now," he explained in a lazy drawl.

Not pleased by Kara's obvious distaste for their plan, Acuña bent down to open the safe concealed beneath a removable panel in the hardwood floor. He removed what Aidan had demanded and then added more, but as he stood up he made a new request. "I'm willing to pay a generous sum, but I want her taken care of as well. She'll never go along with this. Get rid of her right now, and then I'll hand over the first half of your money."

"Are you crazy?" Aidan responded with a frown. "You get blood all over a floor like this and you'll never get rid of the stains."

"Hell, you don't have to use your laser. Just break her neck." When Aidan didn't follow that order instantly, Acuña decided to handle the job himself. He jammed the thick packet of bills into his pocket, but he had taken no more than one step toward Kara when the warrior clamped a hand on his shoulder and spun him around. Extremely vain, Acuña was in superb physical condition for a man his age. Because of his volatile nature, he had fought many a fistfight in his youth, but he would have been no match for Aidan even in his prime.

A slow smile curved Aidan's lips as he landed his first blow squarely on the man's chin. Acuña fought back, and gamely, but the warrior was so quick on his feet he easily eluded every punch the man threw. When he made the mistake of trying to grab the laser pistol from his holster, Aidan responded with his favorite combination of blows. He drove his elbow into Acuña's solar plexis, swung his hand down for a brutal jab to his groin, then brought his fist up for a vicious blow that shattered his nose.

Racked with pain, Acuña was screaming, "No, no! Don't hit me again!" Ignoring the blood gushing from his broken nose, he pulled the money from his pocket and waved it frantically. "I'll give you twice this, just don't hit me again!"

Aidan hesitated a moment, letting the villain think he was considering the offer, and when he saw the light of hope fill Acuña's eyes he grabbed him by the shoulder to keep him from sinking to his knees. "You evil son of a bitch, there's not enough money in the universe to buy your life!" With that final insult he slammed his right fist into the man's broken nose, sending shards of shattered bone through his skull into his brain and putting an end to his miserable life instantly. Aidan dropped the limp body to the floor and turned around to face his wife. "It's just barely dawn now. Why didn't you wait for me in the Banshee? I would have been back on time."

Kara stared up at her husband, unable to comprehend the full import of the gory scene she had just witnessed. "Was that all just an act?"

Aidan laughed as he bent down to draw her to her feet. "Of course it was an act. I pretended to be impressed by his offer merely to get him talking, and he told me plenty. I'm sure we'll find more than enough evidence in his safe or personal computer files to prove the enormity of his crimes. Now when are you going to learn I can take care of myself?"

Kara clung to her husband with a frantic hug. "I'm sorry, I was just so frightened that—" She was interrupted then as Ryan Blake came barreling through the door followed by Matthew Merrill and half a dozen other heavily armed men from Mother's crew.

Without releasing his wife, Aidan explained in a few brief sentences what had happened. "Daya's upstairs, but you needn't worry. I arrived before anything happened to her."

Merrill blushed with embarrassment. "I'm sorry, but she must still be wearing the transmitter and when it sounded like you were actually interested in Acuña's offer, well, I—"

"Thought I'd sold out?" Aidan asked. "Don't apologize, Kara thought the same thing, too."

"No, not really," the disheveled redhead argued.

Aidan regarded her with a quizzically raised brow thinking her bright blush told the true story even if she continued to deny it. "If you're feeling up to it, why don't you go on upstairs and see if Daya needs any help while Matthew and I locate the evidence we came to find? There are six guards tied up in the underbrush and an elderly couple locked in the pantry. They all need to be questioned."

Kara nodded. As she pushed through the men gathered at the door, she couldn't help but notice how disappointed Ryan seemed. "Were you hoping for an excuse to shoot Aidan?" she asked in a threatening whisper. "If you're still aching for a fight, there's a man roaming the garden and I'd like to have someone pay him back for knocking me over the head." She looked back over her shoulder at Aidan, wondering if he had planned to kill Cipriano Acuña from the beginning. Shivering slightly, she realized she would probably never have the answer to that question.

CHAPTER
◊ **XXV** ◊

Kara and Aidan lay on the soft carpet of grass by the pool at *La Casa Contenta*, lazily enjoying the warmth of the morning. Acuña had left no heirs, so the property now belonged to Alado, and the handsome pair were using it for a brief vacation. They had spent a frantic week documenting Acuña's treachery, and now both wished to put the whole ugly incident behind them and get on with their lives. Yet neither seemed to know exactly what they wished to do.

"This is a very beautiful estate," Aidan mused thoughtfully. "Eden could have been no prettier than this."

"Yes, I'm sure you're right," Kara agreed. "I told you my father had the unique ability to create worlds as perfect as God's own, and this is a superb example of his art. It's like coming home, even though I've never lived here." There was something more on the attractive redhead's mind, but she didn't know quite how to approach it.

Seeing her pensive frown, Aidan reached out to draw her closer to his side. Her two-piece bathing suit was so brief it covered little of her elegant tattoo, and he reached out to caress the vine where it swirled around her waist. "What's wrong? We have beautiful surroundings and each other—what more do you want?"

Kara chewed her lower lip nervously, still uncertain how to begin. "Please don't be insulted but—"

"Oh no," the handsome man said apprehensively, "what have I done now?"

"Why, nothing," Kara insisted. "Why do you feel so guilty?" she teased.

Aidan laughed. "I don't feel the least bit guilty. We didn't even have that emotion on 329. It wasn't allowed."

"I am trying to be serious."

"Forgive me. Go ahead and say whatever you like, and I promise not to feel insulted."

Kara rolled over on her side and propped her chin on her hand. "Our marriage was so sudden, and so, well, so—"

Alarmed, Aidan sat up, "Just what the hell is it you're trying to say?"

"You promised you would not be insulted," Kara reminded him.

"So I lied!"

He looked absolutely furious with her and since it was totally without cause, Kara began to giggle. "I'm trying to ask you to marry me and I know I'm doing a very clumsy job of it, but I didn't mean to make you angry."

"But we're already married," Aidan pointed out with a befuddled frown.

"Well, perhaps the citizens of 329 feel a man need do no more than take a woman's hand in public to be married, but I would like to have a more formal exchange of vows. I want to invite all our friends and have the wedding here. The gardens would make such a beautiful setting."

Aidan gave her proposal thoughtful consideration and then asked a question of his own. "Are you sure you really want to marry me again? You've seen what happens when I say I'm from 329. As sweet as Daya is, she cringed, and everyone else will as well. People will probably never really trust me. You had to ask me yourself if I was merely playing a part to gain Acuña's confidence."

Kara was embarrassed by that memory, but now that he had brought it up, she wanted to pursue it. "The man was truly evil, Aidan, and if you had meant all along to kill him you would have been justified in doing it. I would just like to know the truth. Did you come here that night to gather evidence or to kill him?"

"Do my motives matter so much to you?"

"Yes. I would really like to know what you planned."

As Aidan gazed out over the gardens, his senses were assailed by the heavy fragrance of the bright blossoms which grew in such wild abundance. Since they cultivated no plants on 329 strictly for the beauty of their flowers, he recognized none of these, but thought them a glorious sight. "I don't understand how the man came up with such a wicked plot in such an idyllic setting. I don't plan ever to fall into the trap that snared Cameron. I'm not going to be anyone's hired killer—and most especially not Alado's. If I were the bloodthirsty type, I would have slain every one of Acuña's guards and the servants, too, but I didn't. That fact ought to prove something to you. I came here knowing if I told Acuña my name he would mistake me for the same type of vermin he was and confide in me. It worked. It was simply a ploy to learn all I could quickly so our charges would be that much easier to prove. Then when you stumbled into the middle of it, everything changed. It was a very simple choice then: Your life or his."

"Did I ever thank you for saving my life again?"

"No, not that I recall."

Kara leaned forward to begin with a kiss when they heard the new housekeeper, Irma, calling to them. "I'll go see what she wants." Kara returned a few minutes later with a message from the board. "I'm not certain if the fact that we have direct communication with Alado here is good or not. They sent word that Cheryl and Ramon were picked up weeks ago by one of Europa's cargo vessels, but the report of their rescue didn't reach Fleet Command until yesterday. That's wonderful news even if it is long overdue. Here's a message for you too and they request an immediate reply. I hope it doesn't mean our vacation is over."

While Aidan was also relieved the missing scouts had been found, he was worried about the brief note sent to him and glanced over it quickly. "Did you read this?"

"No, it's addressed to you." Kara knelt at his side as he began to study it more closely.

"The board has voted to dissolve itself at the end of this session and has called for new elections in which the majority of the present members have agreed not to run for reelection in exchange for the promise their ties to Cipriano Acuña will not be investigated. His death will be attributed to natural causes." He looked up then. "That's just like them, isn't it? Why is a convenient lie better than the truth?"

Kara understood the board's reasoning perfectly. "The man was a viper, but to disclose the full story would serve no purpose whatsoever except to embarrass the unfortunate victims of his unprincipled ambition. In fact, it might even inspire some other lunatic to try and play one corporation against another until only one is left. I think they're justified in not taking that risk."

While Aidan wasn't entirely convinced, he didn't argue. "What do you think of this? 'For services rendered to the board' I've been awarded not only *La Casa Contenta*, but Acuña's spaceship as well."

"What? Let me see that." Kara took the printout and read

it hurriedly. "My God, that's exactly what it says. That's why they requested a reply." She was thrilled by the generous gesture, but her heart fell as she looked up at her husband's disgusted frown. "You won't accept the house and ship, will you?"

"This wasn't something I did hoping for a fat reward! In fact, it was the one time in my life I didn't even think of being paid. What about you, Daya, and Matthew? Why isn't there any mention of a reward for you three?"

"You still don't realize what you did, do you?" Kara reached out to caress his cheek with a light, loving touch. "You could have walked away from the problems Acuña was creating. You weren't one of Alado's employees, and none of the decisions he influenced the board to make would have affected you. You came here simply in an effort to do some good. You knew you were risking your life, but you never once mentioned that you expected to be paid, despite your usual boast that you always work for the highest bidder."

Aidan waved the message as evidence. "Well it certainly looks like I've been well paid after all, doesn't it? I still say it's not fair for me to have such a large reward while you three get nothing."

"I am your wife, Aidan, and what belongs to you belongs to me as well. As for Daya Crane and Matthew Merrill, well, they are both quite wealthy. We've been invited to their wedding, and I think now that they've decided to give their relationship priority over their separate careers, they already have everthing they could possibly want."

"Well I don't!" Aidan declared emphatically.

Kara swallowed hard, forcing back the lump of fear that suddenly filled her throat. "What is it you want?"

"I want Cameron's name cleared. I want the board to admit the truth about him: That he worked for Alado thinking he was furthering the cause of peace and when he became disillusioned and tried to quit, he was exiled to 329. I want the whole truth about my home told, too. Few of the prisoners were innocent as he was, but none of them deserved to be abused so badly that they welcomed death!"

As he continued, the same fierce anger that had filled him

during their very first conversation brought back the memory of the day they met. Kara held out her hand. "Will you permit me to touch you?" she asked with an enticing smile.

Aidan stopped in mid-sentence, startled by her question and yet delighted by it, too. He pulled her into a fond embrace, loving the warmth of her bare skin next to his. "Well, is it worth a try? I'll take the house and ship and allow them to suppress the real story about Cipriano Acuña's death if they'll admit the truth about Cameron Burke and 329."

That a question of honor meant more to him than the most lavish possessions brought tears to Kara's eyes. "Of course it's worth a try, and I don't see how they can refuse. If they don't reveal the truth about Cameron, then we'll just make them all look like fools when we do it ourselves. I'll send your acceptance with your conditions and request an immediate response."

As she turned away, Aidan watched the fluid line of her graceful walk with an admiring glance. She was gone a long while and the grass was such a pleasant pillow beneath his cheek that he dozed off, not really caring what the board replied when he had such a bewitching mate. He would marry her a dozen times if it would please her, for her happiness was also his. She had never really had a home, but he meant to create one for her now.

When he heard her excitedly calling his name, he rose to his feet and had to cover a wide yawn before he spoke. He could tell by the width of her smile what the board's answer had been. "They agreed?"

Kara rushed forward to give him a hug, but she was so excited she danced around him like a carefree child. "Not only did they agree, but they'll open the records so you can do the research and write Cameron's story yourself. It's such an exciting one it will lead quite naturally into his adventures on 329. It will be the story of the century! Oh Aidan, they gave you everything you wanted!"

When he looked more puzzled than ecstatic, Kara realized he was still half asleep and gave him a playful shove. Tickling his ribs with fiendish delight, she pushed him off the grass into the deep end of the pool. Her lilting giggles swiftly turned to a gasp of alarm when she realized by the frantic way he flailed his arms and his hoarse sputtering shouts that he couldn't swim. She dove into the water, came up behind him and, slipping her arm over his shoulder and across his chest, towed him swiftly to the side of the pool where he could hold on to the bright decorative tile border. "I am so terribly sorry. I had no idea you couldn't swim when we always had such a marvelous time in your big bathtub."

Aidan flipped the damp hair out of his eyes and regarded her with a suspicious stare. "There's not a single pool of sufficient size for swimming on 329. None of us can swim. Blast it all, Kara, you damn near drowned me!"

Despite his fierce expression, the stunning redhead began to laugh. "I finally got to do it, Aidan, I finally got to save your life!" she teased with giggles she couldn't stop.

She was so very pretty with beads of water adding a sparkle to her long thick lashes that Aidan couldn't stay mad at her even though he tried. Still holding on to the side of the pool, he moved around in front of her so she was trapped between his outstretched arms.

"I intend to make you pay for this outrage, Kara. I want your promise you'll leave Alado and come to work for me. I suddenly find myself the proud owner of a spaceship, and as soon as I finish Cameron's story I want to travel as far as it will take us. I want to see everything from Earth to the last star and beyond. I'll need a pilot and I want it to be you. Believe me, your pay will be generous and your benefits extraordinary."

"You're going to spoil me terribly, aren't you?" she inquired with an alluring glance which encouraged him to do just that.

Aidan's grin grew even more rakish as he nodded. "You bet I am."

"Then how can I possibly refuse? I think the only way I'll ever be able to keep up with your adventures is to be your pilot."

"Then you agree? You'll leave Alado and come with me?"

The choice she had once feared would tear her heart in two was an easy one now. "Yes, I'll always want to be with you." As Aidan's lips began a slow, loving trail down her throat, Kara relaxed in his arms, drinking in the affection she longed to return. Whispering in his ear, she purred seductively, "Aren't you afraid we'll drown if we make love here?"

"That's my revenge, woman. I'm going to drown you in love." And for the rest of eternity that's exactly what he did.